Going Back

RICHARD WATT

First Printing, 2013
ISBN: 978-0-9919247-0-7

www.richardwatt.ca/goingback

Book cover design by Scarlett Rugers Design
www.scarlettrugers.com

Author photograph by Philomena Hughes
www.phughesphotography.ca

For Zoe, who tolerated all this for so long; and for Cameron and Conor, who grew up alongside it, in the hope that it might inspire you to create things.

CONTENTS

ACKNOWLEDGMENTS

No story exists or grows in a vacuum; many of those who inspired or helped with it may never have known what they brought to it, while others may feel part of something which to the author feels like a solitary pursuit.

I'll miss some, I'm sure, but here goes:
First, to those – many forgotten, I'm afraid – who once shared a bus to Germany with me: without you, there would never have been a story, and while almost none of the things I describe actually happened, *something* put the idea in my head. (Actually, I know exactly what put the idea in my head, but I think I'm the only person who remembers that incident, reproduced more or less faithfully here, albeit with added plot points.)

Many have offered their time and patience to get me to this point; readers, in particular, are gratefully thanked: Zoë, of course, who pointed out with her usual kindness just why certain parts didn't work, and helped me fix them. Emma Lindsley who nailed my worries about Andrew, and by doing so, changed him for the better. My sister Heather, Dave Hendon, Steve Staves, Sandy Graham, Judy Clark, Patricia Roy, Rob Long, Wayne Osteen and Joe Thomas, whose encouragement came at exactly the right moment.

Frieda Munro was present at the aforementioned incident, although she doesn't remember it; she's not in this book, but something of her influence stayed with me all these years for some reason. Fred, if I had one, I'd raise a plastic cup full of vodka and orange in your general direction.

Dmitri Shostakovich: there was other music, but the bulk of the first draft of the story was written whilst listening to all of the symphonies in order, except for one bit which will, I imagine, be obvious…

It bears saying that this is a work of fiction. The places are not real, although if you are sufficiently interested, it isn't too hard to work out where the places they are based on are; the people are entirely figments of my imagination and any resemblance to real people, living or dead, is entirely coincidental. Nevertheless, some research was necessary; to those who helped, anonymously or otherwise, much thanks – I'm not going to do the usual 'errors are entirely mine' bit; if something doesn't fit with your experience of the world, it's nobody's fault; it's fiction!

RICHARD WATT

PART 1: ANDREW

AUGUST 2003

Andrew was tense, sweaty, and lost. His memories seemed to be conspiring against him. He thought he knew why he was doing this, but the more he worked the thoughts over in his mind, the less clear they seemed. He knew that he wanted to return to the place where it had happened to him, but he was unable to explain why, even to himself.

His ex-wife had scoffed at the idea initially, and then had sent a strange, almost pleading message, asking him not to go stirring things up. Andrew had considered giving in to this - there were a number of other places he'd also like to visit - but he had made plans, and sticking to plans was one of the few things he felt he was really good at.

He snatched at the gear lever, mistiming the gear change once again, but grateful this time that he had not first reflexively punched the door with his left hand. Eventually, he supposed, he would get used to things being on the wrong side, but he had so many other things to worry about that he was genuinely surprised not to have already ploughed into the back of some expensive-looking Mercedes. Another unfamiliar German road sign came into view, and he peered at it, hoping that he would recognise one of the place names or road numbers, but the same mixture of vaguely familiar names whipped out of sight just as he began to decipher them.

He wondered at what point he would have to admit to being lost, and what he would do about it then. Thankfully, Friday evening traffic in Frankfurt seemed slightly more forgiving than the London variety he was used to, and he took advantage of the forgiveness to veer wildly from lane to lane in search of something familiar. After half an hour or so of surging round impenetrable gyratory systems in ever more random fits and starts, he spotted a sign for the airport, and feeling confident that he could find his way from there, set off in entirely the wrong direction.

He found the exit for the airport, realised too late that it was the cargo side of the airport, and seriously considered just returning his rented Golf, and calling the whole thing off. He could still be home in time to catch the late Prom on the radio, and he'd have a free weekend.

Trouble was, free weekends weren't all they had cracked up to be when he had been married, and something in him insisted that he had come this far, and there might be at least one question he could have an answer to. He knew that he had been suppressing the memory, but he wanted to know the truth about Karla, and why she had done what she had done to him. Then perhaps he could get to like free weekends; maybe even get to know his children a little better. He had a suspicion that it might even explain why he was no longer married, and why he had always felt like a spectator in his own life. Someone had once told him – or had he read it in a book? – that feeling detached from one's own life was perfectly normal; that everyone experienced that, but he didn't believe it.

He stopped at the side of the road, pulled out the poorly photocopied map which he had made before leaving London earlier in the week, and squinted at it until it made vague sense. He fixed on a couple of likely place names – places which were both on his way and liable to appear on direction signs. He repeated them out loud three times each, in the hope of making them stick, then tore off his tie, opened his shirt collar, turned up the air conditioning, and set off in what was surely the right direction. The fact that, ten minutes later, he passed the building where he had spent the previous two days he took to be a good omen.

He allowed himself to think back to the last time he had been in Germany, and smiled at the memory of the dreadful bus. He wouldn't be here on the Autobahn headed for Kassel had it not been for that bus, and the sudden, shocking, realisation several months earlier, that 25 years had passed. Prompted partly by the unexpected lull in his life which the finalisation of his divorce had brought him, he had written both to his old school, and to the school they had visited, expecting only that someone, somewhere, might remember something. What he had received was a non-committal, vaguely interested reply from the school in Chester, and an entirely unexpected greeting from Hohenügel; the place which nagged at his memory for so many reasons. He hadn't intended to actually go there, but finding himself in Germany for work reasons, he managed to shuffle dates and flights enough to be able to spend the weekend stirring up some ghosts. Which was not going to happen unless he began to concentrate on the bewildering pace of driving, and the way the road numbers seemed to keep changing.

Andrew Macintyre was, he knew, slightly taller than what people generally considered 'tall'; his height had been a curse throughout his adolescence, and he still found the world generally not designed for someone of his build. He thought he looked pudgy - bland and inoffensive - but had been surprised to learn in an exit interview he had carried out for one of his staff the year before that most people considered him stern and forbidding. His heavy black eyebrows and even darker eyes probably had a lot to do with that, he thought, since he felt that he was easy-going and mildly eccentric.

His eccentricities were well hidden, since he lacked the confidence to carry them off, but he liked to think of himself as slightly out of the ordinary. And, in as much as most people seemed to think him slightly odd, he was out of the ordinary. Notwithstanding a comfortable and well-paid job in a well-respected company - which these days mainly involved getting people below him to do what people above him wanted done, rather than the technical work which he so enjoyed - and his divorce, he did feel different from most of the people he socialised with or met through work. He liked music which his few friends thought unlistenable; he read great, complex novels which he could never discuss with anyone; he refused to be interested in sports or cinema; he went to the opera more often than he could reasonably afford; and he drove a sports car which he couldn't actually quite fit comfortably into. Which at least meant that his rented Golf felt spacious, and he could change gear – when he remembered where the gear lever was- without getting his knee wedged in his ear.

After half an hour or so the road signs began to make more sense, and he nurtured the feeling that he had been here before. He thought the forest looked familiar, and then thought about how much the forest and the surrounding landscape – particularly in this part of Germany - would have changed since he was 15, and laughed at himself. He caught himself yawning, and tried the radio again. Having spent the last two days immersed in technical German, he was hoping to tune his ear to more conversational language. When he had been given this project to look after, he quickly discovered that his claim to have 'conversational German' wasn't entirely true. He had forgotten most of the German he had known back then, and if he was honest, that hadn't been much to begin with. But he still had a good ear for language and picked up enough to get by in meetings, even if he didn't always have the confidence to actually join in conversation. The radio seemed to be offering light classics, noisy Europop or impenetrable politics, and he turned it off again. He tried to squint at the roadmap on the passenger seat, but in doing so, earned himself a blast of expensive and rapid German horn. He sat back up, and concentrated on the road.

And then, suddenly, the forest – or, rather, the road - really did look familiar. Because they had used the school as a base and visited several places by bus, they must have traversed this particular piece of Autobahn around a dozen times, and something stirred in his memory, just as he saw the first sign for Fastlose. This was where the road ended, he thought. Just about here. He saw the junction flash past, and recognised that a memory had also slipped just out of reach, and then caught sight of the church between the trees – still exactly as it had been in the photograph he had found when removing himself from the family home. He smiled as he drove on to the next exit, where he hoped he would be able to summon enough German to check himself into his hotel.

Motorway hotels turned out to be the same in Germany as in England – spartan, functional affairs with just enough amenities, and a low background rumble audible wherever you were. Andrew negotiated the reception quite well, he felt - although the receptionist switched effortlessly to idiomatic English once she saw his passport, he was pleased at having initiated the conversation and established who he was and what he wanted. He showered quickly, and sat on the end of the bed for a few minutes, contemplating his situation. The hotel was just over the line of the old border, and there were some long-suppressed memories nagging at him now. He had been here, or somewhere close to here, before, and he suddenly felt cold and scared for reasons he wasn't able to properly digest.

The cold hand which suddenly appeared to have grasped his heart belonged to Karla, he knew. He also knew that he was going to have to finally face up to why he was here; not because of Matthias, or some romantic idea about retracing his youthful steps, but because Karla had changed him in a way he still felt uncomfortable thinking about, even 25 years later. And because he still had trouble even thinking about his encounters with Matthias' sister. He shook his head as if to clear it, and then reached for his travelling bag.

A large part of him didn't want to bother with dressing and going out again – he'd even forgo dinner if necessary, but he knew that he had to face up to why he was here. It wasn't that he didn't want to meet Matthias again – he had genuinely fond memories of his German shadow – but he was now properly alarmed about who else might still be in the village.

His email to the school in Hohenügel had been more hopeful than anything else. He had tried to write it in German, and was not too unhappy with the result; he had managed to get a colleague to proofread it for him, and the changes had been stylistic rather than grammatical. Still, it had been a surprise when he had received a reply almost immediately, and seeing Matthias' name on it had been quite startling.

In Andrew's mind, the process would have been something like this: he would write to the German school, receive a bland reply from some office functionary explaining that there was no-one still there who remembered anything, but that if he was ever in the area, he was welcome to come and visit. He would then happily drive out there after the Frankfurt meeting, look around for a day or so, and go home, satisfied that nothing terrible lurked in the unassuming rural village, and that whatever he thought had happened to him while he had been there was a product of his overactive teenage imagination. *After all,* he thought, *it was every teenage boy's dream. Wasn't it?*

He was, therefore, truly taken aback to see Matthias' name appear in his inbox the following day. Before he saw the message, he would have been hard pressed to say for sure what Matthias' last name had been, but in spite of the fact that he was regularly receiving emails from German colleagues in conjunction with the current project, and that sometimes messages came from people he had never even heard of, as soon as he saw *From: Matthias Schneider,* he knew exactly who it was.

Matthias. The boy who was so determined to get away from Hohenügel, away from something he had never been able to properly explain to Andrew. Matthias' dedication to learning English was because he felt sure he could learn to be a pilot, had even saved up enough money for a handful of flying lessons, although his father had seemed scornful to say the least about this whole idea.

Matthias was, for some reason, still in Hohenügel, and worse, was on the staff at the school, the same school he had hated at the time, although Andrew always felt that was because of being taught by his overbearing father. Perhaps the old man – Andrew remembered that Herr Schneider had been considerably older than his own parents, older perhaps even than old man Cartwright – had something to do with it; perhaps he had forbidden anything other than going into the same profession. Perhaps –

And perhaps Andrew should go and meet Matthias, as arranged, and find out for himself.

The pub was exactly where he remembered it to have been – not in Hohenügel itself, but a couple of miles along the road in the next village, which appeared to be called Witkreuz, although the name seemed new to Andrew. Although it looked quite different from the outside, inside – once Andrew's eyes had adjusted, it appeared still to be very familiar. The bar was where he remembered it to be, and if he looked over his shoulder as he stood at the bar, he could see the room where he had first experienced being drunk. This memory had been one of the few he had tested out with his German colleagues earlier in the week. He had explained how he remembered being able to go in a pub and buy beer at the age of 15, and had been assured that this was perfectly normal; that the legal age was 16, and that even in a pub like that, it was fine at 14 if you had a responsible adult in charge. Andrew was finding some of the teachers who were on the trip fuzzy in his memory, but he felt sure that at least one of them would have been classified as 'responsible'.

Matthias had not sent a photograph, and Andrew spent some time peering cautiously at the few unaccompanied men in the bar, but none of them seemed to recognise him. He managed to order some of the local brew, and stood at the bar, confident as always that the person looking for him would not mistake his 6'5" frame.

"You remembered how to find it, then?" – Andrew looked along the bar, and saw a vaguely familiar, but bearded, face grinning back at him.

"Matthias? Of course it is." The two men shook hands warmly and laughed. Matthias looked middle-aged; his hair was more grey than not, and his beard, although neatly trimmed, was almost white. Andrew wondered how old he must look to someone who hadn't seen him for a quarter of a century.

"You haven't got any shorter in 25 years, then?" Andrew laughed again.

"And you haven't grown any, I think!" The height difference between them had been one of the main talking points of the whole trip for everyone. Andrew had always suspected that the match had been made deliberately, to give the teaching staff some light entertainment; in truth it had given the two shy boys something to laugh about from the first, and had seemed to cement their friendship.

"Shall we sit; you must be tired?" Andrew agreed gratefully, and let Matthias lead the way to the back room. He gazed around him

"You remember this? We were supposed only to use this room, because we were school pupils. You remember – we weren't very good at staying here!" Andrew's memory served up another image – he remembered sitting around a long table in here, translating rude jokes back and forth. He smiled. Matthias started to interrogate him about his life since they had last met, and in spite of his normal discomfort at talking about himself, Andrew found the conversation remarkably easy – it was good to have someone else to talk to about his life, and he used the time to try to frame some reciprocal questions which wouldn't seem too prying. Andrew had an abiding and, he felt, well-founded, fear of asking the wrong question at the wrong time. Although he knew many people who could get away with the most outrageous lines of questioning, he never felt he had the confidence, and often simply never asked the things he wanted to know.

So the long explanation of how he had married one of the girls from the bus – Matthias said that of course he remembered her, and Andrew began to piece together some more memories – and how their marriage, like so many, had simply run out of steam because they had married too young, and had turned out to have quite different expectations of one another, proved to be a useful conversational buffer. Andrew gradually realised that he was being fairer to her, and harder on himself, than usual, and some part of him wondered whether this was him actually coming to terms with it, and accepting his share of the responsibility.

The conversation turned to children, and the two men compared stories. Matthias had a daughter of 13, and there was shared fearfulness over what girls of that age get up to, since Andrew's daughter was 14. He pulled out his photograph of his children – the boy younger, but seeming older thanks to his father's genes – at 12, he was approaching six feet tall, and already attracting the kind of comments Andrew remembered only too well.

"I think we have not done so badly," Matthias commented. "I had a time when I was almost not married, but it passed, and things are good. I think you are quite happy, too, no?" Andrew agreed – whatever he felt about his life, he was enjoying being back here, enjoying Matthias' company, and slowly relaxing as he understood that nothing dramatic was about to happen. He was about to say something to that effect, when Matthias suggested some dinner.

"You remember our food?" He laughed. "Of course you do – all those sausages; I remember your complaints!"

"Complaints? Only because we thought we might burst. I remember your sausages very well." He allowed Matthias to order for them, and watched him as he went to the bar to collect more beer.

Matthias seemed outwardly cheerful and relaxed, but Andrew wondered about his demeanour. He remembered that the two of them shared a kind of social awkwardness which manifested itself in simple things like the inability to maintain eye contact. Andrew noticed that Matthias spent most of the conversation looking anywhere but directly at him, and he noticed that he seemed to have some nervous tics, constantly rubbing his arms and patting his legs. He had seemed particularly distracted when they talked of his ex-wife, and Andrew remembered that Matthias had seemed genuinely fond of her at the time – *perhaps he's embarrassed about his schoolboy crush*, Andrew thought. Matthias returned and Andrew watched him tug on his sleeves and smooth down his sweater as he sat. *Has he always been like that?*

JUNE 1978

'Andrew bloody Macintyre,' boomed the voice from the front of the bus, 'we've all got cramp son; stop whining'

'Yes, sir' he replied, not entirely respectfully. When he'd signed up for this seemingly endless bus trip, he'd been under the impression that only the younger teachers had been assigned to it. He hadn't reckoned on old man Cartwright, half-moon specs, tweed jacket and all, being in charge of the whole damn thing. And he did get cramp worse than the others, being about six inches taller than them. As if being 15 wasn't bad enough. It had been Cartwright who had spotted him the previous night in the duty free shop on the ferry, and ordered him out with a lecture about responsibility and respect. He shifted once again in his seat and tried to concentrate on the dreadful thriller he'd brought – he was supposed to be reading Graham Greene for A Level English, but the pull of nonsense about German spies in England in 1944 was stronger than that of anything which required him to actively think about the motives of the characters.

There had been a startlingly explicit scene about fifty pages back, and Andy had worried about how red he was getting, and about whether he could justifiably stay in his seat if they had to stop again, but the moment had passed without comment from Mark sitting beside him, and – he was fairly sure – without any of the girls, especially *her*, looking over at him. He folded the book over his thumb, and allowed himself to wonder about things for a few minutes. He wondered about the standard things which adolescent boys wondered about, projecting what he had just read onto the object of his unspoken desires, and he wondered about his motives for being on this trip.

He wasn't particularly good at German; almost none of his friends were going, although Mark's presence was a relief, and if he'd known that the bus would have no toilet facilities, he would certainly have stayed at home, and he suspected he would not have been alone. He leant out to his right to look ahead, but saw only endless German autobahn stretching into the distance. *She* was behind him somewhere; he wondered if she was looking at the back of his head right now, then he wondered if his ears were red, and then he understood that they were now, and hauled his upper body back upright. He thought he saw another of the girls look round at him, but couldn't be sure.

The thrill of the journey had left them all about 24 hours previously; now, all anyone wanted was to get there. All Andy wanted was to straighten his legs again. And to find a way of at least talking to *her*.

"Andy, look – there – I saw it!"

"You're imagining it – there's too many trees." Andy wanted to go back to his book, but Mark had his attention now. "It's the other side of the town, isn't it?" Mark smiled.

"Well, the road doesn't go any further, so it must cross here somewhere". Andy stood up, and craning forward could just see where the autobahn was fenced off, and then stopped. The bus, and all the other remaining traffic, was siphoned off down the slip road signed for Fastlose.

"Fast and loose," proclaimed a voice from behind – one of the girls; Andy thought it was Victoria, but he didn't look round to check – "very promising." Andy grinned. Judging by the conduct of the past two days, he was going to experience a different side to a number of his classmates. Mark prodded him again:

"Look – there! It's a fence, and a tower! I saw a tower! I bet they can see us." Andy strained to see, but apart from a flash of something white, saw only trees. The border – the Iron Curtain – could wait another day. Right now, there was the terrifying prospect of meeting this strange German family and having to make conversation in a foreign language. Cartwright was proclaiming from the front of the bus about logistics - waiting on the bus until your name was called; that sort of thing – and lecturing everyone on behaviour and respect. The bus was uncharacteristically quiet for this little speech. The tension was getting to everyone.

Andy peered out of the window at what had to be the school building. It was considerably more modern than their own Victorian pile, and seemed to have several discrete parts to it. There was a knot of people gathered on the front steps, and the bus driver appeared to be having to pick his way through a mass of parked cars. Andy swallowed drily; he had always known that this would be the most difficult part of the entire trip, but he wondered if everyone else was also suffering from palpitations and sweaty palms. *She isn't*, he thought. *I don't think she is affected by anything. I can hear her laughing.* He turned to say something to Mark, but his companion was staring fixedly out of the window, and Andy understood that.

His was not the first name called out, but it was close enough to it that he felt self-conscious about it, and there was a certain amount of gentle ribbing from one or two of the boys as he tried to organise himself and get off. He stepped off the bus and turned to his left, to look for his impractically large suitcase, and it took Mr. Cartwright's sharp rebuke for him to understand that he ought to say hello to his hosts first.

He turned slowly round to see a short, even by Andy's standards, and stocky boy looking up at him, or more accurately, at his shoulder. Matthias introduced himself brightly in good English, and Andy relaxed a little. The German boy's parents were standing stiffly some way behind him, and Andy made to go and introduce himself, but was pre-empted by Mr. Cartwright, who was effusively greeting Matthias' father. Andy remembered that he had been told at some point that Matthias' father was the head of English at the school, so this was a natural thing, but it threw Andy for a moment, and he didn't know where to look. He turned away from Matthias, who seemed in no hurry to talk to him, and helped the driver look for his suitcase.

By the time he had been reunited with his luggage, the introductions were over. Andy briefly shook the hand of Matthias' father, who was otherwise not introduced to him, and he thought he detected a certain coldness in the atmosphere. Later that night, as he tried to get to sleep in the unfamiliar bed, he wondered if it had been caused by the fact that the two men seemed to be of a similar age, and had possibly both been in the war. Matthias' father – *I really should find out his name*, Andy thought – seemed distant and somewhat stern, and his mother appeared to be timid and quiet. Matthias was pleasant enough, though, and seemed to be quite similar to Andy in outlook, if not height.

All of which was by now of secondary importance to Andy, who had briefly met Matthias' older sister. Her name he knew, and he tried to stop himself from muttering it out loud as he drifted off to sleep. *Karla.*

The first day in the foreign environment was just as much of a culture shock as Andy had expected. The food was different, the television was incomprehensible, the bed was not his own, the village was quiet, even the toilets were different – much to the amusement of 15-year old schoolboys – and the school, although much newer, was sufficiently like their own for the differences to appear stark. Where the school at home had a playing field, this one had an athletics track and a covered stand; where they were used to blackboards and chalk there were whiteboards and marker pens; where the school day ran from nine to four, here they were in school by eight, and in return for having free afternoons, were expected to attend on Saturdays. After the first morning of this regime all the English pupils congregated next to the running track, debating whether they would all be able to withstand the strangeness. Andy was outwardly relaxed – he had mainly been in an English class of a sufficiently high standard that he had been able to participate – but inwardly, he was as disorientated as most of the others. He joined in the jokes about the food, and waited for Matthias with a little trepidation.

Matthias was carrying his lunch, cold sausage and black bread. 'I suppose you would like to see the border?' Andy nodded. 'Well, come, then; we can walk up there.' The walk was perfectly normal at first: they passed through a quiet residential area where the houses were not so different from the ones back home, and then came to the centre of the village, which had a curious red brick clock tower in the middle of a small public square surrounded by small shops, one of which even operated under the same logo as the local grocer which Andy passed on the way to school each day. That familiarity helped him to relax and put the place into some kind of context, but then Andy was confronted by a sudden feeling of dislocation; the buildings stopped suddenly at a road junction, and on the other side of the crossroads a rusty old sign proclaimed that the unwary pedestrian was about to enter the Soviet sector. Beyond that, to Andy's amusement, there really was a slightly faded sign which read *"Vorsicht. Minen!"* Andy stopped to photograph it – there's something Dad will like, he thought. Beyond the crossroads, the main road simply faded out into an overgrown wilderness. There was one more house on the right with a tired-looking old Fiat parked outside of it, but the house had no neighbours, just an overgrown field with an alarming-looking concrete tower in it. The top of the tower bristled with antennas, but Andy could not see the fence, or wall, or whatever it was. He stood and stared, but could make no sense of it. Beside him, Matthias laughed.

"There is a gap here." Andy turned and stared, but Matthias held up his hand. "No, this is the wrong word." He mimed something and Andy puzzled over it for a moment. Then light dawned.

"A dip?" Matthias nodded. "I understand – the wall is in a dip. Can we go closer?" Andy looked across at the signs – they may have been old, but they still carried a potent message.

"No, we must go up. I will show you." Andy looked where Matthias was pointing, and thought he saw something white. They started to walk, then Matthias stopped them.

"A few months since, something happened here." Andy looked at him, wondering if he was about to hear a spy story or some such. "The border was moved, so this house can have a car." Matthias pointed at the Fiat, and smiled. "I think if this is possible, many things can happen."

Andy thought about this. "So, the East Germans moved the border?"

"Yes, although only a few metres. But I think it is a good thing."

Andy pondered on this, and on the precise location of the border, all the way up the hill.

As they walked, Matthias fell silent, and Andy felt no urge to talk. He looked around him as they went, taking in the landscape. The houses in the village looked alien, but not in a way he could easily identify; there were houses in Chester which had white walls and a red roof, but something about these looked foreign. The countryside was not so different to what he was used to, but small things stuck out – the way fences were made; the fact that the pylons holding up the power lines were painted red and white. He kept seeing glimpses of the border, but couldn't properly resolve it until they came over a rise, and there it was, not quite what he had expected, but unmistakable.

The wall he had half expected, extrapolating from pictures he had seen of Berlin, was not there – this was just a fence – a tall fence, but one you might see surrounding a warehouse or factory where dangerous or valuable goods might be kept. *Or round a prison,* Andy thought morosely. Behind the fence there was a nondescript area of scrubland, almost sandy in appearance, then a concrete track way, and what looked like another, smaller fence which ran in front of the tower Andy had seen earlier.

Matthias stopped and pointed.

"See the guards? Right there, they are watching us." Andy shivered in spite of the heat, and squinted at the tower. He could just make out that there were people inside it, and he fancied he could see binoculars being trained on them. They were quite close to one of the red, yellow and black posts in the middle of the field, which seemed to mark the beginning of the border zone. He started to wander over for a closer look, and Matthias shouted after him.

"Careful, don't cross the border!"

Andy laughed. "Not likely – I don't fancy the climb"

"No – the post. It is the actual border." Andy stopped, suddenly unsure, and a little afraid.

"Really? Can't be. Is it?"

"Oh, yes. The whole fence is inside the DDR" – he pronounced it in German; day day err – "the real border is just there. I think it's safe to cross, but people don't, usually."

Andy peered at the nearest post. It clearly had a 'DDR' shield on it, and he took a deep breath. He looked back to Matthias, who was looking at him with a curious smile on his face. "Do not worry – they do not lay the mines on this side, but they are interested in you."

Andy looked up at the tower again. One of the guards, or whatever he was, had come out to stand in the open and was obviously watching him. Andy stuffed his hands in the pockets of his jeans and walked back over to Matthias.

As he did so, he considered the German boy. He was dressed oddly, to Andy's inexpert eyes – a long sleeved shirt which even looked out of place among his German colleagues, and a pair of the widest, most outrageously flared jeans Andy had seen for a couple of years. Even Andy's parents, not entirely comfortable with teenage fashions, had allowed that a pair of straight leg jeans would be acceptable, and had only complained a little when Andy had torn a hole in one of the knees. Matthias seemed – old-fashioned, he supposed, but in a way which seemed different from his peers. Andy sat down beside him.

The peace was suddenly broken by a raucous two-stroke engine on the other side of the fence. A drab green motorbike rumbled past, the rider looking fixedly ahead.

"Do you ever get used to it?" he said, looking at the white expanse slicing through the landscape before them.

"I don't know what you mean – it's always been here." Matthias was concentrating on excavating his lunch bag, and seemed to have given the fence barely a glance since they arrived. Andy sat and stared, burning this extraordinary sight into his memory. It wasn't until after the trip was over that he realised that he hadn't taken a single photograph of it.

AUGUST 2003

The food was as filling as memory insisted, and Andrew ate heartily – he hadn't really understood how hungry he had become. The conversation faltered at first, then, as Matthias gently resisted talk of his family, turned to the border and the startling difference in the landscape since 1978. Matthias shrugged at first, as if bored of talking about it, but quickly warmed to the story.

"We didn't really know what was happening, you know. We sat at home with the TV on, watching all this madness, and no one really connected to the fence here. That first night was about – what can I say – symbols, not action. Not here, anyway. The next morning, everyone opened their doors and windows, as if to let in the new air, but when we looked, it was still there."

'Still the big white fence?"

"Yes. It just sat there, like always. Some people got in cars and drove up to the border crossing – you remember, up at Herleshausen?" Andrew nodded; there was another memory, but one he tried to shake off. "Well, they didn't come back until the evening – just kept crossing and crossing, with no one to stop them. There were hundreds from the East wandering about – not really trying to cross, just seeing that they could if they wanted to. Here, there were still guards for a few days, then they just went away one morning, and never came back."

"And the fence came down, and –"

"Well, not at first. There were mines and wire – what is it?"

"Barbed wire?"

"That's it. Barbed wire, and concrete, and so much to demolish. And the Autobahn had to be completed – you remember it used to end here? In the end, it took more than a year."

"And is there nothing left?"

"Not really. You can see some tracks if you know where to look. There is a tower still, down by the railway. We can go up tomorrow. I would like that." They talked for a time about the economic problems which reunification had brought, and Andrew was genuinely surprised to find how difficult things had been for several years; he had imagined the end of the border as a simple, good event which had benefited all – after all, that was how it had been reported. Or how he remembered it. He was beginning to understand that he could not fully trust his memories. Until Matthias mentioned the border crossing, he had entirely suppressed the memory of Karla and the motorbike. Now, however much he wanted to be part of this conversation, he was having a hard time shaking it off. Matthias continued to talk for a time about the early nineties, but Andrew was suddenly tired, and needed to sleep. He wound the evening up as gracefully as he could, and the two men agreed to meet again in the morning, to go and look at a fence which was no longer there.

The following morning, Andrew drove his rented Golf into Hohenügel and waited for Matthias by the clock tower. He had smiled to see it again, trying to remember why it had seemed such an important landmark. He was piecing something together when Matthias hailed him from the opposite side of the road.

"Come, Andrew – we can walk; see if you remember!"

Andrew crossed the road, remembering just in time to look the other way first, but there was no traffic; Hohenügel was as sleepy and quiet as he remembered it. Matthias led the way, and Andrew tried to piece together what he remembered of the village.

He could see the church spire some way off behind the street they were walking along, and he remembered that Matthias' house was close to it. Then he remembered lying on his bed, looking out at the steeple, and shivered – he thought he had remembered everything about that Friday afternoon, but it seemed not; seeing the church alarmed him, and made him look away.

He was staring fixedly ahead, then, as they reached a crossroads which he thought seemed familiar. He thought for a moment, and remembered a little Fiat 500.

"This was it, wasn't it?" he asked. "Just here – the road stopped, and there were – I have a photograph of the signs."

Matthias nodded. "Yes – the road ran out here, and the field there was overgrown. The tower is still there, you can see."

Andrew looked properly at the scene in front of him. The road curved off to the right behind what had been the last house in the West. He could see that some new houses had been put up beyond it, and that the road led down a hill to an industrial area. He squinted against the strong morning sun, and could make out the tower which he had remembered as being tall and stark. It was difficult to pick out now, in the mass of new industrial buildings. He asked Matthias about it.

"Some of them were kept. I do not know why that one, but perhaps it was difficult to take down, so close to the railway. My pupils say it is haunted, but children believe anything. Imagine; I teach boys and girls who do not remember the border here. It is so strange for me."

Matthias set off again, retracing the walk the two teenage boys had taken in 1978. They were quickly in countryside again, and Andrew supposed that it was not so different.

He searched his memory for clues to what he had seen before, but the remembrances were overwhelmed by the reality; the mundane, ordinary reality of a plain, clear countryside, dotted with villages and farms. They walked slowly down the hill, until they came to a faint line in the grass. Just beyond it, Matthias pointed out some concrete slabs.

"They ran between the fences, I think. They used to run motorcycles along them. At night time, too"

"I remember a motorbike once," Andrew murmured. Matthias seemed unsurprised.

"You know, you once asked me if I would get used to it, but it's this which I can't get used to. This – normalness. It seems wrong."

Andrew gazed out at the villages in what had been the East. He remembered that the closest village, just visible on the lower slopes, had been connected to this one in some way, and asked Matthias about it.

"Yes, we are Hohenügel; they are Niederhügel. The fence came right between us."

"And now?"

"Now, the memories come between us. Not for the children, I think, but for us, yes. We are not so different now, but in the early days it was strange." Andrew tried to imagine it, but it was too far outside his experience. He walked up to the concrete, but that held no clues, and he walked on, into what had been East Germany. There was nothing strange about it now; just a field like all the others, a field like the ones he had seen from the aeroplane earlier in the week as his flight had approached Frankfurt. He turned and walked back to Matthias, who was staring down at something in the grass.

Andrew looked down, following Matthias' eyes, and saw a faded wooden post, still painted in the German colours, but he could see no sign of the 'DDR' badge he suddenly remembered having seen before. Matthias explained that most of the posts had been removed further north, but that they were expensive to shift – set in concrete, and bigger and heavier than anyone had expected, so many of them were still in situ. The metal shields, however, had made good souvenirs in the first year after reunification, and he didn't know of any which were still in place. He took a deep breath, and looked out to the east, then turned away, and started to walk back into the village. Andrew turned and looked one more time at what was no longer there, then followed. They walked for some time in silence, until Matthias broke it.

"For my parents, it was worse, I think. My father would say that even this is temporary, and that we should wait and see what comes next. He died ten years ago, and I don't think he ever got used to it. You know he was in the war?" Andrew suddenly remembered – Matthias' father had been older than his own, and had shown him some photographs of him as a young man in Wehrmacht uniform; something which had alarmed his younger self – how was he supposed to react? His own father had been too young to have seen active service, and Andy had no real knowledge of that time apart from war films and the dreadful military comics which still, even then, portrayed Germans as 'the filthy Hun'. He realised that he had been frightened of his friend's father, imagining him to be some kind of monster, when in all probability he had simply been a conscript, like almost all the men of his age.

"And your mother?"

"She is still alive – you say "she is still with us", do you not?" Andrew smiled encouragingly, and Matthias carried on:

"She lives in a kind of old person's house near Kassel – she has friends there, and she was born in Kassel, so she feels as if she is home. She is well, but-" Matthias tailed off, and Andrew turned to look at him.

"You do not know about my sister, do you?" Andrew felt himself flush; he hoped his face did not betray him, but Matthias smiled faintly – "I thought so! All these years, I thought you must have been – ah, I don't say "in love" – but you liked her more than she liked you, I think?" Andrew felt his face burning. This was not going well; not at all how he had planned it. He mumbled something about teenage crushes, and Matthias laughed a little, then stared thoughtfully at him. Andrew felt sure that there was something important to be said, but he was not about to volunteer anything about that Friday afternoon unless Matthias showed any sign of already knowing about it. Would Karla have said anything? To her brother? Andrew tried to remember what their relationship had been like, but came up with nothing. He walked on, and Matthias quickly caught him up.

"She certainly knew about crushing younger boys, I think. She was not so kind to you, I remember." Andrew winced. He wanted to change the subject, but he also wanted to know about Karla, and this might be the only chance. He forced himself to ask what his friend had been about to say.

"Ah, Andy, it was all very long ago. You know she was a little – what do I say? Rebellious? Is that good?" Andrew thought hard about it.

Rebellious was certainly one word which you could use, but he would probably have gone with something stronger. "She left us soon after I came back from England that time – when I lived at your house." He sighed. "You know, this is difficult, and yet it will sound so silly to you, I'm sure.

"She had been away before, of course; sometimes planned, sometimes not, - she went to England one summer - and this was just another missing time. But it lasted for a week, then two, then we heard that she was in Bremen, living with a gang of – ah, I don't know, anarchists and drug dealers, I suppose. Maybe something worse – it was a strange time in Germany.

"We thought she'd get bored and come back, but it seemed to be for real. Then Father got the idea that she had been captured; kidnapped? Yes, kidnapped. He got it in his head that they were some kind of cult, and that she had to be rescued. The police were sympathetic, but they did not really want to get involved – I suppose that someone was watching this gang, and they did not want to interfere; I don't know for sure." Matthias looked pained; clearly this was troubling for him, and Andrew wanted to tell him to stop, that it didn't matter, but the truth was, it did matter, more than he had anticipated it would, and he kept silent, save for general noises of sympathy and encouragement.

"After six months – it was the springtime – Father decided we would go and find her. We had to wait for the holidays, since he could not take time off from school, and we went to Bremen, just he and I. We thought we could talk to her, and maybe she would come back with us." He laughed; again, that dry, humourless laugh. "We were wrong. We found her quite easily, she wasn't really hiding, and she had written to one of her friends with the details of her new life. But she didn't want to talk, and at first wouldn't even come to see us. When she did, the next day, we saw why she didn't want to see us. She was pregnant – very much pregnant. She was so big, I thought she must be ready to give birth, but that was just Peter. He was a very big baby; like his father, I suppose."

Andrew blinked and said nothing. This wasn't where he had though this was going – he had visions of Baader-Meinhof and Karla being involved with that somehow, not the domesticity of a baby. Was this what Matthias was so concerned about? An illegitimate nephew? Something continued to nag at him, and he realised that he wasn't paying attention. He recognised that Matthias had stopped, wondered what to say, and then satisfied himself with a simple 'go on', but they had reached the village again by this time, and Matthias suggested coffee.

"We can go to my house," he suggested, "you might recognise it." Andrew nodded and walked on, preoccupied – he kept stealing glances at Matthias to see if the other man had noticed how bewildered he must seem because his thoughts were running away with him now, but Matthias continued to walk without making any kind of eye contact.

It was not until they were standing outside the door that Andrew realised that Matthias must have inherited his parents' house, and that he was about to cross the threshold he had last crossed 25 years earlier. He made polite conversation about the house, and his fond memories of the time he spent here, which gave him time to organise his thoughts and to appear calm and politely interested by the time the two of them sat down again. The rest of the family were visiting Matthias' wife's mother - a task which he seemed to be glad to be relieved of – and the two men had the house to themselves as they settled in the comfortable armchairs. Matthias began his tale anew.

JUNE 1978

Andy lay on the pavement beneath the odd-looking clock tower, his head and arm expertly bandaged, with most of the blood having been mopped up. The crowd around him had, if anything, grown and he was a little bemused by the whole thing. Matthias was nowhere to be seen; having volunteered himself and his exchange student for first aid practice – something to do with Saturday morning classes, but Andy hadn't properly understood it - he had almost immediately been summoned back to school by one of his cousins, leaving Andy a house key and clear enough directions for getting back to the house. Eventually the first aid teachers proclaimed themselves satisfied, and Andy was released from his bandages. Having earned himself effusive praise and thanks – and having probably marked himself down as a soft touch – he felt in need of a rest and to at least read some English, if not hear some spoken.

He found his way back to the house with no difficulty, and let himself in. He stood in the entrance hall for a moment, just listening to the silence, and appreciating the difference between rural village life and the urban noises he was used to. He was thinking that the one thing he would most remember of Hohenügel was how quiet it was, when he realised that it was not entirely silent. Somewhere in the house, a radio was on. He coughed loudly, and clumped noisily up the wooden stairs, so as not to take anyone by surprise. Halfway up, he heard Matthias' older sister, Karla, laughing at something she was listening to. She must have heard him, and yelled out "Hey! English boy! Come and talk to me." Andy felt his face redden, and thought of feigning deafness, but she could see him from her bedroom, and was staring at him quizzically. "Come on; I don't bite."

Andy had had next to no dealings with Karla, other than to be introduced to her on the first day, and to be tongue-tied by her presence at every mealtime. She was small and slim, almost boyish, with a severe close-cropped haircut and a stare which made him most uncomfortable. She also appeared to speak idiomatically perfect English, and had instantly supplanted *her* as an object of desire, although that situation seemed to be complicated, and he had not even begun to try to work it out in his own mind. He knew that if he opened his mouth to talk to Karla, he would ruin everything, and had resolved to keep silent whenever he was in her company. However, she now seemed determined to give him an opportunity to expose himself as a naïve, clumsy 15-year-old; and there was no way out.

Karla was sitting on the edge of her bed. She had a battered old transistor perched on a shelf in the corner of her room, and she leaned over to turn it off. As she did so, her t-shirt rode up her back, and Andy was paralysed by what he saw. He didn't, however, have time to think about her skin, because she abruptly sat back up and turned to face him.

"It's OK," she said, smiling, "I just want to practice my English on someone."

Andy heard himself say that he thought her English didn't need practice, and then stop and not say anything stupid, and as her smile broadened, he thought that maybe he actually could carry this off. He tried something else:

"Actually, I think your English might be better than mine – how did you learn so well?" He cringed inwardly at his sentence structure – after nearly a week in Germany, he was habitually simplifying some of the things he said, but was only now aware that it might sound patronising. Karla, however, was explaining how she seemed to have a natural aptitude for languages – "I don't know where I get it from, although *he* has taught it for a long time" – and how she had spent two months in England the previous summer, and forced herself not to use any German at all.

"My accent, though, needs some work, I think."

"Oh, many English people are much harder to understand. Anyway, your accent is nice. It's very" – Andy stopped, aware that he was an unflattering shade of beetroot, and that Karla was laughing. Her laugh made him feel uneasy, for some reason, and he mentally compared it to *her* laugh, which he had heard so often on the bus and several times during the week. This train of thought was uncomfortable, however, and he felt for some reason that he needed to be paying full attention to Karla.

"Hmm, English boy, I think I like you – you're sweet and kind." She got up and walked over towards the door. As she passed him, she took hold of his upper arm, and murmured "and a little bit smitten, no?" He heard her walk slowly down the stairs behind him, but he was unable to move. Her voice floated up from below:

"That's right, isn't it? Smitten is the right word?" Was she asking about vocabulary or the state of his emotions? He stammered something and fled to the safety of his room.

Matthias showed up an hour or so later, accompanied by his two female cousins, Erika and Liezl, and also their exchange students; two of the girls from Andy's class. One of them, Anne, he knew quite well – she was studious and introspective, and they had many classes in common. Anne was one of the girls at school Andy could talk to without getting tongue-tied or feeling stupid, and she seemed to enjoy his company most of the time. Andy wouldn't have claimed her as a friend, exactly, but he suspected Anne thought of him in that way.

The other girl was, of course, *her*. Clare. Andy had been stunned to discover that Clare was billeted with Matthias' cousin; delighted to discover that this meant spending time in her company for parts of the week, and terrified that any conversation he might have with her – there hadn't been many – would turn out as disastrous as the one he had just had with Karla. So far, she had mostly ignored him; now, it seemed, she was watching him closely. Andy felt the colour rise in his cheeks again.

Anne was solid and somewhat old-fashioned; Clare was tall, outgoing and effortlessly cool. The two of them had, as far as Andy knew, nothing in common, and moved in quite different circles. He was aware of the complex social arrangements girls had, and didn't begin to understand them. But he did understand that the most unlikely of friendships could be forged when you were a long way from home, and forced together by the fact that your exchange partners were close.

Andy stared at Clare for longer than he would normally have felt comfortable with, then glanced over at Anne. Anne seemed concerned, and he dimly understood that they must have been talking about him before he came downstairs. Clare coughed softly, and as he looked back at her, grinned – not Karla's grin, which his feverish imagination had been deconstructing for the last hour, but a playful and friendly grin; the smile of someone who wants to share your secrets.

"Matthias tells us you've been alone in here with his sister all afternoon, and someone" – she glanced sidelong at Liezl – "says she's a bit of a maneater. What have you been up to? Something you want to tell us?"

"No, not really," he replied, in what he hoped was a cool and matter-of-fact tone of voice; the kind of expression which says 'nothing to see here; move along'. But it came out in a much higher register than he'd intended, and everyone laughed. He cleared his throat and tried again, painfully aware of the colour he was turning.

"No, honestly – she was here when I came in, but she went out soon after – I've been alone; waiting for someone to turn up and tell me what's going on this evening. That's all." He almost added "Honest!" to the end of that, but realised in time that he was over-egging things. Anne was staring at him oddly, but when he stared back, she smiled and changed the subject – Liezl's parents were hosting a barbecue for the exchange group that evening, and they had all come back to collect Andy and figure out how to acquire beer – something for which an extremely tall English boy might come in very useful – and how to smuggle it in to the party without being spotted.

This prompted much discussion in high-speed German, which Clare seemed able to keep up with, so Andy and Anne took themselves over to the front window and looked out. He knew he should say something, but couldn't work Anne out at all. Normally, she was not a complex person – what you saw with Anne was what you got, and Andy liked that about her. This afternoon, however, she seemed distracted and a little distant. He tried to get her to translate what was being said, but she professed not to have even been listening. He tried again.

"You're not comfortable with this, are you? The beer thing?"

"Well, no – not really. But I don't have to be involved, so I don't really mind."

There was a long pause, which Andy really didn't want to fill, but gradually realised that he would have to.

"So, how are you? Had a good day?" Normally, their conversations were a little more intelligent than this, but he was already disconcerted by what had happened with Karla, and Anne's unfathomable demeanour, coupled with Clare's playfulness, threatened to derail him entirely, so he retreated to safely bland ground.

Anne seemed to have to think about the question, which struck him as odd.

"I suppose I have, really. A little strange, but most days this week have been strange. I did something I never thought I would ever do earlier, and – well, this week has been full of things like this. You know me, Andy – I don't do new experiences."

Andy recognised this as a cue for him to ask what it was she had done, but he was always wary of getting in to those kind of conversations, so he simply nodded, and looked out of the window at the houses across the street. He thought about Anne's week – paired off with Clare, someone she probably couldn't stand, although she would be far too polite to say anything; and forced to undergo all kinds of alarming experiences. He thought he had caught sight of her in the pub earlier in the week, which struck him as deeply uncomfortable territory for her; he had been preoccupied with dancing to some awful out-of-date music, and had only recognised Anne when she had looked away.

He smiled at the memory of the pub excursions; it seemed that it was normal – or at least not frowned upon – here, and he and the other boys in particular had thoroughly enjoyed their beer-drinking evenings, even if they had been regularly cut short by one or other of the teachers.

Anne asked him what he was smiling at, and he told her.

"Oh. Well, yes; I suppose that was also a new experience. I actually quite enjoyed that evening, if you want to know the truth. I can't say I want to repeat it too often, but it was fun, in a strange way." She started to say more, but Clare interrupted them, explaining the process by which Andy was to buy beer, and which tree it was to be hidden under. Andy felt himself captivated by having Clare talk directly to him, and almost forgot that Anne was even there. Anne walked away from them, and Andy concentrated really hard on being polite and normal with Clare. He somehow felt a lot calmer than he would have expected, and wondered if that had been Karla's doing.

The barbecue turned out to be a relatively sedate affair. All of the exchange students were there, most of the teachers, and a smattering of German parents – mainly, Andy supposed, the friends of the hosts. The beer had successfully been acquired, but given the size of the gathering, it had not lasted long, and Andy had been left with a curious sensation of having been comfortably relaxed before gradually sobering up as more and more orange squash was consumed.

Liezl's parents had been able to host the event because they owned several large fields on the edge of the village; clearly one of the wealthier families in the area, they had arranged for a marquee to be erected, caterers to do the barbecuing, and this left the responsible adults in the party to actually act responsibly, and wander around the gathering breaking up anything which looked to be getting in any way interesting. There was, for a time, a relentlessly jolly camp-fire singalong, which Andy quietly ducked out of; in searching the fringes of the crowd for anyone he knew, he came across Anne, sitting on a tree stump with her back to the party.

He sat on the ground beside her, and she looked down – or, more accurately, across- at him.

"Hi, Andy. Not your thing, either?"

"No – I hated it when I was in the Cubs, and I hate it now. And this is worse – they don't understand our songs, and we don't understand theirs. It's tragic." 'Tragic' had been a fashionable adjective among the fourth form that year, and it raised a laugh from Anne. Andy stared at her. She was, he supposed, not really his type, but he liked that they could talk to each other. That had to count for something. He had, rather unkindly, described her to one of his friends as being middle-aged already, and in truth, her dress sense and hairstyle, even this far from what she had once told him were oppressively 'upper-middle' parents, left a lot to be desired. Most of the English girls, and all of the German ones, were in jeans, the English ones mostly painfully tight, the Germans' tending to the more voluminous, with creased t-shirts or, in some more daring cases – *her*, for example - leather motorcycle jackets. Anne, her hair as always tightly permed, had on a long cotton dress, white ankle socks, and a severe bottle green cardigan. It was a fair approximation of her school uniform, and about as casually dressed as Andy had ever seen her.

However, she was someone to talk to, and someone he liked to talk to, so they talked. They swapped impressions of German life – Anne's more luxurious than Andy's, thanks to the vast house she was billeted in – and of the fence, the giant scar on the landscape, which seemed to be ever-present, even when it was out of sight. He told her of his trip to see it earlier in the week, and of the fact that he had almost strayed into East Germany. She asked him to show her, and they walked the length of two of the fields until the great white curtain came into view. He pointed out where he had been the day before, and they watched the guards in their watchtower staring back at them. Both fell silent, and Anne shivered, although it was not cold.

Later that night, alone in his bed, Andy realised that the shiver had been a signal for him to put his arm around her shoulders, but he was too inexperienced, and way too preoccupied with Karla even to have noticed it beyond commenting that they should be getting back if Anne was feeling the cold. They walked back in silence, and merged separately into the crowd once back to the main group. In Matthias' father's Mercedes on the way back, he realised he had not even said goodnight to Anne.

AUGUST 2003

Matthias started to speak, then stopped himself. He did it again, then looked Andrew in the eye and apologised.

"This is hard for me. I have not thought about it for so long, and I don't know what to tell you, what you will want to hear. It is not so important now, I think."

Andrew, still in a state of heightened alert, became even more alarmed at this. He wanted to know everything. The more he thought about Karla, and what she had done, the more he understood that he needed to know exactly what had happened. She had a baby? Andrew suddenly remembered the name of Karla's boyfriend – Dieter. Was Dieter still here? Was Karla? Was Matthias about to produce them both, with a smiling Peter, to prove that whatever he was thinking, life just carried on as normal for everyone else?

He realised with a start that Matthias was still staring intently at him, waiting for an answer. He tried to collect his thoughts.

"No, Matthias, go on – I am interested. I remember Karla, and I would like to know what happened to her."

Matthias continued to stare, and Andrew began to feel uncomfortable, as if he was being judged for something. Eventually, Matthias broke the gaze and looked out of the window. Andrew suddenly remembered standing with Anne at the same window, and tried to remember what they had talked about.

Matthias cleared his throat, and Andrew looked back at him.

"Very well, I will say it. I told you that Father and I went to find her? Well, that was not a good journey. She did not come home with us, and Father was very angry. I suppose he wanted us to be all together. He was – you remember, perhaps; he was a difficult man, and he got very, very angry."

There was a pause, and Andrew ventured a question.

"Because she was pregnant?"

"I do not think so. No, he said – I remember it; he said he knew this would happen, but she must come home."

"He knew she would be pregnant?"

"I suppose so, yes. We came home, and he did not tell my mother anything. She tried to make me tell her, but he - ah, you remember him; I could not disobey him."

Andrew remembered a forbidding man with a short temper and a genuinely frightening air about him. He remembered Matthias' mother spending a lot of time at her sister's house, where the atmosphere was more relaxed. That house was where Clare had been staying, and he smiled to remember it. Matthias appeared not to notice Andrew's inappropriate smile; he was visibly struggling to get the next part of the story out.

"I am sorry – this is not so easy. After some days, I managed to tell my mother where Karla was, and then everything became much worse. My mother would go away for some days – I suppose she was visiting Karla, but I don't know this for certain. Father – there was much shouting and it was not a good time for me." Andrew noticed that Matthias appeared to swallow the word 'shouting', as if he meant to say something else, but Matthias moved on, and the moment passed. "And then one day, I decided that if my parents could not do it, I must. So I did a very stupid thing; I went to get Peter."

"When was he born?" Andrew still wanted some kind of assurance about something he couldn't quite put his finger on. Matthias looked surprised at the question; clearly not what he had been expecting. He had to pause for a moment before replying.

"Peter? His birthday is May 1st, so I must have decided to go just after that – I know I missed some school, which was a very bad idea. I went to get him, or perhaps I went to get Karla; I don't know, now." Matthias continued to stare quietly out of the window, and Andrew looked round to see what he was staring at, but there was nothing unusual out there. He looked back at Matthias, this time ready to tell him that it really didn't matter; he could just tell him where Karla was now, and they could talk about something else.

Matthias, however, was working up to something.

"So, Andrew, I don't know what to say. I went to get them, or to run away, or something, but I don't remember a lot of it. I do know that it destroyed my family, and I still cannot talk to my cousins because of it."

"I got to Bremen easily – it is not really so far away, on the train. I left before dawn, and was in Bremen by the middle of the day. I did not have much money, and I did not know what I would do if I could not find Karla.

But my adventure was not so much of an adventure yet, and I found her still in the same apartment, with Peter. When I went in, I could see she was miserable. I think her comrades, or whatever they were, had no time for real life and a baby, and she was alone for most of the time. She was feeding him, and I tried to ask her to come home with me, but somehow it wouldn't come out properly. She was not interested, anyway."

Andrew stared at Matthias, who had turned a deathly shade – almost grey –and was clearly distressed. Andrew wanted again to tell him to stop, but there was something important here, and he sensed that the other man needed to tell his story. He made encouraging noises, but Matthias was gazing out of the window again. Andrew tried a question.

"You couldn't persuade her?"

"No. You didn't know Karla – she did not really like me, or ever try to, I think. I was always her *verdamptes* baby brother – even when she was in trouble, and I could help, she did not want my help. So I did not even try. Instead, I told her that our mother was going to come and take Peter away – absolutely the worst thing I could have told her. She started to pack her bag – Peter was asleep now – and she told me to come with her. We were going to Hamburg, where she had another friend, and another place to sleep. It was a terrible journey – we hitch-hiked, and two young people with a baby is not so attractive for most people. It was worse, because Karla would not get in certain cars, and I had to try to explain to the drivers why we did not want to have the ride. In the end, I would just say that she was a little crazy – the baby, you know, and people mostly left us alone.

"In the end, I spent some more money, and we got a train from Buxtehude in to Hamburg. We found the place – it was disgusting; I think you call it a 'squat' – this is right?" Andrew nodded – "and we could have a space on the floor. I never had a worse night, not even with my own children. Peter was cold, hungry, and uncomfortable. Karla was too tired to help him, and I could do nothing; I could not feed him, and even to change him was too much for me; I was helpless, too. At some time in the night, she and I talked – maybe for the first time in our lives, we talked properly; we even talked about Peter's father - she didn't tell me, but I could tell it was Dieter - but in the morning, she was gone; she left me with Peter." Andrew was suddenly aware that Matthias was staring directly at him, seeking out the eye contact he normally avoided. Andrew stared back for a moment, sure he knew why he was being scrutinised, but not at all clear how he was supposed to react. He got Matthias back on track, and the German looked away again.

"What did you do?"

"What could I do? I waited for her to return, and when she was gone for three hours, and Peter was crying again, I tried to leave."

Andrew did not know how to respond to this. He tried to think of himself at that age, the person he became after his trip to Germany, and the way he felt about himself. He remembered that he did feel more grown-up, and that perhaps he had a reason to, but also that he would not have been prepared to travel halfway across the country to kidnap his baby nephew.

"I think I would have done that, too," he ventured, after a moment's thought.

"Yes. I was young. Also, I was stupid. I had not much sleep, and I could not think properly. I think I was going to get on the train with him and go home. I wanted to protect Karla, I suppose – let her still be 'free', if that was her desire. But of course, it did not work out."

Andrew guessed: "Karla came back?"

"Yes. Right when I was leaving, she came back. She had bags of supplies for us and for Peter – I suppose she thought we would all stay together in Hamburg. She – she went crazy. I don't remember this part so well – I think I was in a kind of shock. All I know is that I left her there and went back to Bremen. You have to understand; I was scared for my own life – the people in the squat were threatening me because I couldn't make Peter be quiet"

Andrew, absorbed in this tale, quite forgot his normal reticence: "These people; they were armed? Dangerous?"

"Ah, I do not know. Later, they told us it was a small group with wild ideas, but harmless. At the time, perhaps they were more dangerous than anyone understood. It was a strange time; anything was possible.

"So, I was thrown out of the place I suppose, and maybe my adventure should have ended there. I took the train to Bremen and waited for my father – I guessed that he would know where I had gone. But it was my mother who came. She did not drive often, and I was very surprised to see her there. I got in the car, and told her it was a waste of time, but she said nothing; just sat silently staring outside the front. In a short time, I started to get out, because she would not talk to me, then she spoke. She asked me to take her to Peter – to let her see him.

"I should have said no. I should have left it there, even if it upset my mother – I knew Karla was not ready to see her, and that it might even be dangerous, but what could I do? It was my mother. We went to Hamburg – now it was late, and I said we should find a hotel and come back the next day. She said nothing – the only time she spoke to me was if she needed something – some food on the drive to Hamburg, or the directions.

"She stopped the car where she could see the entrance to the building, and she just stared. I think perhaps she sat there all night – I do not know because I slept: it was a very long day, and I was very tired, so I slept in the car. In the morning, I heard the door shut, and she was gone."

Matthias stood up and stretched. Andrew gaped – *what happened next?* he wanted to say, but he knew he wouldn't be able to, and perhaps it was as well that Matthias took this at his own pace. Andrew also stood, and smiled as if Matthias had completed some amusing anecdote.

"Come, Andrew, I want to show you something."

They left the house again, back into the bright August sunshine, and walked back into the centre of the village. Ahead, Andrew could see what had been the end of the road; there were no signs warning of mines or anything else; just the last few houses in the village on the right, then a broad sweep of tarmac and beyond it, the beginnings of an industrial area. Superficially, it was unremarkable, unless you had the overlay of the old border in your memory. Like so much on this trip, Andrew thought.

Matthias led him to a small restaurant – more of a café, in truth - in the centre of the village. From his seat in the window, Andrew could see the open space where he had been bandaged all those years ago - now converted to parking bays - and beyond it the solid red municipal buildings – all of it having been until this morning merely a faded memory.

Matthias came back with coffee and some highly sugared pastries. "I hope this is OK for you." He said, "I always eat this, because I am not allowed to at home. Once this is done, I will take you back to the school. Would you like that?"

Andrew would; he had been looking forward to the possibility of seeing the school again. For now, being in public had made Matthias more reticent; he spent some time chatting with the tall young man who had served him. Andrew tried not to listen in, but it seemed to be a conversation about sports, and he had little or no interest in any case. He stared out of the window at the traffic, and tried to piece together what he had heard, but all that he could hear was Matthias insisting that Dieter had been the father.

Then why am I so uncomfortable? Andrew wondered. *Something here doesn't quite add up.* He looked back to where Matthias was still deep in conversation. The young man behind the counter was remarkably tall, and something about him nagged at Andrew for a moment, then he realised what it was, and smiled.

They walked to the school in silence. Andrew was too startled by all he had heard to suggest any topic of conversation, and Matthias appeared lost in his own thoughts. As they neared the school, Andrew began to recognise parts of it: there was the low wall where he and – someone, was it Mark? – had tried to tune a shortwave radio to the BBC World Service one morning while they waited for the bus to take them on some trip or other. There was the curve of tarmac where the bus turned, and where they had all been soaked during a late afternoon thunderstorm after one of the trips. They had all had to shelter – there, under the canopy at the front of the school. It looked superficially the same, although whether any changes were real or merely the effect of his faulty memory, he couldn't be entirely sure.

Matthias led him around the back of the main block, to a new extension – its age clear from its construction, and not merely its absence from Andrew's memories. He ducked into a covered passageway between the two structures, and fumbled in his pocket for a set of keys. Clearly Matthias had some kind of administrative privileges here; he opened the door, unset the alarm and flicked the lights on with a practised ease.

"After I got your email, I started to search for things," Matthias explained. "I found a few items about the visit, and there were some more visits by different schools around that time. But eventually, I found the photographs. They were kept in this office – I wanted to have them put on the website, but no-one else seems to like the idea. I suppose I can understand; I am almost the only connection here to those times."

He led Andrew into the back of an office area and hauled on a large, deep drawer in a filing cabinet of what struck Andrew as unfamiliar design. The relevant files were easily found; Matthias had been in here only a few days previously, after all.

"Here, take a look – I think they are fun, especially the clothes. My children laughed about that!"

Andrew found a seat and studied the fading images. Although they had presumably been more or less out of sight for 25 years, the colours appeared to have washed out, and some of the group photographs were fuzzy and difficult to resolve properly. However, with perseverance, and a magnifying glass Matthias excavated from a science classroom, Andrew was more completely transported back in time even than he had been thus far.

There were several pictures of the bus, and various pupils getting on and off it; Andrew could clearly identify himself in one or two of those, thanks to his size, and then a whole set of group pictures – some of only the English students, and others of the whole mixed group – Andrew always in the back row, and Matthias always in the front. In these, he could, eventually pick out familiar faces; Anne, of course, but several others whose names came back to him as soon as he saw them. He took his time finding Clare; she was always turned slightly aside, or otherwise obscured, and he wondered about this for a moment. Then he tracked down the boys he had been closest to, and surprised himself by realising that he had kept in touch with none of them over the years.

The final group of pictures were of the exchange pairs; he skipped several who he only vaguely recognised, and smiled to see Anne and Liezl together with Clare and Erika: those four had been inseparable for the whole time, he remembered; even to the extent of being photographed together. The picture of he and Matthias made him laugh out loud – the disparity in height was even more pronounced than he remembered, and then he somewhat guiltily recalled being dared to stand on the bench which had been provided for the group shots. No-one seemed to have noticed at the time, but he could feel himself colouring as he looked again at the evidence of the practical joke.

Matthias laughed, too. "I remember you were moving around, but because you were a little bit behind me, I never knew what you did. Until I saw the picture; then it was too late."

The final group of pictures had been taken on the morning of their departure – groups of new-found friends self-consciously hugging and sheepishly looking away from the camera, in case their faces revealed something other than teenage ennui. But the final picture drew Andrew up short. Most of them were on the bus; he could make out Anne clearly; she had probably been ready to leave for half an hour or more, and was simply sitting there, staring fixedly ahead. He couldn't see himself clearly inside the bus, although he had a good idea where he would have been, but what startled him was the face in the crowd outside the bus. Karla; staring directly in through the front windscreen, as if burning something into her memory. He still hadn't properly absorbed all that Matthias had told him about her, and neither had he properly thought about what had passed between them that second week, but seeing her there, like that, exactly as he remembered her, caused him to freeze.

Matthias laughed again: "I am right – you did feel something. She was so cruel to you, I remember, but you know you were not the only man she hurt – just one of a long list."

Andrew found his voice. "I hadn't remembered she was even there that day. I was too busy with other things, I suppose. I don't know what I really thought of your sister – I was so young; certainly not yet a man, and she seemed so much older –"

"She was 18; it's a big gap at that age, I think"

"Yes, it was. You're right; she was cruel – or maybe just unkind – to me that week, but I was – I don't know; it was just a crush, I think. I never forgot about her – you don't when it's something like that, but I hadn't thought about her for a long time."

Andrew paused and then said something uncharacteristic for him: "I would like to hear the rest of your story. If you don't mind, that is"

Matthias sighed. "I don't know if I can tell you all of it today. My wife will be back by now, and we should go back there. You will have dinner with us, I suppose?"

Andrew suddenly thought of something. "Your wife – you didn't tell me her name. Is she – I mean, was she someone I knew?"

"No – I am not like you, my friend; I married from well outside my school friends – someone I knew from just after I was in prison – but that must be for tomorrow." Matthias walked back along the corridor to the door they had come in, leaving Andrew, open-mouthed, staring after him.

JUNE 1978

Andy was woken the following morning by church bells. He had been surprised by the frequency of bells rung in the church, but thought he had got used to them. Normally, he would have been woken by Matthias before this in any case, and he lay for a few minutes trying to figure out what was different. Slowly, he remembered that it was Sunday; Matthias had explained that the family would be going to church, and that Andy was welcome to join them; this said with a vigorous shaking of the head, which left Andy in no doubt that he would be better off staying in bed. He lay there for a time, enjoying the stillness which followed the end of the bell-ringing, then got himself up, and walked along the corridor to the bathroom, where he could enjoy a hot shower.

This walk took him past Karla's room, but the door was closed, and all seemed silent. Andy luxuriated in his shower, and took his time drying and shaving – this last a new experience for him. He really only needed to shave about once a week, but he had been scrupulous about it on the trip, since the consequences of allowing the fuzz to remain were beyond embarrassing. He wrapped himself in his enormous bath towel, and walked back, only to be stopped in his tracks. Karla's door was now open – open enough for him to see inside. Karla was lying face down on her bed, with the covers up to her waist. All he could see of her was the back of her head, and an expanse of bare back, but he felt he had been electrocuted, and stood rooted to the spot. He clutched frantically at the top edge of his towel, terrified that it might fall, or reveal him in some other way. As he stared, he saw that she had a bruise on her lower back, off to one side. Once he had noticed it, he was grateful to have something to fix his attention to, and stared at that.

He stared for what felt like an eternity, before realising that she must

41

have arranged this – she was awake (or how else would the door have been opened?), and was, in fact, propped up on her elbows, reading. This slowly-dawning realisation was worse than the fear that his towel might fall; she knew he was there, and was waiting for him to say or do something. He cleared his throat – an entirely reflex action; since he would rather have fled silently, and she laughed.

"Hey, English boy; have you read this?" She half-turned to show him what she was reading, and he gave an involuntary gasp as the side of one small breast came into view. He tried to see the title of the book – something to do with a rat, as far as he could see, but his focus was wandering – look anywhere but directly at her, he told himself, but this only occasioned more laughter. Karla pulled on her covers as she turned to face him, and he caught sight of - what, exactly? Something darker than the surrounding skin, perhaps – as she covered herself.

Andy felt like a fieldmouse in the gaze of a kestrel – unable to move, unable to save himself in any way. Karla was, as far as he could tell, naked; he had only a towel to protect himself, although his pyjamas and sponge bag were doing a reasonable job of covering what would otherwise have been a source of even greater embarrassment. He was, he knew, bright red, and more than anything in the world, he wanted to get away to the security of his room. Instead he was going to have to stand here and have a conversation about – he could see it now – a book called *Dr. Rat*.

"It is very good; I like to read in English, and your friend Clare gave it to me yesterday. It's about –" she peered at the blurb on the back cover – "vivisection; a good word, I like to learn new words. I like it; have you read it?"

Andy had not even heard of it, much less read it, and he managed to say so in more or less comprehensible English. Karla laughed at him again. "I think you are so young in some ways, but maybe not in all. No?" He simply stood and stared as he tried to work out what she meant. She was looking pointedly at his waist while she said this, and he belatedly understood that this was the kind of situation which generations of 15-year-old boys had fantasised about. The reality, however, was more than a little terrifying, and in spite of having written the script for just this kind of thing in his head, he slowly backed out of her room. As he did so, Karla looked him in the eye and began to raise her arms above her head in a languid stretch. The covers slid down, but before they could reveal anything more than he had already seen, he fled.

He reached the security of his room and closed the door behind him. He had expected to have been pursued by her mocking laughter, but perhaps the pounding of the blood in his ears had covered that. He leant against the door, in some kind of protective reflex – no-one was coming through that door – and threw his pyjamas and toiletries onto the bed. The vision of Karla's back appeared to him, and he was happy to let it do so, now that the danger was past. He reviewed the encounter. Had he been an idiot? Was she teasing him, or was she serious? What would have happened if....

His reverie was interrupted by Karla's soft voice on the other side of the door.

"Hey, English boy – I'm going to have my shower now, then I can take you to the East. If you like. It's OK, I really don't bite."

"Oh, and no peeking!" He felt, as much as heard, something brush gently against the other side of the door, then soft footsteps trailing off into the bathroom. Andy dressed, somewhat awkwardly, then, taking a deep breath, slowly opened his door. Karla was nowhere in sight; indeed, he could hear the shower running at the other end of the corridor, and he walked past the bathroom. The door was firmly shut, and he could hear Karla humming loudly over the sound of the running water. He went downstairs and found some breakfast.

Karla didn't appear to need breakfast, and her peremptory manner once she appeared downstairs – to Andy's relief, fully dressed – left him scurrying to tidy up after himself. Karla was not impressed: "Come, leave that – she can do it when she comes back".

She, Andy surmised, was Karla's mother. Even he, not normally well tuned to relationships, could tell that Karla and her mother were not exactly the best of friends. Of course, his relationship with his own parents could be strained at times, and many of his school friends had their own horror stories, so it didn't seem to be so unusual. Still, there was something about Karla's manner which alarmed him a little.

That alarm, however, was nothing compared to what he felt when she turned into one of the other houses in the street, walked around the side of it – Andy staying, uncomfortably, at the front gate – and returned wheeling a large BMW motorcycle. He tried to express his concerns, which were many, but she simply shrugged. "It's OK, we just cannot tell my father. Get on."

Andy pondered this for a moment, then decided that at least he would have something to tell the others about, and that perhaps they might even believe him this time. Karla was already on board, and Andy swung one of his long legs over the pillion seat. She turned to face him; closer than he had been to her before now, he could smell the toothpaste on her breath: "I will go slowly, but you must hold on tight." She demonstrated where she wanted him to hold, and he complied. He had somehow expected their first actual contact to be accompanied by electric sparks, or to be in some other way momentous, but it turned out that she was just another human being, flesh and blood like anyone else, and holding on to her waist was probably the least embarrassing outcome he could have anticipated. At first, he sat upright, watching the village roll by; then as she left the buildings behind, he found it was more comfortable to lean forward into her back, and look out over her head.

The level of comfort was, of course, relative – he had nothing to shield him from the wind and insects, and it wasn't long before he was contorting himself to try to get into Karla's slipstream a little. She had no helmet, either, and he wondered what the experience must be like for her. He found out sooner than he had expected. Karla pulled off the road no more than two or three miles out of Hohenügel – they had crossed over the abbreviated autobahn, but were still within sight of the church. She sat up and shrugged him off, before turning to look at him.

"I suppose you have never been on a bike before?" Andy shook his head. Karla sighed. "OK, then – you need to work with me a little. You are so big, you are making me fall over, and slowing things down. You need to work with the bike; lean into corners, and keep out of the wind if you can. Can you do that?" Andy nodded this time. "Good. Well, do it."

She started the engine again, and Andy had to scramble back into position. This time, he tried to clear his mind of all the strangeness, and just concentrate on doing what Karla asked. He leaned with her – raggedly at first, but with increasing confidence, and after a time, he found that he was enjoying it. He had not really been able to focus on where they were going, but had noticed an increase in traffic, particularly commercial traffic, and he was not altogether surprised when Karla once again pulled the bike over to the side of the road.

This time, she also dismounted, and looked up at him. "So: you think you can ride this?"

Andy stammered: "M-me? No. No, I don't think so; I can barely ride a pushbike."

"Pushbike? I don't know this expression. You mean a pedal bike, I suppose? A bicycle. Well, interesting. Perhaps you can teach me something, after all. OK, so this is what you do…"

Andy noticed that his refusal had simply been ignored; whatever else she was, Karla was clearly a force of nature and not to be gainsaid. He straddled the bike once more and tried to understand what Karla was telling him, but the intricacies of the clutch and the gear changing baffled him, and she had to get back on and demonstrate. All the while they were standing at the side of the road – buses and lorries thundered by only a few feet from them, and he kept looking nervously over at them. Karla finally appeared to register his discomfort, and smiled, rather than laughed at him:

"No, not on the road – I like this bike. You'll go down here –"she indicated a trackway he had not noticed until now "– there's a big field on the other side; you can practice there."

Andy swallowed hard, then did as he was told. He walked the bike into the field, then got on. He got it started, worked out how to select a gear, slowly let the clutch out, and promptly fell over. Fortunately he was tall enough to stop the bike hitting the ground, but only just strong enough to hold it there. Karla came to his rescue, grabbing the clutch and getting it back upright. Although she was much smaller than he, she handled the bike with a confident ease which Andy knew he would never be able to copy.

After half an hour or so of struggle, Andy managed to ride one length of the field, even changing gear as he did so, although the stop at the far end was less than dignified, and he managed to stall it trying to turn round. At that point, mildly humiliated, he turned the engine off, put the bike on its stand, and sat down to look out over the undulating countryside bisected by that great white fence.

"Perhaps it is not your best activity." Karla had come up behind him silently, and he jumped slightly to hear her voice. She laughed quietly again, and sat beside him.

"I meant what I said – I can take you in to the east, if you would like."

Andy, thinking this highly unlikely, simply stared back at her. She wasn't exactly pretty, he was thinking; there was a hardness to her face which made her look almost cruel, and her hair was much too short for his taste. But she was intoxicating. And dangerous; very dangerous. He understood that her flirting and teasing had been designed to embarrass him in one way or another – during the course of the morning, he had come to understand that she would use his timidity against him at some point, just as she would have used his boldness, had he actually been bold enough to – to what, exactly? To drop his towel and climb into her bed? He almost laughed out loud at the thought of it: he was 15, for God's sake; you might have more-or-less innocent fumblings with girls at that age, but no-one was actually having sex. Were they? Perhaps he was just hopelessly naïve.

While this was thundering through his mind, Karla was watching him with interest. Finally, he realised he should say something.

"I don't know. I'm not even sure I should be here – your parents don't know where we are; I don't know whose motorcycle that is, and I'm sure I can't get in to East Germany without a passport. Maybe you should just take me back -" he almost said 'home', but stopped himself in time. For all of this trip, he had not once really thought about home – he was having too much of an adventure – but now he was suddenly intensely aware of how far away from everything he was.

He stood up, and began to walk back to the road. Karla must have watched him for some time, because he didn't hear the bike start up until he was nearly back at the road. Karla rode up alongside him as he reached the edge of the road. He looked down to his right, where he could see what he hadn't noticed before, the crossing point into East Germany. He didn't really have any experience of border crossings, but as far as he could tell, it didn't look so different from the ones they had passed through in the bus on the way here. Of course, there were high fences and watchtowers here, and probably more armed guards if he looked closely enough, but there were lines of traffic, inspections and an air of bureaucracy about the place.

Karla eventually tired of watching him fail to decide anything. She gave him one last opportunity to get back on, then gunned the engine and shot off down the hill towards the border. He stood and watched as she skirted the lines of commercial vehicles and approached one of the less-used booths. He saw her get off the bike, and go inside. Then, unsure if he was really seeing it, he thought he saw the bike, with a dark-suited rider, on the far side of the border fence. He stared, amazed, as it disappeared around the bend in the road.

After half an hour or so, Karla was back. He had stopped watching the crossing closely, so the first he knew of it was the distinctive sound of the bike's engine racing up the hill towards him, and then suddenly she was beside him, grinning a genuine, open smile – the first time he had seen her like that.

"So. It wasn't so hard, was it – you should have come, because I won't offer it again. Get on." Her face closed up as abruptly as it had broken into a smile, and he silently resumed his pillion position. Karla raced back towards the village; whether she feared being late for something, or was simply trying to frighten him, he didn't know, but he more than once wished he had just stayed in bed that morning, or gone to church with the others; anything other than sitting on the back of this bike with this crazy girl –no, woman.

Once they were across the autobahn again, and close to the edge of the village, Karla suddenly stopped.

"You can get off now. I don't want anyone to see us; they might think I stole you, or something." She suddenly switched to rapid German, and Andy only caught something about his friends and the swimming pool before she sped off.

"Kidnapped," he shouted at her retreating back, "the word is 'kidnapped'".

He stood for several minutes, wondering if she might come back for him, but it was hard for him to shake off the feeling that he had yet again failed one of Karla's intricate tests. Whatever game she was playing with him, he understood only that he didn't know the rules

He found the open-air pool with a little difficulty, despite having heard that it was on the far side of the school athletics track. As soon as he entered the village and passed under the railway bridge, he had turned right and walked confidently to where he thought the school was, only to discover that his sense of direction had completely let him down. He wandered for a time, and then heard sounds coming from somewhere off to his left. All he had to do was to follow the sounds of yelling and splashing once he located the school, and before long he was surrounded again by familiar faces. He was not entirely surprised to see Karla there, lying on the grass with a couple of older boys, laughing uproariously at something.

Mark came up to him. "We wondered when you'd show up – she" – nodding at Karla – "said you were walking." At this, several of the English teenagers laughed, and Andy understood instantly that Karla's humiliation of him had begun. She would have arrived noisily on the bike, and – having everyone's attention – announced something or other to the assembled crowd. He looked around, and saw that many of his friends were unable to quite meet his eye. He reddened, and caught between a desire to go and confront Karla, and an equally strong urge to just slink off and go back to his bed, essentially did nothing.

He looked around for a sympathetic face, but Anne was not there – he was sure that open-air swimming was not really her kind of thing, either – and in the absence of Matthias or anyone else he could use as a pretext to go and get involved in conversation with, he simply sat down where he was, and for more than an hour, looked around him as everyone, consciously or otherwise, ignored him.

He was aware that certain of the other boys were being mercilessly teased about rubbing sun lotion into the backs of the girls, and even vice versa, but the whole high-spirited, hormonal thing left him cold, and he made up his mind to walk back to Matthias' house, to see if he could find his exchange partner, and to get out from under the stares of his classmates.

Of course, Karla got up at the same moment – had she been waiting for him? That way led to paranoia, so he did his best to ignore her.

He would have succeeded, too, but for the fact that he had to pass behind her, getting back on the bike, to get out, and as he did so, she started up, covering him with a light coating of first exhaust smoke, then fine gravel as she rode off without a backward look. He knew that to stop would invite further humiliation, so he walked off, all the while trying to make it look as if nothing had happened.

Later that evening, after a quiet dinner, and an evening of excruciating German television variety programmes, Andy was reading Graham Greene in his bed when there was a knock on the door. His heart began to pound – surely Karla would not be so brazen? But it was Matthias' voice which came through the door. Andy called for him to come in.

Matthias – dressed in an ill-fitting robe – almost sheepishly sidled up to the bed, and sat on its edge.

"I want to say sorry about my sister," he offered, "I heard what she did, and I'm sorry. She is not a kind person, sometimes." Andy considered this.

Matthias appeared to be the opposite of his sister; kind and thoughtful – it couldn't have been easy for him to come in and say this; teenage boys are not normally good at that sort of thing – and Andy did appreciate it, but part of him didn't want to even think about the day's events. After a minute or two, however, he spoke.

"It is also my fault, Matthias. I let her take me out on that motorbike, and I should not have. I don't understand her, but I think I have maybe upset her somehow."

"Only, I think, by being a man, and being in this house. This is what I think; I have to be here every day with her. She is this person all of the time. I am sorry."

Andy thought about it. He could never tell Matthias all that had passed between him and Karla, even though it would simply have reinforced what Matthias already knew about his sister. He thought for a moment, then asked the one question which had been bothering him since that morning: "Whose bike is it? I am worried that she just stole it."

Matthias smiled. "No. She says it is hers. She got it from a boyfriend last year, but father does not allow it to be even near this house, so she keeps it at the house of a friend."

"She has a boyfriend?" Andy hoped his voice didn't betray whatever strange emotions were coursing through him on hearing that news.

"It is hard to say, sometimes, but always there is Dieter – you have seen him, I think? He is very tall – almost like you, but he has" – Matthias stroked his chin. Andy had no memory of a Dieter, but nodded anyway.

Andy lay back against the oddly uncomfortable pillows, and Matthias rose to leave. "I go now, my friend. You must sleep, it is an early beginning tomorrow, I think." Andy agreed – he had set his little travel alarm for 5.30, as the bus was due to leave the school at seven the next morning to take them to some outlandish castle or other. Just another day trip.

AUGUST 2003

Wilhelmshöhe was all that he had remembered – a mad, baroque extravaganza, with follies, fountains and landscaped gardens. Matthias had suggested he get out and explore on Sunday morning, since he and Gerda had many church-related duties, and they had arranged to meet again in the afternoon, as soon as Matthias could reasonably get away.

Dinner the previous evening had been a slightly odd affair. Andrew had, with no particularly good reason when he thought about it later, expected that Matthias' wife Gerda would have English as good as her husband's (or indeed her children, who appeared to have inherited the family's knack for languages), but this turned out not to be the case, so the evening was spent telling anodyne stories of family life, translating them painstakingly between the languages until Andrew's head, fuzzy with good wine, and full of Matthias' remarkable tales, had begun to spin, and he had excused himself around 11.

He had not slept well, and had not expected to, given all that he had been told, and when he was fully awake at 5.30 in the morning, resolved to drive back to the scene of the day trip he remembered most strongly. This meant fortifying himself with hotel coffee, and using his laptop to try and figure out a reasonable route which would not get him lost too often. It turned out to be a remarkably straightforward journey, and he arrived outside the gates to the park before 9am, with over an hour to wait before he could gain access.

While he waited, he considered the previous time he had been here. He was trying to understand why it figured so strongly in his memories; it was, he remembered, the first time he had taken Anne seriously as a friend, and he knew that there was something else, but he couldn't quite remember what it was. The day, he knew, had been hot and sunny – his memory suggested that all of the days had been, but he suspected that was also not entirely true. He remembered that there had been a great deal of walking, and of messing around in fountains – or near fountains, given that the ever-present teachers would have been frowning on them at every turn.

It was not until he had managed to gain entry to the park that more of it started to come back to him. He had spent a lot of the afternoon just walking with Anne; he remembered counting ducks at one point, and thought he could identify the pond where that had happened; he looked up at the ridiculously overblown cascade, and remembered a group of them trying to climb the hill alongside it, and he wondered just what the educational value of the day had been, given that they spent it all tearing around, yelling at each other in English, and generally blowing off steam. Perhaps that was the actual point of it – to keep everyone sane.

Walking sedately around the parkland this morning was having much the same effect on him – he wasn't exactly blowing off steam, but he was clearing a lot of the fog from his mind, and as he thought harder about what had happened all those years ago, he realised that there were repercussions in his life to this day which he perhaps ought to do something about. He knew that as soon as he got home, he was going to have to have a conversation with his ex-wife, for example. And he now had a sudden urge to try to trace someone else who had been a more important part of the trip for him than he had remembered, and he felt he might have some things to say to her, as well.

In the Golf, the drive back took only just over an hour, and he was, once again, early. He had arranged to meet Matthias back in the same café as they had visited the day before, and he used the time to ensure that he was well fed – the walk had left him hungry. The tall young man from the previous day was nowhere to be seen, and he was served by a cheerful teenaged girl whose hairstyle reminded him of Karla's, but whose disposition could not have been more different. He was pondering this when Matthias sat down opposite him.

"Still like the girls with the short hair, then?" Matthias teased. Andrew could feel himself blushing again – he did not redden quite as furiously as he had done as a teenager, but it was still noticeable when it happened, and Matthias immediately apologised: "I'm sorry, Andrew – I should not tease you. My sister did enough of that before, I think."

"I got over it in the end," Andrew said, not sure if he was telling the truth or not. "I can take it now."

"Still, I am sorry. Let us explore – you have eaten, I suppose?" Andrew nodded; yes, he had, and they left, Andrew leaving a larger than warranted tip – something else he did not want to think too hard about.

Matthias suggested a trip into the East, which these days merely involved crossing the border between Hesse and Thüringen. Andrew drove, and Matthias, in between giving directions, continued his story from the previous day.

"What happened after my mother left, I do not properly know. I might have been asleep again, I think, because the next thing I know is a policeman knocking on the window. He did not tell me so much, but asked me to come with him. I wanted to know about my mother, but he said nothing. He did have the keys to lock the car, so I guessed it was OK.

"When I look at it now, I think I must have been so stupid. All I needed to do was call my father and let him do what was necessary. But I did not – I waited to find out what my mother was doing, and in the end I had to answer some questions. I thought they would let me go then, but there was some problem which I did not really understand. Eventually, someone brought me some food, and told me that my mother was going to be arrested. I could not believe it, but they did not tell me why then. In the evening, Karla came to see me. She told me that Peter had been taken away from her, but that it was mother's fault, and she was going to pay for it. Look – here we are."

Andrew stared at what looked like an abandoned motorway service area, but something triggered in his memory, and as Matthias directed him around a complex series of right turns, designed to get them facing back the way they had come, he understood that this expanse of tarmac and concrete must be the site of the old border crossing. They parked and got out of the car. There really was nothing left here now; if you had not known, you would have been unlikely to guess what this had been. The border, he remembered, was further back, so this must have been the eastern side. Matthias confirmed it.

"Yes, you know that the fence was over there" – he pointed back beyond the service area "- and there was a corridor of road before this, where you could cross into the DDR. Here we used to come on the weekends and the brave ones would take their passes to try to go in – sometimes it was possible, but not always. You could always get past the West border, but to get in the East was much harder – it was only supposed to be for travelling to Berlin, or visiting family; you could get the special pass, and most of us had one. Even the ones without liked to try, though – we thought it was safe, because the East did not want to make a fuss about Western teenagers. Now, I wonder if we were right, or just lucky."

Andrew now understood what had happened with Karla that Sunday morning. She must have had one of those passes, perhaps it even had permission to take someone else across; he resolved to look it up when he got back. She must have just gone across and waited – just staying out of sight long enough for him to wonder what was happening, then come back. He tried not to think about what any of that meant, if indeed it meant anything at all.

Matthias led him back to the car. "Come, we will go back the old way – you can see Niederhügel, if you like." Andrew got back behind the wheel, and allowed Matthias to direct him, as he listened.

"After that, it was very strange – my mother had been charged with something – is 'assault' the right word?" Andrew confirmed it "- and then later they said also kidnapping, or trying to. When that happened, I was also accused of kidnapping, and then my life changed, I suppose." He was silent for a time, and Andrew looked over at him. "I know, it sounds so strange, but some things happened in that place which I did not understand. There were some things – evidence, I suppose, and they said that my mother and me were working together to steal Peter away. She would not say anything, and I could not; I did not know what had happened." He sighed heavily. "Because of this, my family does not talk to me. I could have changed everything; explained that it was my idea, but my mother did not talk, and people do not understand that – they think it was all my fault. Perhaps it was. My mother was never well again after – after she was in prison, and I accept that it was down to me."

Andrew was aghast: "But you did nothing! You were 16 years old; you went to try to help! How did it end up so badly?"

"If my mother was well enough to talk about it, then perhaps I could tell you, but she has never talked."

"I didn't know she was ill," Andrew said, "I mean, you said she was in a home, but –"

"I know; I still think it is easier to say that, and I did not expect to talk about this, really. She does not know us now; any of us. My father believed that prison broke her health, but I think now she was sick before all this – some things happened before this which I think I understand now. Everyone blames me for all of this, but it was my sister, I think. She was the one who made sure that both of us had to pay for what we did. I understand why, but it is still so hard for me."

"How long were you in prison? It sounds so unreal."

"For me, about three years in all." This sounded absurd to Andrew, and he said so.

"There were some other reasons, but it was a long process. My mother; she was longer, and then she moved to the – the place where she is now. She never came home, and when I came out, my father was also gone – but that is a different story, not so interesting. So I live here in my old house, and I have my own family. All my old family are around, but I do not see them. My fault, I think."

"What happened to Peter? And to Karla?" Andrew had managed to get them back to Hohenügel without incident during this explanation, and he now pulled up outside Matthias' house. Matthias looked over at him. "Well, that is not so long a story – perhaps, if you have some time this evening, another beer before you go?"

JUNE 1978

Monday was another day of extraordinary heat – perhaps the hottest so far – and the bus was by now becoming an extremely unpleasant place to spend any time. Andy had been dreading spending the first part of the day cooped up with everyone who had witnessed his humiliation the day before, but he was rescued principally by Anne, who latched on to him before the bus arrived, shepherded him to a window seat, and effectively fenced him off from his compatriots. Normally, he detested the window seat on account of his size, but on this occasion, he was grateful for the way he was being protected. Anne was silent for most of the journey, content to read her *Tess of the Durbervilles*, and leave him in peace, but after an hour or so, as the noise level in the bus indicated that everyone was waking up properly, she leant in to him and quietly told him that she was sorry about what had happened.

"But you weren't there," he replied, "what do you know?"

"We were there when she came back without you – we heard what she said about you. I know you better than that, though; you wouldn't have done any of that."

Andy, who had merely been depressed up to this point, now began actively to worry.

"What? What did she actually say?"

Anne hesitated.

"I can't say, but it wasn't nice. People are going to say things, but - " Anne was blushing now, and made a pointed effort to go back to her book, but mumbled something about not listening to any of it. Andy, as ever too polite to interrupt, simply stared out the window in bewilderment and confusion. As the rowdier elements of the bus came to life, he began to hear comments – mainly, from the sound of it, those who had been at the pool conveying the details to those who had not. All of this was conducted in a kind of murmured code, however, from fear of alerting any of the teachers at the front of the bus.

Something must have been said by someone at one point, however, because Mr. Cartwright got up and delivered a vague, unfocused lecture on respect and comradeship, the general point of which must have got home, for the rest of the journey was conducted in relative silence, save for the occasional outbreak of giggles.

Once they arrived at Wilhelmshöhe, the party scattered. Instructions had been given regarding timetables and so on, but mostly, they were free to wander and explore at will. As Andy got off the bus, he had his elbow grabbed from behind by Cartwright, who must have understood something of what was going on.

"Walk with me, son," the old man said, "and stop frowning; you're not in trouble."

"Yes, sir."

The two – the giant pupil, and his shorter, slightly stooped master, walked amid the gardens for what seemed like Andy to be an age, while Cartwright pontificated about the plant life and the different species of duck, some of which were not native to northwestern England. Even restrained Andy was on the verge of asking if there was a point to this diversion, when Cartwright indicated a stone bench for them to sit on.

"I know I may seem an old fool to you -" he held up a hand to forestall Andy's inevitable and insincere protest "- but I have, in my years of service to this school, seen most everything. I do not understand what was being said in the bus this morning, and I believe I do not wish to find out more, but I must ask you one thing, for you are my ward; I am the one who signed the documents making me *in loco parentis* for these two weeks – I feel sure it is the only reason I was encouraged to come at all – and so I have a duty and a responsibility to you and to the school."

Andy chewed this over for a moment, discovered that there hadn't, in fact, been a question embedded in it at any point, and replied "Sir?"

"I must ask, Andrew. Are you in any kind of trouble? Anything which would reflect badly on the school, or indeed, yourself? Because, whatever it is, I am able to act as a surrogate parent, and offer advice or discipline, as necessary."

Andy suppressed a laugh, and tried to concentrate. Cartwright may have been a brilliant scholar of Modern Languages – Andy had no way of knowing, in spite of having sat through two entire years of the man's teaching – but he was no-one's idea of a surrogate parent, and the idea of confessing to him that Karla had tried to seduce him, and when that had failed, had publicly humiliated him in a way which he did not yet fully understand, was absurd. However, he had to say something.

"Um, no, sir. Not really. There was an – no, let me see. My host's sister – his older sister, you understand – was teasing me about something yesterday, and some of the boys might have got the wrong idea; that's all I can think of."

"I see. Girls will, in my experience, do this kind of thing. It is most unkind, but I suppose it serves some kind of evolutionary purpose. Well, alright, then. You may confide in me further if anything more untoward happens, but otherwise, you are free to enjoy this magnificent place. You know where to find me if needed. Good morning." Cartwright stood smartly, almost to attention, and walked briskly away. Andy sat on the bench, unable to hold in his giggling any longer. *'Good morning'*? No teacher – no, no-one at all said that kind of thing any more, especially not at the end of a conversation like that. Andy reflected that Cartwright must have been a military man at some point in his life, and wondered how that had shaped his life.

Still, the encounter had put him in a much better mood than he had thought possible at the start of the day, and he devoted the remainder of the morning to avoiding the worst of the potential troublemakers.

At lunch, however, he was not so lucky. One or two comments were made which at least allowed him to understand the nature, if not the details of Karla's broadcast the day before, and he tried to slip away unnoticed – no easy feat for someone of his size. He was arrested by Mark; good old Mark, the closest thing he had to a best friend on this trip – his actual 'best' friends having been left behind in Chester through a combination of indolence, poverty, and not knowing any German.

Mark seemed uninterested in the gossip and instead tried to interest him in a race up to the top of the 'Herkules' statue which loomed over this end of the park. Andy thought about it for a few moments, and then politely – more or less – declined. Mark accepted this at first, then said something under his breath which Andy thought he understood. Something in him seemed to snap, however, and he challenged Mark:

"What? What did you say?" Andy wasn't confrontational by nature, and he felt absurdly unsure how to proceed now he had started. Mark's eyes widened, but he stood his ground.

"You heard. Thimble prick, she called you. Not surprised you don't fancy a race – you're probably not up to that, either". Andy reached suddenly for the front of Mark's shirt, and the smaller boy gasped. Andy didn't know what happened next in these situations but heard himself threaten to "tear your fucking head off" before he came to his senses. Mark looked intimidated enough; Andy let him go - he was in enough trouble; he didn't want to attract any more attention.

Mark was unhappy, but left well alone. Some minutes later, Andy heard a commotion which suggested that some takers had been found for the race, and shortly afterward, the unmistakable sound of a teacher spoiling everyone's fun. He sat forlornly on a stone bench, far enough away, he hoped, from the action that he wouldn't be spotted by anyone. His heart sank, therefore when he became aware of someone standing next to him.

"They can be such children sometimes. I'm glad you didn't get involved." It was Anne's familiar voice. She sat down beside him, and he turned his head and smiled at her – her kindness that morning had not been forgotten, and he was genuinely happy to have an ally alongside him. Anne suggested a walk, and Andy agreed, provided that it didn't involve climbing any of those steps.

They strolled back downhill, towards the castle. This was not quite as straightforward as it looked at first, because although there was a clear, straight line of sight to the main building, the footpaths meandered around lakes and ponds. But they had all afternoon, and neither of them was in any hurry. As they walked, they chatted inconsequentially at first, and then Andy, feeling comfortable with Anne, asked her if she was alright.

"You seem a bit – I don't know; sad?"

Anne appeared to have to think about this, but eventually she answered him.

"I am, a little. It's nothing important, but thank you for noticing."

"Homesick?"

"I don't really know. I suppose that might be some of it – I have never been away from home this long before. In fact – don't laugh, will you?" Andy promised. "I've never been away from my family more than one night in my whole life. I know we're odd; I'm odd, but that's just how we are." Andy, who had been on Cub and Scout camping trips since he was around 8, found this surprising, but refrained from saying so. He was rapidly being made aware of just how different people could be, and didn't feel qualified to make any kind of comment in any case.

Instead, he tried something else – another conversational gambit, which pushed him a long way outside his normal comfort zone. He hesitated, but then asked the question he had been asking himself over the past couple of days:

"Anne, do you feel like you're having to grow up this week?" Silence. "I mean, I'm not saying you're not already grown up –" he was blushing now, but once on this path, he felt he ought to keep going "- I just think – well, away from families, and so on, we're kind of exposed to all these other things; do you feel that?"

Something in what he had said had caused Anne to giggle, but she quickly suppressed it, and tried to cover it with a cough. She made some vague, noncommittal noises to cover her thinking time, but eventually took the question seriously.

"I do know what you mean. I think I felt grown-up already – my parents try to encourage me to be an independent adult" -

"Except that you're never out of their sight"

"- well, yes – that's what I was going to say. Normally, that independence is enough, but I think, being here, and having time to think about things has made me wonder. I'm going to tell you something else which you mustn't laugh at, OK?"

Andy put his hand over his heart by way of reply.

"Liezl took me out on Saturday, and I bought a pair of jeans. Don't laugh! You promised. I know; it should be no big deal, but I've never owned anything like that before. I don't know when I'll ever wear them, of course; mother would faint, and I don't even think I look very good in them."

"Anne, you're a rebel! This is what I mean by growing up, I think – whether or not we feel ready to make decisions about things, we're making them. Well, I think you've made a good decision, even if you don't wear them."

Anne stopped and turned towards him. Andy, noticing a little late, had to turn back ; as he did so, he noticed that she was – not exactly crying, but obviously not far off it. They looked at each other for several minutes, Andy wondered if he was supposed to do something here, but his mind was full of Karla and Clare, and he really didn't have the mental strength to even consider Anne as anything other than a friend. The moment passed, and they walked on. Anne drew closer to Andy's side, and grabbed his arm. "Thank you, Andy – I think that's all I needed to hear – someone who thinks I'm not a fool."

"I don't – I never have."

Anne clearly wanted to say something else, but she must have suddenly realised that they had walked back into a crowd of their peers, so she restricted herself to "save a seat for me on the bus." Andy nodded, and they went their separate ways.

Soon after, he found himself watching ducks with Mr Finch, the youngest of the teaching staff. He was strongly rumoured to be 'seeing' Miss Lee, whose presence on the trip – she was a maths teacher – would otherwise have been hard to explain. Exactly what 'seeing' meant, Andy was not sure, but he liked Finchy, and they stood together for some time, counting ducks and chatting about how over the top this whole castle and park were. Andy at one point was convinced he had seen a duck go down and not come back up – Mr. Finch was sceptical, but they did agree that ducks must drown sometimes, and perhaps Andy had just got lucky.

As the day drew to a close, everyone began to gravitate towards the bus, and Andy kept an eye out for Anne. When he saw her, however, his heart sank. She was deep in conversation with Cartwright, and although he could hope otherwise, she had clearly become his chosen victim for the trip back.

Any moment now, she would hear him say "sit with me, and we'll talk further" – Andy had been caught by it on one of the interminable sections of motorway driving on the trip over, and had been spared only by the need for a sudden stop after one of the girls complained of feeling faint.

Sure enough, Anne and Mr. Cartwright were quickly ensconced in the front pair of seats, and Andy suddenly panicked at the thought of being surrounded by the mickey-takers. He thought briefly of cornering Mr. Finch, but he was, of course, already settling into his customary seat beside Miss Lee. He froze for a moment, unable to decide, and earned some rough shoves from behind for his pains. Eventually, though, he decided on an aisle seat – leaving a space beside him which he could control access to – near enough the front that someone in authority would have been able to hear anything untoward. No-one from the first group even looked at the seat beside him, and he was beginning to relax when he heard a distinctive female voice ask if that seat was taken. Clare.

Through all the batterings his psyche had taken over the weekend, nothing had dimmed his long-standing low-level crush on Clare, and he acted before he thought, standing up with a smile to let her in.

Ordinarily, being this close to her would have left him tongue-tied, but she broke the ice immediately, and he was talking to her before his brain had even begun to consider all the ways that he might mess this up:

"So," she said as she sat, "how was your day? Not as dull as mine, I'll bet."

He laughed: "Not dull; I like this place, and there was some silliness at lunchtime which livened things up, so no – did you not enjoy it?"

"I'd have enjoyed it a damn sight more if it hadn't been for all these spotty teenagers I had to hang out with" Andy was slightly taken aback; Clare was well-liked, and there were a number of boys and girls on this trip whom he would have assumed to be close friends of hers; appearances, it seemed, could be deceptive.

"And I saw your 'silliness' – thought you were going to kill him. Didn't know you had it in you" Andy flushed, and mumbled something about it being a misunderstanding, but Clare simply grinned at him, and he fell silent, staring out of the front of the bus for a time.

"Anyway," she continued, once the bus was under way, and their conversation was less likely to be overheard, "I wanted to tell you; your friend's sister is a cunt." The word, in that context, almost literally sucked all the air out of Andy's lungs. Sure, boys of his age liked to bandy around swearwords – who didn't - but to hear a girl – a girl he liked – using it in such a vitriolic way about another girl; it shocked him to the core. He was speechless long enough to cause Clare to turn her head and look at him:

"But you do need to grow up a bit, Andy. Try not to be so scandalised that I know words like that; you'll find me much easier to get on with if I'm not going to shock you rigid every time I open my mouth." Andy just stared. "But I'm right, aren't I?"

He nodded – for all its brutal crudity, the word had summed up his feelings towards Karla. One thing still nagged at him, though:

"Clare? What exactly did she say? You know, at the pool." On reflection, the clarification was probably not necessary, but who knows where else Karla might have been spouting off yesterday. Clare sighed.

"She came in on that bike – nice bike, by the way – and came straight over to Matthias. She told him not to worry about his boyfriend; you were walking back from East Germany – of course, she said this in German, so I might have got it a bit wrong, but then she switched to English, and made sure everyone could hear. She said – hm, I can't believe I'm going to tell you this – you sure you want to hear it?"

Andy wasn't, but said he was.

"OK, well, she said she'd tried to seduce you in a field, but that you weren't up to it, in more ways than one – those were her exact words; she does have a good command of English, doesn't she? And then, just in case any of us didn't quite get her meaning, she said 'he showed me his dick' – again, her words – 'I hope other English ones are a bit bigger' "

Andy had thought it must have been something like that, and had expected his face to be providing enough illumination for those around him to read by; but he was calm, for some reason. He leaned into Clare, and quietly said "thank you; I thought no-one would have the guts to tell me. Oh, and I didn't. Show her – that. You know." She smiled, and hooked his arm in hers.

"You know, Andy, you're actually a really nice guy. Hang on to that – it's more important than you might realise."

Several hundred thoughts, many of them contradictory, collided in Andy's head at this point. He felt he must be getting some kind of signal or other from Clare, although he also remembered that she could be this tactile with people she had never met before, and in his confusion, resorted to his normal tactic – sit still, and say nothing.

They sat like that, arms entwined, for some time, then Clare leaned in to him again. "One other thing, but you didn't hear this from me, because she doesn't want you to know. Anne over there," – she actually pointed, as if Andy wouldn't know who she meant – "she tried to come to your rescue."

"What do you mean?"

"I mean, she had to be held back by Liezl, or she might have done some damage." Andy was, once again, stunned.

"Anne did that? For me – I mean, on my behalf?" This time, he did turn red.

Clare smiled. "You know, she's not who people think she is." She turned her face to the window, and said, almost off-handedly, "at least, she isn't now – we've been corrupting her!"

Andy smiled: "I heard about the jeans. Was that you?"

"Those, and some other things, but she probably won't tell you about those."

He thought for a moment. "I was going to say don't tell her this, but you just told me stuff, so..."

"I won't. Look at me."

Andy did.

"I won't – I told you that because it was more important for you to know than for her not to be embarrassed – she'll get over it. Anyway, I can guess what you're going to say."

"You can?"

"You're a 15-year-old boy, Andy; you're pretty much an open book. You're going to tell me that you like her as a friend, but that's all, and you're now worried that you'll hurt her."

"Pretty much, although – oh, I don't know; this is hard."

"You are so lucky I think enough of you not to make a joke of that." – Clare smiled as she said this, and Andy's heart flipped; now she was flirting with him. If that's what it was – he really needed to work this stuff out, he thought, before he got into any more trouble.

He cleared his throat, in an attempt to mask his confusion. "I mean, I do like her, and she has been so kind today" *So have you,* he thought, but did not say; he was a little way away from being able to compliment Clare to her face, "but she doesn't make me feel– " here, he stopped, before he said something really stupid.

"I'll just pretend you said something clever there, shall I?" Andy nodded. "OK, well, that's OK; time sometimes deals with these things, and sometimes it doesn't. In the meantime, look after her, Andy; she's breakable."

Andy was about to say something pithy and significant when he was interrupted by the weather. For the past half hour or so, the conditions had been slowly deteriorating, and the bus driver was now dealing not only with the general autobahn madness, but also torrential rain. With no particular warning, since it must have happened more or less overhead, a peal of thunder detonated like a bomb going off. Andy leapt out of his seat and banged his head on the luggage rack above him; Clare grabbed his arm so tightly that he feared she might dislocate it. Some tiny part of his brain filed her reaction away for later inspection; perhaps she was actually just a scared schoolgirl, too.

The thunderclap broke whatever mood there had been on the bus, and Mr. Cartwright felt it necessary to get to his feet and lecture them all on meteorology for a while, punctuated at regular intervals by thunder – not ever again quite as loud as that first burst, but still quite significantly louder than any Andy had heard in his life before.

The thunder, but not the rain, had abated by the time they were back in Hohenügel. None of them was dressed for rain – it had been another hot, sunny day – and they all had to scurry for the shelter of the canopy over the school's front entrance while they waited for various lifts and alternative arrangements to be made. By the time Andy reached the shelter, he was soaked through, as most others were, although he saw Clare briefly, and she appeared as untouched by the rain as he was wet.

"How does she *do* that?" he heard Anne ask. He didn't know, and turned to tell her so, when he caught sight of her. She was as wet as he was, and the sight of her, smiling at him with her normally tightly controlled hair plastered to her skull, and her dress –

He paused at the sight of her dress. Anne was about as modest a person as he had ever met, but the rain had undone a certain amount of that modesty, and Andy simply stared. He had, quite honestly, never thought of her as even possessing a body until that moment. Now, there was no getting away from it. He forced himself to look up into her eyes; she was smiling back at him. He expected a rebuke, but she even allowed herself a little grin. "Funny thing, rain, isn't it?" she said. He could only agree.

AUGUST 2003

Bube's bar was quiet – probably a regular Sunday evening; Andrew ordered for himself and Matthias, and found a corner seat before the man who had been his host so many years before arrived.

Matthias seemed much more cheerful than he had been all weekend, and Andrew commented on it.

"I think I am. You know, this part of my life has been sitting like a stone in my stomach all these years – no-one talks about it now, so I think it has been good for me to tell you these things. But now, I want to ask you one thing before I finish the story. You don't mind?"

"I don't – go ahead – I feel like I've been very rude, letting you do all the talking."

Matthias smiled. "Do not worry; I think perhaps I have more to tell than you, no?"

"Perhaps." Andrew let that hang, and Matthias appeared not to notice it.

"I wanted to know – all these years, I wanted to know one thing. And you must say if it is not something you want to talk about." Matthias looked up, but Andrew was impassive.

"OK, then – you remember the day at the swimming pool? Of course you do; it is not easily forgotten, I think." Andrew agreed with a laugh which came out more nervous than he had planned. He also felt his familiar blush begin to spread over his cheeks, but he ignored that. Matthias noticed it, however:

"Oh, it is too hard – I will not ask it."

Andrew demurred: "No, no – it is only fair; I have heard all your secrets this weekend. Please; ask."

"Well, one thing. Karla was very cruel to you. I know you told me she

63

only left you outside the village, and you said nothing else happened, but is that true? I always wondered what else she might have done to you."

"No. Really, nothing else happened. She – ah, what harm can it do now?" Andrew cleared his throat. "That morning, she did try to seduce me – in the house, I mean; before we went out. It was mostly my own fault; I was very naïve, and I almost fell into her trap. But nothing happened then, and I think the rest of the day was her revenge."

Matthias nodded. "I thought so; she had a – reputation, I think you say. Yes?"

"Yes. Whatever she said about me that day; I didn't show her anything; in fact I never offered her any kind of encouragement at all."

"I thought so – it fits with who she is. She never needed any encouragement, I don't think. It was just – but no, it is stupid."

"Go on"

"I only thought of this when I saw you again on Friday – it suddenly seemed possible that you might have been the father."

"Of Peter, you mean?" Andrew could now feel the blood pounding in his cheeks. Matthias smiled, and raised his glass, as if in a toast.

"No, I knew it was absurd. Forgive me; this weekend has given me many strange thoughts."

Me, too, Andrew thought, but did not say.

"So, I should tell you how the story ends; although it never really ends, of course. Karla stayed in Hamburg at first, but she was finding everything very difficult; her comrades were always being in trouble with the police for something or another, and she had some good legal advice to get away. So she came back here."

Andrew was puzzled. "How? You were in prison? You and your mother?"

"Ah, but she did not live with us. There was Dieter; the father. They moved into an apartment in Witkreuz – just around the corner here. She kept away from everyone, especially family. They were only a few kilometres away, but – I think – she never saw anyone."

"Your father was here?"

"Some of the time. He stopped teaching, and I do not know what he did while we were in prison. He – he did not come to see me. My mother also, I do not think. She was very far away in prison, but Karla told me after that he did not go even once. After, he went away – he did not live here any more." Matthias looked away, and Andrew had the clear sense that there was more to this than met the eye, but he felt it didn't concern him, and said nothing about it.

"And you? Were you far away in prison, too?"

"Yes – but not for so long, and it was a young person's prison. Not so bad, really – I studied English more there, and I thought I might study this when I came out, because nothing else would really be open to me. After I was out I spent time passing examinations – it's where I met Gerda; she was my fellow student in the course – we were in Fulda, and I lived there with her for some time. The house was empty all of this time, and eventually I was told that it belonged to me – because my mother was not able to – you understand? After my father died; then it was my house, and we decided to move here for a short time – now it is ten years. Karla left one day; just walked away from Peter and everyone, and we did not really see her again. I have not spoken with her since. I suppose this, also, was my fault, but I cannot ask her. We never speak"

"Not even when your father died?"

"Especially not then. She was away – out of the country, I think, and I had only a message: 'Good. I am happy today'. That was it."

Andrew went and ordered more beers while he thought about this. On his return, it seemed to him that Matthias had not moved. He smiled as he passed the beer over, and said "well, that certainly sounds like Karla. I am so sorry for everything that happened, Matthias. I cannot imagine what your life has been like."

"Ah, do not worry, my friend – my life has been not as bad as you think. I have a good family; my mother is looked after, and I do not worry about her; Peter is here with us, and I am happy to do the work I thought I would hate. It is more interesting than I thought, and I enjoy to see young minds learn. I was taught well, and I am happy to pass it on."

Andrew almost missed the reference in the list of Matthias' blessings, but his brain caught up with him after a moment or two: "Peter is here? How – I mean…"

Matthias smiled. "Yes; Peter is why I made you come all the way to the café yesterday. That was Peter who gave us our coffee."

Andrew's default position over the weekend had been one of mild astonishment; now it evolved into open bewilderment. "*That* was Peter? How? Why?"

"How is he here? Easy, really – it is Dieter's place. Dieter brought him up after Karla left – he is a very lucky boy to have such a father. It was very hard for him, because everyone knew Dieter was the father, but Karla made a lot of trouble – she even said Dieter was not the father, and there were blood tests, there was a lot of fighting to make things OK again. Dieter worked so hard to keep him; when he married in the end, Peter was adopted properly, and although he has something of his mother in him – he was a lot of trouble as a teenager – he has settled down to life here. I think he will run the café one day, and perhaps develop it into other things, I don't know. I am proud of him, he has turned out to be maybe the best of us.

"He is the only link I have to my family – my cousins, I mean. They do not speak to me, but Peter tells me some things. He does not blame me for anything – how could he? He was too young." Andrew looked Matthias in the eye, which caused both men to instinctively look away, but Matthias must have understood that there was a question in the glance.

"Why I did not introduce you? Because I needed to ask that stupid question from before. You are not his father, so it is OK; but I wanted to know for sure. I'm sorry you did not meet him properly; perhaps next time?"

"Perhaps." Andrew's head was spinning, and that was the only word he could force out. In an attempt to cover his confusion, he ordered more beer, forgetting that it would mean not being able to drive back to his hotel. He had been here before, he thought, if only he could remember how.

In the end, Matthias offered to put him up for the night; they made some complex arrangements to ensure that Andrew would be delivered back to his hotel in time to check out, and still make it back to Frankfurt for his flight in the morning, and after a nightcap – schnapps, which triggered another whole series of memories for Andrew – he was shown to his 'old room' – the very one he had slept in all those years before.

And, he thought, as he undressed and sank into the same soft old mattress, almost certainly the same bed on which Peter was conceived.

JUNE 1978

Monday had felt in some way momentous, but the remainder of the second week seemed to just drain away listlessly. The routines were familiar now; a morning in various classes, the afternoon free to mess around, often hanging out by the track, or walking up to the fence. One afternoon, Matthias took Andy to the village graveyard to peer at family gravestones. Andy was surprised to see that many of the stones had photographs inlaid into them — something about this seemed ghoulish to him, although he couldn't precisely explain it.

There was one more day trip — to Fulda, for souvenir shopping; Andy loaded his bag up with pewter beer tankards and, lacking inspiration, some slightly odd-looking kitchen implements which his mother would almost certainly toss in a drawer, never to be seen again. The evenings were spent in the back room of the pub; the arrangement was that they could stay in there and have some kind of 'social club', but it quickly became apparent that, as long as you looked older than 16, and did not cause any actual trouble, you could not only get served at the bar, but dance the evening away to Genesis and Gerry Rafferty - music you would never admit to even being aware of at home.

Andy took part in all of this with a kind of detached amusement; something in him had changed over the two weeks, and he really wanted time to assess it, and to decide how to deal with it. He generally sat on the outside of the groups translating crude jokes back and forth; he chatted with Mark and one or two of Mark's friends; he spent some time in the company of Clare and her friends, or 'friends', as he thought of them now, and he generally tried to be as inconspicuous as possible. The taunts and barbs faded as the week went on; his humiliation had been just another of the many events of the week — as much time was spent, in those last few days, analysing the various relationships which had sprung up between English students and their hosts, or their hosts' siblings and assorted other relatives, as appropriate. Andy watched these conversations with a wry amusement – tales of illicit snogs in laundry rooms seemed a little tame to him.

The Thursday evening was spent en masse at an open-air theatre production of some obscure 18th century Harlequin play – by chance, Andy had actually seen an English performance of this same play only a few months before, as part of his parents' relentless drive to improve him. This meant that he was virtually the only one who understood what was going on, and his muttered explanations along his row drew some sharp rebukes from teachers at first. Once they understood that he was actually able to follow it, and help others follow it, the comments stopped, but he could see one or two puzzled looks among the staff. This suited him just fine, and he was in no rush to explain himself to Mr. Steel at the end of the evening.

Throughout these few days, he was conscious of spending a significant amount of time in the company of both Anne and Clare, but never in a position where he could really talk to either of them – the pressure of the group pretty much overwhelmed everything else. He wasn't sure whether he was grateful for that or not.

Friday morning dawned grey and cool, and the normal routines were observed for one last time – the solid breakfasts, the packed lunches, the trek to school. Karla had been, to all intents, absent from the house during the week. Andy knew she was around from time to time, but if he saw her at all, it was as a background figure. He occasionally hear her crashing around in her room late at night, and on this final Friday morning, she was a sullen and silent presence at the breakfast table. Everything happened around her while she stared morosely at the bottom of her coffee cup. None of them, not even her parents, spoke to her on interacted with her in any way, but this didn't seem so unusual, and Andy simply accepted it. He glanced at her from time to time – what she had done to him didn't seem so bad by this end of the week, and he was able to identify in her just what it was that had caused his infatuation.

He shook his head, as if to shake out the thoughts, and followed Matthias out the door. On the way, Matthias explained to him that he had no intention of actually going to school that morning.

"I talked to Liezl and Erika, and we have a plan to do something else." He explained that they would have to turn up at first, attend the first class since it was taught by Matthias' father, but that after that, they would slip out and go back to Liezl's house, where there would be a guarantee of no-one being in.

Andy was up for this – the classes outside the language-based ones, were mainly incomprehensible to him, and he really wasn't sure of the value of them. And, in any case, it was the last day – what could anyone do?

The English class, however, dragged. Andy was several times invited to write translations on the board, and he struggled with the unfamiliar marker pens and was hopelessly lost when asked – not for the first time – to make phonetic transcriptions of his pronunciation of certain words. The German school system seemed big on phonetic script, but it hadn't yet reached Andy's corner of England, if indeed it ever would, and he tried to convince himself that the class were laughing with, rather than at, him. Once the ordeal was over, however, Matthias ushered him into a corridor he had not seen before, and they met up with the two German girls and their English shadows – Clare and Anne. Matthias led the way, and Andy fell in beside Anne.

"Are you OK with this – it doesn't seem like your kind of thing", he asked Anne with a smile.

She looked straight ahead, but answered "I'm not sure, but I guess we can't really get into trouble for skipping classes we don't understand in the first place. And it's the last day."

"It's the last day," he agreed.

They escaped with no particular incident – one of the school staff looked at them quizzically when they passed the office, but they looked as if they knew what they were doing, and nothing was said.

The walk to Liezl's house passed in a flurry of excited chatter – for all their pretended sophistication, they were, at heart, just naughty schoolchildren, and they allowed themselves to behave like naughty schoolchildren. Once there, however, seated around Liezl's parents' expensively furnished living room, the conversation ran out of steam.

Matthias rescued it by pulling a bottle of something out of his bag.

"Schnapps," he announced. "And I managed to get it without my very tall English friend here." He seemed extraordinarily pleased with this, and everyone gave him a short round of applause. Glasses were found, and the bottle passed round. Everyone save Anne poured themselves a little, and Erika proposed a toast. Matthias stopped them. "No – everyone must have a drink before we can do this. Anne, will you have some?" Anne flushed, but said nothing. Liezl offered to get her some water, but this just made the situation worse. All eyes were on Anne, and she plainly didn't know where to look.

Andy saw her look to him, and he smiled briefly and shrugged, trying to convey to her that it was not a big deal either way to him; whether that worked, he didn't know, but she looked at Matthias:

"Ok, I will – but only a tiny amount; I have never- well, you know." She looked down at her hands, folded in her lap. Erika seemed delighted – "everyone has new experiences this week, I think."

"So, we drink – to friends – we should stay friends after this, I think."

Everyone drank, all of them trying not to look directly at Anne, which made the whole thing more uncomfortable than it already was. Andy was able to watch her without turning his head, however, and he saw her take the merest of sips, react to it, but not cough, which he had been half expecting, then straighten up and try a little more.

Once the awkwardness had been dealt with, the morning descended into deep but meaningless conversation. The bottle was slowly drained, although no one seemed to be getting out of control; however Andy recognised that his ability to think straight was not quite as good as it had been.

At some point during the morning, Andy finally got the odd relationships among the Germans sorted out – Liezl was Matthias' cousin, or something along those lines, and Erika was somehow related to both of them, although it seemed to involve at least one remarriage, and a different generation. Clare leaned over to Andy when he looked his most puzzled, and explained.

"Erika is actually Liezl's aunt, because of a second marriage. They are all related, and they all grew up together. Kind of nice, I think. Although Erika told me that she sometimes feels uncomfortable about it, because Liezl's mother is her sister – it must be strange, don't you think?"

Andy had enough trouble putting this all together, without having to venture an opinion on it, so he simply agreed and left it at that.

He then spent some time repeatedly checking whether Anne, who had by no means drunk as much as the others, was still OK. She seemed tired and distracted, and Andy allowed himself to worry about her a little. After his fourth or fifth solicitous enquiry, she smiled at him. "Andy, I'm fine. In fact, I think I'm going to change."

She stood, and walked out of the room. Andy watched her go; looking to see if she was in anyway unsteady, but she did, in fact, look fine. She was gone for some time, and the girls were debating whether one of them should go and see if she had fallen asleep somewhere, when Anne reappeared, wearing her new jeans, and what must have been a borrowed t-shirt of Liezl's.

Conversation stopped, and five pairs of eyes followed Anne's progress back to her seat. She stopped to drain her glass, then looked Andy in the eye, and asked "well, what do you think?"

Without the help of the alcohol, Andy might not have been able to say anything, but the schnapps had done something to him, and he ventured an opinion.

"I think it's great – I mean, I think you're great. You look – ah, I don't know. It's great. Have you really never worn jeans before?"

"No, not really. It's not how we were brought up. Women don't wear trousers. In fact, women don't do a great many things, but I'm changing that." She refilled the glass, and drank a little more. Matthias got up and applauded. "You see, my friends – we have changed one life this week. We should try to change more!" They all cheered, and Clare came over and laid a hand on Andy's arm. "Well done, that's what she needed to hear. You could be a natural at this!"

Andy grinned at her. "Well, now you should go and put on a dress, and I'll tell you how – ah, never mind." He was suddenly aware where that train of thought might lead him, and he stopped himself. Clare smiled at him. "OK, big man – don't overdo it!"

From that point on, the conversations got more relaxed and sillier – there was some good-natured teasing of Andy, some mildly rude songs in both languages, and – at Erika's prompting – some lunch: more of that solid German bread, which seemed to help calm things down a little. After they had eaten, and aware that the rest of the group would be out of school, and probably looking for them, they decided to go out and find out what was going on, if anything.

They walked back into the village, all six of them a little unsteady, but none of them actually drunk. They encountered various groups of pupils, but no one seemed to have any clear idea of anything inspiring to do, and mostly they all wandered around for an hour or so, peering into shop windows and giggling about everything and nothing. As they drew close to Matthias' house, Andy, conscious that they were all expected to attend a farewell disco in the school later, announced that he was going to go in and pack. Anne felt that was a good idea, and that she would probably do the same, "and maybe have a nap – I seem to be very tired, all of a sudden." The others laughed – Anne had held her own with the schnapps, but that, and the undoubted stress she was feeling being out in public in what she had claimed her mother would call 'improper dress', must have been enough for one day. Matthias, Erika and Clare all decided to go back to Liezl's house, leaving Andy feeling temporarily left out of things, but he arranged to meet them all later, and as Erika said, "we will probably all fall asleep watching TV anyway"

Andy grinned to himself as he walked back inside – whatever else had changed over the past two weeks, he was feeling a self-confidence he barely recognised, and in spite of what he thought of as feeling a bit flat after the fun of the morning, and the realisation that the end was upon them; this time tomorrow, they'd be somewhere in Belgium, heading for the ferry, he was in a remarkably good mood.

Having let himself back in, he wandered through to the kitchen, and fortified himself with an apple from the fruit bowl on the table. The normal routines seemed to be in place; Matthias' mother would be back in about two hours – he never had established quite what she did all day, but her routine never varied; she was home at 4:30 every afternoon. Matthias' father would be doing whatever it was that teachers do in the afternoons, and would be back around 3. Andy had been in the house alone with the old man several times now, but he had never found any useful topic of conversation. Matthias had explained that, as a much older father, he had never seemed to be able to interact with Matthias' friends, and that Andy should not worry, and let him be – as a rule, he seemed to spend his time doing crosswords, and watching news programmes on television.

Andy wandered upstairs, not taking particular care to be either conspicuous or otherwise; Karla's door was closed, but that could mean anything. Once in his own room, he listened out for her, but heard nothing. Still, he closed, and on an impulse, locked the door behind him.

He packed, forcing things into his big suitcase so that he wouldn't have to carry them around in his undersized duffel bag over the weekend. All he left in that bag were two books, and a change of underwear. He remembered to change and dress for the evening, so that he would have minimal work to do either at the end of the day, or first thing in the morning. He looked down at himself, and decided that these clothes would do for the journey as well – judging by the outbound trip, everyone would be somewhat less than fragrant in any case after a couple of hours, so it really wouldn't matter too much.

Once packed, he sat on the edge of the bed and read. He contemplated lying down, but that would invite sleep, which he wanted to avoid. He also thought about going back out to Liezl's house, but felt altogether too tired for any more walking, and decided to stay put.

He heard Matthias' father come in a few minutes later – the television was switched on, and the smell of coffee wafted up from below. He considered the book he was reading – a Graham Greene novel about priests and donkeys, part of his required reading for A levels next year – if he gave it a solid hour now, he'd have it finished, and could reward himself with something he actually liked reading for the bus trip.

Some time passed – he couldn't say how long, but he didn't seem to have got much further in the story – when there was a soft knock on his door. Alarmed, he sat upright, and then froze – should he open it? It was probably Matthias, back home and checking up on him. On the other hand…. But her father was downstairs, what could she do?

The knock came again, more forceful this time, but no words; nothing to help him identify who was on the other side of the door. He rose, crossed to the door, unlocked and opened it.

Karla stood there, in sweatpants and t-shirt, looking as if she had just woken up. Andy had never seen her look vulnerable before, and he hesitated for long enough that Karla took it as an invitation to come in. She pushed the door closed behind her, causing him to become even more alert, but she was smiling, apparently genuinely, and holding out something which could even be seen as a peace offering – Clare's book.

"Would you take this back to your friend, please? Tell her I enjoyed it." She held it out, and Andy tentatively reached out for it, fearful of what might happen if he touched any part of her. Once he had safely retrieved it, he sat back down on the end of the bed, but Karla made no effort to leave. He looked at her, and she smiled again.

"I also have something for you." With that, she slid one arm into the sleeve of her shirt, and pulled it off over her head in one smooth motion, dropping it to the floor. Andy gaped – Karla stood before him, bare-chested. He could feel the pages of his book crumple in his hand, his legs seemed to have turned to liquid, and he tried to stop himself staring at her nipples. He looked lower, and could see that the bruise he had noticed before was larger than he had thought; he tried to focus on that detail to distract him from what Karla clearly wanted him to look at. She stood silently before him until he looked up at her face, then looked him in the eye, and said, clearly and as if she had prepared it:

"If you will not give me what I want, I shall have to take it." Her hands, already on her waist, pushed smartly down, and with little extra effort, she stood before him naked. Andy could now hear nothing but the pounding of his own blood. She was between him and the door, but he was bigger and – surely – stronger than she was. He could do nothing other than stare. If he had not been so profoundly shocked, he might have tried looking away, giving as clear a signal as he could until he regained the power of speech, but he was undone by her body. He looked at it as if he had never seen anything like it in his life before, which, in truth, he had not. Creased and battered photographs, passed around in the schoolyard, and the odd glimpse of top-shelf magazines had in no way prepared him for the reality of what stood before him. Karla seemed to glow; she was radiating heat and light, and he was dazzled by her. His eyes, unsure where to look at first, became fixated by her trimmed and shaped pubic hair. He had never even heard of such a thing, and it astonished him.

Karla broke the spell by turning to lock the door, and then marched confidently over to him, put her hands on his shoulders and pushed. He fell back on to the bed; he had no control over his own motor functions any more, and what happened next seemed to take place in a place where the laws of time and space had been suspended.

Karla manoeuvred herself into a position where she could pinion his legs, yet have access to his belt. She wrenched it open, then efficiently unsnapped and unzipped him. He winced as his jeans and undershorts were wrenched down, but what was exposed gave Karla pause.

"Hmm. I'm sorry, English boy – I was not fair to you." She took the object of her contemplation in her hand, almost as if weighing it, and Andy gasped. The things which he told himself he should be feeling were mostly absent – this was not joy and wonder at a magical experience, but more the feeling of being a specimen on an examining table. However, the basic impulse which had asserted itself at the sight of Karla's breasts remained, and seemed to meet with her approval.

She moved gradually up him, until she was straddling his hips, then leaned forward, as if to kiss him. Instead, she leant her head to one side, to try to get a view of what she was doing, fumbled with him almost painfully for a moment then raised herself upright and sat down hard.

Andy almost screamed, then found himself overwhelmed by sensation. He had no words to describe what he was feeling; complex feelings of humiliation and anger surged through him, mingled with the extraordinary physical sensations. Karla sat upright, looking down at him; she did not appear to be moving, but *something* was happening – he could feel a subtle churning sensation, and he knew that, irrespective of anything else, at least this would not last long. He looked away, but his control deserted him when Karla really did start to move, and he looked back at her, gazing fixedly at her small pink nipples until he felt his rage and his desire burst from him in one simple jolt.

The aftershocks surprised him, not their intensity, but their duration – she seemed to almost be milking him as he lay there, gasping for breath. Once satisfied that he was done, she briefly lay forward onto his chest. Had he moved a hand at that point, he knew that he would give her what she wanted – his submission, so he lay rigidly, staring at the ceiling. Karla must have understood this, and rolled off him. She got up, reached for her shirt to hold between her legs, picked up her sweatpants, unlocked the door, and walked out, apparently unconcerned that her father was watching television at the bottom of the stairs. She did, at least, close the door behind her, so Andy did not have to move.

Minutes passed. Andy stared at the ceiling, then slowly turned his head so that he could see out the window in the far corner of the room. Once the blood had stopped pounding in his ears, he once again was able to appreciate just how still and silent this place was. He could hear only the faintest murmuring of the television downstairs; otherwise, nothing.

A fly buzzed softly against the window, and Andy tried to look for it. He could not see the fly, but he did finally focus on the window. He could see one edge of the church steeple outside, and beyond it a sky of deep blue; a colour which he had never seen in a sky back home. As he stared, a white streak caused by an aircraft scored the view, followed shortly after by another at right angles to it. Belatedly, he understood that these trails, so obvious in the clear skies since they arrived, were probably not commercial flights, but the markings of opposing air forces, fighting silent border skirmishes above him. Up there, a war was being fought. It may not have involved bullets, rockets or fiery deaths, but it was a war nonetheless, and he briefly wondered at his own place in such a world. He had lost his virginity, more or less against his will – what did that matter to the pilots up there, each working to protect people like him, or Karla, however much she may have resented the fact, from what the people on the other side of the fence might want to do to him?

Gradually, he became aware that he was cold, damp and sore. He sat up, then – after a moment to stop the room spinning - stood. He cleaned himself up as best he could, pulled up his jeans and made himself presentable, then cautiously opened the door. Seeing the way clear, he almost sprinted down the corridor to the bathroom. He only just got the door locked, and his head over the toilet bowl before he was violently sick; all the schnapps from the morning burning his throat as it came back up. He lay there gasping, and only with a supreme effort did he prevent himself from crying; never in his life had he felt so alone.

Had Matthias not come back for him an hour or so later, he would have simply crawled into bed and stayed there until it was time to leave in the morning. As it was, his friend had to work hard to persuade him out of his room; he said nothing, but his overwhelming fear was of encountering Karla; once out of the house, he relaxed a little, and began to take notice of the rest of the world. Matthias was cheerful and full of life; and enough of that rubbed off on Andy for him to feel that he might be able to get through the evening.

Once at the school – the disco was taking place in some previously unnoticed hall across the yard from the main buildings – Andy felt his familiar defences fall into place. He sat at the side, quietly nursing a large glass of water, and studiously ignored everyone who came near him. After an hour or so, he was aware that Liezl and Erika were dancing, and that therefore Clare and Anne must be somewhere; in looking for Clare, he found Anne, apparently as quiet as he, also drinking water. She looked up at him and managed to trace a smile, although it quickly vanished. She was once again wearing one of her dresses, and he fumbled with the idea that the progress she had made up to the last time he had seen her had all been reversed; it was as if the real Anne had been let out to play for a bit, but had since been carefully packed back up in a box, and put away. He could find no way of even beginning to express this, however, and he said nothing; just sat with her watching their friends having fun.

Eventually, he asked her if she was OK, and she replied in a way which told him that she was not He simply stared at her, aware that he should say something, but his mind drew a blank, and he looked away, unable to meet her gaze. After a lengthy pause, she asked him the same question, but he couldn't think of a suitable answer, and simply nodded.

Some time later, he was coming back from the bathroom when he encountered Clare. She was apparently thrilled to see him, and planted a kiss on his cheek. He looked at her. "You're drunk!" he deduced.

"Sure am, big man. There's beer outside. Come on – do you good; sitting there with a face like thunder." He resisted, feeling sure that in other circumstances he would have confessed something to her, but as it was he'd rather she just got on with whatever she needed to do and left him in peace. Eventually, she got the message, and after what felt like several hours of dire music, the lights went up, everyone was ushered out, and the trip more or less came to an end. By the time he and Matthias got back to the house, it was in darkness, and the pair went to their separate rooms in silence. Andy's last conscious thought was to remember to set his alarm, but he lacked the strength to undress, and slept in his clothes, something he was vaguely aware he'd regret in the morning.

AUGUST 2003

25 years later, Andrew woke in that same bed, spent several minutes working out just where he was and why, then proceeded to dress and try to leave. There was some comedy with the bedroom door until he remembered the lock *–How could I have forgotten the lock?* he wondered – and more farce as Matthias tried to help him get some breakfast without waking the rest of the household, in spite of not being entirely awake himself.

On the doorstep, Andrew turned to face the man who had been his exchange shadow, and extended his hand. "Matthias, it has been a wonderful weekend. Thank you for sharing it with me; and thank you for sharing your life with me. I keep thinking there should be something I should say, but I don't know what it is. I think you were a good friend all those years ago, and you have been a good host this weekend" *Stop wittering,* his subconscious told him; *say what you really think.* But he couldn't – Andrew was still Andy, even after all this time – perhaps more than usual, having been back in that bed – and he couldn't quite get out what he was thinking.

Matthias reached out to shake his hand, then seemed to change his mind and put his arms around Andrew. Andrew in turn, stepped back off the step in an attempt to make the embrace a little less farcical, and possibly to avoid scandalising any neighbours who had been woken by the exchange. Matthias laughed and stepped back. "I didn't really think that through! Goodbye, my old friend – please come and see us again, and I will show you how we are happy now, not how we were sad before – is that OK?"

Andrew agreed, and automatically extended the reverse invitation. Matthias seemed to give this considerable thought before agreeing that it might be a good idea; then Andrew turned and walked quickly away; he still had to find his car before he could begin the long drive back to Frankfurt. He knew from long experience that the best way to get a lengthy and tedious journey over with was simply to get on with it.

The autobahn was relatively straightforward early in the morning; the traffic still moved faster than Andrew was comfortable with, but he found a classical music station playing Brahms' *German Requiem*, and he was able to sing –or at least hum - along for large parts of it, which prevented him from thinking about anything else. He found his mood improving, but whether that was because of the music or the fact that Hohenügel was slipping away behind him, he couldn't say.

The final part of the journey, to the airport, was familiar to him – he realised that he must have covered a good part of this stretch on Friday, trying to find the way out towards Kassel. He smiled at his own incompetence that afternoon – some things, he thought, never really change. The car hire return and the check-in procedure both went smoothly, and he found himself in one of Europe's biggest airports with around two hours to kill. Once he had exhausted the possibilities of the 'retail environment' – buying things for the children was next to impossible these days, but he managed – he settled into a corner seat in one of the bars and ate another breakfast. The general activity of the airport, and the constant low-level panic he always felt at the thought of missing a flight meant the he could not properly relax, but he was grateful for that, since it also meant he couldn't think about the weekend.

As if to perpetuate a national stereotype, German airlines are extremely efficient at loading passengers – rather than doing it row by row, they do it from the window seats in, meaning that Andrew was almost last to board, but this suited him, since he would not have to spend so long cooped up in his seat, unable to stretch his legs out for fear of being mown down by a passing drinks trolley. Eventually, however, he was seated, strapped in, and pressed rather uncomfortably against his neighbour, an overweight German with a bad haircut, and no apparent desire to converse. Andrew was left to his own thoughts. On the way out, he had bought a new copy of *The Power and the Glory*, thinking it would be amusing to read it again in the place where he had first read it, but the weekend had passed so quickly that he had not even picked it up. Now it sat in the seat pocket in front of him, and seemed to mock him.

He closed his eyes, and began to think. His knees ached, as they always did after more than five minutes in an airline seat, and that prevented him from drifting into any kind of sleep; instead he began to turn over in his mind all the ramifications of what he had learned. He kept trying to recapture the brief sight of Peter he had had on Saturday afternoon; the tall young man had nagged at his subconscious at the time, but he had not followed it up; tall people generally caught his interest in any case, and now he tried to work out what he had noticed even before he knew it was Peter.

He had, of course, looked a little like Andrew's 12-year-old son, or was that simply projection? No, he was sure of it – he remembered smiling at the resemblance. But something else was bothering him, if only he could concentrate…

The relentless efficiency of the cabin crew repeatedly interrupted his train of thought, and he feared he would get nowhere, when it suddenly struck him. Peter was left-handed. Andrew had been surprised to see it at the time; a lefty himself, he was always aware at some level when he met others, and something long-suppressed now resurfaced. Left-handedness had been a talking point on the trip, since it seemed to be something of an anomaly in that corner of Germany. Andrew remembered now that part of his discomfort at being asked to write on whiteboards, for example, was that the German students would mutter among themselves at this freakishness. Left-handedness was more than unusual in that part of the world; if Peter favoured his left, it confirmed what Andrew had subconsciously known as soon as Matthias had started to tell the story.

He thought about what Matthias had and had not said about blood tests, and being sure that Peter was Dieter's son. How evasive had he been? Did he actually say outright that Dieter was the father? Why did he feel he had to – so awkwardly – ask about Andrew and Karla, and what had happened? And, indeed, why had Andrew felt the need to evade the truth?

And that thought led him down another path – he had a problem, but exactly what kind of problem was it? Did he have any kind of responsibility to Peter? Surely Karla had known what had happened – he froze at this point; what had Karla's intentions actually been? He now vividly remembered every detail of that last afternoon; her words to him: *if you won't give me what I want…* What had she wanted? Sex, he had assumed at the time, and in all the intervening years – on occasion, when he allowed himself to remember it, he wondered if his inertness had put her off sex altogether, or perhaps just English men. Now, he saw that line of thinking for the avoidance it was, and pondered properly what had really happened that hot Friday afternoon.

Had Karla intended to get pregnant? If so, was he simply the nearest available donor who provided no complications, or was there something more; something he was missing? Although his recollections of the event were vivid, he had always been conflicted about them; it had been in many ways the ultimate teenage boy's fantasy – an older woman stripping off and throwing herself at him – but it had also been a source of much anguish and self-doubt. Had he done something to provoke it? Why had he not reacted with enthusiasm once he realised what was going to happen? Why did it still sometimes cause him cold sweats and sleepless nights?

He needed to talk to someone, and his first thought was that he would have to finally confess it to his ex-wife when he got home. Then it slowly dawned on him that he was no longer married to Anne, and he wondered if that would make the confession easier or harder. How, exactly, do you go about telling your ex-wife that you were unfaithful to her long before you were actually married to her? Andrew realised with a start that he had always felt it as an infidelity to Anne – the trip had been the beginning of their relationship, and although it had been close to a year before they were officially 'going out', and considerably longer than that before they were sleeping together, he had never said anything because he felt in some way that it would have been a betrayal of something or other, but he never knew what.

He allowed himself to think through what he might say, and in the course of working that out, he realised that he had a much more pressing need to talk to someone else – Karla.

Matthias had not actually told him where Karla was now, and what she was doing – he thought he had picked up that Matthias did know, but now he began to wonder about that – he supposed that a psychiatrist would have some clever technical terms for his need to see her, but he didn't want 'closure' or anything like that; he just wanted to know why it had happened, or even if it had been, in any way, his fault.

That whole concept of being at fault for things kept him occupied for most of the flight; it wasn't until he was being instructed to fold his tray and to sit up straight that he managed to shake himself out of it. He looked past his neighbour at the view out of the window: he could see vaguely recognisable bits of London slipping by, and that brought him back to the present. He needed a plan; to see Anne, to figure out how to contact Karla without alerting Matthias or Peter; to decide what to do about Peter; to find out the truth about the blood tests, if they even existed, and – this sprang to mind with such clarity that he supposed it must have been sitting in his subconscious all along - to talk to the only person he had ever told the whole story to.

JUNE 1978

Another early start; another grey morning – this time, however, was the last such. Andy had slept soundly, mainly, he thought, due to exhaustion. This meant, however, that he was slow to get going, and the awkwardness of having to undress, shower, and then put the same clothes back on almost defeated him. He ended up slightly damp, and disguised under rather too much deodorant, standing in the hallway of the house, waiting for everyone else to finish breakfast. He had woken with what he would only in retrospect diagnose as a hangover, and had not wanted to eat anything. He drank close to a pint of weak orange squash, something which he understood immediately he was going to regret for the rest of the morning, and then had gone back upstairs for his bags. On the way, he saw that Karla's door was open, and her room empty. Had it been open before? He had no idea.

In the back of the Mercedes, he questioned Matthias in a whisper about his sister's whereabouts. Matthias knew nothing: "sometimes she stays out all weekend – it's normal". That might have accounted for the expressions on Matthias' parents' faces – his father, in particular, looked murderous, but that, Andy reflected, might have been due to having to get up earlier than normal on a Saturday morning and drive his son's odd English friend to school.

The loading of the bus was a familiar procedure by this time, but it still managed to take an eternity. There were many sad and prolonged farewells; Andy watched with amusement at the number of German mothers hugging plainly embarrassed English boys, and stared openly at the amount of tearful hugs and kisses being shared by pupils. He and Matthias shook hands awkwardly; Matthias looked as if he just wanted to be back in bed, and turned to head for the car as soon as he reasonably could. Anne arrived at about the same time, and she stopped to say something to

Matthias. They both seemed distracted, but he knew that Anne was not comfortable with any kind of personal talk, and Matthias was probably trying to explain how nice it had been to get to know her, so it was not unexpected.

Andy hung around the door of the bus for as long as possible – his knees were going to be enough trouble as it was, without prolonging the torment unnecessarily. He already could feel pressure on his bladder, and excused himself to Cartwright, who distractedly gave him permission to duck into the school toilets.

When he came out, the scene had altered only in that there seemed to be even more people swarming around the bus. He saw Mark, already seated. Mark shrugged at him, as if to say *sorry, mate – you're too late*, and he realised he was going to have to negotiate a seat beside someone he didn't particularly either know or like.

However, when he finally managed to fight his way on through a gaggle of parents, he saw that Anne had saved him a seat. She was, as she had been on the Monday trip, quiet and almost unfriendly, but he attributed this to the hour, and smiled gratefully at her.

Once they were under way – around half an hour late, as might have been expected - he tried to talk to Anne, but she pointedly kept reading, and he soon settled down to his own book, willing the time to pass for the sake of his knees, if nothing else. After an hour or so, he noticed that Anne was sleeping with her head against the window, and he solicitously tried to rearrange her so that she had something softer to lean on. The only available item was his upper arm, and in tipping her over, he managed to wake her briefly, but she seemed to understand what he was doing, and smiled at him for the first time that day.

It was lunchtime before everyone was properly alive, and the normal rowdiness of the bus reasserted itself. Their last German packed lunches were eaten, for some reason, on the grass field of a gliding club somewhere in the hills of western Germany. Anne and Clare wandered off to some quiet corner, heads bowed in conversation, and Andy sought out Mark and the knot of boys he had assembled. They were still some way behind schedule, and Cartwright lectured them sternly about not drinking too much for the rest of the day, so that as few stops as possible would be required.

Most of the afternoon seemed to be spent crawling along through industrial suburbs, still on autobahns, but not reaching the speeds of the first part of the day. Borders were crossed – Andy noticed them this time, and was surprised to see that they passed through Holland on the way to Belgium. He stared at the border crossings, trying to fit their seeming normalcy with the one he had briefly glimpsed with Karla the previous Sunday. Eventually, after what seemed like hours parked in a traffic jam on the outskirts of Oostende, they were all decanted into a kind of primitive terminal building, with strict instructions to be back on the bus at a certain time, or to find themselves swimming back to England. Andy joined most of the other boys in the cafeteria, clearly designed to cater to the tastes of returning Brits who had missed their baked beans and chips, and they all ate heartily before wandering the terminal in search of pinball machines and some way of spending the last of their German currency. Of course, this was fruitless, given that they were now in Belgium, and Andy was dispatched to the Bureau de Change with a long, complex list of monies owned by various boys. He returned triumphant, having discovered that the exchange rate had worked in their favour in the past two weeks, and disbursed familiar-looking British coins and notes to everyone, although he felt sure that he had managed to short-change himself somewhere along the line.

They gathered back at the bus in time, only to be ushered off again and loaded on the ferry on foot. It was hard to be certain, but Andy thought that it was probably the same ferry as the previous crossing; it certainly seemed to have the same layout, and so the group scattered to their favourite places – places where they would be unlikely to be discovered by teachers should the promised duty free purchases materialise.

Andy headed for the upper deck, where he was able to watch the sun set over Belgium as they set sail, and then went in search of Mark and the promised alcohol. On the outward trip, Andy had been volunteered to do the shopping, but had been quickly and easily caught, so the plan this time was to be a little more subtle about it. One of the boys Andy didn't know that well had been cultivating some five o'clock shadow in the last couple of days, and he was dispatched to browse while the others kept watch for teaching staff.

The operation was completed quickly, however; the teachers appeared to have given up on monitoring their charges by this stage: Mark reckoned they would all be in the bar. Whatever the reality was, various bottles of spirits were procured, and once some plastic cups had been liberated from the restaurant area, a merry time was had by all.

Andy took his cup of orange juice, flavoured with vodka, up to one of the open deck areas, hoping to find some peace and to perhaps allow himself to start to think about what had happened the day before. He stepped over the sill of the outside door, however, to be greeted by the sight of Clare leaning out over the rail, looking back at the way they had come – it was dark enough now for the lights of Ostend and other towns on the Belgian coast to be the only visible points of reference. He came up alongside her, and offered her his cup.

"I have vodka, if you're interested"

"No, it's OK, Andy. Thanks." He looked at her, and saw, to his shock, that she was – or had been – crying. Nonplussed, he reviewed what he might say which wouldn't sound crass or immature, and came up with nothing. So he said nothing.

After a few minutes, Clare turned to look at him. "I'm not normally like this, it's just- well, I don't know. I'm homesick for Hohenügel, not Chester. Does that make sense?"

In a way, it did, thought Andy. He might have been glad to get away from Karla, but it was slowly dawning on him that the trip had wrought a huge change in him, and that he wouldn't be able to develop that at home – life would probably just drift back to normal. He said something to this effect, and Clare agreed with him

"You're right – but I think it's more than that for me. I just want to travel – to go somewhere which isn't home. There's a whole world over there, and I want to know more about it."

Andy sighed. Two weeks before, Clare had been an unattainable ideal; someone he could admire from afar, but never even consider approaching. Now, here she was, confiding her inner thoughts in him. He wondered how this had come to pass, and what he had done to bring it about. He also realised that he ought to say something, or risk having her walk away from him.

"Clare, I – at least, um. Sorry; I just want to tell you something, but you have to keep it to yourself." *Oh, great,* he thought. *I've blown it. She probably thinks I'm about to declare my undying love for her or something, and she's just going to laugh and walk away.* He drained the vodka and tossed the cup over the side. "I mean – look, could we go inside somewhere?"

Clare looked at him, and seemed to come to some kind of conclusion. She nodded, then led the way inside and then upstairs to a small lounge area, where only a handful of people were huddled under coats and blankets trying to sleep. They sat at the back of the seating area, out of earshot of anyone, and more or less out of sight of anyone unless they were deliberately searching.

Andy steeled himself to tell his tale, but Clare interrupted him.

"Andy, don't get me wrong. I like you, but I don't… well, you know."

This threw Andy for a moment, but he recovered:

"I know. I just don't know who else to talk to about this, and you helped the other day, and -" This wasn't going where he wanted it to, so he stopped talking, and instead fished in the pocket of his sweatshirt and produced the copy of *Dr. Rat.* Clare looked at him.

"She finished it?"

"As far as I know. She said to tell you that she enjoyed it, anyway." He handed it over, and Clare caused it to vanish somewhere about her person. She was wearing her customary oversized leather jacket, and he supposed it disappeared into one of the internal pockets.

He started to say something else, but was suddenly overwhelmed by a sob which seemed to just burst out of him unbidden. He looked away as tears began to flow, and Clare shifted in her seat to put her arms about him.

"You don't have to tell me, Andy – just let it out. You'll feel better." After a moment's thought: "did you fall in love with her? Did she break your heart?"

Andy shook his head, then thought about it. "Well, maybe in a way. I thought she was something – you know; what you just said." His voice was not as shaky as he had feared, but it was closer to the reedy treble he had grown out of the year before than he was happy with. He took a deep breath, and told Clare what had happened; the truth about Sunday, the way Karla had manipulated him, and then – with no little embarrassment – the whole story about Friday afternoon on his bed. He blushed deeply and stumbled around the description of what Karla had done to him. Clare had to ask bluntly if they had actually had full sex, and he admitted that, yes, they had, and no, he hadn't had any protection.

She sat in silence for a long time, just holding him, and he slowly reciprocated the hug as his embarrassment subsided, leaning down into her shoulder, and closing his eyes. He felt himself begin to drift into sleep, and her low, gently spoken words came to him as in a dream.

"It's not your fault, Andy – I told you what I thought about her before. You mustn't blame yourself, or let it change you. Most of us have come back from this trip with broken hearts in some way or another." He wondered if he should ask her about that, but was unable to stir himself from his torpor, so let her carry on.

"Just sit here with me for now. We'll work this out." He smiled at her words, and slipped into a kind of semi-doze, still leaning against her. He vaguely hoped that he was not crushing her, but couldn't have moved if he had wanted to.

Some time later, the pitch of the ferry's engines changed, and roused him. Clare was still there, curled up with him, and he tried to figure out how to uncurl and ease his cramp without disturbing her. She, however, was awake, and perhaps had not slept at all. She murmured "I think we should get back downstairs. I think we're coming into Dover. He started to uncoil, then froze as he realised with horror that he had had his hand cupped around one of Clare's breasts. She turned her face to his:

"Ssh. Our secret." She smiled, then gently unhooked him, and helped him up. He tried to stretch without making much noise, and without drawing attention to one part of himself in particular, but Clare stepped in to him, and hugged him tightly. He had a sinking realisation that she must be able to feel it, but all she said was "it's not me. I'm not who you need. Be happy, big guy." She looked up, kissed him briefly but firmly on the lips, then led the way back to the bus.

The remainder of the journey passed for Andy in a kind of dreamlike state; he was conscious of motorways and headlights, and at one point he felt sure that they were going through one of the tunnels under the Thames on the wrong side of the road. Most of his companions were asleep, but he, having unburdened himself, had a kind of raw energy buzzing in his head, and he didn't even try. Anne slept peacefully on his arm, and he looked over from time to time to see Clare looking tranquil and serene in her seat a few rows back. During the hours of darkness, he thought of many things, but none of them seemed important or worth remembering. By the time they stopped for breakfast at a motorway service area, he almost felt like he was the old Andy again; ready to take part in the banter of the bus, and ready to be home.

In the final hour of the journey, he and Anne shared a conversation which seemed strange and intense to him, but he wasn't entirely sure what it had been about – Anne seemed to be trying to tell him something, but unable to come out with it. He felt it was in keeping with the rest of the week – normal on the surface, but full of things he didn't properly understand - , and tried to contribute, but only felt he had sounded foolish. As the bus approached Chester, he tried to lighten the mood with a cheery "well, back to school tomorrow," but Anne stared at him, and he reddened and turned away.

Homecoming was as chaotic as expected – several groups of parents hadn't got the message about when the bus was returning, and there were groups of students hanging around the bus. Clare was among them, and Andy tried to say something to her, but his mother spotted him at that moment and swept him off in about as embarrassing a way as he could have imagined. Clare looked over at him and smiled sympathetically, but that was more or less the last time he had any meaningful interaction with her for 25 years.

PART 2: ANNE AND CLARE

AUGUST 2003

Andrew sat heavily in his office chair and stared morosely at his coffee. He knew it had been a mistake to come in to work instead of going straight home – most of his team were already winding down their days, and he had earned a couple of ill-tempered stares from people who didn't like to leave before the boss. He had shut his office door behind him, but he knew what the muttered conversations out on the office floor were about. He called the team leader, and told her that it was fine to send people home; that Andrew would only be working on his notes from the meetings in Germany, and they'd start fresh the following morning, and this seemed eventually to calm the buzz from outside his door.

He sighed; he had never been good at office politics, and knew he was an inept manager at times, but in spite of several expensive training courses, still was not clear why that should be. He checked the time – was it too early to call Anne? He tried to remember what her working day was like; she had a new job at the library in Godalming, and he couldn't remember what time she got home, what time she fed the children, or anything about her post-divorce life.

He thought of Anne, picked up the phone, and then put it down again. He dug his notes from the meetings out of his laptop case, and started reading them through. He stared at them without comprehending much for what must have been some considerable time until he was startled by a knock on his window from his team leader letting him know that she was going home. He checked the time, and decided it was late enough.

Anne answered after several rings, and he apologised for obviously being inconvenient. Anne stopped him:

"Andrew, it's fine. I was just finished with dinner. Let me sit down." He listened to her move around, picturing his ex-wife in what had been their living room. When she spoke again, Andrew was struck by how strained her voice seemed. He almost asked about it, then decided it was none of his business, and made small talk until she asked him about his trip.

He had thought he would come straight out with the news of Peter, but hadn't been able to figure out a way of making it sound natural, so he talked about the village and the lack of a border, and briefly about Matthias and Gerda. He heard himself petering out, and wondered what Anne must be thinking – this conversation would be over before he had a chance to explain anything if he wasn't careful.

Anne surprised him, however, by starting to talk about the bus trip – asking him if he remembered certain things which, in truth, he mostly didn't. She paused, and he heard her take a deep breath. He suddenly, irrationally, wondered if she already knew about Peter, but stopped himself from asking anything. Anne spoke quietly:

"Andrew, I don't know what you've heard from Matthias this weekend, but some things happened to me over there which you should know about. Are you OK to carry on talking?"

He thought about this – he was in the clothes which he had travelled in; he was tired, hungry, and probably in need of a shower, but he thought that if they didn't have this conversation now, it might never happen. He told her that it was fine, and reclined his chair.

Anne began to tell her version of the bus trip, and Andrew was surprised to hear how much her perspective differed from his, but after almost an hour of what sounded like a prepared script, he felt obliged to interrupt.

"Anne, I'm sorry to stop you, but I'm tired and hungry, and I don't think you're telling me anything I don't already know."

This was met with silence before Anne sighed in the way which had become so familiar to him during the final years of their marriage. He felt he should say something more, but his ex-wife stopped him.

"You're probably right, Andrew. There are important things I need to tell you, but you need to understand how they happened."

"Anne, what happened to you? All this stuff – I even remember the fuss about the jeans; you were changing, and then…"

"And then I changed back. I know, Andrew. I was trying to tell you why, but it's taking a bit longer than I expected. Why don't you come round for dinner on Friday, and I'll try to explain." Andrew felt that his own agenda had been derailed by this strange conversation, but looked at the time and agreed – there was no way he was going to start telling Anne about Peter at this time of night, and she seemed to have her own story to tell, which might also take long enough. He hung up and stared at the blinds covering his window for a long time, trying to absorb what he had heard. He became aware of the sound of the cleaners working their way towards his corner of the office, and discovered that the excuse he had given Anne about being tired and hungry was actually true. Still bemused by the conversation with his ex-wife, Andrew gathered himself and headed out.

AUGUST 2003

Anne hung up the phone and promptly burst into silent tears; she wasn't about to alarm her children by giving vent to what she was actually feeling, but she needed some kind of release, and a small part of her mind gave thanks to her counsellor who had effectively given her permission to cry whenever she felt the need. Anne couldn't take all of the advice she had been given to heart, but she had stopped feeling guilty about showing some emotion, and after a few minutes she composed herself, and began to think about what had just happened.

First, and possibly most important, Matthias appeared not to have told Andrew any of it. She had been terrified from the moment Andrew had first proposed his ridiculous trip that he would find out what had been so carefully hidden from him for so long, and it appeared that had not happened; she knew him well enough to know when he was hurt or upset with her, and she heard no trace of that in his voice; she would have to see him face to face to confirm it, but she was confident of that at least.

Of course, it gave her another problem: she had expected accusations and bitterness, now she had to prepare a confession. This had caught her off guard, and she knew that by trying to organise what she wanted to say, she had rambled badly, and said nothing.

She busied herself for several minutes making tea and checking on her children, then retired to what had been Andrew's office to think. She knew that Andrew needed to hear all of it; to really understand what had been in her mind that Friday afternoon, and how things could have gone so badly wrong for so many years because of a sauna, a pair of jeans and a boy who wore his scars on the outside, but his pain so deeply inside.

She thought back, as she had done so often, most recently with her counsellor, to those two weeks when she had 'kicked over the traces', as her mother would have put it, and tried to reconcile what she needed to tell

Andrew with what she still wanted to conceal, and how any of that would make sense alongside what she had already told him in her inept and incoherent way that afternoon.

Only one person could help her with this, she thought – at least, only one person who might answer the phone at this time on a Monday evening. Her oldest friend and the one she had tried hardest – perhaps unfairly, she sometimes thought – to keep from Andrew.

She drained her teacup, idly wondered if there was any wine left in the box on the kitchen counter, then picked up the cordless phone and dialled Clare's number.

JUNE 1978

After their first morning of classes, Anne was happy to tag along with whatever Liezl had in mind. Her mild bewilderment at being in this alien environment was mostly gone now, and she genuinely liked her German shadow. Liezl was strikingly pretty, and wore clothes which showed off more of her body than either would have been tolerated at school back home, or indeed Anne was entirely comfortable with, but she was kind and thoughtful, and fun to be with.

There had been only one moment of real unease on the Sunday evening. After what seemed like an open house party to which half the village had been invited, during which Anne had met almost all of Liezl's extended family, the two girls retired to Anne's room to talk. Liezl good-naturedly teased Anne about Andy – apparently, Anne's friendly affection for her tall friend seemed a little more than just friendship to an outsider – and about Matthias, who was Liezl's cousin, Andy's shadow, and who had quietly made quite an impression on Anne.

Anne had even felt emboldened enough to ask Liezl about him, and was dismayed by the yelp of delight this had elicited. Clearly, she was going to have to be more guarded around her new friend; she was very sharp, and noticed things Anne thought weren't even there.

The disconcerting moment came when Liezl's mother called up to them to go to bed. Liezl disappeared to her own room for a moment, and then, without knocking, and with Anne down to her underwear, simply walked back in, carrying what must have been her nightclothes. Anne swallowed her impulse to scream, but sat down quickly, covering herself, to Liezl's delight. The German girl began to undress before Anne's appalled stare – was something else going on here? Anne was not well versed in the various sins of the world, but surely Liezl wasn't about to – well, what was she doing?

Anne turned her back and covered herself with her nightdress, to Liezl's delighted laughter, and when she dared to turn round again, discovered that her shadow was dressed, although in nightclothes which seemed positively indecent to Anne. She realised that she was blushing, and a little shaky. Liezl looked concerned.

"You are OK? I do not want to miss talking, so I changed here. This is not a good thing?"

Anne nodded, then shook her head, then understood that she was giving off mixed signals and tried to explain that she wasn't comfortable with changing in front of anyone, never mind someone she had only known for a few hours, and Liezl looked genuinely upset.

"I am sorry – this is normal for me. I do not think about other people sometimes. You must tell me. You are tired, I think. We sleep now, and talk more in the morning. This is good?"

Anne nodded, and was grateful to see Liezl leave. It was nearly half an hour later, however, before she felt confident enough to undress properly and put her nightdress on again.

By the following lunchtime, however, the previous night was mostly forgotten, and Anne was happy to follow whatever lead Liezl suggested. However, this seemed inevitably to mean spending the afternoon with Liezl's cousin – Anne thought cousin was the correct description, but something was not quite right about it – Erika, and her shadow, Clare.

Clare was not someone she would ordinarily have any dealings with. Anne prided herself on getting along with everyone, but knew she would struggle with Clare, as they had almost nothing in common. Clare was social, gregarious and outgoing. As far as Anne knew, she smoked (and the school gossip led her to believe not just tobacco, either), had had a string of boyfriends, all of whom were older and more sophisticated, and was in most ways the antithesis of Anne.

Anne resigned herself to this, ready as always to make the best of whatever situation she found herself in.

The four girls ate their lunches in the covered seating alongside the running track – Liezl insisted that these were called 'bleachers', but it was not a word which Anne had ever heard before, and Clare suggested that it was probably an American word, which sparked a debate among them about the differences.

After lunch was done, they all walked up to the cemetery. Erika wanted to do something which Anne couldn't quite work out, but it soon became clear that it was her turn to tidy up the family plot. Anne and Clare sat some distance away on a stone bench, and watched as the two Germans – aunt and niece, they had worked out, although they were essentially the same age – weeded, tidied and polished. Anne was profoundly uncomfortable at being in Clare's company, but soon had her preconceptions confounded.

"What do you think?" Clare asked her.

"About what?"

"Well, everything. It's about as weird as I'd expected, but somehow I thought I'd be more uncomfortable. They're all really nice though, aren't they?" Anne agreed, and then ventured an opinion of her own:

"I'm not sure about weird. I just thought it would be a different experience – and I think I'm going to be right. You know, I'm actually enjoying myself, sitting here in a cemetery with three people I don't really know."

"Well, you know – nobody really knows you, either." Clare smiled at her. "You're a bit of a mystery to us. I think… No, that's not fair. You're not interested in my opinions; I like to shoot my mouth off before I think about things anyway."

This took Anne completely by surprise. Clare had always struck her as superficial and self-centred; there was clearly more to her than met the eye. She smiled. "No, I'd be interested to know what you think. I honestly don't know what people think of me, other than thinking I'm some kind of throwback."

Now it was Clare's turn to smile. "Well, yes; I hear that. But, you know, people are mostly a little intimidated by you; you know so much, and you seem so in control of everything" -

"Buttoned up, I'm told."

"Yes, I hear that too, but I think that's only the ones who don't know you. I guess you're more complicated than you look. I'd really like to see the real you – maybe you should let her out sometimes"

Anne felt somewhat taken aback by this. Why, for instance, was this person so interested in her? Why would she even have an opinion? Anne needed to think about that; right now, Clare was looking at her expectantly.

"Well, I – I think this is the real me. The buttoned-up person; that's actually who I am on the inside as well. I don't really want to conform to what others expect of me, and -"

Clare interrupted. "But what people expect of you is what you give them. It might be worth exploring the other person, the one who would be unexpected. Just a thought, anyway. My motto is that you should do what you want; be who you want to be."

Anne wanted to know who Clare wanted to be, but the conversation was ended by Erika dumping a pile of weeds into the bin beside the bench. They stood and admired the work, then strolled back toward the village.

AUGUST 2003

Clare answered on the first ring, and Anne automatically and absurdly apologised; no matter how often Clare had told her over the years that if she didn't want to be interrupted, she wouldn't pick up, Anne always felt she was intruding on her friend's glamorous life.

Clare, as always, laughed. "It's fine – I thought it might be you; I take it Andrew is back, then? Does he know?"

Anne sighed. "No, at least I don't think so. But I know I need to tell him. And I've already had a good go at messing that up. Tell me what to do, Clare; I'm going to get this wrong. He's the father of my children, I'd like him not to hate me, if he doesn't already."

Anne could tell that Clare was smiling on the other end of the line, and started to feel better. Clare was good at this stuff, even if she had never married or even looked like settling down; she seemed to cruise through life negotiating relationships and friendships without ever hurting anyone's feelings or getting in difficult situations. Apart from that once, of course…

She focused more closely on what Clare was saying:

"You need to talk to him, let him tell you if he's found anything out, or if he's just had a nice time with Matthias, and it's all in the past now. Maybe you don't need to tell him anything – he might not want to know."

"No, Clare; I've lived with it for so long and it's time I was honest with him. If he's struck up a friendship with Matthias again, the truth will come out eventually. I'd rather it was from me."

Clare paused, then asked about the conversation Anne and Andrew had already had.

"Well, I messed it up a bit. I thought he was going to accuse me and I had a story ready for that, but he didn't say anything, so I started to ramble. I told him about the sauna, but he didn't seem interested."

Clare burst into her usual delighted laugh at this. "Anne, he couldn't care less about you in a sauna, unless he wants some mental images of all of us in there to help him sleep!"

Anne blushed, and nearly rebuked Clare, but she could never get cross at Clare's way of expressing herself; it usually was closer to the truth than Anne's way of looking at things.

"It was important to me, Clare – you know it was. That, and our shopping trip, changed everything that week. None of it would have happened otherwise; you know that as well as I do."

Clare fell silent at this. "Yes, I do, Anne. I never understood it, but I always believed you.

JUNE 1978

The evening's entertainment turned out to be a trip to the pub in the next village. Anne was tired, and had the beginnings of a migraine. She was also uncomfortable with the idea of spending an evening in a pub, and after she and Liezl had walked over to Erika's, she pulled Clare aside to tell her so.

Clare suggested playing up the migraine, and offered to cover for her. She also offered Anne a book to read – *Sons and Lovers*, but it was Anne's turn to surprise: "I've read it," she said.

"And? Clare wanted to know.

"And most of the others, although I didn't like *The Rainbow* as much"

"That's not what I meant, but.... OK, another conversation for another day. Do you have something to read right now? It seems to be my day for lending out books." Anne was staring at Clare's stack of well-thumbed paperbacks in some surprise. This was clearly not the person she had expected at all.

"No, I'm fine – I'm working my way through *Tess* at the moment. Thanks, though – I appreciate the offer."

Clare smiled at her: "No problem – if you see anything you like, though, just ask. Oh, and don't take it too seriously – he's just a man."

This last puzzled Anne for some time, but she finally decided that Clare meant Hardy, rather than either Andy or Matthias.

Liezl's parents were surprised to see her come back so soon, but sympathetic rather than suspicious. Anne had intended simply to go up to her room and read, but Liezl's mother had a different suggestion, which thanks to her pronunciation of the word 'sauna', puzzled Anne for a time. Once she had worked it out, however, she was tempted. She had heard that saunas could be good for relaxation, and she thought that, having denied herself one new experience that evening, perhaps she should try another.

She was shown the sauna, which was in a kind of half-cellar arrangement Anne had not seen before now, was given several fresh towels, and left alone. It was painstakingly explained to her that she would not be disturbed, so that she could be 'in privacy', and then she was left alone.

Anne then walked all the way up two flights of stairs to her room, which earned her a puzzled look, changed into the swimming costume she hated, but which she had brought anyway – just in case, her mother had said, although Anne had rarely worn it in public, and had no intention of going swimming with people she didn't know. She hadn't, however, brought a robe or any kind of dressing gown, so she pulled her dress back on, and wrapped a towel around her shoulders to hide the obvious incompatibility between the costume and the dress.

Once back in the half-cellar, she shed the dress and hung it up, then showered, as per instructions, and pulled the door of the sauna open to check the temperature, which caused her to gasp audibly and close the door again. She was supposed to sit in that? She went back to pick up her towel, and tried again. The heat was overpowering, but she found that she adjusted to it remarkably quickly. Sitting down was painful, until she figured out that she could sit on the towel, and then she closed her eyes and tried to relax.

After a minute or so, she remembered that she was supposed to set the timer – a kind of egg-timer gadget on the wall, by turning it over, so that she didn't spend too long in there. There had also been some pantomimed instructions about pouring water on the coals, but when she tried this, it caused the temperature to rise alarmingly, and she opened the door a crack to try to regulate it.

Once it seemed bearable again, she returned to her seat, and lay down. There was room for two – or three at a pinch - people on the bench along one side, and one more seat on the short side directly opposite the door. Anne could lie on her back on the long bench with her knees bent relatively easily. She closed her eyes again, and began to appreciate the stillness, and even the heat.

Another problem slowly asserted itself, however – she was uncomfortable. The detested swimming costume had metal loops of no apparent purpose around the waist, and these were beginning to be painful against her skin. In addition, various seams and edges were causing her to fidget with them, and she thought perhaps she should just abandon the whole idea, when it occurred to her just what the 'privacy' speech had been about. Was she expected to be naked in here? She gave a little nervous laugh, telling herself not to be so silly – she was naked in the shower, for example, every morning, and that didn't cause her any issues, other than the fact that she really didn't like to see her own body in the mirror; she felt odd-shaped and unattractive.

After a minute more, the issue became pressing – she was either going to have to get out of the sauna or strip off. Taking her courage in both hands, she did the latter. When nothing terrible happened after two or three minutes, she began to relax, and even enjoy the experience. She lay still and sweated out a lot of her anxieties and worries, and when the timer ran out, she turned it over, although she kept a sharp eye on it this time, so that she only had another five minutes. Self-discipline was her guiding principle, and even in a strange situation like this, she was not about to lose sight of it.

She thought about dressing before opening the door, but, reasoning that the shower was less than three feet away, and that she had been guaranteed her privacy, she decided to risk it. The shower, oddly, had no obvious temperature setting, and it wasn't until she had waited for a full minute for it to warm up that she understood that it was supposed to be cold. *Another new experience, then,* she thought, and stepped in. The cold contrasting with her elevated body temperature made her want to scream, but – that self-discipline again – she contained it, and suffered. As soon as she was confident that the sweat had been sluiced off, she shut the shower off, and looked down at herself.

She was covered, painfully, in goose pimples, but felt vastly better than she had before the sauna, and actually delayed drying to just experience the sensation of slowly coming back up to room temperature. Eventually, she dried herself, pulled the dress back on, and slowly walked upstairs, feeling like she was floating. *Well,* she thought, as soon as she was back in her room, *that was certainly worth the risk: perhaps some of these new experiences will turn out alright.*

The next day, on the bus back from some picturesque but otherwise forgettable town, she told Clare about the sauna.

"No-one told me about this! We must sauna together, what do you think?" Anne wasn't so sure about this – one of the most enjoyable things about the previous evening had been the solitude – and when Clare and Erika turned up to sauna later that evening, Anne politely declined, and left the other girls to it, faintly irritated by the various shrieks and giggles she could hear from below.

Anne was alone in the enormous house for most of the following afternoon, and she read in the garden for much of that time; not just her copy of *Tess,* which she was beginning to find tedious in places, but also a German magazine which she had found in the sitting room. It appeared to be mainly devoted to television shows, and its bright simplicity made it fun for Anne to try to decipher, even if most of the articles were about people and shows she had never heard of.

After some time had passed, she felt hot and sweaty, and considered the sauna again. She was alone, and unlikely to be disturbed, and she felt a thrill run through her at the thought of it. Within minutes, she was comfortably relaxed in what could easily become her favourite part of the house. She even came close to sleep, but roused herself, fearing that sleep would be dangerous. She had just turned over to lie face down, and facing away from the door, although this was less comfortable because of having to bend her knees and place the tops of her feet on the wall, when she heard movement in the house somewhere. She stiffened, but reasoned that the ruse she had devised of hanging her dress on the outside of the outer door would suffice for privacy, and tried to relax.

Which made her shock all the greater when the door suddenly opened. She gave a cry of alarm, and sat up while trying to cover herself. Liezl stood in the doorway, having pulled it quickly shut behind her, laughing.

"Ah, my friend, you must learn to relax, I think." Liezl came over and sat very close to Anne, who was shakily trying to do just that.

"I am sorry to frighten you, but I thought you would not mind. I think you like our sauna. No?"

Anne nodded, not yet trusting her voice. She still sat hunched over, with her arms folded about her in a most uncomfortable and, frankly, ridiculous pose. Liezl nudged her with an elbow.

"Come on, only you and me are here. Try to relax. I think you will like it."

Anne stared, but slowly sat up, and even more slowly, unfolded her arms. She tried to affect her usual studied calm, but it would not come, and her expression caused Liezl to laugh again.

"This is better. I was thinking you had no reason to hide. Except perhaps if you were really a man!" This caused more uproarious laughter, which Anne, slightly giddy after the adrenalin rush of being discovered, joined in with. Once that had subsided, they sat in companionable silence for some time; Liezl paying attention to the state of her toenails, and Anne simply staring down at her knees and trying not to think too much. *Four days in Germany, and I am sitting in a sauna with no clothes on, talking to someone else as if it was the most normal thing in the world.* She could not yet decide if this was a good or a bad thing.

Anne excused herself after another few minutes, showered and dried, then had to face the issue of how to retrieve the dress without being seen by the crowds of people she felt sure were on the other side of the door. Liezl got out of the sauna and showered after her, and Anne decided to wait – safety in numbers seemed to be the best policy. Liezl dried, then picked up her clothes and, wrapping the towel about her waist, opened the door. Anne almost shouted after her.

"You're not going out like that, are you?"

Liezl turned and smiled. "No-one is in the house, and it's OK if they are; it's my family, not strangers. She held Anne's dress out to her, and the English girl considered it. She was soundly wrapped in her towel, and the idea of now spending time unwrapping and dressing, only to undress once more when upstairs did strike her as slightly absurd. She bundled all of her underwear in the dress, then followed Liezl upstairs, wearing only a towel.

The house was, as promised, deserted, and the girls retreated to their rooms. Anne sat heavily on her bed as soon as she had closed the door, and for no clear reason that she could identify, began to sob.

Liezl must have heard this, and came in. Anne, not really in control of her emotions, yelled: "Don't you ever knock? In England, we are more considerate. Please knock before you come in!"

Liezl stared, then solemnly retreated and knocked. Anne, realising what had happened, laughed through her tears, and said "come in". As soon as Liezl was in the room, she began to apologise, but Liezl halted her.

"No, no, Anne, I must say sorry. I do not think about you – it is different. I mean, you are different to us. Here, we always had a lot of family moving around this house; we always do this. You are not us, and it is wrong. I am sorry." Now she looked more carefully at Anne. "I think we are making you frightened, no?"

Anne shook her head. "No; I'm really sorry. I don't know what has happened. Perhaps it is all still too strange. And.." She faltered, and Liezl simply waited for her.

"I cannot change who I am so quickly, I think," Anne said. "it is too hard. In Britain I cannot even change in the same changing room as other girls – I don't know why. I hate to do any sport or gym because of it."

Liezl watched her thoughtfully. "Are you *beschämt?* – What do you say?"

"Ashamed?"

"Yes, I think. Ashamed. Is this right?"

Anne thought about this for a long time. "No. I mean, I don't like my body, I think it is a stupid thing, but I am not ashamed. It is just wrong, that is all. You should not be – like that; not dressed – with other people. It is how I was brought up. I don't think it is so unusual in England."

"But your friend Clare – "

"She is not like most people in England, she says." A long pause followed, before Anne could find more words. "I want to change things a little, but I must do it on my own – I can't let other people change them for me. Is that - does that make sense?"

Liezl thought that it did, but suggested that perhaps other people might be able to help and advise, which struck Anne as sensible. Anne had by this time, recovered her poise, and suggested that they dress and help to make dinner. Liezl found this amusing, but Anne explained that she loved to cook, and it would be a way for her to thank the family for their hospitality.

AUGUST 2003

Clare laughed when Anne reminded her of that evening's meal.

"You made a shepherd's pie – I remember Erika asking me what on earth it was! You made a big impression, although I don't think you realised that at the time."

Anne agreed, although she wasn't sure she believed that.

"So, that's mostly what I told Andrew. I don't think he was interested, but it still seems so important to me, even after all this time. That and the jeans, of course."

Clare was quiet, and Anne had to prompt her: "You remember that, don't you?"

"Yes, I do. I think we went too far."

Anne objected, but Clare would not be diverted.

"We pushed you so hard – do you remember how we ganged up on you in that department store? We weren't going to take no for an answer, and I think, deep down, I knew it was wrong. The sauna was one thing, but this was way more public. I didn't get what a big deal it was for you. I've always felt bad about that."

Anne sighed. She was wearing a pair of comfortable jeans right now; it really wasn't that big a deal, she thought, but then remembered how she had been brought up; how strict her mother in particular was about the rule: women do not wear trousers under any circumstances, she declared; it's an important distinction, we are different from men, and we should not be afraid of it.

Anne's counsellor had described it as a form of brainwashing, but it wasn't – not in Anne's mind, anyway. It was just the way I was brought up, she would say. Every family has rules; that was one of ours.

The counsellor had shaken her head in exactly the way Clare had all those years ago when Anne had first tried to explain.

Clare was talking again, and Anne made herself snap out of her reverie.

"I know that the jeans were a big deal for you, Anne. How much better it would have been for you to have gone off to university and been allowed to gradually find your own way, instead of me trying to make you fit my idea of who you should be." Clare sounded genuinely upset, but Anne was having none of it.

"No, that's not it at all. I wanted to be different; you just showed me a way. Maybe it would have been better for me to try some other paths, but I did what I did. No-one actually made me change; I did that myself."

Clare was unconvinced, and said so, but Anne knew her own mind, and realised that she felt much better. She told Clare, who seemed a little puzzled.

"Not sure I did anything, but I'm happy it's helped. When are you seeing him again?"

Anne had to think for a moment. "Friday; he's coming after work."

"And do you know what you'll say to him?"

"Now I do." She took a deep breath. "I'm ready. Thanks, Clare."

AUGUST 2003

Dinner at what had until the year before been his home turned out not to be as terrible an experience as Andrew had imagined. He had been keen to see the children, and in a way Anne, but he did suffer pangs of doubt as he parked in the driveway.

Anne lived with the children in the house he had bought ten years before in Godalming – Godforsaken Godalming, as he had come to call it. He wondered if the move out of London had been the beginning of the end of their marriage, since he almost immediately began to spend less and less time at home; commuting to London to work, to socialise, and to have a cultural life which he had been used to before children, and which he continued to enjoy on his own – finally, in the last year of their marriage, moving into a tiny flat in town - while Anne raised their children in a bubble of suburbia far from his daily life.

The children had been pleased to see him, mildly and briefly distracted by what he had brought back for them, and then made themselves scarce. They appeared to have eaten long before Andrew's arrival – it was already eight in the evening – and they clearly had important social events to plan, and television to watch. Anne managed and marshalled them throughout the rest of the evening without ever having to leave her seat or raise her voice, something which astonished Andrew, who remembered endless shouting matches and tantrums not so long ago. He remarked on it.

"Well, they are growing up, and – oh, Andrew, you know why they don't fight."

"I suppose I do – we aren't fighting so they aren't. I've been thinking about that…"

Anne cut him off. "Don't. I don't think we can change our situation now, do you?"

"I guess not." Andrew looked around the dining room. The house had been little altered since he moved out – not surprising, he thought, since it had always been furnished entirely to Anne's specifications in the first place. He had already seen the only major change – the empty space which had been his study had become a sort of den for the children, although it appeared mostly unused; a new and comfortable-looking chair stood where his desk had been, under the window, but the toys and games arranged on shelves and around the walls looked too carefully arranged, and mostly seemed to be the kind of thing his children would have grown out of by now.

He drained his wineglass, and looked at Anne. "Did you want to carry on your story from the other night? I do have some things to tell you as well which I didn't quite get round to"

Anne looked down at the table, and then suggested moving to the more comfortable seats in the living room. Once they were settled there, she asked him about Hohenügel as if she hadn't already heard one version of the tale.

"Well, Mathias sends his love, and says he would like to meet you again." Anne smiled thinly at that, and looked away. Andrew – now attuned to his ex-wife's moods in a way he had never been while he lived under this roof, asked if she really wanted to hear any of this, but Anne brightened and said that of course she did. Andrew worried over this for a moment, then pressed on:

"You'd probably still recognise the place, except that the wall is gone, of course," and he then retold the story he had already told her once, relating everything except what was actually important and relevant to why he was here. Eventually he realised that he was going to run out of time and excuses not to tell the story of Peter, and he took a deep breath.

"Anne, there's something else. Something important and fairly difficult to believe. And I'm going to need a stiff drink – have you got anything?"

There was half a bottle of whisky which had sat at the back of a cupboard since before he had moved out, and he helped himself to a generous measure. Anne regarded all of this with a curious expression – she seemed almost afraid of what he was going to say, and again he looked at her quizzically. Had he missed something?

He tried to begin, but saw immediately that Anne was crying. He hesitated, then stopped. Anne got up and went into the kitchen, and he almost went to follow her, but reasoned that she wanted to be alone, and sipped solemnly at his whisky, wondering if he could take the rest of the bottle home with him.

When Anne returned, she was a little brighter, but Andrew was still concerned about whatever it was he was missing. Instead of carrying on where he left off, he asked Anne what the problem was.

"It's almost too hard to explain, Andrew. I have something I need to tell you as well; something I should have told you 25 years ago, but I need to tell it in my own way. Is that OK?"

Andrew looked at his watch, then nodded. It was Friday night; he certainly didn't have plans for Saturday. Anne called up to the children to come and say goodnight, then head to bed. This domestic interlude seemed to help them both regain some equilibrium, and Andrew took a deep breath, finally ready to tell his tale, but Anne got there ahead of him, and he remembered belatedly that she wanted to tell him something.

JUNE 1978

Sunday morning was quiet – most of the extended family went off to church, but the girls ducked out of it, reasoning that it would have been difficult for the English girls to follow, to Anne's slight disappointment, and instead they sat around the garden of Liezl's home, and chatted. Lunch – less formal than an English Sunday lunch might have been, and more fun, according to Clare – was taken after the various families returned, but Anne was slightly distracted by the fact that Andy wasn't there.

Matthias had gone home to collect him, but had returned with the news that he and Karla were nowhere to be seen – "probably they are already at the pool" was his verdict – but this news seemed to agitate Clare a little, and it made Anne uneasy for no reason she could put her finger on. The five of them agreed to head over to the pool as soon as they politely could. Erika was, it turned out, the most skilled at family politics – Anne supposed this made sense, given her status – and soon they were on their way.

Anne worried about what the trip to the pool might entail – she was not swimming in that ridiculous costume in front of anyone - but Liezl reassured her that it was more of a place to hang out than an athletic activity, although the heat probably ensured that an amount of swimming would be going on.

The pool turned out to be next to the school, although Anne had not noticed it there before now. Some of her classmates were swimming, but most of them were sprawled on the grass in groups, watching the world go by. The five scanned the area for Andy, who would surely be distinctive even if he was lying down, but there was no sign of him, and Anne began to worry. Liezl went over to a group of older girls – presumably friends of Matthias' sister, whose name Anne had forgotten again – but she came back shaking her head. They debated what to do, and decided to stay put for the time being.

It was not long before a motorbike arrived, roaring up on to the grassed area and scattering the girls Liezl had talked to earlier, causing them to fall about laughing. Matthias groaned and stood up.

"This is Karla," he announced, but stood and waited for her to make the next move.

Karla parked the bike, then walked back over to her friends. On the way she spotted her brother, and yelled something to him about his friend. Anne didn't quite catch it, but Matthias went pale and then puce in alarmingly short order, and she was truly terrified for a moment – had something awful happened?

Matthias started to run over to Karla, but she spun round to face him, and he hesitated. Karla then switched to what sounded to Anne like remarkably good English

"Oh, don't worry; he can find his own way back. He may not know his way around a woman, but he can find his way back here." Matthias said something to her, and Anne also noticed Clare moving in her peripheral vision. Karla laughed out loud.

"No, he was useless. I tried to show him what to do, but it was no good. He showed me his dick – I feel sorry for you English girls. Unless all the others are a bit bigger. It is no wonder you are all frustrated." She laughed again, and Anne was startled to see Clare running at Karla. Anne went after her, propelled by a sense of comradeship more than any rational desire to defend Andy. What would she do, in any case?

By the time she got there, Clare had grabbed the startled Karla by the front of her t-shirt and was snarling viciously at her in what sounded like a mixture of German and English. Karla wrenched herself free, spat in Clare's general direction – Anne supposed it was intended to hit Clare, but it sailed wide of its target – and stared at her. The two antagonists stood like that for what seemed an eternity to Anne, but can only have been a few seconds, then Karla broke off the stare, and stalked back over to her friends.

Anne wanted to reach out to Clare, who was calm on the face of it, but must be in turmoil, but she could do no more than ask over and over if Clare was OK. Liezl pulled her gently aside while Erika walked Clare back to where Matthias was still standing, dumbstruck by what he had just seen.

The crowd took some time to settle back to what it had been before, and Anne was sure that she could hear the scandalous story of Andy being recited over and over; gaining in lurid detail each time it was retold. Because of this, she wasn't truly paying attention to the other girls, who were working out what had just happened and what to do next. Matthias was sitting with his head in his hands, and Anne felt she ought to go and speak to him.

She sat down heavily beside him, in the hope that he would look up and break the ice for her, but he didn't flinch. She cleared her throat, and then dared to speak.

"Matthias, what just happened?" He said nothing, so she tried in German, hoping that *passiert* was the correct word. He looked up at her blankly, but this time spoke:

"I am sorry, Anne. I should know that this will happen. I really thought she was not at home, so Andy would be safe. She is dangerous woman, and he is not – *ach,* he is young. It is my fault."

Anne felt herself put her hand on Matthias' arm, and tell him that he wasn't responsible for Andy or Karla. He looked at her.

"I know what you say is correct, but I must feel this. I apologise; my English is not so good. We should find him, yes?" Anne agreed, and went to get the others, to discover that they had independently arrived at the same conclusion. Mathias explained that if he truly was walking back from the border, he could be anywhere, but Clare interrupted him.

"She did not leave him at the border. He is not far away; she told me this much." Liezl nodded, and suggested they go round the school to try to intercept him; if he was walking back into the village from the direction of the autobahn, then he might not be far away.

Their searching proved fruitless, however. Erika pointed out after they had been walking for close to an hour that they could easily have missed him, and probably it was better to go back to the pool. Anne, in particular, was not keen on that idea, and Matthias said that he didn't particularly want to face his sister again. He offered to go home and see if Andy was there; the group agreed to this, and went their separate ways, although Clare, after hurried consultation with Erika and then Liezl, came back with Anne and her shadow. She would explain later, she said to Anne.

Once back at Liezl's house, it was not long before there was a phone message from Matthias to say that Andy was back, and apparently OK – he had gone to the pool, but had apparently just missed them, so went home. Anne wondered whether he actually was all right, and even considered walking over there to see him, but Clare dissuaded her, suggesting that Andy probably needed time to himself to work out what had happened to him today.

"I think the last thing he needs right now is any female company. Leave him alone for tonight; Matthias will help him, I'm sure." Anne wasn't so sure; she felt that boys weren't as good at this kind of thing as girls, but Clare almost insisted, and Anne demurred.

They retreated to Anne's room for a time, until Clare wondered if she could use the sauna again.

"I think I could use some time alone – Erika's place is so crowded." Anne negotiated this with Liezl, then sat glumly in her room for what seemed like an age, staring out of the window at the countryside.

Eventually, it occurred to Anne to wonder if Clare had been in the sauna too long, and set off downstairs to look for her.

Clare was still in the sauna, although she claimed to have come out and showered a couple of times. She offered to vacate it for Anne, and Anne found herself agreeing, then negotiating the still awkward task of undressing in the vicinity of someone else. She expected Clare to laugh at her, but the other girl seemed subdued, and Anne worried about that.

She spent less time in the sauna than she intended, and came out to find Clare showered and dressed, and plainly waiting for her. Anne sighed at Clare's apparent ability to adapt to German attitudes toward nudity, but showered and dressed with less embarrassment than she would have expected. As they walked upstairs, Anne asked Clare what was wrong.

"I'm still trying to work out what happened back there. I know I can be impulsive, but that was unusual, even for me."

Anne diverted them to the kitchen, and sat at the table. She found herself unable to look at Clare, and studied the placemats instead.

"I thought you were very – what? Brave, maybe"

"Or stupid."

"No. I think it was right, what you did. She shouldn't be allowed to do that. What did you say to her?"

Clare was silent for a time. "Well, it's complicated. I already had a fight with Karla this week. She's a piece of work, that one."

Anne looked up. Clare was sitting there calmly – serenely, Anne thought – but her voice betrayed her tension. "A fight? What – no, forgive me; it's none of my business."

Clare didn't seem to mind, however. "No, it's fine. It was really a silly argument about my jacket, which is leather, and she thought it was hypocritical of me, or something."

"I didn't realise you were vegetarian."

"I'm not – we were talking about animal experimentation, because of a book I lent her. It was a silly argument, but she turned it very personal very quickly, and I called her a few things; she was obviously looking for a reaction, and it all got a little silly. No serious harm done, but I guess I won't be getting a Christmas card from her."

Anne didn't really want to know, but asked anyway. Clare told her what she had called Karla, and Anne laughed.

"I'm sorry; I don't mean to appear rude. I should be shocked, I guess. No, wait – I *am* shocked. But I also think it's funny. I suppose she knew what it meant?"

"Oh, her English is very good – she knew. She called me some things first – she knew what it meant."

Anne considered this. "Why did she do that to Andy, do you think?"

Clare laughed drily. "Well, it's not out of character for her – she seems to be naturally cruel. But I was worried about it because she told me – she told me she was going to get something from him. I thought I was being paranoid, but perhaps not."

"Something?"

"I assume she wants to use him for sex, or something." Now Anne really was shocked. Fancying a boy was one thing, and she was not naïve about the impulses and drives involved in that, but *sex*? It was a long way out of her comfort zone, and Clare could clearly see that.

"I think poor Andy has landed in a difficult situation purely by chance. He's big and – I suppose – strong, and she sees him as some kind of conquest. Good luck to him if he turned it down, though."

Anne's mind was a whirl. She tried to figure out what she thought, and eventually her subconscious, she supposed, prompted her to ask Clare if she thought Andy really had turned Karla down.

"Of course; I mean, I don't know him at all, but he's not the sort of person to get involved like that, is he?" This appeared to be a rhetorical question, but Anne looked over to check if she was expected to answer. She didn't think Andy was that kind of person, but what did she know? She wasn't the kind of person who undressed in front of someone who was a complete stranger a week ago. She wasn't the kind of person who bought jeans. She wasn't the kind of person who went to pubs. Anything seemed possible. Clare continued.

"Anyway, there's compelling evidence that he didn't. You think she'd have been that angry; that vindictive if she'd got what she wanted?"

Again, Anne felt no pressure to answer; she carried on listening.

"No, he's innocent. My guess is she took him out there on the bike to show off and impress him into fucking her – sorry." Clare looked over, checking just how much that word had offended Anne, but Anne waved it away. "He's turned her down, or whatever, and you saw the result. Poor Andy; he's going to have such a hard time tomorrow."

Anne had been thinking about this. "What can we do?"

"Tomorrow? Well, I don't know him, but you can help him."

"Me? How?"

"Just be his friend. You'll need to take charge of him; keep him occupied, let others see that you're his friend, and that you won't stand for any nonsense."

"Sounds all very good, but I don't think I can –"

"Nonsense," Clare interrupted, "you're exactly the right person to do it – people are intimidated by you, and you won't get drawn into the silliness. You can always enlist support from the teachers in any case."

Anne thought about this. The idea frightened her, but interested her at the same time. If she was going to make a connection with Andy, this might be the way to do it, when he needed a friend. A thought struck her.

"Clare, why are you getting so involved? Is he - I mean, do you...." Words failed her, and she only slowly looked over to Clare. She wasn't sure what she felt about Andy, but she knew in some primal part of her that she didn't want Clare to feel that way about him.

Clare reddened and looked away, but quickly looked back and smiled at her. "No, Anne, I don't. Like I say, I barely know him, for one thing, and for another, he's...."

Clare faltered, and Anne felt a sense of panic. Her face must have betrayed her, because Clare suddenly smiled.

"You'd be better for him in any case. He's probably not my type. I think I'd like him if I knew him, but I'm not sure he does it for me."

Does what? Anne wondered. The things she had read in Lawrence? The things she had read in some other books? She had read something in a recent novel which had astounded her; did women all feel like that? And if so, how? That was surely a conversation for another day. Anne was beginning to feel tired, and said so to Clare, who looked relieved to be offered a way out of this conversation.

Anne, as always looking to be helpful, found some coffee cups to tidy up, and was rinsing them in the sink when she heard what she thought was a heavy sigh – almost a sob - coming from behind her. She turned, drying her hands. Clare was clearly unhappy.

"Clare, what is it? Are you OK?"

"Yes. Yes, I am. It's just one hell of a lot of growing up seems to be going on this week, don't you think? I'm only beginning to understand what a naïve child I still am. Sorry, I'm probably not who you think I am, Anne. Don't worry." She stood.

Anne stared and then took a deep breath. She wasn't sure what she was about to say, but decided to open her mouth and find out:

"Clare, it doesn't matter who I think you are. I thought I knew all about you, but that was before I ever spoke to you. You've helped me – and Andy, I think – this week, and I'm so glad to be your friend"

The girls hugged before Clare left, and Anne, normally uncomfortable with displays of affection like that, felt that it cemented some kind of bond between them.

AUGUST 2003

Anne realised Andrew was staring at her, and stopped. He opened his mouth, then closed it again. She waited for him; she was finally mentally ready to tell the truth, she could wait for him to catch up.

He coughed, then spoke: "Wait. *Clare* took on Karla that day? Not you?"

Anne laughed, then caught herself. This must have been important to him.

"Yes; Clare. Do you really think I would have had the guts to face down that madwoman? You remember what she was like, don't you?" She paused – Andrew surely did remember what she was like, then she felt as if the blood had drained from her face. Was he about to confess that he had done all those things Karla accused him of? That something had happened last week, and now Karla was going to – what, exactly? She was going to sue him for sexual harassment? Confess her love for him?

Anne couldn't formulate a way of asking him that, and the pair of them sat staring at each other for a moment, until Andrew found his voice.

"Yes," he said quietly, "I remember. That's not all I remember, Anne. I remember Clare telling me how you had stood up for me that day, and how that set me off on a path... That and the rain, I suppose."

Anne felt herself blushing, even after 25 years.

"Me standing there, looking like a cheap tart? I lost about a year's worth of sleep over that, as I recall."

Andrew clearly did remember; Anne saw an all too brief flash of the expression she remembered from that day pass over his face, and she almost laughed to see it.

"I knew it! I knew there was something!" Andrew shifted a little uncomfortably in his seat, then looked her in the eye.

"You want honesty?" Anne said she did, although she wasn't sure she believed it.

"OK, then – that was the first time I had ever thought of you in that way – you know, as someone.... You know, as a woman, I suppose. It was just so much for me to take in. First Karla, then Clare on the bus, then you. And....

"And, I suppose I might have done something about it, but things changed. Permanently and I don't think I ever really recovered. I need to tell you about it, Anne, before I lose my nerve."

Anne was startled. In her mind, she had been leading up to her confession. Whatever Andrew had in mind was clearly going to derail that conversation. Again.

Slowly, haltingly, he began to tell his story; to unburden himself, and as Anne heard exactly what Karla had been like, and what she had done to Andrew, she felt as if she was having some kind of out of body experience. She listened intently to his description of how he was seduced, although that didn't seem the correct word to her.

As she listened, she realised that she was analysing his words as if they had no connection to her; that she was visualising the whole thing as if it was a second-rate soap opera, and she forced herself to try harder to connect with his story. Suddenly she understood that this must have been happening at exactly the same time as her own story; the thing she had never confessed to Andrew, and she began to cry again. She was unable to stop herself, so when he was done and looking at her for a reaction, she simply stared back, tears flowing freely down her cheeks.

When no reaction came, he started to say something about their courtship, and about changing Anne, which made no sense to her, so she waved him into silence while she composed herself.

"Do you know, I always knew something must have happened. Not the baby, but something. You changed so abruptly after the trip; I wonder..." she tailed off, then composed her thoughts and began again.

"I tried to change you, Andrew. I thought I was trying to get back the boy I fell in love with, but now I understand that he was gone; seduced by a woman who should have left well alone. We talk about being damaged goods, Andrew, but I don't think either of us really understood how badly damaged we were." She gave a short, mirthless laugh.

"Still, it explains one or two things, don't you think?"

She had lost him again. He clearly didn't think it explained anything, and began to say so, but she cut him off again.

"No, actually, I suppose it doesn't explain anything to you. But then, you only know half the story."

JUNE 1978

Liezl woke her on Friday morning with a plan. The plan seemed to be to skip out of school as early as possible and to come back here to – well, just to come back here and enjoy their last day together. Anne weighed up the shock factor, and decided that this would do nicely for her final day.

As they calmly walked out of the school later that morning, she found herself calmly explaining to Andy that she really didn't mind the odd bit of rule-breaking. He looked at her, and she gave herself a mental pat on the back. *This might all go according to plan,* she thought.

However, she had not been prepared for Matthias' bottle of schnapps. Alcohol really was a line she wasn't ready to cross, she thought, and she felt herself begin to panic a little as all eyes turned to her. Matthias had asked her something, and she really didn't know what to answer. She slowly looked around the group. Aside from Matthias, who she liked well enough, but hadn't really got to know too well, these were the closest friends she had right now – perhaps the closest friends she had ever had, and she didn't want to let them down. She looked at Andy, who shrugged, which wasn't much help. Then she looked at Clare, remembering how helpful she had been in previous sticky situations. Clare smiled, and mouthed something which she worked out was "a sip". She thought about it, then agreed to "a tiny amount." Once she had agreed to it, she felt herself over-explaining everything, and she had to force herself to be quiet.

The tiny amount barely touched her lips before it evaporated. She had a fleeting burning sensation, an aftertaste she couldn't really describe, and then – nothing. She thought about this, and decided to try to get at least a proper taste. She could always say that she hadn't enjoyed it.

The second sip had more substance to it, and she had to bite down hard on a cough, which would have been disastrous, even among friends. Once it settled, however, she felt a warmth spread through her, and she decided not to be too judgemental just yet.

With the spectacle of Anne's First Drink out of the way, the group discussions turned to other things, and Anne felt herself relax. Another test passed, and tomorrow it would all be over, she told herself. I've survived it, and I'm still feeling good about it. She barely noticed that she was still sipping at the schnapps until Andy asked her something, and she found that turning her head caused her to feel light-headed. The room wasn't exactly spinning, but it wasn't quite as stable as it might be, either. This intrigued, rather than alarmed her, and she found that she had tuned Andy out while she contemplated it. A little while later, he asked her the same question again, and she mumbled something at him, lost in thought.

The next time he asked, however, she felt herself snap out of her daydream. He was only being kind, and checking if she was still OK, and she had been ignoring him. She smiled at him and told him she was fine. On an impulse, she decided that she was going to change her clothes, and she told him so. He smiled, and she stood.

Standing seemed to have become a slightly more complex set of movements than it had ever been before, but she managed it, and also managed to leave the room and walk upstairs without tripping over anything, which seemed suddenly to be a very real danger. She reached her room, and collapsed on to the bed. She would probably have slept, had it not been for a spark of something which seemed to have asserted itself along with the light-headedness. She felt odd; not at all Anne-like, as if she wanted to surprise a few people and see what happened. She thought of Clare, and grinned; her new friend would help her do this, she decided.

She looked up and leant over the edge of the bed to pull the lid of her suitcase open. There, on top of the packing she had done earlier, were the jeans which she had not had the courage to wear yet. She supposed that her idea had been to come up and put the jeans on and get everyone's opinion. She stood, and somewhat unsteadily undressed.

When she was down to her underwear, she forced herself to look in the mirror on the wardrobe door. She really didn't like how she looked – there seemed to be lumps and bumps in odd places, and the width of her hips had made her feel like a cartoon representation of a woman ever since she had first been aware of it. Still, she had seen Andy's reaction to seeing an outline of her body the other day, and she would have to say that she felt she was in better shape than Erika, who seemed to have no hang-ups about *her* body. She realised that she had been there for some time, and ought to get dressed and go back down. The jeans fit well; she was absorbed by the sensations involved in all of this, and had actually opened the door before realising that she had no shirt to wear.

She stood there in the doorway for a few moments, not properly aware that anyone might come upstairs and find her there, then she walked along the corridor to Liezl's room, and let herself in. The feeling of wearing something so unfamiliar was mildly alarming, but she registered that the spark was there as well, and she allowed herself to take it all in. She quickly found a t-shirt of Liezl's which had looked baggy on the German girl, and pulled it over her head. It was somewhat less baggy on Anne, but it didn't constrain and emphasise the way Clare's shirt did. She pronounced herself satisfied, and walked back to her own room.

At this point what she wanted more than anything was the bottle of schnapps. The edge may have just been wearing off her confidence, and she was sure that a little more alcohol would restore it. She debated this with herself for a minute or two, then, understanding that the situation wasn't going to improve by simply standing there, set off downstairs.

The reaction was all she could have hoped for. Andy, in particular, looked stunned, and complimented her more than once. She drank more of the schnapps to help get a grip on things, but after a few moments she couldn't tell if the buzz was coming from the drink, or from her own self-confidence. Matthias drank a toast to her, and she saw him, too, looking at her when he thought she might not notice.

They ate a little lunch, and Clare talked to her for a few moments; partly supportive, and partly warning her to stay inside her limits.

"You've never been here before, and you just need to watch out – don't get into a situation you'll regret." Anne understood that this was good advice, but she only half heard it, and it competed with the spark, and her own thoughts, which were about never turning back. Perhaps she would wear the jeans all the way home. What better way to announce her change to her parents?

After lunch, they all wandered around the village for a bit. Had it not been for the alcohol, and the alarmingly unusual experience – freaky, Clare would have called it – of being out in public dressed like this, Anne might have been bored. She felt the euphoria of the morning wearing off a little, and she was suddenly tired and in need of some solitude. She heard Andy peel off the group and go back to pack his case; she thought this was a splendid idea, and announced that she would do the same.

The other three walked back with her; Clare in particular keeping a steadying hand on her arm when needed. Once back at the house, Liezl brewed coffee, but Anne felt she needed sleep, and excused herself. Once upstairs, she could barely keep her eyes open. She dropped to the bed, holding back sleep only long enough to pull the shirt off over her head.

A little while later, she felt there was someone in the room with her. She heard Clare's voice, and tried to tell her she was just fine. After that, silence again. The village was still and quiet at the best of times, but something about this Friday afternoon felt almost oppressively so. It was hot, and there was no air, in spite of Anne having opened all the windows.

A little while later, the door opened again. Anne was neither asleep nor awake, and she couldn't really make out who was there. She sensed whoever it was standing over her, watching, and she smiled – these were her friends, they were concerned for her.

Then the someone was on the bed with her. She looked up and turned her head, to find Matthias' kind face smiling back at her. He said something about the others having gone into the sauna, and that he was left alone, so he thought he would keep Anne company. This struck her as kind, and she made a little room for him. She considered the fact that there was a boy in her bed with her, and felt, rather than outrage, the reassertion of the spark. Something nagged at her; something someone had said, but she couldn't quite focus on it.

She must have dozed again for a while, because when she was next aware, Matthias' arm was around her shoulders, and he was gently stroking her back. This set off some alarm bells, but she restricted herself to trying to push up on one elbow to look at him. He stared into her eyes and said, very clearly, she thought "forgive me; I will leave now."

He stood, and as she focussed on him, she saw that he had taken his shirt off. This struck her as amusing for a moment, then terrifying, and she started to scream, then almost as quickly stopped herself. What good would it do? The others were in the sauna in the cellar, and Matthias wasn't about to attack her; he was standing there crying.

Anne sat up, her head slowly clearing, and patted the bed beside her. Matthias shook his head, but she insisted, and he sat with his back to her. She suddenly felt pity for him, and put her hand on his back. He flinched, and she drew away again. She looked at his back; it had several bruises, oddly grouped together. *What are they?* She wondered, *some kind of sports injury?* Finally, she gathered enough wits about her to speak.

"Matthias? What is it? Why are you here?" He took a deep breath, but no words came out. She saw his shoulders slump, and then he tried again.

"I am sorry; I am ashamed. I should not have done this, but…." He sighed again, and she could hear the tears in his voice. "It is only that I am so lonely. You are so kind, and I thought that you need a friend. I came here to talk to you, but you are sleeping, so I want to sleep too. I am sorry about this; I did not think; I only did." He held his arms out to her, and she felt the memory of his skin on hers; something she wanted back.

She did not know what to say. All of the thoughts and impressions of the last two weeks crowded in on her, and she wondered if it was possible for a head to explode from the pressure of thoughts. She looked at Matthias' arms, still stretched out, and saw why he wore long sleeves all the time. She had no mental space left to process the marks she could see, but her attitude to him changed. As all of this turmoil raged in her head, a calm voice told her what to do. She got up, not too unsteadily, she noted, walked to the door, and locked it. She stood there, looking at Matthias, who was crumpled in shame and sorrow, then calmly went back to him. She pulled the covers down the bed, and then she lay down, and patted the bed beside her. He lay too, also still in jeans, and Anne got the clear sense from him that he was as unsure about what to do next. She thought about the sensation of skin on skin she had briefly felt, and opened her arms to him.

"We hug, I think. Nothing more. You understand?" She felt like she was talking to a 5-year-old, but he did not seem to mind, and they hugged, clumsily and self-consciously, for some minutes. She spent the time absorbing the physical sensations – the feel of his skin, the feel of – well, *that*, pressed against her hip – and the dull ache at the centre of her which told her this was wrong, and that this was what Clare had warned her about. She thought about Matthias, and how something in him seemed broken. She knew that this was why she had done this, but she struggled to make her thoughts coherent. She tightened the hug.

They lay for some time like that, Anne in her sensible bra pressed against Matthias' bruised chest. She gently stroked his back for a time, which produced some tears from him, then stopped when he began to reciprocate. That way lay all kinds of things she wasn't ready to deal with.

They must both have fallen asleep for a time, and when she woke fully, Matthias was gone. She had a memory of him moving her, and supposed this was what had woken her. Her bra felt uncomfortable, and she looked down to see that one cup was pulled aside – perhaps by the way she had moved to let Matthias get up – and a nipple was partially visible. Her heart pounded at this – had he done it; had he…

This was what she had been warned about. This was why she had all these defences. Everything in the last two weeks had eaten away at those defences, until she was left in this position. The words *fallen woman* flashed through her mind, but she knew that wasn't right – her jeans were still in place, and she would have known if anything had happened. All that had happened was –

What, exactly? She had slept with a boy. Not 'slept with' in the way the books and the newspapers meant, just actually laid down and gone to sleep. She felt a shame deeper than anything she had ever known before. She needed to shower, but not to wash him off her; the stain she felt was deep inside. She would, she thought, never be the same again, but she meant by this that she would never be this way again – instead, she would go back to the way she had been – the 'same again'.

She showered, and then hid in her room until Liezl came to take her out to the evening's entertainment – a farewell disco at the school. She wanted nothing more than to cry off and crawl into bed, but Liezl, surprised to see Anne back in her 'English' clothes, insisted, and Anne thought it might actually be a good idea; to get back out into the world and face things.

She had, however, overestimated her ability to cope with the world. The disco was torture; more so than these events normally were, and she could find nowhere to sit which didn't either put her in the path of well-meaning fellow students trying to get her to dance, or in sight of either Andy or Matthias. After some time spent lurking around the door, she decided that perhaps talking to Andy, who looked as bad as she felt, might be preferable to anything else. At least other people would leave her alone, she thought.

But Andy was not in a conversational mood. He eventually noticed her, asked if she was OK, to which she replied that she was just fine, intending for him to get the opposite message. Andy just stared at her for a while, then looked away. She fought the impulse to cry again, or hit him with something, and eventually asked him the same question. He looked past her shoulder and nodded, and shortly after that, got up and walked away. Anne felt that the world had ended. She looked for Clare, but shied away from her when she smelled alcohol. Her head started to pound and she managed to summon the energy to let Liezl know she was going home, then walked out.

The walk back should have been refreshing and calming, but it was the opposite. She fought tears of rage all the way back, and by the time she reached the house, she was ready to scream. Liezl's mother kindly offered the sauna again, but Anne couldn't face it. Everything different about these past two weeks would have to go. The only way to get through the rest of her life, she felt sure, was as the old Anne; the real Anne; the person she had been all along.

She packed everything away, ready to just get up and leave in the morning, and looked around the room. She finally let her gaze fall on the bed, still unmade after the afternoon. She made it up, hoping to erase something by doing this, but it only made her feel worse. She suddenly felt more tired than she could ever remember, and simply curled up on top of the covers in her dress. She heard Liezl come in, and feigned sleep in case she was looked in on, but the next thing she heard was the alarm.

The early morning was almost unbearable. All Anne wanted was to be on the bus and under way, and the polite leave-taking was putting a great deal of strain on her.

Once they arrived at the school, and the bus, things actually took a turn for the worse. Almost as she turned away from Liezl, she literally bumped into Matthias. She gave a start, and tried to walk past, but he had a hand on her arm, and she was forced to stop. He was looking at his shoes, and an irrational frustration bubbled up in her for a moment, but she swallowed it, and looked at him. She knew she had to say something, but didn't know what it would be until she heard herself.

"Matthias," she tried, in a very soft voice, "you are forgiven. It was not your fault, but I have been very stupid. I am sorry." He looked up at her, startled. Whatever he had expected to hear, that wasn't it. He recovered himself enough to say what he had obviously prepared:

"I wanted to say thank you, Anne. I should not have done what I did. You were more kind than I deserve." He stopped and looked up at her. Anne froze for a moment, afraid that he expected her to kiss him, but he merely smiled sadly and turned away. She wanted to ask him why he had been so happy the night before, but he was gone, melting back into the crowd. She turned and boarded the bus, looking out for Andy; afraid that she might have missed him and messed up her plan – the idea of sitting next to Victoria for two days filled her with dread.

But Andy was nowhere to be seen, and she decided that saving a seat for him would still be possible. She scouted the seats a little more carefully this time; trying to find a pair with a reasonable amount of leg room, and by the time she was done, she could see him, towering over the others, on his way towards her from the front. Before Andy arrived, Clare passed her. Clare was in dark glasses, and gave Anne a rueful-looking smile and a pat on the upper arm. Anne needed to talk to Clare, but this was clearly not the time. Andy arrived and got himself organised with little prompting from Anne, for which she was grateful, having no idea what she would say to him.

Most of the first part of the day was spent in silence. The majority of the bus passengers were sleeping off something or other, and Anne was no exception. At some point, Andy tried to turn her over to sleep against his arm. This reminded her slightly too much of Matthias, but she smiled up at him; he was only being kind.

As soon as the bus stopped for lunch, Anne searched for Clare. For a panicked few minutes, she thought she would fail, but Clare must have been able to read her signals, and was waiting for her by the back of the bus. Anne looked at her, then walked on, hoping this would get the message across that she wanted to be away from anyone who might overhear. Clare caught up with her quickly, and took her arm.

"What's up, Anne? You look like the world's coming to an end."

Anne sighed. Either she had no tears left, or the old Anne was reasserting herself, because she felt calm as she told Clare of the disaster of the previous afternoon. Clare looked at her with an expression Anne couldn't interpret, then asked:

"Just how naked did you get? Did anything, you know, happen?"

Anne was shocked, although she knew her explanation had not been clear because of her embarrassment: "No, no – Clare, he took his shirt off, and I did, too – no, mine was already off. I think he saw more of me than I meant him to, but no – we just, you know, lay there."

"What do you feel about it? "

Anne had to admit that she didn't know what to think – she felt that she had closed this experimental Anne up, and put her away, but Clare begged to differ.

"The old Anne wouldn't have sought me out and told me these things. Don't be so quick to retreat. Also, I think you'll look back on it and understand that it really wasn't so bad – he could have – no, that's not what I mean. I mean, it could have been someone a lot more fucked-up than Matthias who got into bed with you. Poor guy; I wonder what has happened to him."

Anne didn't quite follow this, and said so.

"I mean, it was some kind of cry for help or something. He needs someone to love him, I think. Add that to the mess that his sister is, and I wonder if there isn't something going on in that family."

Anne nodded. That actually made some kind of sense. She remembered the marks on his arm and his back, and almost said something, but understood in time that this would be a betrayal. She wondered if she would ever be able to talk to Andy about it. *Not today*, she thought.

Not the following day, either, it turned out. Anne spent an uncomfortable sea crossing in the same seats she had used on the way over. She saw Clare and Andy come in at one point, but didn't like to pry, and left them alone. As they all got up to get back on the bus, she noticed them hug, but Clare had spotted Anne, and gave her a reassuring smile. As their paths crossed in the bus, Clare whispered to her. "Talk to him, Anne. You're a lot more alike than you realise."

Anne nodded, but she couldn't bring herself to say anything. Her thoughts had crystallised overnight, and she understood that her wariness of Andy was because she thought she had, in some way, betrayed him. As they neared Chester, she tried to explain this without ever actually saying anything.

"Andy, I'm sorry."

"Sorry about what?"

"Just – I'm sorry. I think I've let you believe in something that isn't true. I didn't change what I needed to change, and you must think me so foolish"

Andy looked puzzled. "I'm not with you."

"I don't know; this trip was supposed to be about one thing, but it turned into something else. Now I've spoiled it all by being something else again. It doesn't make sense to me, so you don't have to understand it, but I wish it had been different. Do you know what I mean?"

"Not really, no."

"Tell me what you'll remember about it."

"This trip? I don't know, Anne – it'll mostly be impressions of things, I think. A look at a different life, I suppose – the fence and everything."

Anne had thought for a moment that they were on the same

wavelength; now she wasn't so sure. She picked up one of his thoughts and tried it out.

"A different life; well, I saw that. I saw that it was still mine, though, and I am not sure about the differences now. Maybe I tried too hard."

Andy tried to respond to this, but she had become frustrated by her inability to think straight, and the conversation fizzled out. Not long after, the bus pulled into the familiar school gates, and Anne got off and walked back to her parents without a backward glance.

AUGUST 2003

Andrew sat there, in what had once been 'his' chair and tried to recover his thoughts. Anne looked calmly at him; not once during her telling of the tale had she been emotional. Eventually, he looked up at the mantelpiece clock – it was past one o'clock in the morning now, and what he really needed now was to go to bed, lie down and think about things. Instead, he was going to have to react calmly to this story. After another few moments thought, he thought he could manage it.

"You slept with him?" *No*, he thought; *that's not calm!*

"No – not then. It was all touchingly innocent, in reality. I don't know if he was as naïve as I was, or if he was just paralysed by shame and fear, as he claimed, but no, we didn't have penetrative intercourse."

'Penetrative Intercourse' (Andrew always thought of it as having Capital Letters) was Anne's way of referring to sex; it had made him smile for many years, but latterly he had wished she would lighten up a bit. Now, he wondered if he could see what the distinction was for her. Then something else hit him.

"What do you mean, 'then'? You did later?"

Now Anne's face did betray some emotion. "I don't quite know what to tell you, Andrew. I never have known, and the longer I left it, the harder it was. If I had said something to you at the time, I was sure I would have chased you away. If I told you when we were first together, - well, it's the same story. I have lived with the shame of it for all my adult life, and yet…."

Andrew was silent. He seemed to be unable to control his thoughts; he needed to be alone to work this out, but Anne was now silently weeping, and he knew her well enough to know he couldn't leave her. He got up and went over to her, sitting awkwardly on the sofa beside her but not actually touching her. She looked up at him

"You know, this is what I was thinking about earlier. You remember the afternoon in the park? The day after what Karla – the day after that? We walked, and you said some things. All I wanted, with every part of me, was for you to…." She stopped. Andrew was bemused.

"Oh, Andrew. Hug me, you fool."

He did so, and her crying became more intense. He sat there, feeling as if he was in some play to which everyone else had a different script from him. None of this was making much sense, and perhaps this had been his problem all along. He genuinely didn't know why Anne was so upset about something which may or may not have happened – he really wasn't clear on that from what she had said – 25 years before, before they had so much as held hands, and after he had been with Karla that afternoon…

Then he made the connection. He had never said anything to Anne about Karla, because he was deeply ashamed and embarrassed. At times over the year or so afterward, he might have blurted it out to any of his friends during one of the infrequent conversations boasting of their real or imagined sexual conquests, but he had kept quiet. For a time, he had even managed to convince himself that he had imagined it; that it had all been a particularly perverse wet dream, but as he matured the whole incident had become something vaguely unreal to him; something which had happened to another version of him, but which still affected him somehow. He realised now that the shame he had felt then was what Anne felt about her altogether more innocent time with Matthias, and that Anne – the inner Anne, the one which had been buried, rather than evolved from, as he had fondly imagined for so long, still felt a kind of grief about it. He tried to express this, but this only caused Anne to disengage the hug.

"You don't understand, Andrew; you can't. No-one does. I know you had a bad experience, and only tonight have I understood just how bad that was, but what happened to me actually destroyed who I thought I was. I've always believed that."

A long silence followed as Andrew collected his shattered thoughts. He thought of a number of things he could say at this point, but could not find one which wouldn't cause Anne either to break down again or yell at him. It wasn't an entirely unfamiliar situation for him, but at least in the past he had always known something of what he had done to provoke it. This time, Anne seemed to be as angry at herself as anything, and he had no frame of reference for that.

Eventually, Anne spoke.

"Why did you go back, Andrew? What drove you?"

He had been thinking about this, and hadn't really figured it out. He started to say something, then hesitated. Anne looked expectantly at him, and he took a deep breath.

"Honestly, I really don't know. I only started to think about the bus trip by accident – I was talking to someone in Germany on the phone, and he asked me where I had learned German. It kind of popped into my head then, but I only began to think about it later. What I remembered most was that I had come back from Germany, changed all my A-Level plans, dropped German, picked up Maths, and, I suppose, changed my life.

"All I knew was that Karla had changed me. I didn't want to think about what that meant, or try to analyse why I had dropped German, or why I dragged out my flu during the return. I thought about finding someone else who had been on the trip, and asking them, but you weren't exactly talking to me, and I had no idea where to find anyone but Mark, and he was no help."

"I didn't know you had spoken to Mark."

"I didn't – we exchanged a couple of emails, but he remembered stuff that had happened to him, and almost none of it related to me, as far as I could see."

"So you wrote to Matthias." Anne shivered slightly as she said his name, but the crying storm appeared to have passed now, and she said nothing more.

"No, not really. I wrote to the school – actually, to both schools. I got a message back from Germany almost immediately, and it was from Matthias. I was astounded; I'm not sure I could have told you his last name after all that time. He was excited, and hoped I would be able to come over soon."

Anne laughed at this, and Andrew looked quizzically at her.

"Oh, come on Andrew. He had no way of finding you, I guess, but you fell into his lap. It must have been killing him all this time."

"What? What did I miss?"

Anne sighed. "He must have known almost from the first time he saw Peter. Or suspected, at least. Once it was clear that Peter is left-handed, he knew. Don't you think?"

Andrew paused, catching up with this. "I don't know, Anne. He seemed relieved to have worked out it wasn't me. He asked me, and I – "

"Lied to him."

"No; no I didn't. If he had asked me if she and I had ever had sex, I would have told him. I think. But he didn't – he asked me about the day on the motorbike, and I told him the truth."

"So, did you know, at that point?"

"No. I tend to take things at face value, as you know -," Anne nodded, "- but it did not cross my mind until I realised why he was asking. At that point, I knew. I assumed that he didn't – he told me it was Dieter, more than once, I think. Now I don't know what to think; he must know.

Anne had a theory for this. "I think he knew – he knows - and he got you over there to see if you wanted to do anything about it. I don't know, but I'm guessing he was worried you might come and try to disrupt things."

"I suppose it's possible. But what would he have done if I'd come to assert my rights as a parent?"

"I don't know, Andrew. But now he knows you won't, so I suppose it has satisfied him."

This caused a lengthy silence. Eventually, Andrew broke it.

"He doesn't know I won't – he might think so, but he doesn't know for sure. After all, if you're right, and he knows, then my failing to tell the whole truth won't have changed his opinion."

And this isn't what I want to talk about, he thought. He continued to think it for several minutes, and then, to his astonishment, he heard himself say it.

Anne looked at him in alarm. "Well, what is? It's very late, Andrew, and it's really a little late for this kind of conversation, don't you think?"

In more ways than one, Andrew thought. "Anne, I want to know about you and Matthias. I want to know, because – actually, I don't know *why* I want to know, but I do. I need time to work out what to do about Peter and so on, but I can't stop thinking about what you said before."

Anne looked at him, calmly. "I'm not sure I'm ready for that, Andrew. But I'll make you a promise. I will tell you all of it, and soon. Just tell me one thing – when you said that Matthias sends his love, did you mean it, or is it just one of those things you say? Did you even tell him about us?"

"Of course I did – you were one of the first things we talked about. He said he remembered you; now, I'm thinking that of course he did!" Andrew felt suddenly very tired. How had Matthias actually reacted when he mentioned Anne's name? Oddly, he could recall details from 25 years before much more clearly than he could from last week. Anne was looking at him expectantly, but he had more or less forgotten the question.

"I should go," he said, standing. "I do want to have this conversation with you, and maybe we should have dinner again soon. You know, I enjoyed that part of this evening." A few hours ago, he had wanted to stay, see if Anne would let him share their bed again, but now he needed to be out of the house. *Did Matthias really send his love?* What did that mean? What did it imply? He didn't know, and right now, he didn't want to know. What he needed now was to not think about any of it.

Anne kissed him goodnight at the door. Not in the impassioned way he still remembered from their courtship, but equally not in the perfunctory way he associated with most of the years they had lived in this house. This was a kiss between old friends, and he smiled at her as he left. For all their faults, they had loved each other once upon a time, and he felt good to have re-established some thread of connection to that love.

In the car on the way home, however, he worried at that thread. What had their love really been about? He knew why he had fallen for Anne; he had always known. She was the only real friend he had in those last two years at school. He had seen her in a different light in Germany, and he knew that the inner Anne was there, just waiting to be released. He had not really so much as looked at anyone else for all those years; not until they started to live separate lives after the children were born.

He understood that Anne, for him, had been about the puzzle; the question of how to unlock all the doors and coax the real Anne out. Even after he had done this; after they were married and happy together, he had genuinely enjoyed her company and her personality, for all its quirks, and it had never occurred to him to wonder what she saw in him; whether she felt the same way as he did about the changes. Now, as he struggled to keep himself from either falling asleep or surging wildly over the speed limit, he thought about Matthias and about how his family had entwined themselves into his life: just what *had* happened that summer? Were they all still affected by one Friday afternoon in 1978?

The next morning, Andrew woke to the feeling that he had done something very stupid the night before. He had expected to feel better; to have explained everything to Anne and got something in return from her – he thought at first that he wanted forgiveness, but he reconsidered this; there was, in his mind, nothing to forgive. He wanted her to understand, he supposed; to say to him that it didn't matter, and that his slow separation from his family in the final years of their marriage was somehow tied to the experience in Germany.

But none of that actually made much sense, and now he had the feeling that the tables had been turned. Anne had not been the person he thought she was, and hadn't been that person almost from the moment they set foot in Germany. Had she actually slept with Matthias? It still seemed inconceivable to him – she simply wouldn't have done that. He thought back to their prolonged courtship – there was no sexual activity of any kind until they were actually engaged, and he still remembered Anne's confusion and discomfort. She had struggled with sex until after they were married – the whole Penetrative Intercourse issue had come from that time – and hadn't, Andrew felt, really relaxed about it until they were actively trying for children, almost ten years later.

So how on earth had that person got into bed with someone she didn't really know? And when she said "not then", did it mean that they had done later? Perhaps when the Germans came to Chester, and he had been so ill? He sat at his desk that morning resisting the urge to call Matthias and ask him about it. At lunchtime, he closed the door to his office and called Anne.

"Hi, it's me. Are you alright?"

Anne was silent.

"I mean, I'm sorry to have sprung all that on you last night. You probably thought I would just have had a jolly time and wanted to share it with you."

Still silence. He pressed on. "I've been thinking about -." A sob this time, and he stopped. Anne took a long time to recover her poise, and he could picture her, straightening her shoulders and recovering her bearing before she trusted her voice. When she spoke, however, her voice was clear and strong.

"No, Andrew. I had been dreading it from the moment you first told me you were going. You surprised me with your news, certainly, but only because I thought you were going to come back and tell me that you had found out about Matthias and me. When you told that other story, I didn't know what to say. I still don't. I'm in shock, I suppose."

Andrew waited, but this seemed to be all she had to say on the subject.

"What do you think I should do?"

Anne laughed, although the laugh was not exactly full of warmth. "I don't know, Andrew. It's not really my business any more, is it? You should do whatever you feel is right. If it was me, I suppose I would leave well alone now. You've found something out, but you can't really change anything, can you?"

"You're right, but I want to try something. I feel – no, damn it, I *am* responsible for Peter. I could have stopped her if I had been strong enough, and everything which happened after that was because I didn't do anything, or even say anything."

"Not all of it, Andrew. Matthias was not the person you thought he was, either. I have to bear some of that responsibility, too. I hurt him – not deliberately, but I did. I didn't understand until last night just how much damage I had done, because I didn't really understand – not properly - what he had been through, and how damaged he already was."

This threw Andrew. *Anne* was responsible for Matthias? For Peter? What was she telling him?

The signal dropped for an instant – Andrew had another call coming in.

"Anne, I'm going to have to go. I need to talk more with you; I'll call you back."

He didn't find the time to call until the end of the day, and before he could, he saw Anne's name in his email inbox. He printed the message off and took it back to the flat with him, sure that he shouldn't call again until he had read it – Anne was much better at putting things in writing than saying them out loud.

Dear Andrew,

I am sorry if this is difficult for you. I do have more to tell you, and it is mostly about the return trip, which I suppose you remember little of. I want to write it down and send it to you, but I know that my counsellor would advise against it. I need to face what I did, and I need to face it with you, in spite of everything.

I am sorry that I am imposing my issues on to you – you have had a big shock, and you must be confused and angry about it. My reaction is not helpful, I am sure. There is one person you could talk to – someone who knows the whole story, and I am going to put you in touch with her. I will leave it to you when you want to talk again, but you should know that I will need a few days to come to terms with all of this.

I'm sorry,

Anne.

He read it several times, but could not see how it was moving anything forward for either of them. He was vaguely aware that Anne had been seeing a counsellor since the divorce, and guessed that this was who she was putting him in touch with. He tried not to think too much about the fact that a complete stranger had known about Matthias before he had. He, at least, understood why Anne was talking about 'issues' and 'coming to terms' with things rather than putting her normal brave face on it and just getting on with life.

Two days later, he was startled by the name which appeared in his inbox. *Not the counsellor, then*, he thought.

Dear Andrew,

Well, this is freaky, isn't it?

I can't begin to tell you how glad I am to finally talk to you. Anne and I had an agreement, and I always kept up my end of the bargain, even though I wanted to hear your side of the story. So, she told me about Karla and Peter, to which I can only say – oh, shit!

Let's have coffee some time – I think it's allowed, now.

Love,

Clare.

Below Clare's name were several rows of text explaining her position in the Foreign Office, that this correspondence was privileged and belonged to the Queen, or something, and a thinly veiled threat of legal proceedings if its contents were divulged to anyone at all, as far as Andrew could see.

He had known little about Clare's life after school, and she had mostly faded from his mind after a couple of years – at least, that's what he liked to tell himself. He thought he understood at the time that something odd had happened to her, but Anne's explanation that she had 'run away to join the Civil Service' might actually have been the truth. He was, however, startled by the implication that Anne and she had not only kept in touch for all this time, but had, for whatever reason conspired to keep him out of the loop. Even if there had been nothing else to talk about, he would have agreed to the coffee to find out just what had been going on.

The following Friday, he found himself sitting in the courtyard of Somerset House in the centre of London, enjoying the fountains, and laughing at the young children scampering in and out of the jets of water which perforated the flagstones and soaked anyone who was foolish enough to get too close. It was a hot day, and he tried to imagine having the freedom to strip down to your underwear and just run around in the cold water. He was absorbed by this, and therefore missed Clare's approach.

"She told me I wouldn't need a photograph. You know, I'd actually forgotten just how bloody tall you are."

Andrew looked up, and grinned in spite of his determination to keep cool and calm. Clare appeared not much older than she had been the last time he had seen her. If he had been asked to describe her, he would have struggled, but now he could see her, it was as if they had never been apart. She was as slender and poised as he remembered, and looked, frankly, stunning. He stood, intending to shake hands, but was swept into a fierce embrace.

Ah, yes, he thought, *I remember this....*

They sat. Clare had brought her coffee out with her, which meant that Andrew didn't have, as he had hoped, any time to adjust to the sudden presence of Clare and how he was supposed to react to her. She sat and studied him for a time, seemingly enjoying his confusion, then smiled and put her hand on his arm.

"It's nice to see you, too!"

"Sorry, Clare – I'm a bit.... Well, bloody hell; here you are! It's nice to see you; I'm not sure what else to say. Sorry, I'll get my act together in a minute or two."

Clare laughed, and he was taken back in time. Her laugh had always entranced him; she seemed to totally abandon herself to it – when Clare laughed, the world stayed laughed at, he always thought. He felt like his fifteen-year-old self for a moment; entranced by this sophisticated woman. He nearly said so, but recovered his wits in time to bite his tongue. Clare sipped her coffee, then appeared to understand that she would have to steer the conversation.

"So you've been back? It's not really changed much, has it? Except for the wall, of course?"

"You've been there?" Andrew was thrown by this. "Recently?"

"Recently, and reasonably often over the years, really."

Andrew heard himself start to talk about Hohenügel, and how he had found it, when his brain caught up with what Clare had actually said.

"Wait – hold on. Fuck."

Clare stared at him.

"Fuck. You knew?"

"About Peter? No, not really. Not for sure. I mean, it's all a bit complicated. Matthias isn't really close to the rest of the family now, and I only saw him a few times as he grew up. Peter, I mean. I – hang on; I'll go back to the start, shall I?" Andrew nodded.

"I kept in touch with Erika. When I left school – you might remember that – I went back to see her."

"I don't know, really. I remember that you were around for the return trip, but my memories of that are fuzzy."

"Not surprising, really. You really did have the flu, didn't you? Well, after the Germans went back, I kind of went with them. It's a long story, but I ended up staying with Erika for about a month while everyone fought over me, then I came back, went to Sixth Form in Kent, then joined up."

"The Civil Service?"

"Yes. It's a long story, and it involves Erika, and I'm not sure it's all that interesting, but I wanted to travel, and that's how I did it."

"So you're still in touch with Erika?"

"Oh, yes. She and I - ah, you're not going to believe this."

"Try me. There's no limit to the amount of unbelievable stuff I've heard in the last few weeks."

"I guess so. Well, we both did the same thing. She went to Bonn, and I went to London. We did similar jobs, we missed each other for years as we were sent round the world, then about three years ago, we ended up in similar positions – she's in Berlin, and I'm here, and we're kind of unofficial liaisons between our respective governments. Don't ask; I'm not allowed to tell you."

Andrew smiled. "As weird stuff goes, that's pretty tame, really. But you've been in touch with her and the family, and Hohenügel all this time?"

"More so in the last few years; we were kind of peripatetic before that, so I'd only see them very occasionally. Now, Erika lives in Berlin with her family, and I'm more or less permanently here, so there's more opportunity. If I go to see her, I go to Berlin, but we sometimes drive down and see them all."

"All? Including Matthias?"

"Not so much – I think I've seen him two or three times over the years. He kind of keeps himself to himself now; there was a lot of bad blood for a long time."

"Because of Peter?"

"In a way. I think that a lot of them thought that when Matthias went off the rails, it destroyed the whole family. Me, I'm not so sure it wasn't already destroyed. I think what he did was a reaction, not a cause."

"I think I may have a slightly different story than you do."

"Not surprised, old friend. I think Matthias is well now, and probably generally in control of his life, but I'd be surprised if he was able to talk about the whole truth. But then again, I'm just going on what I've heard; I'm only getting one side of the story as well."

"Spoken like a true diplomat!"

"Why, thank you sir!" Clare smiled at him, and Andrew felt calmer than he had been since before he went to Germany. He thought about this for a moment, then shook his head once, quickly, as if to shake the thought out. *Don't*, he told himself. *Just don't.*

Clare was looking at him, her head cocked slightly to one side, as if she was trying to decide something about him. He fussed with his coffee for a moment, to give him something to do, and Clare broke the silence.

"Ah, I was going to say something about feeling sorry for you, but I don't think I do, really. I feel – I don't know; mostly intrigued. We all had our lives blown out of the water that summer, and I don't think any of us suffered more than the others, do you?"

Andrew didn't know, and said as much. He had known that this conversation was going to be strange and something of a minefield, but now he was in it, he didn't want it to end, and his brain seemed to be trying to help him with this by refusing to say anything meaningful.

Clare carried on: "I'm looking at you, and I'm thinking that you're not to blame for what happened with you and Anne. And, believe me, that's not something I expected to say. I've only had her side of that story, of course, but I had a nagging feeling that you weren't doing half the things she imagined you were."

Andrew didn't want to know, but he asked anyway.

"Oh, you know – the 'other woman in the London flat' thing; the drink problem, the 'pretending to be out of the country' thing. I look at you now, and I think she got you wrong. You just failed to talk to each other, I'm guessing."

"Mostly true, Clare. You want to know what I was really doing all that time?" Clare nodded, and Andrew paused for a moment to watch her. Normally, he found eye contact difficult in conversation, but he was magnetised by Clare's eyes, and he had to fight to get his own attention back where it belonged.

"I was sitting alone in my one-room cupboard, trying to get a signal on the world's smallest television, or going out eating sad, lonely dinners in cheap restaurants before going to see operas I could neither afford nor understand, and wondering when exactly my life had turned to shit."

"And it never occurred to you just to get the train home and talk to your wife?"

"Honestly? No, it didn't. I felt like a stranger in that house; still do: I was there last week - which you know; sorry – I just couldn't face the commuting day after day; pressed up against the great unwashed of London."

"OK, now I feel a little sorry for you. I still don't see what's wrong with talking to your wife, but I used to say the same thing to Anne, so I'm not judging either of you. I think it's sad, because you were good for each other once upon a time."

"But we each had secrets. I didn't even know how much of a secret I had, and you – wait. You never told her?"

"About Karla? No, of course not; that was your job. It made life a little difficult, because for a long time, I had to try to figure out if you had said something, and she wasn't telling me, but eventually I realised that you hadn't, and never would, and that she would never tell you about Matthias, and so life went on. And then when she was going through – sorry; when you were going through the divorce, I just kept thinking about how if you just talked to each other, you might understand things a bit more."

"But you didn't say anything?"

"I told her she should tell you, but she always felt it had been some kind of betrayal, and I think she was advised not to at some point. And I promised not to contact you, so – no; I didn't say anything. Maybe I should have."

"So her lawyer knew about it?"

"I don't know; you'd have to ask her. It's too late now, in any case, isn't it?"

Andrew thought about this. It had been on his mind since he had seen Anne the weekend before. "Yes, I think it is. She's happy there without me, and I don't feel – well, I thought about it. I like Anne; I always did. But I don't love her, and I'm not sure if I ever really did."

"Poor Andrew, Karla really fucked you up, didn't she?"

"I thought about that, too, and I don't know if that's true." Andrew was briefly annoyed by this, but thought about it, and recognised it. "Sorry, I don't mean to be defensive. You may be right; I thought it was just one of those things, but I don't suppose it really was, was it? I mean, I never told anyone. Apart from you, that is, and I don't even know if I meant to tell you; I just needed someone to tell me it was OK, and I couldn't get through to Anne. Of course, now I understand why."

"And I understand now why your marriage was doomed from the start. OK, I officially feel sorry for both of you now. That family was in your marriage from the start, but neither of you even recognised it. What a mess." She drained her coffee, and stood up. "I have to get back, Andrew, but I'd love to carry this on some time. Call me." She handed him a business card, and turned to go. On an apparent impulse, she turned back and leant down to his ear. Andrew could feel her breath on his cheek, and had to suppress a shiver. He felt, rather than heard her whisper.

"Be happy, big guy." Andrew sat there, staring after her as she walked across the forecourt. She walked directly towards the furthest of the fountains, and as it erupted, neatly dodged out of its path. *I bet she didn't even get a drop on her*, Andrew thought.

He sat there for another hour, watching the world go by and gradually burning the top of his head in the strong sun. He thought about many things, none of them related to the conversation, then pulled out his phone and called the office to explain that he would be another hour or so, but he'd be working late to catch it up, as if anyone really cared.

He stood and walked out the river side exit. From there he could just make out his office on the South Bank, squeezed in behind the National Theatre. He stared at it, then began to walk slowly in that general direction. He crossed Waterloo Bridge, but on the far side, instead of cutting across the theatre forecourt, he doubled back under the bridge, and wandered among the bookstalls set out on long trestle tables.

He often spent lunch hours doing exactly this, and he was a regular enough patron to be able to recognise who had new stock, and who had simply rearranged what they had had the week before, to make it look new. He wasn't looking for anything in particular, but as always, several things caught his eye and detained him for a few minutes each time. Nothing which would make him want to part with actual money, however, and he was about to turn away and head back to his desk when he spotted a title out of the corner of his eye.

He picked it up, and stared at it. He had never read it, but he recognised that it was the same edition. He looked inside the front cover, in case it might have something written there which would identify it as the same book, but he didn't know whether Clare wrote her name inside books or not, and in any case, it was blank. He flipped it over to read the back cover blurb, as if he was contemplating whether it was worth the investment, but there was no way he could not buy *Doctor Rat*.

He paid for it, shoved it roughly in his jacket pocket, then made his way back to work. He had planned to spend the afternoon working on a presentation for a meeting the following week, but instead locked himself in his office and called Anne.

She answered on the first ring, as if she had been waiting for him, and he was momentarily taken aback. He heard Anne's voice asking who this was, and realised he needed to say something.

"Well, I saw Clare. We spent an hour talking about our divorce, as far as I can tell. Weird doesn't begin to describe it."

"Oh, it's you. Well, I'm glad you saw her, but I don't suppose that helped you much. Did it?"

"No. Not really." Silence, then he blurted out, "Anne, why did we get divorced?" As soon as he said it, he felt like hanging up, but he was in this car crash now; he would have to see how it ended.

"What do you want me to say? Because 25 years ago we both had sex with people we didn't really know? Because being happy wasn't enough for you? Because - oh, Andrew, do we have to do this now? You know why – you signed the papers, too."

His ear, attuned to Anne's turn of phrase, picked up on the *had sex with* – not PI, or any other euphemism. Was that a confession? Or did she really consider lying on the bed with Matthias equivalent to having sex? He had never known how to ask her things when he was married to her; now, he wondered if he even had the right.

"I know what it said on the papers, Anne; I just wondered if I had missed something." He wanted to explain what he meant, but he was interrupted by Anne's almost hysterical laughter. He thought about it, and supposed it was pretty funny, but it didn't exactly help him make sense of any of this. Anne stopped laughing.

"I'm not going back over this, Andrew. We're divorced because you made it plain enough that you didn't want to be married any more, and I finally stopped caring about that. End of story. If you want to beat yourself up over it now, please be my guest."

"I'm sorry, Anne." This was the first time he had been aware of saying this in the context of his divorce, although he wondered if he meant that he was sorry for calling her up in the middle of the afternoon when she probably had children to collect from school, or something. Anne's response, he realised after an uncomfortably long time, was to cry down the phone at him.

"Oh, fuck off, Andrew. Just fuck off. Do what you want. I hope you can be happy, but I wouldn't hold my breath. None of it makes any difference now; it's all gone. All under the bridge, or whatever. You're messed up; I'm messed up, but we did it to ourselves; don't go looking for excuses now." She hung up, leaving Andrew in a state of shock. In all the years he had known her, even through the bitterest periods of their divorce, he had never once heard Anne swear; not at him, or at anyone else. Even when she had broken her wrist one winter, slipping over on ice which he had forgotten to clear on their front step, the worst she had managed was 'oh, bother,' and 'fiddlesticks'. He felt like crying but couldn't figure out why.

He called Clare, but got voicemail. He left a rambling message which would probably mean she would never want to have any further contact with him, and went home.

He was in mid-presentation on the Monday when his phone began to vibrate in his pocket. *Oh, bugger,* he thought, *not only am I woefully under-prepared for this, but I forgot to turn the damn thing off.* He struggled to regain his concentration, and felt sure he had blown a vitally important part of persuading the committee to divert more budget to his current pet project.

His mood was not brightened by the vague and non-committal response to the presentation, and he had to sit through another three hours of counter-proposals, all of them better researched and better presented than his had been, before he could escape. He turned the phone on and waded through half a dozen old messages before he heard Clare's voice. She sounded amused, rather than offended, by his message, and suggested that he might like to meet him for a drink after work. He was greatly cheered by this and emailed her back to accept.

They met in the Coal Hole on the Strand, a pub which he had only dimly been aware of, but which she appeared to know well.

"I'm a bit of a theatre-goer," she explained. "This is pretty much the best place in town for pre-theatre drinks." It did, indeed, seem to be full, even on a Monday, of a slightly excitable crowd. Andrew bought drinks for them, somehow unsurprised that Clare drank pints, and even managed to negotiate a table for them. The crowd thinned quickly as curtain-up approached, and they were able to talk without raising their voices, to Andrew's relief. On the walk over, he had figured out a number of things he wanted to ask Clare, but these had disappeared from his mind as soon as he saw her; she was as in control and elegant as she had been on the Friday. His carefully planned conversational gambits dried up as he was simply content to watch this person he thought had gone from his life a quarter of a century before, matter-of-factly drinking beer from a pint glass. Clare smiled at him.

"You know, I'd quite like it if you didn't just stare at me as if I had just beamed in from Mars, or something." Andrew blushed and looked away.

"I'm sorry. It's just – I'm a bit confused by life at the moment. I think I finally destroyed what relationship I had left with Anne on Friday, and -"

"I know; she told me. She's not as mad at you as you might think, Andrew. She needs time, though. Peter's existence" – she pronounced the name as a German speaker would – "has thrown her quite a bit. She'll get there, though. She's tougher than you give her credit for."

"I suppose she is. I know this sounds silly, but I wish I knew her better."

"Not silly, but a bit sad, don't you think?" Andrew supposed so, and he sat in silence for some time, sipping morosely on his pint. Suddenly he remembered something.

"Clare; I have something for you." He fished in his pocket and drew out the book he had bought on Friday after their meeting. Clare laughed.

"Well, thank you! I can put it with my other one, I suppose."

"You still have it? I kind of assumed..."

"I never throw books away. Even in the upheaval after I left home; even as we travelled around the world, my books stayed with me. Best I ever do is lend them out, not expecting to see half of them ever again, of course. This one, though, I got back, as I suppose you remember."

"I do. I feel kind of stupid now; it was just such a surprise to see it straight after seeing you. I had to buy it."

"Well, thank you for the kind thought. I never lent it out again after we got back. It's been on a shelf in my bedroom for years now. I shall put this one alongside it. Unless you want to borrow it, of course."

Andrew thought about it. "Well, I think I might. I bought a new copy of the book I was reading back then, but I didn't even open it all the time I was there. It got a little busy, as you can imagine."

Clare passed it back to him. As she did so, their hands touched briefly, but whatever he was expecting to happen failed to materialise; her hand was just like any other hand he night have touched during the course of an ordinary day. He had to remind himself that he had long ago discovered that Clare was just a person like he was, and that being temporarily dazzled by her didn't change that; she had been a good friend in the past, and with luck, could be a good friend again, but that was all.

Clare was staring at him this time, and he looked away. The plan had been that the book would lead them on to talking about Karla, but he had managed to derail that, somehow, and he tried to rearrange his thoughts so that he could get back to where he wanted to be, but Clare beat him to it.

"Remember the last time you gave me this book?"

"You know, until I went back to Hohenügel, I had kind of forgotten about it – I wonder if I had blanked a lot of things out."

"You were so scared. I've never forgotten that. We were just children, but we suddenly had to deal with all this – stuff. I can still see that lounge; the seat we curled up on. You know, in all that trip, that was the one time I felt calm and in control of things. It's kind of a fond memory for me."

Andrew was staring into his beer, remembering how terrified he had been, and how Clare's kindness had brought him round and calmed him down.

"You were so thoughtful," he said, "you looked after me, and I never really thanked you. In fact, I have been wondering if we even spoke again after that."

"We did, but you probably don't remember too much about it. You dropped out of German, remember? And then there was the whole flu thing – you spent most of the return trip in bed, as I recall." Andrew knew: he *had* had flu, or something like it, for a few days, but he had dragged it out because something in him which he couldn't quite identify now had made him want to avoid the whole return trip. He wanted to talk about that, for some reason, so he suggested they find somewhere to eat, if that was OK with her.

"Suits me fine; I'm not going home to anything in particular, and it saves me cooking. Come on; there's a little Italian I know…"

They walked along the Strand for a few minutes, Andrew wondering how to work the obvious question into the conversation, or complete lack of conversation, but Clare beat him to it.

"I know what you're wondering; there's just me at home these days. I like it better that way, and, no – I'm not about to talk about it to a more or less complete stranger. You can ask Anne if you really want to know; she's heard all the sordid details over the years." She turned and grinned up at him, and he, having assumed that he had his emotions under control, had to re-evaluate things once again.

The restaurant was one he had noticed over the years, but had never been in. Clare, on the other hand, appeared to be a regular and was greeted effusively and fussed over. As soon as they sat down, she began to talk. Andrew was more than happy simply to sit back and listen.

SEPTEMBER 1978

Clare sat glumly on the platform at Chester station. She had imagined that the return trip would be fun, but she had lately been feeling tired and vaguely sick, and the distinctive diesel smell of the station really wasn't helping that. She ascribed the nausea to nerves; so much had happened in June in Germany, and now, after a summer of relative calm and quiet, they were about to be invaded by all these people who had caused so much turmoil.

She reviewed her thinking on that; a habit she had got into recently. The turmoil, she supposed, was restricted to Anne, Andy and herself – they had been embroiled with the same family, but although there were bound to be issues with Andy's shadow, Matthias, the principal sources of trouble would not be on the trip.

At least, she hoped not; she wouldn't put it past Karla to pursue whatever vendetta she imagined to the point of tagging along with her father. Again, Clare reviewed this. Karla, however dedicated she might be to her vendetta against Clare, would not suffer two weeks in the company of her father, a man she had made a number of wild allegations against. Clare tried to relax, but something gnawed at her.

She looked in vain for a friendly face, but saw only her parents, dressed in their Sunday best, waiting almost, but not quite, out of sight. A full hour before the train was due to arrive, her father had insisted on being on the platform. He had said that parking would be awful thanks to the number of families meeting this train, and had wanted to bag a prime spot for his Austin Maxi. Clare had mostly rolled her eyes and said nothing. She actually was fond of her father and his eccentricities; unlike many of her peers, she tried not to be too insulting about 'the old man' and 'the old girl', although some of the parts she felt inclined to play at school sometimes demanded it.

With only half an hour to go, she was finally joined by a friendly face. One or two other of the party had arrived, but they were boys Clare wasn't terribly familiar with, and she affected her cool, aloof expression which successfully kept them at bay. She saw Andy turn up, look over at her, but join the group of boys. She would have smiled at him, but for the presence of his friends. She still didn't know how to deal with her feelings for Andy. On one level, she had made a powerful connection with him on the boat, but she had told Anne that she would keep clear of him. He was clearly infatuated with her, although she tied to discourage that, and hope this would push him towards Anne. Since they had returned from Germany, she had only spoken to him once or twice, and never alone.

She thought back to the ferry on the way back in July. He had been so scared and vulnerable, and she saw in his eyes something which she could relate to. They had both suffered at the hands of the same vindictive person, and they had shared a quiet hour or two just being supportive of each other. She smiled to remember how sweet and innocent he had seemed – in other circumstances, she might have been tempted to do something she'd later regret with him; indeed, the thought had crossed her mind for other reasons afterwards. Perhaps they should have sneaked back on to the bus and....

But that was pointless speculation. Andy wasn't the solution to any issues she had, and for all that she had been so achingly lonely and scared that night – so much so that she had not only slept with him curled up around her, she had moved his hands so that she might imagine how it felt to be held lovingly and tenderly. She remembered his embarrassment on waking, and his endearing attempt to cover it up, which had at least distracted him from noticing her own confusion.

Andy wasn't the friendly face, however; Anne was. Clare had hoped that her own group of friends would be as fashionably late as always, and that she would have an opportunity to talk with Anne before the train arrived. It seemed that Anne's parents were only half as paranoid about parking as Clare's, but they tended to hover around their daughter, and this made conversation difficult. She could see Anne's mother appraising her and evidently not approving of the ripped jeans or the leather jacket, but Anne ignored this, and sat down beside Clare, who felt impelled, as she always did when anyone sat beside her, to take Anne's arm.

"I think Mother's going to pass out on the spot!" Anne said, "she probably thinks you're going to sell me drugs or something." Clare laughed for the first time that day. "Would you like some? I've got –" She stopped to enjoy Anne's expression. "I'm kidding, Anne – relax! Calm down; it's OK, she didn't hear me." Clare genuinely enjoyed Anne's company, a little to her own surprise. She had always been the kind of person who could get on with anyone, but had made a number of false assumptions about Anne which had led her to believe that they would simply have nothing to talk about. It was true that they had little in common in areas like music or films, but they were sisters under the skin – in their skin, Clare liked to tease, remembering the sauna in Germany – in a great many areas. They hadn't spoken much over the summer, and Clare desperately wanted to know how Anne had coped, and whether any of the changes she had tried in Germany had become permanent.

To look at her, Clare would have bet that none of them had. Anne still dressed the same way; pleated skirts or long dresses with sensible – there really was no other word for them – high-necked blouses or, like today, a modest cardigan. Plain flat shoes and a hairstyle directly out of the fashion pages of the 1950s completed the picture, but Clare had seen under Anne's carapace – literally so, she reminded herself – and she knew that there was a late 1970s teenager in there, waiting to come out. Clare listened to Anne complain about her parents' fussing over her while trying, as casually as possible, to appraise the parents. They looked staid and unremarkable; church-going folk, as she knew; but nothing in their manner really suggested that they were deliberately oppressing the 'real' Anne, and not for the first time, Clare wondered just how much of Anne's outer shell was of her own doing.

A loud group of painfully trendily dressed boys and girls arrived; Clare's group. Anne took the opportunity to stand up and rejoin her parents. Clare shouted to her that they could catch up later in the week, and effortlessly – or so she hoped – switched personalities to join her gang.

In truth, while she enjoyed the status of being in this group of teenagers, Clare was coming to understand that they were essentially phonies. She liked many of the things that they liked; she prided herself on being a little ahead of them in liking the next big thing, but that whole scene seemed like too much effort at times, and she knew that when she had been in trouble in the first week in Germany, she had not felt able to turn to any of them.

The London train finally arrived, and out of it poured a stream of tired-looking, but familiar faces. Clare spotted Erika almost immediately, and the two girls embraced enthusiastically. One of the most pleasant surprises of the trip to Hohenügel had been how well Clare and Erika had got on. Erika's English was not particularly great, and Clare's German not much better, but they had found that they operated on the same wavelength and had become fast friends almost immediately. They had exchanged a couple of letters over the summer; Erika keeping Clare up to date on the village gossip, and Clare's earlier anxiety was swept aside by her genuine pleasure at seeing her friend again.

They were seated in the back of the Maxi and halfway back to Clare's house before she realised that she hadn't seen Liezl or Matthias, or any of the others. She asked Erika how everyone was, and once they had figured out that Clare meant in general, rather than how the journey had been, Erika began a long, halting tale of family infighting.

What Clare mostly wanted to know, of course, was what Karla had been up to, but since Erika only knew sketchy details of the feud, she didn't give Karla's doings any particular significance, and the moment passed.

The English students didn't live as close together as the Germans did – their school had a reasonably wide catchment area in a moderately sized city, rather than being the only school in a smallish village, and this meant that there was less wandering from house to house, and less time spent in groups. Clare noticed that the six who had been almost inseparable thanks to the family connections in Germany spent relatively little time together in the first week. This was partly down to Andy being in bed with flu, meaning that Matthias was billeted with his father, to try to minimise the risk of infection. Matthias, in the few occasions she saw him, seemed to be taking this particularly badly, and she got the impression that he was not enjoying this trip at all.

On the Sunday afternoon, however, they finally managed to spend some time together. Andy still wasn't well enough to join them, but it seemed that it would be possible for them all to pay him a quick visit before catching a bus into town and spending the afternoon in Grosvenor Park.

The visit with Andy was somewhat surreal, in Clare's eyes. They were ushered into a front room of some description which didn't look like it had been used for years, where Andy was propped up next to a coal fire in an armchair wearing an ill-fitting dressing gown and a pair of ridiculous slippers. He looked pale and appeared to be trying to prevent himself from drifting off to sleep as they all crowded round him, trying to outdo each other with tales of what he had missed. After half an hour of this, Andy actually did fall asleep, and they left. On the bus into town, the German girls sat together, as did the English girls, leaving Matthias looking as if the weight of the world was on his shoulders, sitting alone at the front. Clare took the opportunity to grill Anne about him.

"Have you seen much of him? How has he been? Is he embarrassed, or – "

"Hold on, Clare. One thing at a time. I spoke to him yesterday on the way back from Liverpool. He made no mention of anything. Mostly he's just furious about being left with his father the whole time. I really wonder what's going on there, don't you? He seems in a permanent state of rage. I think I feel sorry for him."

"Are you...?" Clare didn't need to finish the thought.

"No! No; I don't think so, at least. When I see him like that, I mostly want to feed him, and try to cheer him up. He seems to bring out a kind of mothering instinct in me. So, no, I don't fancy him, or anything."

"How about Andy? Did he bring out your mothering instinct, too?"

"Yes, of course; seeing him like that. But I'm more confident about how I feel about him now. I like him, and I would like something to happen, but I'm in no hurry. What happened just showed me that I'm not ready for that yet. Really not."

Clare nodded and pondered this. She had lost her virginity to a boy two years older back at the start of the year. She hadn't meant for it to happen, but she didn't regret it. She hadn't enjoyed it much, but hadn't expected to. Subsequently, she had had more enjoyable experiences once or twice, and one which she really tried not to think about. She imagined that Anne thought of her as being vastly more knowledgeable about this kind of thing, but she didn't feel that way. In a way, she envied Anne's certainty. She considered Matthias. If he had climbed into Clare's bed, what would she have done?

A sympathy fuck, she supposed. She wouldn't have seen the harm in it, and it might have done the poor boy some good; to think that someone might be able to show him some unconditional affection for a while. He was short, and not really her type, but he was harmless enough. When Anne had related her tale, however, Clare had mostly felt sympathy for both of them. They were neither of them ready for what had happened, and there didn't seem to be much to say.

Now, however, she felt an urge to warn Anne again.

"You still should be careful. I know you're not likely to be drinking schnapps again any time soon, but things can happen, you know" – Clare certainly did – "and if he's that lonely...."

Anne nodded. "I'm aware of what could happen, I think. I can't say I wasn't warned." Anne grabbed Clare's arm, and Clare almost jumped in surprise.

"Anne, you really have changed! You'd never have done that a few weeks ago."

Anne looked momentarily confused, then understood.

"I know, but please don't go around saying I've changed. I'm trying not to let it show." She smiled at Clare, but Clare wasn't at all sure how to interpret that smile. She let it pass.

The park had seemed like a good idea that morning, when the weather was looking promising, but it had clouded over and become colder during the day, so that by the time the five were walking across the neatly manicured lawns, there was a definite chill in the air. Clare had expected to be able to sit out and enjoy autumn sunshine, but they were forced to keep moving by a breeze which had the edge of winter in it. They admired the flowerbeds and peered at the waterfalls, but pretty soon the novelty had worn off, and they all looked to Clare for some idea of what to do next.

"There's not much to do in Chester on a Sunday afternoon," she heard herself say, "but there's a café down by the station which might be open."

This seemed to be the preferred option, and they all followed Clare. Erika and Liezl flanked her and the three of them cheerfully complained about the complete lack of anything worthwhile to do on Sundays. Clare was conscious that this left Anne and Matthias together, but she resisted the temptation to turn round and check up on them. As they crossed the canal, with the station in front of them, Clare stopped to look over the parapet, but there was nothing much to see. She looked back and saw Anne and Matthias apparently deep in conversation. That, at least, seemed to be going well.

The café was dingy, damp and steamy; the coffee on offer was not much more than warm brown water, and what food there was seemed to have been left over from the day before. But it was warm and had enough seats for them all, so they sat and chatted happily. All of them missed Andy, and speculated whether he would be fit enough for any of the activities later in the week. Clare thought not, but kept this to herself. She felt distant from the group, and preoccupied with something which she couldn't quite put her finger on. She moved them on as soon as she reasonably could, the coffee sloshing around unpleasantly in her stomach. All she wanted to do was go home and sleep.

On the bus back, she sat alone behind the others, noting warily that Anne and Matthias were sitting together, still lost in their conversation. She wondered if she should have paid more attention to Anne during the afternoon, but decided that she was overreacting and concentrated instead on her own discomfort.

Once home, she and Erika repaired to Clare's room. They had shared Erika's room in Germany, and this had bonded them more strongly than Clare had expected. Now they were sharing Clare's impossibly tiny box room; Clare on a camp bed which had to be folded away during the day so that there was somewhere to stand up. She had expected to hate it, but it felt like their own little private space, and they spent a lot more time than Clare had anticipated in it with the door shut against the world.

Clare asked Erika about Matthias.

"I think he is – um, I do not know. He is liking – no; he *likes* her!" Erika was delighted to have got this syntax sorted out, and Clare smiled

"I think so too, but I am worried. She is easily hurt, and she is not ready for…." Clare tailed off, not sure exactly what she was about to say. Erika switched to German and said something about Matthias needing someone to protect him.

"That is what I worry about. Anne is not that person, I think. We must watch over them." Clare was careful to use expressions which they had worked out between them before, and Erika understood what she meant by 'watch over'.

Erika began to ask a long and complicated question, which had to be ported over into German for a stretch. Eventually, Clare understood that she was asking why Anne was the way she was.

"I don't really know. She seems to be happy that way, but I cannot understand her. When she was with us in Germany, I thought she was changing, but she says that it was not true, and she is back to the way she was before now." Erika pondered this, then smiled

"Perhaps Matthias will change this." Clare hoped not, but said nothing.

The entire return trip seemed to Clare to be something of an anti-climax. There certainly didn't seem to be as many dramas and crises as there had been in Germany – *perhaps they are happening to other people,* she thought – and the Germans spent a lot more time on trips and a lot less time in the classroom with them. This probably accounted for her sense of unease and discomfort, she felt. She had expected all this to be a lot more momentous, and essentially nothing was happening. She had assumed that her own problem, which she was only dimly beginning to realise that she was going to have to admit to herself first, would have been somehow magically addressed by having Erika in the house with her, but nothing was happening, and she could feel the opportunity slipping away.

The Monday passed without incident, as the Germans were on a shopping expedition somewhere, and the Tuesday had seemed likely to be similar. Erika had been looking forward to the day trip, although Clare had warned her that Rhyl in mid-September would probably not be the seaside experience she was hoping for. Some of the English students had been 'volunteered' to go along, but Clare checked with Erika, and since Anne wasn't accompanying Liezl, Erika felt sure that she would be fine with her 'cousin' – she still struggled with the word 'niece', and in any case, felt it didn't properly explain their relationship:

"I feel like cousin," she explained, "so I say cousin. Not the other word."

Clare saw the two girls on to the bus and headed back to the classroom. She realised that she hadn't seen Matthias or his father, usually the first two on the bus; Matthias sitting glumly at the back, and the old man barking out orders at the front. She could, however, hear them. She followed the sound of yelling around two corners before understanding that it was coming from the boys' toilets. She looked around, but everyone else was already in class, and she was unlikely to be seen.

Won't be the first time, she thought and tiptoed through the door. The shouting was incredibly loud once she was inside; it was rapid-fire and strongly accented German, and she could only catch a few words at a time. She was stunned to hear several clearly enunciated swearwords, however. If this was Matthias and his father, the old man was really letting rip. This didn't particularly surprise her, she thought – Herr Schneider seemed to have a temper permanently close to boiling point, and his rage had seemed to be barely contained at the best of times. She heard a couple of dull thuds, then had to quickly duck back out of the door as it was flung open. Matthias' father strode past her without so much as a glance, but of Matthias there was no sign. She waited for a couple of minutes, then pushed the door open. This time, she ventured fully in, bracing herself for the sight and smell of boys' toilets. They really were unpleasant animals, she thought.

Matthias was sitting on the floor with his back against the wall. He looked up at her as she came in, then buried his face in his hands.

"Please go away," he said quietly, "I don't want you to see this. Just go; I will be OK." Clare ignored this, and went over to him.

"What did he do? Did he hit you?" She looked carefully at him, but there was no obvious sign of anything untoward.

"Please. This is ashamed. I mean…"

"I know what you mean. Don't worry; I will look after you. You do not need to be ashamed. He is a bully, and it is not your fault." She didn't know what to do or say beyond this. She tried to put an arm around his shoulders, but he shrugged her off. She stood up and grabbed his arm.

"Come on; you need to get out of here, and there is no-one around now. I will help you. I suppose you are not going on the bus today?"

"Yes. I was late because I wanted to talk to Mark, and – so, this is how he is."

"All the time?"

"All the time. Since I can remember. Always this."

Clare was shocked. She had supposed that the old man was a bully, and prone to fits of temper, but Matthias seemed broken by it. What kind of man could do this to his own child?

Matthias winced as he stood, and rubbed the back of his head gingerly. He looked at his hand. "No blood. Always, no blood. No-one can see, so no-one will believe me."

"How – I mean, how often does he hurt you?"

"Most days, in some way. Not always with the hands, but most days something bad happens. Please do not tell anyone; I am happy to be away from him for today."

Clare walked him out, and they found a low wall to sit on just outside the school gates. She offered him a cigarette, and he laughed. "You think he wouldn't notice? He can smell it from 400 metres. No, thank you."

He sat in silence for a while, and Clare looked at him. He had seemed to her to be a tough, wiry character. She supposed that daily abuse will do that to a person, but wondered how hard he had to work every day to keep a lid on everything. Could he fight back? Probably not, in truth – his father was taller and powerfully built; probably no-one had ever fought back.

She heard a bell ring and had an idea. She told Matthias to stay where she was and walked back into school. The exchange pupils had reasonably free reign during these two weeks; they were supposed to keep the office and their teachers up to date with what they were doing, but Clare hadn't bothered, and had even been greeted with surprise by one or two teachers on arriving in class. However, she had a problem. She needed to be in her history class this morning to retake a paper she had missed the week before – for all her apparent rebelliousness, she worked hard to keep her marks good, and knew that getting this one done would make life a lot easier for a few months to come. She headed down to the English department where Anne should be just coming out ….

Clare explained roughly what the problem was, and could see Anne struggling with her emotions. She desperately wanted to help Matthias, but skipping class for Anne was a momentous thing, not to be undertaken lightly, or at all if possible.

"Come on, Anne, you know it's not a problem. If we need to be out of class this week, everyone turns a blind eye. I'll cover for you. He needs a friend, Anne, and Andy's not here. Just until lunchtime; I'll catch up with you outside at lunchtime, and I'll take over."

Anne considered this, then nodded. "OK, Clare; I'll do it. Thank you for looking after him." Clare smiled

"Oh, it was my pleasure. Walk him around for a bit, let him talk – I think that's what he needs."

The two girls hugged briefly – *she wouldn't have done that before*, Clare thought – and Clare headed back to History.

There was no sign of them at lunchtime, which alarmed Clare a little, but there was not enough time to do anything about it without skipping the first class of the afternoon, and what good would that do if she didn't know where they were and couldn't find them?

But all through her compulsory Latin hour, Clare fretted. Once it was over, she headed out the gate and walked to Anne's house. At first there was no reply, and she was about to go home when she heard a window opening above her. Anne's voice floated down from above

"Oh, it's you. OK, well, you'd better come in."

Clare tried the door, but it was locked, and she had to wait for Anne, still in her school uniform, to come down and let her in. Anne had plainly been crying, and Clare was suddenly terrified.

"What happened, Anne? Are you OK? Where is he?"

"He's gone back over to Andy's – I sent him. Everything's OK, I suppose." Everything plainly wasn't OK, and Clare said so.

"No; you're right. I have done something very foolish, Clare. Perhaps unforgivably so. Come on, I'll make some tea."

Clare sat at the kitchen table and watched Anne as she boiled the kettle and organised tea. On the surface, aside from the redness around her eyes,

Anne looked calm and in control. Clare would have been fooled; she wondered if someone who knew Anne better would be taken in.

Anne poured the tea, offered several types of biscuit, then sat down and took a deep breath.

"We went to see Andy. On the way, Matthias told me what you had seen. He seems to think it is normal, and part of life, but it's wrong, and he needs to do something about it. His father is a monster." She paused, but Clare could only nod. Her heart was pounding because she knew as surely as she knew anything what Anne was about to explain to her, and it was all her fault.

"So, anyway. We saw Andy; he's better, and he made us soup, if you can believe that. He might even be back at school tomorrow. Matthias asked if he could come back, but Andy wasn't sure – when Matthias was out of the room, I tried to explain why, but Andy was not really taking things in. He said that he hadn't seen anything like that when he was staying there, but there wasn't time to talk more.

"So we sat with Andy, and then we came back here. I couldn't think what else to do. And it was so stupid, and so easy, but we talked a little, then we…. Oh. Clare; I can't even say it."

"You don't have to. Oh, fuck, Anne. I'm so sorry. This was all my- "

Anne interrupted her. "No; I knew you would say that. It's not your responsibility. I got him back here" – Anne was crying now, but they were silent tears of self-recrimination, rather than the racking sobs and wails Clare might have expected – " and I took a decision, and then I got it wrong. It's my fault; I could have just kept walking, taken him back to school; gone into town; I don't know. I didn't have to do it."

Clare sat and looked at Anne. "Anne, I'm sorry, but I'm going to have to ask. What exactly happened? Did you" – Anne interrupted her.

"Yes, we did. We had penetrative intercourse, and yes, we used something. He had a packet of these things. I've never seen one before, and right now it's my biggest problem."

Clare laughed, firstly at the expression Anne used, and then at the absurdity of the concern.

"Well, they don't really flush, if that's what you've been trying."

"I know that now." Anne laughed through her tears, and Clare felt her heart might break.

"OK, let's go. We need to clean you up, and sort you out, and then we need to think about what this means."

"I can't do the thinking now, Clare. It's too soon. I don't love him; I wish it had never happened – it hurts and the hurt won't go away. I've ruined everything; my life, his life, maybe Andy's life, maybe even your life, it's just…"

Clare stood and dragged Anne upright so they could hug.

"No-one's life is ruined, Anne. Not unless you want it to be. Lots of people have sex when they don't mean to; lots of people have sex when they're not ready. Some of us even learn to enjoy it after a while. It feels like the worst thing in the world right now, but that will pass. Your life is only ruined if you want it to be; Matthias' life is probably vastly improved right now; Andy doesn't ever need to know, and my life has problems of its own right now; I can carry a little extra burden for now; it makes almost no difference. Come on, show me the evidence."

Anne took Clare upstairs, where they made short order of rearranging the bed, straightening Anne out, and wrapping the offending article in tissue paper and stuffing it in Clare's bag for safe disposal later.

By the time Clare was ready to leave, she felt Anne was looking and sounding much brighter.

"I'm going to sort a few things out now," she told Anne, "don't worry; I don't think any permanent damage has been done."

Anne reached out and hugged her again. "Thank you, Clare. I don't know what I would do without you. I don't agree about permanent damage, but – oh, Clare; you should see his bruises." Anne took another deep breath, but retained her composure this time.

"I can imagine. I think, for what it's worth, that you might just have been the best thing which has happened to him in a long time. The trick now will be to make it into a fond memory for him, not an obsession. I'll let you know what happens."

Anne looked at her. "What are you going to do?"

"I'm going to go and find Matthias and sort some things out, then I'm going to figure out how to stow away on the bus going back to Hohenügel. There are a few things I need to do."

AUGUST 2003

Andrew had stopped eating at some point in Clare's story. He had been enjoying the food, but had gradually simply lost interest in it.

"I remember them coming to see me. I remember wanting them to go away again; something about it all just made me think of Karla. I don't remember Anne telling me anything about Matthias. I think I would have remembered that, because now I'm just thinking how much it explains. I had no idea about anything else. Matthias did come back to ours after that, I remember."

"Andy – sorry; Andrew – I did that. You don't remember? I came over, we sorted some things out with your parents – your mum was very understanding – and we moved Matthias back in before his father came back. You don't remember it?"

"Not really. I knew there had been something going on, because I remember that you had been in my house, which I couldn't really explain, but no; I don't remember the rest of it."

"You were very ill, to be fair. Still, I'm surprised."

"I wasn't. Not really – mostly I was just pretending it wasn't happening."

"Or daydreaming about Anne. You remember her visit, but not mine!"

"I don't think so, but maybe. How did you sort it out with his father?"

"We didn't. I went to see Finchy; you remember him?" Andrew nodded. "He took it all on board, and promised to straighten it out with Cartwright – you remember Matthias and his father were staying there?"

"I did." A waiter came and hovered, looking for Andrew's permission to clear his plate. Clare had to prompt him, he was so lost in thought. He passed his plate up and then began to fold his napkin. Clare looked at him.

"What's the matter? Don't want coffee? Or dessert?"

"I don't know, Clare. Spending time talking to you; it's all a bit disorientating, to tell you the truth. Right now, I don't know what to think. I feel like I need some mental space – a bit like after I've been locked in a room with a programmer for half a day."

"I think I'll take that as a compliment, even though I'm not sure it is." Clare was smiling. "I'm sorry, Andrew I've had 25 years to process all this; you've learned it all in about two weeks. Come on; let's walk for a bit."

Clare paid for dinner without much protest from Andrew, and led him out into the London evening.

They walked arm-in-arm along the Strand, and into Trafalgar Square. Andrew was lost in thought; he had assumed that Anne had slept with Matthias, but Clare had removed any doubt, and he wasn't sure how he felt about it. It was really none of his business, he supposed, but it nagged at him and made him feel that he should apologise to someone for something, but he couldn't figure out quite what.

Clare seemed content just to walk with him, and she seemed to be steering him in some direction or other; he was happy just to let her lead. Gradually, his mental churning eased, and he found he had more questions for Clare.

"Can I ask you something?"

"Depends – I'm not allowed to tell you lots of things, but that's mostly for reasons of state security." Andrew laughed.

"No, I mean that I don't understand what happened to you. You disappeared – Anne said you had run away to join the Civil Service. What happened, Clare?"

"That, my old friend, is a story for another day, I'm afraid. It's one of those tales of teenage angst and over-reaction which all seems mildly ridiculous now, but I'm happy to tell you about it another time, if you like. Your treat next time, though."

"I would like that, Clare. I'm so happy…" Andrew caught himself. He was about to say something without thinking, and he knew even as the thought formed in his mind that it would be something he'd regret. He tried to cover his confusion with a cough, but Clare must have seen through that. She stopped, and turned to face him.

"I know; me too, big guy." She stepped back and looked up at him. "I'll call you this time, shall I? I'd really like to hear more about your story, too." Andrew agreed, although he wasn't sure he even had a story. Clare hugged him briefly, then walked off up Haymarket, leaving Andrew to figure out the quickest way back to his own flat.

Work consumed him for the rest of the week. There had been fallout from his trip to Frankfurt which he hadn't properly dealt with, and then a great deal of fence mending to be done in the wake of his half-hearted presentation on Monday. By the time Friday afternoon came around, he felt in need of someone to talk to. He sat at his desk and considered this;

when he had been married, he had spent most weekdays in London, only braving the train on Friday evenings. He had always dreaded the Friday commute; it was unbearably crowded, and at the end of it, he would have a week's worth of domestic problems to deal with. Somehow, he never did find a way of listening properly to Anne, or having her listen to him – Friday evenings were spent working out the domestic timetable for the next two days; dealing out appropriate punishments to children who had transgressed in some way, and pouring himself larger and larger measures of Scotch until he fell asleep by the fire.

And when he really needed to talk; to have Anne listen to him and advise him on something or other, it would generally end up being done over the dinner table on Sunday while the children grew more bored and restless, and Anne wasn't able to give him all of her focus. *It's a wonder it lasted as long as it did*, he told himself.

He considered calling Clare. What would she be doing on a Friday evening, he wondered. Out somewhere having a good time? Perhaps she was at the theatre – pretty much all he knew about her was that she was a theatre-goer. If so, and he cut through the foyer of the National, perhaps he would run into her.

He actually stood up and put his jacket on before he realised how silly he was being. He had her number; he could just call it. If she was there, all well and good; if not; well, he could leave a message.

He dialled, but got her voicemail, which explained that she was out of the office until Monday, and gave him a bewildering array of options to contact someone else who might be able to help, even if his problem was to do with passports or visas.

Andrew's problem, however, was to do with broken hearts and damaged people, and there wasn't a number for that. He turned his laptop off, and headed home.

Andrew wasted the entire weekend. Several times, he picked up the phone to call Clare, but he only had her work number, so that was pointless. He dialled Anne's number twice; the first time he got a generic recorded message and left no message; the second time he heard his son's voice and hung up before he was recognised. He even dug out Matthias' number and tried to call that, but he must either have written it down wrongly, or was transposing some numbers as he dialled, because all he heard was a piercing howl. He took this as a sign, and spent much of the rest of the weekend hunched over in front of his computer, trying to find some meaning in random internet surfing. Late on Sunday evening, Anne's name appeared in his inbox. He smiled to see it – Anne had been a recent convert to email, and he wondered how much she still had to rely on their children to get it to work. He went and poured himself a drink, then settled down to read.

Dear Andrew,

I spoke with Clare, and she tells me that you have met and discussed some things. I am glad that it has finally happened, and I am sorry that you had to hear it from her, and not me. However, I have been so angry with you for so long that I can't bring myself to feel too sorry.

The other day, you told me you were sorry. For what, I don't know, but it was the first time I had ever heard you apologise for anything, and it upset me a great deal. I want to talk to you again, but I need that talk not to be about our marriage or our divorce, or even about our children. For years, I believed that I had betrayed you with Matthias; in later years, I understood that it was not true, but it was too late to change anything. Now, I don't know what I believe. Perhaps I betrayed Matthias; I don't know.

I need to talk it over, and I think I need to do it with you. I will come to you when I can arrange a sitter. Please don't reply.

Anne.

Andrew read this several times, then closed everything down and retreated to his bed. He did not sleep well; every time he felt himself going under, some other detail from 25 years before surfaced in his mind, and caused him to try to see it from a different angle. For all those years, he had genuinely believed that he had been the only person affected by the trip; to have to re-evaluate all of it at this stage was deeply disconcerting. Had it not been for the existence of Peter, he would almost say that he had been the one who got off lightly.

Anne accosted him in the foyer of his office building on Tuesday evening. He had been half expecting this, but wondered aloud why she hadn't called in advance.

"I don't know why, Andrew. For years, I imagined doing this – coming to meet you after work. At one time, it would have been to surprise you; after a while, I thought of spying on you – trying to catch you out."

"You would have been disappointed."

Anne thought about this. "Do you mean that I wanted to catch you, or that I wanted *not* to?" She paused. Andrew said nothing. They hadn't even left the building, and they were already on dangerous ground as far as he could see. This was what she had said she didn't want to talk about. She stared at him, started to say something, then appeared to change her mind.

"You know, let's not go there. I don't want to know now, and I can't see what good it would do anyway. Take me out to dinner, Andrew."

They walked together along the embankment, past the bookstall under Waterloo Bridge, and all the way along past the London Eye to the old County Hall buildings. In recent years, a number of restaurants had opened in what had been at one time the seat of government in London, and Andrew chose an expensive-looking Japanese restaurant, remembering that

Anne had liked Japanese food once upon a time.

They had walked in silence. Andrew found this comforting, since they had often walked together in silence over the years. He wondered if he was supposed to have been talking; asking Anne about her life – he wondered, now, if he had always been supposed to be asking Anne about her life – but he said nothing. Anne seemed in no mood to talk, and said nothing until he had got them seated.

"I haven't had sushi for a long time. I'm impressed that you remembered."

Andrew felt himself flush slightly. "I remember well – especially when you were pregnant. I was convinced it couldn't be good for you."

Anne looked away from him. He wondered what was going through her mind, but had no way of asking. He sat and contemplated the menu until she seemed to be ready to talk again.

Once they had ordered, Anne seemed to relax. He asked her about the children, but she said little other than that they were fine, and doing well at school. He tried to figure out a way to break into Anne's inner thoughts, but all he could come up with was talking about Clare, and he somehow felt that might be dangerous ground. Anne looked at him, and he was sure that she was encouraging him to say something, but his mind was a blank. What did she want to know, anyway?

Eventually, the food started to arrive, and Anne smiled. She thanked him again for bringing her here, and then started to talk. It felt to Andrew like a prepared speech, and he wondered briefly just how long she had been waiting to say it. He knew that he didn't want to hear the details of what she and Matthias had done, but she spared him that, launching instead into what she no doubt thought of as the aftermath.

SEPTEMBER 1978

After he had gone, she lay on her bed and tried to analyse what had happened. He had been prepared; had he planned the whole thing? Did he carry those *things* – contraceptives – around with him, or had he got them especially for today? She looked down at her floor. The thing itself was there, neatly knotted at one end, and full of – well, *stuff*, but she could see no sign of the wrapper he had torn off so hastily. Had he taken it with him? She panicked about this and tore at her bedclothes until she found it. It was ripped in half, and had very little identification on it, but what there was was in German, which she supposed proved something. If only her head would clear enough for her to understand what.

She lay back on the bed, examining her situation. She had not expected the passion and overwhelming feelings she had read about, but she had expected to feel something more than pity, and a sense that this was what Matthias needed her to do, so she had better lie back and get on with it. She carefully considered how she should be reacting. She had done something which she had expected not to have to deal with until her wedding night; it had felt wrong before, and it felt wrong now, but there was a grey period in between during which it had felt inevitable and almost right. It had been uncomfortable, but not painfully so. There had been little or no blood, which had surprised her – no sense of being battered at until something gave way, but equally no feeling that she had been desperate to have him inside her. It happened, and once it was done, they both cried.

She had told him, as gently as possible, to leave her; to get dressed and go back to Andy's. She had told him that they would talk the following day, and that she was sure this didn't mean anything more than that they had both been weak. She didn't think he had really understood what she meant, but that was fair – she wasn't entirely sure what she had meant by it, either. Before he had left, he had leaned over and kissed her once, on the back, just below her left shoulder blade. The memory of that now brought her to tears – it had been an unexpected and tender gesture, almost an unspoken 'thank you'.

Only the thought that her parents might discover her here like this prevented her from drifting into sleep. She was, however, drowsy and not entirely focussed when she heard the knock on the front door. This shocked her into full alertness. She ran to the bathroom and tried to flush the evidence away, then ran back to her room to find something to pull on over her shame. The second knock prompted her to find out who it was, and when she leaned out enough to recognise Clare she almost collapsed from the relief. Clare was here; Clare would sort it out.

But talking to Clare only seemed to make it worse. Every detail screamed to her that she had got it all wrong, so badly wrong. In the midst of the conversation, she dimly registered that Clare had had sex at some point, and more than once, and claimed to have enjoyed it, but this was no comfort – Clare was the sort of person who would be able to enjoy it; who would be able to deal with it and move on. Anne still felt scarred by having shared a sauna with other people; how would she ever deal with having had penetrative intercourse with someone she pitied rather than liked?

Clare swept off to deal with things, and Anne undressed again. All of her clothes went in the laundry hamper, and she got in to the shower. She stood there and howled at the wall until the water ran cold, then she continued to stand there until every nerve ending screamed at her but she felt better, then she got out, tidied up, got dressed, and made dinner.

She quickly found that the only way to deal with what had happened to her was to pretend that it had not happened at all. Her parents came home, thanked her for making dinner, and she found she was able to converse with them as if it had been a normal day. Every time her mother went upstairs, Anne cringed a little, sure that she or Clare had missed something incriminating. Her father asked her, as always, how she had got on at school, and she discovered a talent for stretching the truth which surprised her. She explained that the Germans had all been to the seaside (and hadn't returned yet, she suddenly thought – where was Liezl?), and that it had therefore been a quiet day, enlivened only by her performance in English, which she embroidered a little so that it overshadowed anything else she might have wanted to talk about, and the conversation moved on.

Liezl did eventually return. Anne had saved some dinner for her, but Liezl was full, she said, of fish and chips – apparently the seaside trip had been a great success. The girls retired upstairs as soon as was practically possible, and Anne then faced an enormous dilemma. Should she tell Liezl? This problem hadn't even crossed her mind until now, so caught up had she been with presenting a normal face to her parents.

Liezl was full of tales of the sea – she had never actually been to the seaside before, although they had, of course, come across the English Channel on a ferry. This took a great deal of time to explain, during which Anne's attention wandered a little as she tried to figure out what might happen next. She understood that Matthias couldn't have said anything to his cousin about what happened in July, but would he be the same now? Was he about to tell everyone? Wouldn't that inevitably get back to his father? She didn't know, and in the meantime, Liezl was rattling on about funfairs and sand.

The phone rang somewhere downstairs, and Anne was truly startled to hear her mother calling up to her a moment later.

"Anne, dear, it's for you. Someone called Clare?"

She almost bolted down the stairs, but caught herself in time – just a normal call about school issues was the image she was trying to convey. Fortunately, the phone was in the hallway, and her father had the television turned up loud enough that her conversation would probably remain private. Nevertheless, her heart was pounding as she said hello.

"Anne, don't worry. I've sorted a lot of things out, and I think it's going to be OK. Matthias is back at Andy's, his father is furious, but there's nothing he can do, and I think he will be... look, you're going to have to talk to him tomorrow, but I've laid down some ground rules for him; I think it'll be OK."

Anne wanted to ask about ground rules, but she was terrified of anything being overheard. Instead, she said "OK, thanks, Clare," in as offhand a way as she could muster, and hung up. She would have to talk to Clare in the morning as well, she thought. She looked up, worried that Liezl would be at the top of the stairs, but her shadow was in the bathroom, apparently preparing to shower the salt and sand off. Anne hoped that there would be enough hot water.

The following morning stood fair to be one of the worst of her life, and she could feel herself almost dragging her feet as she walked along the road beside a bouncy Liezl. They went through the gate together, and Liezl immediately spotted Erika and ran over to her. Anne stood in the middle of the yard, letting the green-uniformed crowds swirl around her for a time. She didn't notice Clare approach, so was surprised by her voice.

"I'm guessing you could be overheard last night?" Anne nodded, not trusting her voice, which wanted to ask Clare a thousand questions. "No problem; we can talk later. One thing, though – before you go into German, you need to know that I've warned Matthias off for now. He might be a little distant; don't take it personally."

This had the effect of worrying Anne even more, and she approached the German classroom feeling a little shaky. Matthias was there; in Andy's absence, he had been inserted into this German class anyway, and he smiled quickly at her and looked away. Anne tried to smile back, but found it harder than she would have expected, and she wasn't even sure that he would have seen it.

The class was painful, partly because Matthias' father came in halfway through and stood in the corner, a brooding presence impossible to ignore, but equally impossible to engage with. He seemed to be staring at his son, but said nothing, and left a few minutes before the bell. The lesson covered some technical grammatical points which the Germans were a lot more confident about than Anne would have been of the equivalent issues in English, then a reading from Thomas Mann which Liezl and Matthias both contributed to. Anne sat in uncharacteristic silence throughout, never volunteering anything, and prompting Mr Cartwright to enquire after her as they were all filing out.

"I'm fine, sir, thank you. Just a little tired today. Perhaps I'm coming down with the bug that's been going around."

"I do hope not, Anne. Look after yourself."

She smiled; Cartwright was perceived as stuffy and unfeeling by most of her classmates, but she had always found him solicitous and friendly. Perhaps she reminded him of someone, she had sometimes thought.

Outside in the corridor, Liezl and Erika were marching Matthias off to some other part of the school – Anne couldn't remember what they had timetabled for today – and Clare was waiting for her.

"This will have to be quick. Important things you need to know: I've told Matthias that you need time – maybe a lot of time – to think about what happened; he does understand, I think, but he is also hurting. I think he didn't really mean for it to happen like that, and he is worried that he might have hurt you. Second thing; he is back with Andy – I told Andy's mum a little of what I saw, and she organised it somehow. His father, as you probably noticed, is boiling over, but there's not much he can do. Andy's not sick any more, and there's no need for them all to be camped at Cartwright's place – can you imagine – Matthias is pleased to be out of there, but I think worried about what might happen on the way back."

"What should I do, Clare? I just want it all to go away. I would be happy if they all went back this afternoon, and I never had to see him again. I don't want to be unfriendly, but I can't cope with even seeing him at the moment."

"I know; I'm thinking about that. You need to talk to him, I think. But I can't do that for you; you need to find a way. Do it when you are ready, though." Clare hugged her quickly, then stomped off in the general direction of History. Anne was supposed to be doing a study period in the library, but she needed some air. She dropped her bag off at the library, explained that she would be back, and walked down the stairs and outside.

The school had settled back into that dull drone which meant classes were back in session. Anne could hear the odd instruction being given, and somewhere, faintly, a piano being played, but otherwise, it was still and calm. If only she could internalise that calm.

One of the science teachers passed her, and appeared about to say something. He hesitated, then moved on. Presumably, Anne thought, he had recognised her as one of the exchange group, who had a little more dispensation to move around during these two weeks. Anne walked aimlessly for a bit, then realised that she had left the school grounds and was heading for the wall where she had sat with Matthias 24 hours previously. If only she could erase those 24 hours; put Matthias on the bus where he should have been, and simply gone back to class and got on with things.

But she knew life wasn't like that, and she sighed, choked back something which threatened to turn into a sob, then walked slowly back in to the library.

In the end, she didn't meet up with Matthias until the end of the day. She talked briefly and awkwardly to Andy at lunchtime, but she wasn't making any sense, and she could see him keen to get away and go back to something which he could follow. She then looked in vain for Clare, finding only Erika and Liezl, and she found she was able to chat lightly to them without much difficulty.

As they left school, however, she heard Matthias' voice call her name. *This is it*, she thought to herself, *try to keep calm*. But her heart was pounding, and she felt sure he would be able to read her emotions on her face. She looked at Matthias, and saw that he must have been in as much turmoil; his face was red, and he appeared to be shaking.

They sat together on the same low wall as the rest of the school filed past them. Andy stopped briefly, but Anne was able to fob him off with a promise that they would all meet up for ice cream later. Andy seemed reluctant to leave, but eventually did, although he looked over his shoulder at them more than once. Anne steeled herself to say what needed to be said, but Matthias beat her to it.

"I think he likes you, no? I think I have made a big mistake yesterday, but it is hard for me to be sorry."

Anne considered this. Andy, it had slowly become clear to her, did like her, although she wasn't entirely clear in what way he liked her. It could, however, turn out to be a blessing; something she could use to hold Matthias at arm's length. She still hadn't quite worked out how to respond when Matthias took up his theme again.

"I know it is stupid. Stupid to say 'thank you' to someone for that, but that is what I need to say. I like you, Anne, but not the same way that Andy likes you, I think. I should not have done – that. But you have helped me a lot to feel better, so I cannot be sorry."

Hearing Matthias say that ought to have been a huge relief for Anne, but instead she suddenly felt close to tears. She had no time to analyse that sensation, however, because she knew she had to respond; to say something.

"Matthias, do not feel sorry. Two people did what we did yesterday, and neither one should be blamed for it. I only know one thing for sure – I am not ready to be – doing what we did. Not with you; not with anyone. I am not that kind of person, and I feel ashamed and a little scared." She felt him tense beside her, and quickly added, "not ashamed of you and I; but I should not have let that happen to me until the day I get married. I will have some explaining to do then, I think." She looked at her feet, then pressed on. "I need to keep this secret – private; do you understand?"

He nodded "Clare said this to me yesterday, and I understand. I will not be a problem for you."

She looked at him, and he seemed to be sincere.

"Thank you, Matthias. I know I am very old-fashioned, but this is very important to me. I am not who I thought I was, but I need to try to get back to that place. If I can treat yesterday as something which happened once and is now over, then I think I can do that. If not, then I think I will be destroyed. Do you know what I mean?"

Matthias thought about it, then nodded. They sat in silence, and Anne began to feel herself calm down. He wasn't about to declare his undying love for her, or threaten to run away from home to be with her, or anything like that, and she thought, for the first time, that perhaps she would be able to get over this, and live a normal life again. It would always be at the back of her mind, but perhaps she could manage it. A thought occurred to her, and she asked the question before she had properly considered it.

"Was it your first time as well? I'm sorry, I don't mean to pry. Forget it."

"No, it is OK. Yes, also first for me."

Anne couldn't decide if that made it better or not. She decided to think about it later, and stood up. "Come on; we promised Andy ice cream, and he will be very impatient. Matthias stood and stretched. Anne watched him, but try as she might, she couldn't feel anything other than slightly sorry for him. He had a horrible life, and it probably explained a lot, but she knew that she wasn't the answer. And now, she was quite confident that he knew it as well.

As they walked toward the corner shop which was Andy's regular stopping-off point on the way home, she realised that she hadn't asked him about the other problem.

"What about your father? What will happen?"

"I do not know, Anne. He is very angry because I went to Andy's house. I know this will be a problem for me some day. Perhaps not until we are home – too many people might see him, I think. I hope."

"Is there nothing you can do about him? What about your mother?"

"She is not so scared of him, but enough, I think. Enough scared to make her do nothing. Karla fights him; I do not. Probably, we are both wrong. It is my problem, but soon I will be free of it, I think. Soon, I will leave and go somewhere else."

Anne panicked momentarily. "Where? Not here?"

Matthias laughed. "No, not here. I want to train to be a pilot – so I will go somewhere to do this, I think. I need to have good English, so this is why I work hard. But one day…."

Anne had to fight an impulse to take his hand at this point. She kept telling herself she felt nothing more than pity for him, but she would have found it easy to use that pity to establish a physical contact which she knew would be a mistake.

Andy was waiting, somewhat impatiently, outside the corner shop. He explained that Liezl and Erika had gone shopping – he had told them which bus to catch, and was reasonably proud of the fact. He bought the ice creams – he explained that he had missed out for most of the trip, so it was his turn – and they strolled back to Andy's. It was almost possible for Anne to believe that everything was back to normal, and that nothing had really changed. She had faced the biggest crisis of her life, and somehow made it turn out all right. Hadn't she?

AUGUST 2003

Andrew listened to Anne's story while he ate. He had managed to figure most of it out by now, and he smiled to be reminded of the ice cream.

"I really did miss pretty much everything, didn't I?" He thought for a moment. "Can I ask you something?"

Anne nodded, a little warily perhaps.

"What do you think of it all now? Does it all seem like a teenage drama now?"

Anne paled, and Andrew instantly knew that he had read the situation wrongly again.

"Teenage drama? Andrew, it destroyed me. I have never been the same again as I was before I went to Germany. I've tried for most of my life to find that person again, but she was torn apart by what Matthias did." She paused. "No, that's not entirely fair. I had some part in it, I suppose. And you did, and the girls; even Clare, who has been a true friend all these years. We all did things we might regret, but I was the one broken by them."

Andrew sat in silence. He had always known something of this, but to hear it spelt out still shocked him. Anne genuinely believed that she had been 'destroyed' by what had happened. He hadn't understood the depth of it before – he hadn't known about Matthias before – but he still couldn't quite reconcile everything in his mind. Anne was staring at him, and he realised he had missed something again.

"Sorry, Anne; I'm just thinking it all through. I do get how you were changed by it; I really do. I guess none of us really knew who the old you was. It was difficult to see how that worked, I guess."

"But you did," Anne said quietly. "Of all of them, you were the one who knew me before. You were the one who I pinned my hopes on, because you would help me get back there. And it didn't happen. You never seemed to understand it."

"No, I can safely say that I never did understand it. I'm not sure I do now. My life changed, too, that summer. Maybe the old me would have been more sympathetic, but after Karla, I just – was different. I only saw that you can't get what you want, and that the world will change you whether you want it to or not. I just assumed that you were the same."

"I wasn't, Andrew. I wasn't."

They looked at each other. *If I reach out to her now,* Andrew thought, *something will happen, but I don't know what it is, and I don't know if I want it.* He didn't move, and their waiter came to offer them tea. They both declined, each now keen to get out and go home.

Back out on the Embankment, Anne stopped and looked into the river. Andrew stood with her, wondering what he was supposed to do now. She said nothing, and he worried that she might be crying, but when she finally turned to face him, she was as clear-eyed as she had been all night. Andrew ventured a smile, and had it returned. Anne spoke.

"I'm casting you free, Andrew. A tiny part of me wondered if you wanted me back, but you don't. I'm ready to let go of it now; the children are ours, and we'll have to be friends – I think I can manage it now, but I'm letting go of you."

He stared. He thought that the divorce had been a letting go, but perhaps he didn't understand that, either.

"I don't know what to say to that, Anne. I think – I think I loved you, Anne, but maybe not enough."

She smiled at him. "Nowhere near enough, Andrew, but that's not all your fault. Go and work out your life: you need to close some doors, I think. Then you should get on with being you. I think you could be quite good at that."

He walked her back to Waterloo station, then walked home. It took him nearly an hour, and for all of that time his mind was empty – he thought of nothing more than which way he should go, and whether the crossing lights ahead would be red or green. He got back to the flat, took a shower and collapsed into bed. At some point in the night, he came awake to discover that he was crying. He abandoned himself to great racking sobs for a time, then the storm passed, and he slept again.

By the end of the week, he thought he had everything figured out. He said as much to Clare, who had arranged to meet him for coffee on Saturday morning. She took him to the National Portrait Gallery, a place he had not been to in years, and they drank coffee in the new rooftop restaurant and looked out at Nelson atop his Column, and almost at eye level. The view transfixed him for a time, and Clare seemed content to just watch him. He thought about things for a time, then simply plunged in.

"I think I understand some things now, and I'm not sure what to do next." Clare nodded by way of encouraging him to go on. "Well, first of all, I was so caught up with what had happened to me that I know now I was just ignoring everyone else around me. I should have been more aware of what had happened to Anne, and it sounds like I should have been more aware of something which happened to you. But I was in my own bubble of self-pity and doubt, and I'm only now really emerging from it, I think.

"I got Anne all wrong. Right from the start. I remember what she was like before we went to Germany; quiet and polite. I liked that Anne. Not in the way she would have wanted me to, but I did like her. We got on well, and if I hadn't been so blind, we could have been great friends. Maybe more; who knows. Then she changed, and I fell in love with the changed Anne, but I didn't understand that she hated the changes."

"Not all of them, Andrew. Don't underestimate her – she knew what she was doing for some of it. It was just that she had her confidence undermined by what happened with Matthias. Look at it from her point of view: she stepped out of character and put on a pair of jeans; result – well, you know. Then she steps out of character and bunks off school. Again, you know the rest."

"And there are at least two other people you haven't thought about. I think you need to add Matthias to your list. And then we should talk about Karla."

Andrew winced. He had thought this might be coming, but he really didn't know how he was going to react. She was right about Matthias, though.

"Yes, Matthias should be there. I was so blind to his issues that I abandoned him, I think. Even after you got him back into my house, I just didn't know what he was thinking. You know, it wasn't until you told me that story that I realised what had been going on with his father. It probably explains Karla, too."

"It definitely explains Karla. And a lot more besides. For all the time I've been going there, that whole part of the family has been like a blind spot. Liezl is in Munich now, and I haven't spoken to her much, but I saw her parents last year, and they still drew a veil over Matthias and Karla. They only live 15 minutes' walk away, but it's like they are in a different world. That man has a lot to answer for."

I don't even know his name. He was introduced to me as Herr Schneider, and I never questioned it."

"Rolf. If I remember correctly, he was Rolf. Yes, I'm sure of it. He's buried in the village cemetery – you could probably look it up."

Andrew thought about this. "We didn't go there, Matthias and I. We walked around the village a lot, but we didn't go there. Perhaps I understand why. He must have so many issues. Do you know the whole story? Is what Matthias told me the whole of it?"

"I'd be surprised, Andrew. You do realise that there's only one person who does have the whole story, don't you?"

Andrew thought about this. How likely was it that Clare could get in touch with Karla? Not very, he supposed. They had some kind of issue as he recalled. This part was still a little fuzzy, and he said as much to Clare.

"Ah, well, that bit was very simple. I fucked her boyfriend, and she caught us." Andrew looked around, alarmed. This didn't seem to be the sort of place where such blunt talk was regularly heard, but Clare laughed.

"I remember you used to have a problem with my language...."

"No, not at all. I just – ah, what do I know? I think I'm beginning to understand just how much of a sheltered life I've led." Clare laughed again at this, and Andrew sat back and watched. All other considerations aside, Clare's reappearance in his life had been a truly joyful thing. He realised just how much he missed having fun, and Clare seemed to have no problem with the idea of fun. She was talking again, and he had to readjust his focus.

"I was completely at fault for it, and I never complained. I went through a little phase that year of - well, doing stuff - and I thought I was so grown up and mature. I had no idea.

"I met Karla and Dieter on the first night we were there. You remember the Sunday night?" Andrew did, vaguely. "All the relatives converged on Liezl's place to gawk at us, and Karla was there. I got to talking with her, and this incredibly tall, good-looking boy she was with. He had a beard, and a deep, deep voice. He didn't have much English, but he didn't need it. I spent about half an hour with him, and – well, I'm still blushing now!"

She was, and Andrew enjoyed the spectacle of someone else's embarrassment for a moment. Clare continued.

"I saw them a couple of times at the beginning of the week. Always together. Karla appealed to me; she was a rebel and had no respect for authority. She had Dieter exactly where she wanted him, too. It was intoxicating."

"I remember that; she had that effect on me at first too."

"Right. I lent her my book; you know the one. We had coffee and something a little stronger at Dieter's place one afternoon, and then she went off on the bike somewhere."

"And one thing led to another."

"Exactly. It sounds corny, but it was just one of those things. I don't know who started it, but it didn't take us long. It was – ah, now I am embarrassed. Let's just say that my limited experience was broadened considerably."

"And then she came back?"

"Yup. Straight out of every clichéd movie you've ever seen. We got into a fight, believe it or not. She was a fighter by nature, I suppose, and I wasn't about to back down – the vain bravado of youth, you know. She had the advantage, as you might imagine – I was in my knickers, and she had her leathers on. She actually, I found out when we got back, cracked one of my ribs."

"Ouch. So, you never told Anne this bit? She said something about an argument over a leather jacket, or something."

"Well, we had that argument, too. Her positions on things were somewhat more mature than mine, and she kind of wiped the floor with me. So I didn't exaggerate that much. But, yeah, I lied to Anne. And, I suppose, I set the whole thing off by doing that." She drained her coffee. "But I did tell Anne later. Kind of had to, eventually."

Andrew suddenly understood what Clare was telling him. Was she testing him in some way by not spelling it out? Did he have the right to ask? What, exactly, had happened? Andrew felt as intimidated as usual by the idea of asking personal questions, but he felt he had the right, now. Clare, however, was on another tack.

"So, yeah, I didn't exactly have a relationship with Karla. Except – well, long story." She smiled ruefully at him, and he laughed, then faltered.

"Oh my God. I've just thought: is that why Karla turned to me, do you think? Some kind of elaborate revenge?"

"I've always assumed so. She wasn't the most stable of individuals, as you know. I always thought she just picked you because I was your friend in some way, and you were an easy target. Sorry, I don't mean to offend."

"No, no. I guess you're right. But I have another theory, and I've been worrying about this ever since I saw Peter. Do you think it's possible that she just wanted to get pregnant?"

Clare thought about this for a long time. The staff in the restaurant began to give them pointed looks; it was now lunchtime, and there was a queue outside the door. Andrew and Clare weren't exactly contributing to the profits of the place in the way that those outside would probably do. He began to fidget, but she stilled him with a hand on his sleeve.

"Wait a minute – we'll pay; we can stay here. I'm thinking this through. You could be right. You know, Karla was most upset about Dieter not using any protection with me, as we'd say now. She yelled at him for some time in German, and I'm not sure I caught all of it – it was 25 years ago, and I was a little preoccupied with getting my clothes on and getting out of there. But you may be on to something. Did he always use it with her? Was she desperate to get pregnant and he wasn't?" She fell silent. Andrew felt emboldened enough to ask.

"And you? Were you protected?"

Clare laughed, and finally jumped down off the high stool. "Come on; there's more to this than you know. Let's walk."

They meandered pleasantly through the revamped galleries, stopping to peer at famous portraits which Andrew had either never seen before, or completely forgotten about, and it wasn't until they were in the basement galleries, which were evidently more to Clare's taste, that they began to talk again. They sat side by side on a bench and considered a modern-looking portrait of the late Queen Mother. Andrew didn't particularly care for it, but Clare was full of praise, and he enjoyed listening to her being enthusiastic about things, so he listened and learned. Once she was done with techniques in modern portraiture, Clare returned to Karla.

"If Dieter was not playing ball, so to speak, then you must have seemed a very fortuitous alternative. Presumably she thought you would be a pushover, and there was a reasonable chance she could pass it off as his. What better way to rub it in her father's face?"

Andrew was silent. He had been replaying his encounters with Karla, and slowly seeing them in a new light. She had pursued him, but encouraged him to take the initiative. When that hadn't worked she had, in her words, taken what she wanted. Not him, as such, but what he could give her. It was a risky thing to do – not only because she only had one shot at it, but also because her father was in the room directly below them. She probably enjoyed the risk, and presumably was satisfied with the results.

"But what about me?" Andrew said, as if Clare had heard his thoughts. "What did she think I was? I had no say in any of this. Did she just not care?"

"Only one way to find out, isn't there?"

Andrew thought about that, and realised that he had come to the same conclusion. He needed to face Karla, to face up to his past, and something about being around Clare made that seem possible.

They walked out onto Charing Cross Road together, Andrew assuming that it was time for him to make his way home. Clare probably had many more important things to do than babysit an old acquaintance who appeared to be having some kind of poorly executed mid-life crisis.

However, Clare appeared to have nothing better to do than wander around in second-hand bookshops with him until they were both hungry. Since he was paying, he allowed her to choose the venue, and she took him to Cranks in Covent Garden.

As they ate, Clare explained that this had been a favourite meeting place for her and Anne. "When you guys were still living in town, we used to come here now and then; got a bit less frequent once I was abroad more often and you were in Godalming or Guildford or wherever. Still like it here, though."

Andrew shook his head at yet another thing he was unaware of. How many more were there? Should he perhaps stop worrying about them? He decided to change tack slightly.

"So, what should I do now? I saw Peter about a month ago now, and I haven't come to any conclusion about him. Does he need me in his life? Do I need him? I know it's too late to do anything about Anne, but how do I handle that; for instance, I barely see my children now, because she or they are always too busy – I think that needs to change. And I think" – this caused him to pause, but he took a breath and plunged on – "I think I need to find Karla and ask her."

Clare put her fork down and looked at him.

"Well, this is good. This is the Andrew I hoped was in there somewhere. Your life is in your own hands, and you need to grab it and start directing it. Shit. I used to say the same thing to Anne. Feel free to ignore me." She paused, but Andrew said nothing. "But. If you want to know, this is what I think. You need to take care of your children. They're at a difficult age, and they're going to have one full time, in their face all the time, parent. Talk to them; write to them; do unexpected things for them, and be the parent you struggled to be before. And you need to recognise that you have three children, and the first one may need you as well. I can help a little with that, but you're going to have to work it out for yourself. Tell me what I need to do, and I'll do it for you."

"But – but, why, Clare? Why should you do this for me? And how come you know so much about what I need to do for my children? I'm not saying you're wrong – it sounds like you're right. I have spent the last month failing to understand almost everything. Help me understand something."

Clare picked up her glass of sparkling water and drained it. "Oh, Andrew. I'm doing this because I do feel responsible for it in some way. I'm doing it because I should have been your friend, too, all these years, and I want to catch up a little, and I know about your children because I know them. I don't think you've been paying close attention all the time, have you?" Andrew shook his head.

He suddenly smiled, and Clare looked at him quizzically.

"I get it. I mean, I think I got it before, but I was waiting for you to spell it out in some way. Karla wasn't the only one to get pregnant that week, was she?"

Clare grinned. "Bingo! There's hope for you yet. Do you want to hear my sordid story?"

SEPTEMBER 1978

Clare stood on Andy's front step and stared up at him. It was difficult enough, being something close to eight inches shorter than him, but she was also on a lower step. He was essentially looking down at the top of her head, and - as far as she could tell – not recognising her. His mother's voice floated through from the back, asking him who was at the door, and then she appeared, drying her hands on a dishtowel.

"Oh, it's you, dear. Come in. I think things are going quite well, don't you, dear?" This second 'dear' appeared to be aimed at Andy, who didn't really seem to be taking any of it in. He looked at his mother, then at Clare, then sloped off to the living room without a word.

"Poor love; he's exhausted. I told him it was too soon to go back to school, but he doesn't listen. I imagine you listen to your parents, don't you, Clare? It *is* Clare, isn't it? I get so mixed up with all your names, but I remember you from primary. Oh, I'm sorry; I'm rattling on again, aren't I? Come in, I'll put the kettle on. Matthias is upstairs." She yelled up the stairs to Matthias – he got another 'dear' - as Clare shut the front door behind her, and then bustled off to the kitchen.

Matthias came down the stairs almost jauntily, and Clare grinned at him, then hugged him.

"I'm glad you're looking happy. How has it been?"

"Ah, my father is – you know. He does not talk to me now; maybe this is good, I don't know. But it is better to be here."

Two days had passed since the momentous Tuesday, and Clare was simply checking up on what she thought of as her responsibilities. First Anne, who had been subdued but calm, now Matthias and Andy. Andy was plainly still unwell, but Matthias appeared to have changed into a younger and more carefree version of himself. Andy's mother ushered them into the kitchen, served them tea and a remarkable selection of biscuits, and left them alone. Clare hoisted herself up on to the kitchen cabinets, and Matthias stood at the tiny kitchen table. Clare waited for some kind of sign as to whether Andy would join them, but none was forthcoming, so she decided to risk it.

"Have you seen her? Spoken to her?"

Matthias' smile faltered, but only a little.

"No. I thought about you – I mean, the things you have said, and it is right to let go, I think. I know I am not 'in love' with her, and I am a little sorry for what happened, but it is hard for me to explain, I think. I need someone to like me, and she was so kind. I will never forget this. I want to say this to her, but perhaps it is not good."

"I don't know, Matthias. I'm guessing here as well. I think she is still ashamed of what happened, and she is frightened." Matthias became alarmed at this, but Clare calmed him.

"Not frightened of you, or anyone else. She is frightened because it was out of character for her – do you know what I mean by this?"

"I think so – she does something unusual – this is the right word?"

"Yes, more or less. She needs time, and we don't have time. She will be able to deal with this, but you will be back in Germany by then, and I really think this will be over. For you and her, of course. I think if you try to prolong it, it will only hurt both of you."

There was a long silence, which Matthias finally broke.

"No, you are right. I am scared, also. If my father knew, or if anything happened, I think it would be very, very bad. You agree?"

Clare watched him drink his tea. He was plainly drinking it out of politeness, because all these English people drank it, and it amused Clare to see him react to it. She tried to figure out a way of enlisting his help with her own problem, but nothing came to mind. She sighed, and pushed herself off the side.

"Matthias, I need to get going. Look after Andy for me, and if I don't see you before, I'll see you at the station."

She popped her head round the living room door, where Andy's parents were engrossed in something on the television, and Andy appeared to be sleeping. It amused her to see Andy and his father in the room together – they looked as if they were sitting – or in Andy's case, lying – on child's furniture. She said her farewells, and thanked Andy's mum again for her help with Matthias, then left.

As she closed the front door behind her, a gust of wind caught her hair and temporarily blinded her. As she pushed it all out of the way, she realised that it was drizzling. Nothing to be done but to walk through it. She pulled the collar of her leather jacket up to her ears, bent her head, and walked.

As she walked, she tried to figure it out. She needed to go back to

Hohenügel, there was no doubt in her mind of that. She had to confront Dieter, and presumably Karla - however much that prospect terrified her - and then she had to make a decision; the hardest decision she would probably ever make in her life. For now, she was trying to figure out how to get there. She had assumed that she would be able to talk someone into letting her stow away on the bus, but had only later remembered that the Germans had come by train. She had made some quiet enquiries, but it seemed that there was no easy way of buying a ticket all the way to Hohenügel, and there was no way she could afford to buy a ticket in any case.

The whole thing was, of course, ridiculous, since any attempt to travel with the Germans would mean being in the company of Herr Schneider, and there was no way that was about to happen. He would spot her before they even left the station, and probably cause an international incident of some sort.

No, it would have to be done the hard way.

Three days later, Clare found herself at Oxford Circus tube station, having hitch-hiked with varying amounts of difficulty to the outskirts of London, then spent some of her meagre resources on an underground ticket. She felt lost and somewhat overwhelmed by the crowds, but wasn't about to show it. The next step was to get to Victoria station and hope she had enough money for a ticket for the train and the ferry to Oostend.

The final underground leg to Victoria was over relatively quickly, and she reckoned that she was still in good time. She negotiated the ticket office and the issue of boat trains without actually buying anything the first time; she at least knew what everything would cost, and it seemed she would be able to afford it as long as she was able to hitch once across the channel. She found a bench to sit on and thought hard for a long time. This was the point of no return, she recognised. From here, she could call her Aunt Kit, and be back in the arms of her family before anyone really knew that anything was wrong, or she could take the plunge and change things irrevocably.

Until she stopped to think about it, she hadn't expected this to be a difficult situation. She had not even considered doing anything other than going to Hohenügel, but now she was here, it all felt more than a little unreal. She was tired, hungry, and scared. She knew that what almost everyone would advise her to do would be to talk to her parents, who would most likely be angry for a few days, then help her through it, but she knew that if she did that, she wouldn't actually be able to make any of the decisions she felt she had to make. She rehearsed the phone conversation with her parents in her mind for a long time, then took a deep breath and went to find a payphone.

She had expected it to be difficult, especially as she was planning on saying nothing more than that she was safe, had not 'run away', and was intending to come back in a few days – although she didn't quite know how – she was in no way prepared for her mother's hysterics. Even once the howling and sobbing had subsided at the other end – Clare had thought to reverse the charges, fortunately, or the entire conversation would have consisted of her mother weeping and Clare failing to get a word in – she seemed incapable of making her mother understand anything she was saying. Unnervingly, her mother just kept asking if she was pregnant, and getting no useful answer to that, assuming that she was and pleading with her not to do anything 'hasty'. Clare eventually yelled that she would call again once she got to her destination and hung up.

Only once she was on the train to Dover did she realise that she hadn't explained that the next phone call might be a day or two away. So she had to call again from the platform at Dover Marine, and told her father, who was, thankfully, more receptive, if a little stunned, that she was going to stay with friends, and she would call again tomorrow or the next day, and then they would sort it all out.

She felt dreadful at this point; tired, grubby and hungry, and she had to fight an overwhelming desire to just go home. Once that had passed, with the help of more solid British transport food, she looked around for what she needed to do next. Alarmingly, the only signs she could see in the station were for 'Dunkerque', and she had to ask three separate British Rail staff to find out where she was supposed to go.

Once that was sorted out, she suddenly found herself in familiar surroundings. This was where they had all been decanted from the bus three months before, on the first night of the epic journey. She supposed that this would be the same sailing as they had been on all that time ago, and this made her feel a little better. She endured the wait stoically, and then boarded the ferry without a second thought. She even found the upper lounge where she and Andy had passed the night on the return journey. She found the same seats, and curled up on them, remembering how secure she had felt with his long arms around her.

She awoke to a grey dawn in Belgium. She was being encouraged to leave the ferry, and she did so without even having time to wash her face or brush her teeth, which were feeling distinctly fuzzy by now. She had thought this part through, however, and knew that she had to get to where the lorries were being unloaded from the ferry, and find one – preferably an English one – which was going somewhere in Germany.

Her luck held – she quickly found an English driver going as far as Frankfurt, and their journey together passed in silence for the most part. She got out and walked through both of the border crossings – into and out of Holland - and then she remembered little of the rest of the day until he dropped her at a tram stop in the outskirts of Frankfurt. It was late on

Sunday afternoon, and Clare was not entirely sure where to go from here, but she knew that she had some German coins somewhere in her backpack, and used the time it took to rummage for them to come up with a plan.

The plan didn't seem too hopeful, since it involved heading into the centre of Frankfurt, where hitching would be difficult, but she could think of no other. She had enough, it seemed, for a tram ticket, although she wasn't at all sure she had figured it out correctly. However, no-one challenged her, and she got off at the Hauptbahnhof a little more confident. She finally allowed herself the luxury of a proper clean up in the public bathroom at the station, then caught the next train to Bad Hersfeld, after which her German money ran out.

Her backpack was by now beginning to feel as if it had been weighted down with bricks. She hadn't eaten since lunchtime, when her lorry driver friend had shared his sandwich with her, and she was tired beyond measure. She had always known that the last few miles would be the most difficult, and so it proved. She walked wearily to the outskirts of Bad Hersfeld, hoping that she had remembered it correctly, and that this was the right way, then spent over an hour failing to be picked up by anyone. It was dark, and cold, and she was beginning to despair when a dark blue Volkswagen pulled up. The middle-aged man behind the wheel had no English, and she had to work harder than at any time in her life to make herself understood, but eventually she managed to communicate where she wanted to go, and he agreed to take her there, even though, as far as she could tell, he was going somewhere else.

She spent the whole of this last part of the journey – which lasted all of half an hour – in a state of high alert, for once she was in the car, she could smell beer on his breath, and he seemed to be trying to be more friendly than she was comfortable with. She kept her attention on the road, making sure that every sign they passed still indicated that they were going the right way, and finally chickened out as they reached the overpass where all traffic had to leave the road. She could walk from here, she tried to explain, and he eventually accepted this, although he unnerved her badly by sitting stationary in the car until she was out of sight. She thought she heard his engine behind her shortly afterward, but it was someone else entirely, who sped past without even looking her way.

As she walked, she realised that this was the walk Andy had been forced to make on that strange Sunday. She remembered how she had exploded at Karla by the pool that day, and she came close to tears, knowing that she would have to face all of that again in no time at all. She stopped for a moment, and took several deep breaths. She could see lights on in Liezl's house, just up on the hill to her left, and she thought she could make out Erika's house a little further along the road. She tried to clear her mind, and looked at her watch. Eleven o'clock wasn't especially late, even for a

Sunday, as she remembered, but she was nonetheless nervous.

She hid it as best she could, and walked confidently up to the front door. During the two weeks she had lived here, she had had her own key, and could come and go as she pleased, so this was the first time she had actually knocked on the door. The house felt silent, and she wondered what she would do if there was no answer. She then had the startling realisation that Erika would only have got home the day before – she probably *was* in bed; trying to catch up on missed sleep. Clare prepared to shoulder her backpack again, and possibly try Liezl's when the door was opened. Erika took a moment to recognise who was there, then yelped.

There followed much pandemonium and faltering explanations. It was a good hour later before everyone was gathered around the kitchen table and able to try to put the whole picture together. Erika's father offered to call Clare's parents, but Clare felt she ought to do that herself, but not until the morning, when she had time to think things over a little.

Once she was over her shock, Erika was at once bemused and delighted to have her friend back; only three days before, they had hugged farewell for what she might easily have assumed was the last time; to have her back so soon was thrilling. No-one directly asked why Clare had come back, but once they were safely back in the room they had shared earlier in the summer, Erika voiced what everyone must have been thinking.

"It is a boy, no? You come back for a boy?"

Clare smiled warily. "I've come back for myself, Erika, but that's a little difficult to explain. So, yes, you might as well say it was a boy." Erika thought about this for some time, and Clare came close to falling asleep before her friend spoke again.

"Clare, I know about it. Karla told us something. I think this was you, is it right?"

Clare sighed, and propped herself up on one elbow. "Erika, it's not what it looks like," but as soon as she said it, she realised that it probably was pretty much what it looked like. "OK, that's not right. It was one silly mistake. I need to understand if he wants to do anything about it, to – oh, Erika; I haven't even said the words out loud yet." She was close to tears now, but felt that it was partly the tiredness doing that, and she lay back down hoping to sleep. Erika's voice came to her as if from a dream.

"Do you love him? Does he love you?" Clare was too tired to answer, and her last conscious thought was *love? Who said anything about love?*

The morning did not bring much relief for Clare. She was woken by Erika crashing around in the room, and found both sleep and conversation to be beyond her after that. She simply lay still until the house fell silent, then forced herself to get up and take stock. She wished briefly that she kept a diary – at least then she could write deathless things like *well, diary, here I am!* in it. It might allow her some mental space to really think about what she was going to do now.

From the moment when she had first properly understood that she was pregnant two weeks before, she had only had one thought in mind – to come here and sort it out. But she had no clear idea what 'sort it out' actually meant, and now she faced the prospect of facing Dieter – and, worse, Karla – with no clear plan, and no idea of what she wanted to get out of it.

She sat in the kitchen, picking at some dry bread, for a long time, and then remembered that she had intended to call her parents. She then spent some more time trying to work out if either of them would be at home, before realising that the simplest way to find out would be to make the call. She let it ring five times before hanging up the first time, then thought about it some more, and called back.

This time, her mother answered on the first ring. They tried to talk, but both of them burst into tears before more than a few words were exchanged, and not much was said. Clare began to panic about the cost of the call, since she had almost no money left, and managed to calm down enough to explain where she was and ask her mother to call right back.

The phone rang almost immediately, and Clare snatched it up; somewhere in her subconscious, she was alarmed by the prospect of one of the neighbours hearing it. Her mother sounded slightly more fuzzy than she had before, but considerably calmer. They talked vaguely about where Clare was and how she had got there, before her mother broke down again. Clare was prepared to wait this one out; she loved her mother more than she was usually able to admit, even to herself, and right at this moment, what she wanted was to hear the familiar voice.

However, the voice failed to calm, and she heard some commotion on the other end, followed by her father's voice. Her relationship with her father was a little more complex that the one with her mother, but she was nevertheless glad to hear him.

"Clare, listen. We don't fully understand what is going on here, but we were both 16 once. You're pregnant, aren't you?" Clare admitted it – hearing herself say it helped her to gather her thoughts – and listened on. "So, you've gone back to be with Erika, which I think I understand. You will need your parents, though, and we are here for you. We aren't about to disown you. But we'd like you to come home and face it. We need to talk to the boy concerned, and figure a few things out." Clare didn't want an argument, but she heard herself try to start one.

"It's not that simple, dad. Nothing is. I'm sure I know who the father is" - *oh God, what a stupid thing to say right then* – "and it's a little more complicated than you think. Let me work it out for now, and I'll let you know what I want to do." She hung up before she said anything else stupid, and then cursed herself for not having brought up the subject of money. Now her father thought she had a list of possible suspects for impregnating her, and she had hung up on him. Great. This whole thing, she thought, needs a lot more care than I realised.

She cried quietly for a while, indulging herself in something which didn't always come naturally to her, then went upstairs to shower and change.

Erika came in no more than five minutes after the end of the school day, out of breath. She had presumably run all the way home, and took her time recovering – not only was she a little overweight, but she cheerfully admitted to a complete lack of interest in any kind of athletic activity, and was plainly unfit.

Once she had her breath back, however, she wasted no time in preparing lunch and grilling Clare.

"You are in love, I think? It is with Dieter, I think so? Karla is angry with you, so I suppose...?"

Clare stared at her. "Not really, Erika. Sit down, I need to try to explain." She took a deep breath, but her voice seemed steady enough. "When I was here before, I did something bad. I slept with Dieter." Erika looked puzzled, then light dawned.

"You had sex? With him?" She had turned pale, and her eyes were huge. Clearly this was a lot more than she had expected. She fell silent, and Clare felt she ought to clarify.

"Yes; we had sex. And now" – she looked down and made vague waving motions about her midsection. Erika screamed and let fly with a stream of rapid German, the gist of which seemed to be "Oh shit, no."

Once her shock had subsided, she stood and held her arms out. Clare got up and walked into her embrace, suddenly feeling as if a great weight had at least been shifted partly from her shoulders. Someone else knew about it now, and it did feel a little better.

Clare sat and explained what had happened, while Erika fussed over her and asked questions which her English was not quite good enough to keep up with. After a while, however, she came to the crux.

"What will you do? Will you keep it?"

Clare stared at her silently, and Erika blushed. "I am sorry; it is a wrong thing to say."

"No, Erika; it's the right thing to say, the only question, really. What do I do with a – a baby? What do I tell him, and what will he want to do? Nobody wants to be in this situation, but here we are. What now? I have not even asked myself these questions yet, so I don't know what I will say. I think I need to talk to him, alone, first."

"My God, Clare – Karla will kill you! Oh, I am sorry, I don't mean..."

"No, you are right. She will be a big problem for me. I need to understand what she will do. Of course, if she does kill me, that will fix the problem, I suppose."

"Do your parents know?"

"I called them. They've worked it out, although I don't think they've grasped that it happened here. I used the phone, Erika – I hope that's OK."

"Of course it will be. You can stay in this house for - you know. You are welcome to be here if you need it."

"Thank you, Erika – I knew this would be OK. All the rest, I don't know."

The girls fell silent as they contemplated this. After a while, they decided to go and walk up to Liezl's, since she would undoubtedly be pacing up and down in frustration. Liezl waved them all down to the sauna as soon as they came through the door. It was already hot, and Clare supposed that Liezl had had it ready to go from the moment she got home, assuming they would come straight over.

Once they were seated, Clare asked casually if saunas were recommended for pregnant women, which caused Liezl to gasp audibly:

"I knew it! I knew something, and... Clare, it will be OK, we can help. What happened? Oh, and I don't know if it is OK if you have a..." Liezl trailed off, and Clare wondered if she was unsure of the vocabulary, or simply of what to say next. She quickly revisited what she had already told Erika, then Liezl insisted that they all get out, to Clare's relief; she had quickly overheated, and now felt a little light-headed.

The nausea of the previous months had not raised its head since she had started this journey, but it was back now, and she really just needed to lie down somewhere. The German girls looked at her anxiously, and she supposed she must look tired and pale to them. She went to open the door, but was restrained by Liezl, who suggested that she might like to put some clothes on first. At this evidence of her mental fragility, Clare began to cry again.

Liezl seemed somewhat panicked by this, but Erika wrapped her in a towel and led her upstairs to the guest bedroom.

Some hours later, Clare awoke to silence. It was dark, and she had no way of knowing what time it was. She lay still and tried to identify if anyone was up, or whether it was the middle of the night. She took a long, slow breath and held it. She could hear nothing but the sound of her own heartbeat, and she strained to hear another heartbeat mingled with it, but there was nothing there. She tried to decide if that made it feel more or less real, but found no answers.

As she lay there, she remembered that this had been Anne's bed back in June. This was where Anne had her particular epiphany, she thought, then corrected herself; the first of her epiphanies. She thought of Matthias, and wondered if he knew she was here yet. She supposed so; it was that kind of family.

Which meant, of course, that Karla also knew. This finally broke her last connection with sleep, and Clare sat up. She was wearing a loose and not particularly attractive cotton nightshirt, which she supposed belonged to Liezl's mother. She stood, noting that she wasn't as wobbly as she might have expected, and felt her way to the end of the bed, and from there, to the light switch by the door.

Once she had overcome the dazzle, she looked around for her watch, which turned out to be on top of the neat pile of her clothes by the side of the bed. She picked it up and squinted at it. At first, she thought it must be only nine o'clock, but further investigation revealed it to be 3.30 in the morning. She went to the window, pulled the curtain back and looked out. Hohenügel was still and silent. She could see a faint glow, which she remembered marked the line of the fence, and she shivered at the thought of it.

She turned away from the window, and caught sight of herself in the full-length mirror. She stared at herself for a moment, thinking that she didn't look so different, aside from this odd, Victorian-looking nightgown. She pulled it off and stared at herself. She didn't feel any different, aside from the odd bout of nausea, a dull ache in her lower back from time to time, and an almost constant need to pee, and now she looked hard for the first time, to see if she looked different. She ran her hands over her stomach, convincing herself that she must be showing a little, although she was still wearing the same pair of jeans as she had all summer, and she hadn't noticed any real difference. Her breasts were not tender to the touch, as she had half-expected them to be, although she thought they had changed shape, and her bras definitely didn't fit quite as well as before. She had read somewhere that her nipples might change colour, but there seemed to be no sign of this, either. Were it not for the nausea, the missing periods, and the positive test which she had taken, she would be finding it hard to believe.

She turned the light out and got back into bed. *Who am I trying to kid,* she thought, *I am finding it hard to believe.* She went back over her timeline again; she had had sex five times in her life, all of them in the last nine months. The fact that she wasn't about to give birth ruled out the first three times, all of which had occurred in the first weeks of the year, but she continued to worry about the fourth occasion. She had been stupid, sleeping with one of her circle from school some six weeks before the trip. She replayed it in her mind again, and again came up with the same answer – Dieter was the father. And in the morning – in a few hours – she was going to have to tell him.

Morning came with sickening speed after that. Liezl's mother put her head around the door to see if she was awake, and on finding that she was, came in and sat on the bed to talk with her. Clare found this extremely uncomfortable, as she had not put the nightgown on again after her inspection, and so she spent the entire conversation with the sheets drawn up around her neck.

As one visitor left, the next arrived. Liezl at least brought some breakfast and was not in any way alarmed by Clare's state of undress. Clare, in fact, took the opportunity to dress, while they talked about the situation.

Liezl's mother had offered 'anything you need' for as long as she wanted; Liezl now spelled this out a little more.

"We had a meeting last night. Don't laugh; this is what we do. Everyone agreed that you should stay here – or with Erika – as long as you need, but we want to make sure you talk to your family and we can help you to get home if you want to do this. I suppose you want to speak with Dieter?" Clare nodded, and felt her morning sickness reassert itself – unless that was nerves.

"OK, so this is not so difficult. He is at home in the mornings – you know he works with his father at night?" Clare had no idea; she had had two or three conversations with him, all in broken German, and none of them had touched on his line of work.

"Yes, so he is late to come home, but he will be there in the morning. His father is the owner of the bar, you remember?" Now something did come back to Clare. Not only was Dieter often at the bar, but she had seen him helping out serving drinks from time to time. She nodded again; her ability to speak seemed to have temporarily deserted her.

"So, we take you there later. You want me to come in with you?" Clare reacted with alarm, and found the power of speech again

"No! I mean – I'm sorry; no, Liezl, this is not your problem; I will do this alone. You should go to school, and I will work it out."

"Yes, we thought this might be what you do. OK, it is not so hard. I can find you again after. But you should be careful, I think. Only do what you want to do." Clare agreed, but wasn't entirely sure what that might mean.

She remembered where Dieter's house was, and walked past it several times before gathering enough strength to walk up the path and knock on the door. There was no evidence of Karla's motorbike, which was something of a relief. She heard someone moving around inside, and hoped she had not woken Dieter's father, who presumably worked similar hours to his son. However, it was a dishevelled Dieter who answered the door. He was wearing only a pair of faded black jeans, and he took a moment to recognise her. Then he pulled the door open and pointed inside.

She went in and stood in the hallway while he ran upstairs. She stared after him with a sinking feeling. *He's not what I remember,* she thought, *he's not at all what I wanted.* This seemed to stiffen her resolve, and she was more ready for him when he returned, wearing more clothes and having done something to his hair. He spoke in German, but slowly enough that she could follow it.

"I thought it would be you. I heard you were back. What do you want from me?"

She had thought hard about how to answer this question, and had even practised how to do it in German, but when the time came, she stumbled and tripped over her words, and he had to help her out. She began to worry that if she just agreed to whatever he was saying that she would never actually get out what she wanted to say, but he stopped after a few minutes of this and smiled at her.

"So, you are pregnant" – she had looked up the German for 'pregnant', and so she recognised it – "and you think it is mine, and you want me to pay for it, or pay for it to go away, or marry you and make a happy family?" Clare framed her answer carefully.

"None of those. I want you to know about it, and I want to know what you would do."

"I would not want to have a baby now. You told me it was safe; perhaps you are like her, trying to trick me." Dieter sounded angry, but he looked sad and tired, and Clare saw him clearly as a young boy, not ready for any of this.

"No, Dieter, I didn't trick you. It was an accident. I don't think I want anything from you, but it is yours. It will be your baby."

"You will keep it, then?" Clare stared back at him.

"I don't know. I must decide, and you must decide, too."

"I cannot. She wants me to be the father for her baby, but I say no, now you want this for your baby. This is not what I want."

Clare hadn't expected to hear anything different - and would have been appalled if he had offered to run away with her and start a family, or something – but the reality of it still hurt.

"I have no money. My father would help, I think, but this is not so easy for him. He is alone, you knew that?" Again, Clare didn't, but she nodded to keep him talking. He carried on, "so we are always a little bit short of money. I work for him, but he can only just afford to pay me. So I do not have a lot. You would be better without a baby, too, I think?"

Clare didn't know. She hadn't known before she came, and she still didn't know, but she did know that she could never have any kind of relationship with Dieter while Karla was around.

Not that, now she saw him again, she particularly wanted a relationship with him. In the cold light of day, he looked like what he was, a scared teenage boy. One old enough to grow a beard and look the part when on his motorbike, to be sure, but still just another teenager. Older, but not necessarily wiser than she was. She stared at him, then stood up.

"Dieter, I am sorry for this. I have to make a decision, and" – she faltered. She knew what she wanted to say in English, but her German let her down. She tried to work her way around it, but it came out badly stilted. He looked at her, then tried his own version.

"You know what I want, but you don't agree?"

"No, no. I don't know what I want. I will think. I will talk to you again." She felt she had to leave before she lost the ability to stand. She headed for the door, half expecting him to try to stop her, but he just sat there. She almost felt sorry for him, sitting there looking defeated. She let herself out and walked away, not particularly caring where she went.

Later, when she was recounting this to Erika and Liezl, she felt less sure of what exactly had happened. Had she understood him correctly, had she managed to make him understand? She couldn't be sure, and Erika volunteered to go and find out, but Clare stopped her.

"No, it is my responsibility. I will think about this."

Liezl proposed a simpler solution. "We should all three go to the bar tonight, and we can talk to him there." Clare worried about this – would his father be there and overhear? Liezl seemed unperturbed by this possibility, but everything seemed to be closing in on Clare – every possible course of action seemed to be full of dangers.

She sat, alone, in Erika's bedroom later and thought about the encounter with Dieter. He seemed to her to have been inert and uncaring. She wondered if he had been high, which might explain it. Certainly, from what little she knew of him, that wouldn't surprise her. He seemed clear enough that he didn't want this baby, and presumably not any baby, given what she had gathered from the confrontation with Karla in the summer.

She felt no nearer a decision, and worried about this for a time, then changed into her other – now clean, thankfully – set of clothes in preparation for going out. The issue of money still needed to be resolved, and she couldn't continue to depend on Erika and Liezl for everything. Another thing to contemplate tomorrow, she thought.

She was on the point of leaving the room and going downstairs when she heard first the motorcycle, and then the hammering on the door. She was in no doubt what that signified, and froze for a moment, her heart pounding. She heard Erika answer the door, and – as far as she could tell – try to fend Karla off. Clare took a deep breath and went downstairs.

"It's OK, Erika; I'll deal with this," she heard herself say. She felt oddly calm and composed, and her voice was steady and clear. She walked out of the front door, passing a slightly surprised looking Karla, and kept walking. The other girl had to run after her to catch up, and Clare spun to confront her as soon as she felt her close enough. This, too, put Karla on the defensive, and Clare seized the initiative.

"No need to get angry, Karla," she said quietly but firmly, "I'm right here, and we can talk about this all you want. I understand things better now than I did before, and I would like to talk to you about it."

Karla looked at her, astonished. "Oh, do you? Well, I don't think you can begin to understand what my life is like." She was getting back into her stride now, and her voice began to reassert itself with its normal stridency as her volume increased.

"You think you can come here and spread your lies about him? You think he's just going to sit there and believe everything you say? You think I will look away while you steal him away?"

Clare was still calm, and actually lowered her voice, so that Karla was obliged to lean in closer to her to hear properly.

"No, Karla, I think none of those things. I think you and I should talk about things, as I talked to Dieter earlier. Then I will make my decision, and I will have nothing more to do with you, if that's what you want. In the meantime, could we have this conversation somewhere else? This is embarrassing for everyone." She looked back at the house pointedly, and Karla looked sheepish for a moment, then spat back "No, we talk here. I am not embarrassed, but you should be."

"Why so?" Clare began to walk away, confident that Karla would follow. "I have made a mistake, to be sure, but I'm not embarrassed about it. I feel a little stupid, but that's not so unusual, I think."

Karla stood where she was for a moment, then followed. "I would think that getting pregnant when you are hardly old enough to wipe your own backside would be embarrassing. And coming all the way across Europe to try to blame someone you don't even know? That's embarrassing."

Clare remained silent, and Karla stopped. Clare kept walking and didn't look round, sure that the conversation wasn't over. A moment later, she heard the motorbike being kick-started, then it drew up alongside her. Karla wore no helmet, and she turned to look at Clare.

"Get on. We can talk somewhere else."

Clare considered this for a moment. She remembered Andy being left to fend for himself, and wondered just how far she might be taken, and then decided that to get on would show good faith. She looked back to where Erika was still staring at this confrontation, and gave a quick thumbs-up gesture. Erika nodded, and went back inside, presumably to raise the alarm.

Clare got on the bike behind Erika. She had ridden pillion before, and easily settled into a comfortable position, although this obliged her to put her arms around Karla's waist, which caused her a little nervousness; a reaction she couldn't quite explain. Karla wasted no time in turning the bike around and roaring off towards the railway line.

They passed under the bridge, then turned right, as if heading out of the

183

village, back the way Clare had come on Sunday evening. She closed her eyes for a time after that, not really wanting to know where they were going. There were several tight turns, and she had the sensation of being driven slightly too fast in traffic. She kept her eyes closed.

After four or five minutes, she looked up at where they were, and saw the fence off to the left, below them in the valley. This was the road to the border, she recognised; the same one Andy had been taken along. They pulled over into a gravelled area on the right, and Karla killed the engine. Clare dismounted, and looked down the road to the border crossing; busier than she had expected, and somehow normal-looking. Karla almost kicked her in the stomach as she got off, and Clare looked up at her, alarmed, but this seemed to have genuinely been an accident. Karla looked more relaxed and in control of herself.

She let Karla lead the way for the first time, and they walked a short way into a field of scrubby grass, where Karla sat down. Clare sat beside her, partly because she instinctively felt that avoiding eye contact might be a good idea for a time.

Neither of them spoke for several minutes. Clare wished that she still smoked, since that would surely have broken the ice. Karla shifted uncomfortably a couple of times, then began to speak. Her voice was softer and more uncertain than Clare had ever heard before.

"I should thank you, I suppose. Now I can get off my ass and do something. He is actually a nice person; that's why I stayed for so long. But now I have what I want. He will never support me; he will never do anything unless his father tells him what to do. So I have decided – just now, as we were coming up here – what I must do."

Clare was baffled by this turn in the conversation; she had been prepared for almost anything but a confession.

"What is that, Karla?"

"I must do what you do. Get out. I will go to somewhere I have friends. He will not find me, I think. It will be better for me, and better for everyone."

"Why now? Why not before?" Clare was still processing this change, and her responses were automatic ones.

"Because now I am like you. I have a baby too."

Clare turned to look at Karla.

"His?"

"Perhaps, but I suppose no. He – well, I think you know about that. And I have other men, too. I am like you, I think."

"No, not really." Clare suddenly felt very young and out of her depth. "No; I don't have other men. I never meant for Dieter…. I mean, it was a stupid accident."

"So it really is his?"

"It is. I may give certain impressions, but I am not like that."

"Then I think you should be pleased. It is not such a good life, you know."

They fell silent. Clare was gradually coming to terms with what was happening here, and she felt herself relax a little; throw off some of the chains which she seemed to have been carrying since she first met Karla.

The silence lengthened, and Clare felt she should break it somehow.

"I know about your father," she said softly. Karla did not respond, so she pressed on. "I suppose he is as bad with you as he is with Matthias." Karla spat into the grass.

"That boy will never be anything. He has no fight in him."

"But you do?"

Karla stood and shrugged off her jacket. She lifted her shirt over her head, and Clare whistled at the bruises on her body.

"Sometimes it is not so bad. When you people were here in the summer, he didn't touch us for a month before. The day you all left – well, I have still some of those."

"And you didn't leave before?"

"You cannot understand it. It is not so simple. But now, now I have to. In case…." She ran her hands over her belly, as Clare had done the night before. Karla dressed again in silence. Clare struggled to find anything to say, then an appalling thought occurred to her.

"Karla, did he ever – I mean; is it possible…?"

Karla looked at her. "No. He tried, when I was younger, but I fight back, you know. I don't think he was serious about it, anyway. He wants power, not – not the other thing. I think so, anyway. After I was 16, he never tried again."

Clare wondered if she heard tears in Karla's voice, but when she looked, the German girl was staring, clear-eyed, at the fence.

"Every day, I wonder what it would be like over there. Just to live in a different way. But I know there are men like him there, too. Worse, perhaps – they do not have to make excuses, I think."

Clare didn't know how to respond to this, and said nothing. After a moment, she turned to look at Karla. She was still staring at the fence with an intensity which Clare found frightening. She looked away again, and Karla spoke.

"Do not expect anything from him. He is a good boy, but he is a boy. He will not want to know about you – everything is a complication for him, and he does not know what to do when things are complicated. Don't be cruel to him, though."

"But he's the father of my baby," Clare protested, "he has the right…" Karla cut her off.

"No; he has nothing. If you keep it, even then. He fucked you once – I suppose it was only once?" Clare nodded. "So, he should pay for this? Perhaps you will say, 'yes, he should', but life is not so simple. What would you do? Move here, to live with him? What kind of life would that be for you? For the baby? No; I suppose you should just leave him. Make your decision, and leave him."

"Karla, we fucked once; he didn't 'do' anything to me; we both did it. I know this is hard for you to hear" – Clare hoped she sounded convincing, because Karla seemed untroubled by this – "but he has made a baby with me. I will leave if he wants me to, but he gets to make the decision."

"Him? He wants to smoke dope and drink beer; to work as little as possible for as much money as he can get, and to fuck girls when he can. That is it. He is not a complicated person. They never are."

Clare disagreed; the connection she thought she was making with Karla seemed to be slipping away. Arguing with her over this would be easy, but Clare decided to take the other option. She nodded, as if in agreement, then asked Karla what she should do.

"About the baby? You are too young. I think you do not need an excuse to run away, and you don't really want to have it. You should have the abortion, or give it away. For me, this is best for you."

Clare hadn't used the actual word before, and even now that Karla had given voice to it, she wasn't sure she could say it out loud. She tried it out silently, but it made her feel ill.

"Well, I suppose you are right. I have all this life in front of me. But I couldn't do – you know; that thing."

"Abortion? You should say it out loud, Clare. It will make it not so scary."

"Abortion." Clare felt a chill run through her, and her nausea returned with a vengeance. She had to swallow hard several times, and that, she supposed, made one decision for her.

Karla looked at her. "No, I could not do it, either. For me, the decision is easy. For you, I don't know. Good luck." They both stood, and Karla approached Clare and hugged her tightly. Clare returned the embrace, feeling something pass between them. On the ride back to the village, she kept a firm grip on Karla's belly, marvelling at what was going on there, and in her own. Some things had been made harder by their conversation, but her decision was now clear to her.

SEPTEMBER 2003

Andrew stared at her. "And?" he said after a few minutes, when it became clear she was finished.

"And what?" Clare had been calm, even cheerful, during the telling of the tale. Now she seemed amused by his reaction. "I already told you – I have a daughter. Polly will be 25 early next year. I should feel old, but I don't. Not really."

"No, I meant – what happened? You decided to keep the baby – her. Polly; sorry. And you never came home. At least, that's what I thought I knew. What happened?"

Clare stood. "Come on, I'll tell you as you walk me home."

Andrew looked at her. She smiled again. "Sorry; I shouldn't just assume. You have other things you need to do?"

"No. No; I mean. Sorry, Clare. I'm a little stunned. Part of me is waiting for you to tell me that you're also Karla's life-long friend. And mostly, I want to know what happened to you."

Clare made pointed observations regarding paying for things and leaving, which occupied Andrew for long enough that he was able to get his thoughts in order. Once they were outside again, negotiating the lines of people sitting watching the various street entertainers, he gave voice to some of the thoughts.

"So, I suppose I want to know what happened to you after that – after Karla left. I guess that's when she went, isn't it?"

"It was. She left that night, as far as I can tell. Apparently she already had a bag packed, and just took off on the bike after she dropped me back at Erika's. One thing I do remember – in the middle of the night I woke, suddenly sure that Karla's baby was yours. Of course, there was no way of knowing – not for years, but oddly, I think I always knew." Andrew stared at her.

"And you never said anything? To Anne, or to – well, anyone?"

"No. I kept your trust, Andy. Remember Andy? He was a nice guy, a bit out of his depth? He trusted me, and I never broke that trust." Andrew stopped, his eyes suddenly full of tears. Clare looked at him briefly, then wandered over to the window of Stanford's, letting him have a moment to compose himself.

As for Andrew, he was overcome with a collision of emotions. He wanted to say a huge number of things to Clare, but couldn't begin to order his thoughts. Part of him also wanted to know something more pressing. He blew his nose, and walked over to her. They looked at the display of globes for a minute or two, then Andrew felt confident enough of his voice.

"I wonder about Karla," he said, "why she did that. You know, talked to you; made friends with you."

"She was scared and lonely too, Andrew. She hid it better than I did, but that's the truth."

"But she was; I mean…"

"She was a monster. Yes, she was, although some of it was a mask. And a victim of horrible abuse, as Matthias was. Doesn't excuse the fact that she raped you, but it does perhaps explain it."

"Raped me?" Andrew was stunned. For all that the incident had lived vividly in his mind for a quarter of a century, he had never considered it in exactly those terms; never used that word.

"Well, I don't know what else you'd call it. I don't think you were consenting, were you?" He shook his head, and the tears threatened again. He blinked, and swallowed hard.

"No. But rape? I suppose I never thought of it, because – well, it's supposed to be impossible, isn't it?"

"Is it? You tell me." They walked on; Andrew once again following; not entirely sure where they were going. Clare took his arm, as was her custom.

"Anyway, I stayed with Erika for about a month. My parents were frantic for a week or so, then they calmed down. Dieter's father put me to work in the bar"

"He knew?"

"I thought not at the time, but I was naïve. Of course he did – Dieter must have told him I was having the abortion, and he put me to work to help pay for it. Dieter and I – well, it got a bit messy for a few days; his girlfriend had just left him, I was threatening to make him into a father before he was ready, but we had a huge row one evening, then decided that I would give the baby up for adoption, and he would have no claim on it. Once I had enough money to get home, I went back to Kit's."

"Kit? Oh, your aunt." He thought for a minute. "Why not just come home?"

"I honestly can't tell you now. At the time, it just seemed like the worst thing I could possibly do. Kit suggested it as a temporary solution, and I ended up staying there for nearly two years."

"Anne said you went to Sixth Form"

"I did; in Bromley. It turns out that, even in the late seventies, my position wasn't so unusual, and various accommodations were made. I sat A-Levels a couple of months after the birth. Didn't do badly, either, although I still think I should have had an 'A' in German!"

Andrew laughed. "And Polly – how did you…"

"It was the hardest thing I've ever done, Andrew. I had made the decision, but as I got bigger, and I could feel her kicking, I knew I wouldn't be able to do it. It's a dreadful cliché, I know, but she was mine, and we were in this together. I struggled through; I even went back to Chester for a bit, then I woke up one morning and decided that I'd better get on with having a career, and – well, here I am."

"A Civil Servant? Why?"

"Oh, you know – travel the world, see exciting things, meet interesting people, childcare, that sort of thing."

"Childcare?"

"Well, the good old FCO were some way ahead of their time with that kind of thing, and it was actually surprisingly workable. Polly turned out to be highly adaptable, and we saw the world together. It sounds romantic, when it was actually a bit of a grind most of the time, but I honestly wouldn't change it. Came back to Britain about ten years ago; Polly needed some stability in her education, so I said we'd settle down until she figured out what she wanted to do. And I started to enjoy the desk work. I ended up specialising in Germany at just the right time – the early nineties were kind of exciting times in our line of work, I had a contact in Bonn – or Berlin, as it suddenly became, and Erika and I have a working relationship which – well, it still makes me smile. Did I influence her, or did she influence me? I don't know. But here we are."

"So, where is Polly now?"

"Right now, she's somewhere in the south of France, making a film. She's some kind of accountant, so it's not quite as exciting as it sounds, but she spends her time on film sets telling directors that they can't afford to follow their artistic vision."

"Sounds like you have a good relationship."

Clare fell silent.

"I suppose we do," she said after some thought. "She hated me at times; why did she not have a father; why did we have to keep moving around; why did we have to end up stuck in this dump; why wouldn't I let her spend the night with boyfriends when she was 15, that kind of thing."

Andrew laughed at this last. "We turned into our parents, didn't we?"

"Yes and no, Andrew. My parents were younger than most, I suppose. Once they were over the initial shock of Polly, they were kind of cool with it. I only fell pregnant because my mother insisted on putting me on the Pill when I was 15."

"How so?"

"Ah, the old story. I got complacent. You want to know when I knew I was pregnant?"

"When?"

"The next day. I dug my pills out of my bag, and looked at them. I'll remember it all my days – it was Thursday morning; the next unopened pill was labelled 'Monday'. I'd missed three somewhere along the journey; who knows which ones. But it was enough. If I'd not been on the Pill, I wouldn't have had the confidence to go around sleeping with strange Germans."

Something which Clare had said got through the fog in Andrew's mind. "Polly never had a father?"

"Well, not really. Dieter knew, of course, although he was in denial for years. I wanted to do something about it for a while, when Polly was younger, but then fate delivered him Peter, and it seemed apt to me. We were in Ghana, or Malaysia, or wherever, half the time anyway; it just seemed too much like hard work to keep them in any kind of contact. You want to know something funny though?"

"What?"

"When she was 16, Polly ran away to Hohenügel."

Andrew laughed, and Clare joined in.

"Like mother, like daughter – I know. She went to see him, and they got to know each other. She stayed for a month, worked in his café, and they've been close ever since, which is very pleasing."

"She knows Peter, then?"

"She does…." Clare stopped. "I don't know what their relationship is, exactly, but they are friends." Andrew had to think hard for several minutes before he worked out that Polly and Peter were not, in fact, related in any way. He sighed.

"What is it?"

"Oh, nothing. I just realised what I've missed all this time. Not just Peter; but all of it. I wonder if I could have helped Matthias if I'd known more; I wonder if I could have got to know Peter; I wonder if I could have made peace with Karla. I wonder…" he trailed off.

"Go on." They had wandered as far as Soho Square during this conversation, and Clare pointed at a bench for them to sit on. Andrew noticed the inscription on it, and smiled in recognition.

Clare saw the smile, and explained "I knew her, a little. I often come here. Another conversation for another time, I think. Go on; what were you going to say?"

"Oh, nothing. I just – I wondered if I could have been a better person; a better father and a better husband to Anne if I'd known all this. I also wondered if I could have been your friend." He faltered, then decided he had nothing left to lose. "This sounds crazy, because I hardly even knew you, but of all the people I lost touch with over the years, you were the one I missed. You were the one I imagined talking to. You'd always have some sensible advice for me, and I'd usually ignore it, and get into more trouble. Sorry; that's just crazy talk." He looked across the square, at the odd half-timbered hut in the middle of it, and beyond, to where groups of young people were coming and going. Some part of his brain noted that Clare had been silent for some time, but he resolved not to worry about that now, and just sat and watched life go by.

Eventually, Clare spoke. "It's not crazy talk, Andrew. I've been keeping tabs on you all these years, and it's really not been fair, has it? I supposed that you had a crush on me all those years ago." She looked at him, and Andrew could tell he was blushing – still as scarlet as ever, he thought to himself. "OK, consider that one answered. I wondered about you for a while, but Anne needed you more than I did, and it seemed best, especially once I was obviously going to be Anne's friend. Now, I think we missed out on some things, didn't we?"

He nodded, trying to understand just what this conversation was about. He looked at her, and she was smiling at him. "Look, I was a confused teenager, too. I liked you, or thought I did, but I never really got the chance to get to know you. Anne was a much better fit for you anyway, and – I'm sorry, but this is true – once I had gone off to Germany again, you didn't really cross my mind. Not until Anne told me you were together, and that seemed to be a good thing, so I kept my side of the bargain."

Andrew sighed again.

"Clare, I'm horribly confused, tired and frankly in need of a stiff drink. I don't quite know how I'm going to sort all this out in my mind, but thank you."

"What for? Not that I don't think you should be thanking me, I just want to know which bit you're thanking me for."

"All of it; for everything. Let me think." He fell silent for a moment.

"Thank you for helping me to see who Anne really was all those years ago; you gave me permission to fall in love with her – it wasn't your fault that I messed it up; thank you for being a true and loyal friend all these years, even when I didn't know you were doing it; thank you for agreeing to see me now, and for finally helping me understand all the things I missed. And thank you for today; it has been a wonderful day, and I'd like to do it again some time." He paused. "Oh, and thank you for one more thing. I'm going to go red again, but it's important to me. That night on the ferry, we curled up…"

"Snuggled, I like to think of it," Clare interrupted.

"Snuggled, then. And when I woke, I was highly confused and in real danger of doing or saying something stupid and clumsy-teenager-ish. You were fantastic – you extricated us from that and sent me on my way feeling like I had just helped you, instead of the other way round. I don't know how you did that, but I've always wanted to tell you how much I appreciated it." He was scarlet now – his subconscious had rekindled exactly the awkwardness he had felt at the time, but he also felt cleansed of something which he had needed to say for many years. He daren't look at her, though.

"It wasn't as easy as it looked, you know." Clare sounded uncertain now, for the first time he could remember. "I was in a terrible state really – remember all that stuff about being homesick for Hohenügel? Well, I had a pretty good idea what I was getting myself into by going home, and I just wanted to run away. You did help me, you know. You were solid and real, and just what I needed at that moment. It wasn't as easy as it looked, being a teenage girl."

Andrew laughed. "You could have fooled me. You did fool me, in truth. Ah, I wish I'd known you better then, and I wish – all kinds of things, Clare, but wishing won't make it so, and you can't go back."

"You sure?"

Andrew pondered on this. "Well, maybe not. I've been thinking about that. The last time I went, I didn't know any of this story. Now I understand that I talked to the wrong person. I'm not thrilled about the idea, but if you can help me track her down, I'd like to see Karla again; try to understand what she did, and see if she understands it. Once I've done that, I can think about being some kind of father to Peter. And maybe to my own children, too."

"They're all your own children, Andrew. But I think you're right. And, yes, I'd love to help. What do you want to do about Peter, though? What do you think you'll want to tell him?"

"I don't know, Clare. Is he happy? Does he have a good life? Everything he could want?"

"I don't know. I should ask Erika. Or Polly; she probably knows – I bet they exchange emails all the time"

"Only – I don't want to break in to that and disrupt everything. I wonder what would have happened to me if I'd found out about him when I was his age? I think it would have blown everything apart. I'm going to have to think about that one. Like I haven't thought about it every day since I was there."

"Well, my motto has always been to plunge in, and see what happens later. But that hasn't always been the absolute best policy, so I'd think twice about taking my advice, to be honest."

"Fair enough." He smiled, and for the first time since seeing Matthias back in August, felt that something good might come of all this.

Clare looked at her watch and grimaced. "I'm going to be late – I'm supposed to be going out to dinner later, and I have to go home and change. Let's agree to meet again soon, and we'll figure it out." She stood, and Andrew did likewise. She hugged him again, and if she said anything pithy and wise this time, he didn't hear it. He watched her walk across the square, and wondered when he was going to wake up.

An hour passed, and Andrew understood that no waking up was going to happen. He was aware a couple of times that people were coming past and staring, not at him, but at the bench he was sitting on, and he felt eventually that he should get up, and let others appreciate it.

As he walked towards Tottenham Court Road tube station, he allowed his mind to drift back to Clare. He had spent the time on the bench thinking about anything but Clare, but now he was going to indulge himself. He walked along Sutton Row, thinking about who Clare was, and how she had overcome what was a much worse situation than either he or Anne had endured, and had still emerged as herself. She was the same Clare; he would have recognised her anywhere. She had a joy and a freedom about her which he had been overawed by as a teenager, and she still had the same effect on him.

He was lost in thought enough to almost step in front of a black cab, whose driver let him know exactly what he thought of Andrew's ability to walk in a straight line. This snapped Andrew out of his reverie for a while; he looked up to find himself on Charing Cross Road, and turned right. He headed into Foyle's, but his aimless wandering turned up nothing he particularly wanted. He wondered if his subconscious was directing him to look for a book called *Teach Yourself Getting On With Someone You Had A Crush On 25 Years Ago, And Probably Still Do.*

On the tube ride home, he wondered about the whole idea of a 'crush'. Had he ever had a 'crush' on Anne? On reflection, he probably hadn't. He thought of her back then as someone he liked – liked as an equal, as someone to talk to, or to complain about the number of prepositions in German which took the Dative with. Later, he had understood that this friendship allowed him to get into a comfortable place with Anne; one where he could talk to her about things he would never talk to anyone else about.

Except Clare, he now thought. Clare was the one person he had ever told about Karla. Clare was the one person he wished with all his being had still been around during his marriage. He supposed she would have told him a few home truths about what he was doing, and why. And –

And you're going to have to admit it to yourself, at least, he thought as he walked through his front door. He undressed and showered off the London grime, and as he showered he reflected. Clare had been the one. At that critical point in his life when his emotional state was developing, Clare had been the one to fix it for him. He had been aware of her for years; one of the fashionable kids – did they call it 'cool' back then? He couldn't remember. As he reached those awkward years, when he was trying to figure out what he felt about things, he had felt under a great deal of peer pressure to like the things which other boys liked – he remembered pictures of enormously pneumatic Page 3 girls being passed around, and thinking that he didn't quite get it.

But Clare had resolved that for him. He remembered one day watching her as she answered some tricky maths question; this would have been in the Third Form, so they'd have been about 14, he supposed. She clearly didn't know the answer, but her smile, and her confident air alerted him to something. She managed to convince the teacher that the answer was on the tip of her tongue, but that she just couldn't quite bring it to mind. She essentially bluffed her way out of a difficult situation by using her charm, and Andrew understood something about himself that day. He could date the 'crush' from that moment; she had something which he couldn't have defined then, and wasn't sure he could define now.

He thought a little guiltily of Anne; she wasn't as strikingly pretty as Clare; her body was of an altogether more solid and rounded type, and her personality was more sedate and calm. He had never actually cheated on her – despite what she may have assumed – but he had come close on a couple of occasions, and they had been with women who reminded him of Clare – slender, attractive women with spiky personalities. He thought about that, and about Clare now, and he realised that he was in an impossible situation.

But at least that situation now allowed him to spend time with her, and he could find out whether she had always been an impossible ideal, or if there really was something there.

"Who am I trying to kid?" He spoke out loud, to his mild surprise; he really wasn't the 'talking to himself' kind. "She's not only out of my league; she's Anne's friend, and I'm – well, look at me." He stepped out of the shower, and considered his reflection in the mirror. That seemed to bring him to his senses. Clare wasn't about to be swept off her feet by a balding, overweight, over tall senior manager. He stared at himself for several minutes, then snapped the light off, and stomped off to get dressed.

PART 3 – MATTHIAS

OCTOBER 2003

As he watched Heathrow disappear below him for the second time in three months, Andrew wondered again what he was doing on this flight. He had had to take a week's holiday to fit it in, and he really couldn't spare a week off in the middle of a busy period at the end of October. Why was he here? The short answer, of course, was Clare. She had gradually become his friend over the past few weeks, and while he still thought he felt more for her than she did for him, he wondered if that was beginning to change. Under her influence, he had begun to see the world in a different way; feeling more confident in it, and more able to take control of things.

He was going to Germany again because he wanted to, in truth. Clare had facilitated it, but it was Andrew's decision to go, and Andrew's desire to resolve this whole thing. With Peter; with Matthias, and with Karla. All three potential encounters worried him, and he wasn't certain he would have done it without Clare. He had talked to her at length about what to do; how to approach things, and what he wanted to get out of it. He felt safer knowing that Clare would be there to meet him off the plane, and would hold his hand, metaphorically speaking, through the whole thing. She had even promised him a surprise or two along the way.

Only now he was on the flight did it occur to him to worry about exactly what kind of surprises they might turn out to be. He was cautiously optimistic that he knew all the major facts now; he already knew that the plan was to go and see Karla, then trek all the way to Hohenügel to see Matthias and Peter; he couldn't think of anything else which could still crawl out of the woodwork and startle him.

He tried to relax by listening to his iPod. This had been a birthday present from his children – for which, read Anne – a couple of weeks before. He had thought it preposterous; he had only a nodding acquaintance with popular music made after about 1980, and he wasn't sure that you could fit entire operas onto them.

But it had turned out that you could, and he had filled it with Mozart and Verdi, and several symphonies which he had always meant to listen to, but had never quite got round to. He listened to one of these – Shostakovich 4 – and it utterly absorbed him, to his surprise; he hadn't thought of himself as a Shostakovich kind of person, but he could identify with the tormented music; the turmoil and the melancholy resolution astonished him, and he found himself close to tears at the end, and to his bewilderment realised that he had almost missed the landing. They were taxiing to the gate in Frankfurt, and he had to shake his head a couple of times to clear it.

As he waited for his case to emerge, he thought about his birthday. He hadn't particularly intended to mark turning 41, but Clare had called him that morning, wished him many happy returns, and invited him to dinner. They had eaten at some fashionable Indian place in Soho, and it had been a wonderful experience. They hadn't talked about Germany, or about Anne and the children; instead, they taught each other about music, art and the simple pleasures in life. She had persuaded him to listen to The White Stripes; he had urged her to try Mahler. At the end of the evening, they had stood together on the corner of Wardour Street, and hugged. It seemed to him that they were hugging just for the enjoyment of it. He felt no particular desire to take it further; clearly understanding that she was declaring her friendship and not anything else. He disengaged first, and smiled down at her. She smiled back; an open and friendly smile, which he wished he could have photographed, then she had thanked him and walked away. Only later, in the solitude of his narrow bed, did he wonder what might have been. This, he felt, was progress.

He finally emerged from the baggage claim area to be greeted by that same smile. His determination to keep a poker face must have worked, because as she hugged him, Clare whispered in his ear: "Not even a smile? Come on, Andrew, it's not that bad. *I'm* pleased to see *you!*" He blushed and stood back, but she caught him, and kissed him in that multi-cheeked way which the English find so awkward. This gave him time to recover his thoughts, and then to apologise.

"Sorry, Clare – I was thinking of something else…"

Clare grinned at him, and he tried a smile in return, then worried about how it must have looked, because Clare's expression changed to something he couldn't read. She led the way, and Andrew followed her, thoroughly discomfited again. Five minutes in her company, and all the hard work he felt he had put in had been undone.

She led him to a sleek-looking silver Mercedes in the car park. He remarked on it.

"Well, normally we get drivers, and there's not much protocol for hiring cars, but I do it quite often when I'm here – the paperwork would make you faint. But because I rack up points all the time, I occasionally get to upgrade. Nice, isn't it?" He agreed, and got in. Clare drove smoothly and fast, in what he recognised in some way as the German style – no messing around, just get on with it as quickly and calmly as possible.

The hotel she had booked for them was only five minutes' drive away – at German speeds – and appeared to be in the middle of an industrial estate or business park. Clare apologised for this. "There seems to be some kind of convention on at the moment – everything is booked. Best I could do, but it seems OK, and it does have a pool. Hope you brought your trunks." Andrew had, after checking the place out online the day before. He wasn't sure if he was prepared for Clare to see him in swimming gear, but had packed them anyway. Now, he began to worry about that.

As it turned out, Clare seeing him in trunks was the least of his worries. It was early evening by the time they had checked in, reserved a table for dinner, and gone up to their rooms, which were on separate floors. Within two minutes of him throwing his case on the bed, Clare had called him. "Coming for a swim, then? I've had a long, boring day talking to Trade Commissioners; I need to swim." Andrew agreed, and said that he would meet her downstairs.

By the time he got there, Clare was in the water, efficiently crawling up and down the length of it. Andrew fancied himself a reasonable swimmer, but he was sure he couldn't keep up with Clare, so he slipped into the pool and hung on to the side and watched her. She's even elegant in the water, he thought. After several more lengths, she swam over to him.

"Not swimming, Andrew? It's a nice pool, even if it's a bit short. Someone like you will be at the other end before you get into your stroke, I'd have thought. Come on, let's see you swim."

He ducked under, then pushed off and swam lazily across to the side of the pool she had been using. After letting some of the more determined patrons pass, he joined the line of lap swimmers. He felt his shoulders protest, and at one point one of his triceps twinged alarmingly, but he was soon in the rhythm of it. He was right in his assessment of their relative speeds; Clare passed him twice as he plunged along, and by the time he reached the end of his stamina, she was already sitting on the side watching him. He needed some time to get his breath back, but Clare wasn't even breathing heavily. He looked up at her, sitting on the side, and complained about being old and unfit. Clare smiled. "Less of the old, thank you – we are the same age, after all." Andrew felt slightly shamed by this – he was badly out of condition, if indeed he ever had been in condition, and Clare looked like she worked out three times a week. Which she probably did.

He tried not to look at her as she got up and walked over to where she had left her towel. He resolutely averted his eyes, and looked at the clock on the wall at the far end. Suddenly, she was back beside him. He sensed her, and turned, to be confronted by her feet. He looked up, and she asked him if he'd like a sauna.

He thought about this for a moment, before deciding that he would, as long as it wasn't too hot. He had previous experience of nearly passing out in too much heat, and couldn't face the embarrassment in front of Clare. He hauled himself out of the pool, aware that he looked at his most ungainly doing so, and followed Clare to the far corner of the pool, where the sauna appeared to be set into the wall – all that was visible was a large wooden door. Clare held the door open for him, and he stepped in.

As soon as he did so, however, he knew he had made a big mistake. The sauna was large, and not unpleasantly hot, but it was also full of naked Germans of various shapes and sizes. There was a row of hooks just inside the door, and it appeared to be policy to disrobe here, and collect a towel to sit on. Andrew couldn't back out now – it plainly wasn't too hot, and he had in any case only just come in. Clare walked past him, and he looked away. She moved swiftly in the periphery of his vision, then came and stood beside him, holding her towel so that her modesty was mostly preserved. He thought, inevitably, of Karla and the terror he had felt on understanding that she was naked, all those years before. He had no idea what to do, and simply froze. Clare spoke softly to him.

"Come on, big guy – you're blocking the door. Just come in and sit down if you're not comfortable; nobody will mind. They know you're English by now; they'll be expecting it."

He shuffled awkwardly over to the pile of towels. He was rewarded by the rear view of Clare as she walked the length of the sauna, murmuring 'Guten Abends' to everyone she passed. At this point removing his trunks became moot. Although it would be plain enough to everyone who cared to look that he was suffering some discomfort, there was no way he could hide it without anything on. He grabbed a towel, rearranged himself – surreptitiously, he hoped – and wrapped it around his waist, trunks and all. No-one looked up and the conversations continued as before. He walked over to where Clare had been heading, but kept his eyes firmly fixed on the floor as he did so. Once he reached the end, he had to navigate by her laugh. He sat beside her without looking in her direction, and tried to organise himself, so that it might not be so blindingly obvious to everyone just how embarrassed he was.

Clare sat silently beside him for a while. He looked around the sauna without looking at her; she was by far the most attractive woman in here, and he felt no compunction about looking at the other women to verify this. The only place he couldn't look, of course, was to his right. He could feel Clare's skin radiating heat as she sat there, and wondered how long it would be before he could reasonably make a run for it. At least he wouldn't have to stop and put anything on, he thought.

Finally, Clare spoke. "I'm sorry, Andrew – this was thoughtless of me. It's just normal to me; I honestly didn't think twice. I should have warned you. I appreciate that you're carefully not looking in my direction, and I think that's possibly the nicest thing anyone's done for me in a long time, but it's actually OK with me if you want to look. It'll make conversation easier, don't you think?"

Andrew supposed so. He was sure that if he looked he would actually physically turn back into the fifteen-year-old version of himself, but when he finally did, taking care to look into Clare's eyes, he found that nothing terrible actually happened. They talked, about her day, and his flight, and he gradually relaxed enough to be able to look at more of Clare than just the bridge of her nose. She was sitting close to him, and any attempt to look at any more of her would require quite a lot of head movement, and seem blatant, so he compromised by looking away, then returning his gaze toward her slowly.

Naked, he could see that she was not quite the svelte teenage figure she had appeared in her swimsuit. She had aged significantly more gracefully than he had, to be sure, but she still had creases and bits which sagged a little, and this made him feel better. After some more time had passed, he began to feel ridiculous and English, wrapped up in his towel. He unfolded it, but nothing would convince him to take the trunks off – he knew that at least one part of him would not be under his control if he did, and that really would be too much for him to take.

It was Clare who announced that their time was up; Andrew had lost track of time, and had not really noticed as the temperature had risen, but Clare told him that this was long enough for someone who was not used to it, and she got up to leave. Andrew had decided that he should be the first to leave; that way, he could walk in front of her, and be waiting for her outside when she emerged. This plan, however, was scuppered by Clare being quicker than he was. By the time he was up – noticing a certain light-headedness as he did so – she was already walking away from him. He stopped – giving himself time, he told himself, to let the light-headedness pass – and watched as she casually pulled the costume back on. For a moment, he uncharitably wondered if this had been one of Clare's surprises; the ritual humiliation, but he decided that her apology had been genuine. He took a deep breath, and followed her out to the cold shower, which was on the wall beside the door. Clare went first, and he looked away again, as if by reflex. She tapped him on the shoulder when she was done, then jogged back over to the pool and dived neatly in to do more lengths while he lowered his body temperature.

Dinner was pleasant enough; the restaurant was a kind of themed cube inside the foyer of the hotel; the theme appeared to be a Bavarian inn, although the waiter took great pains to explain that it was actually Austrian, and so they dutifully ate Austrian food and drank Austrian wine.

Andrew said little throughout the meal; his thoughts were in turmoil again, and he was acutely aware that he was only a few hours away from meeting Karla; a prospect which would almost certainly alarm him if he allowed himself to think about it too much. Clare was also uncharacteristically quiet; they must, he thought, look like a long-married couple who were barely on speaking terms.

Eventually, he thought he should say something, so asked the question which had been bothering him all along; where exactly they were going tomorrow, and how Clare knew where to go.

"She's in a town called Bretten, which is most of the way to Stuttgart from here. It took some time to track her down, but Liezl found her in the end – apparently, there was a distant cousin who kept in touch."

"What does she do?"

"It's not completely clear to me; Liezl said that she's some kind of counsellor; working with young people, but I don't know any more than that, I'm afraid." This took a minute or two to sink in, then another few minutes while Andrew worked out what he thought about it. Finally, he said, "Well, I suppose she has enough experience."

"That was my reaction, too. I have a feeling she might actually be very good at it."

"Is she expecting us?" Andrew was suddenly worried that they would get there, and be thrown out.

Clare looked uncomfortable. "Sort of. She knows I'm coming, and that I'm bringing someone she might like to meet, but she doesn't know it's you."

Andrew began to ask why not, before catching himself. "Of course; at least this way, you'll get in the door. Does she remember you?"

"We talked on the phone. She remembers me. And you. All will become clear, Andrew. At least, I hope so."

Andrew fell silent again at this. Clare caught the waiter's eye, and dealt with the bill. Andrew tried to protest, but she was having none of it.

"Least I can do, after – you know. I really am sorry about that."

Andrew nodded, and drained his wine. He felt restless and in need of fresh air, so he announced to Clare that he was going for a walk.

"Good idea, Andrew. I'll join you."

He thought for the briefest of moments, then agreed. They walked out of the main door. It had got dark, and colder than they had anticipated. Neither of them was dressed for a chilly autumn evening, and the business park was deserted and a little creepy. The walk, therefore, was brisk and short. Andrew led the way back, Clare on his arm. She spoke softly, and he had to strain to catch her.

"I wonder, Andrew. I wonder if this is all a good idea. I know I suggested it, but you know what I'm like with things; act first, think later. Tell me this is a good idea."

He wanted to tell her that it wasn't; that it was crazy, and they should just stay here, eating schnitzels and drinking unpalatably sweet wine until it was time to go home, but he had come this far.

"It'll be fine. We're here now, and if I don't do this now, I never will. It's time, Clare. It's time to face up to the past, and what it made us."

She hugged him closer and shivered. "Come on, then; let's have a nightcap."

The hotel bar was deserted, and they sat in what now felt like companionable silence, drinking grappa – Andrew had drawn the line at schnapps. Once the drinks were gone, he looked at his watch, and Clare smiled at him.

"Time for bed? We'll make an early start in the morning, so it's probably a good idea. Come on, walk me to my door."

They went up in the lift, and Clare dragged him out when they reached her floor. "Don't worry; I just don't agree with saying goodnight in elevators."

She hugged him, putting her arms up around his neck and drawing his head down to her neck. He felt her soft warm skin against his cheek, and felt like crying. He was suddenly acutely aware that his body was reacting to hers, and he tried to pull back. She gripped him more tightly.

"I know I keep saying it Andrew, but I'm sorry. I really fucked that up earlier, and I know I've messed with your head when you really needed to be left alone. If it was anyone other than you, I'd probably invite you in now – fuck it and forget it has worked for me surprisingly often – but it *is* you, and I need us to be friends. And anyway, it would never work, would it?"

Andrew pulled away from her embrace, to Clare's evident surprise. His heart pounding, he looked at her.

"Clare, what the fuck? I mean, you're probably just trying to be nice to me, and I appreciate that, but could you stop whatever it is you're doing now? I'm not one of your playthings."

He turned and smacked the call button a little too hard. Clare sighed behind him, and he turned again.

"I'm sorry." Andrew had meant to say it, but the words came out of Clare's mouth first. "I like you Andrew, and I want us to be friends. As you can see, I'm really not very good at it, though. You know, if you never wanted to see me again after this, I wouldn't be that surprised. Good night, Andrew. Fresh start in the morning, I think."

The lift pinged softly behind him, and he took that as his cue. Once in the safety of his room he stood and stared out of the window for what felt like hours, wrestling with his thoughts and trying not to burst into tears – of rage, frustration, or just plain sadness, he couldn't quite tell. He thought more than once of calling her room and talking, but felt that would be giving in to whatever it was she wanted, and eventually he undressed and slept.

In spite of everything he slept well, and woke feeling alert. *This never happens to me on business trips*, he thought. He ate breakfast in his room, and headed downstairs well before their agreed start time, only to find Clare ready to go, and having paid both bills. This caused him a great deal of discomfort, but Clare smoothed it away with a smile and an instruction not to worry about it.

He had dressed almost as if for a business meeting, missing only a tie, and Clare, he noticed, was similarly smartly dressed.

"No leather jacket?" he asked. Clare grinned at him. "I have it with me, but no; not today. I feel like having my work head on, and this" – she waved a hand at herself – "helps. Anyway, you're looking businesslike yourself." He smiled, and let her lead him down to the car.

The journey to Bretten passed mainly in silence. He let her entertain him with some of the music she liked, and he was surprised to hear that it wasn't all as bad as he had feared. Clare's iPod was more battered and well used than his, and she had it hooked up to the car radio via the cassette player, which intrigued him – perhaps he could do that in his car at home.

After they left the Autobahn, he felt the tension in the car increase. The countryside they were passing through was unremarkable, and even the small towns they came to seemed fairly nondescript. Perhaps they were actually architectural jewels, but Andrew was preoccupied, and he wasn't really taking anything in.

Bretten, however, interested him. It looked much like any other town as they drove in, but Clare quickly found the centre, and parked close to some distinctively German-looking half-timbered buildings. Even in his distracted state, Andrew could see that this was a very attractive town, and wondered if there would be time to see some of it later.

It was not quite ten in the morning, and Clare had arranged to meet Karla at 11. They wandered through the streets, finding a map by a bus stop. Andrew supposed he should be taking notes or something, but Clare seemed to have it all under control, and he let her lead. They found a coffee shop, and sat there for more than half an hour, nursing espressos. They talked about inconsequential things, while Andrew felt the knot in his stomach grow tighter by the minute.

He managed to get Clare to let him pay for the coffees, and then followed her back along the way they had come, She consulted the piece of paper she had in her pocket only once, and then led them into a dim passageway between two old buildings. This turned into a small courtyard with a solid-looking green door at one end. Clare hauled on this, and led him inside.

Karla's office was up three flights of alarmingly old and creaky stairs, and Andrew had to duck at every turn to avoid being brained by the ceiling. At the top of the stairs, Clare put a hand on his chest, and told him to wait there. She went in alone, and came out again almost immediately.

"Actually, you can come in here – there's a kind of waiting area. Wish me luck." On an impulse, Andrew grabbed her arm, turned her towards him, and bent to whisper in her ear.

"Change of plan, Clare. I'm going in. Wish *me* luck, won't you?"

He pushed open the door Clare had been heading for, then almost apologised and turned back. The woman behind the desk was about Karla's height, he supposed, but entirely grey-haired and old-looking; he was remembering an angular, under-nourished teenaged girl; this was a well-fed middle-aged woman. Andrew stared at her, then as she smiled that lopsided, sardonic smile at him, realised he was, after all, in the right place.

"Well, English boy. It's been a while, hasn't it?"

Her accent was a little less polished than he remembered, but her command of English was still as good as it had been. Andrew had been thinking about this moment for several days; ever since it became clear that it was actually going to happen, but he was robbed of speech, mainly because the Karla who was now getting up and coming towards him was so unlike what he had expected. He started to offer his hand for her to shake before he caught himself. He cleared his throat, and she looked at him quizzically.

Still no words presented themselves. She sighed. "I'm a little surprised to see you here. I – OK, look, sit down. We'll talk about it."

As he sat, he looked around her office, which was neat and ordered. It looked like a business office more than some kind of consulting room, and he wondered what exactly it was she did here. This gave him an idea, so as he tried to get comfortable on the brown leather couch, he asked.

"I counsel. Teenagers, mainly – young people who have got into things which they can't deal with. It might sound familiar to you."

Andrew nodded as he tried to assimilate this. Karla, the vengeful and obsessively predatory girl had turned into some kind of earth-mother figure. He could see the person sitting before him in this kind of role – she seemed like a kindly aunt; someone you could trust with your secrets, and whose advice you could believe in, but he couldn't imagine the self-centred Karla he had known being able to do that.

He tried to formulate a way of asking her about it, but she was ahead of him.

"I'm not the person I was – not the person he made me. It cost me a lot to be rid of him, and he's still in the shadows somewhere, but this is how I'm getting my revenge. He would never have understood."

Andrew finally managed to get his own thoughts in gear. Although he had intended to move on to the subject gradually, he just couldn't help himself.

"But what about your own child? Didn't he need you?"

Karla looked at him evenly. She betrayed no particular emotion, but he fancied her voice was a little strained.

"It's not a simple story. When I left Peter, it was because I was doing more harm than good. I could feel *his* presence in everything I did; I was getting more and more angry, and I would have done something bad. Also, I was on so many different drugs – alcohol too. It wasn't a healthy situation. I left because it was the best thing for everyone. It wasn't easy, but the drugs helped. Later, after I was recovered, I wanted to go back, but I just couldn't. The wall was too high. And there was still a big problem with my brother. He has his father in him, too, and someone could have been hurt. It was a big setback, so I knew." She fell silent, and Andrew looked at her. He tried to feel sorry for her, but it wasn't easy.

"You know that I know about Peter? The truth, I mean."

"I guessed it was so. Or why would you be here?" She looked Andrew in the eye. "What do you think? Do you have other children?"

Andrew felt like getting up and walking out. He wanted something from this encounter, but to be grilled by Karla wasn't it. He took a deep breath, and answered without considering what he was going to say.

"I've known for about two months. I don't know what I think about it yet – it's still too new. Until I came in here and saw you, I'd have said that I would most likely just let it go – he doesn't really need me in his life, and I guess he doesn't know about me. But sitting here, I feel – I don't know; something. Something important. I want to make sure he's OK; that nothing happens to him. He has – oh, I don't know. He has grandparents who don't even know he exists; he has a half-sister and a half-brother; he probably has a right to know this stuff. If he hasn't already been told."

"Told? Who would tell him?"

"Your brother, I suspect. He must know; he must pretty much always have known. He tried to convince me that he knew I wasn't Peter's father, but the more I think about it, the more convinced I am that he knows. He was testing me, I think – trying to see if I would come back and cause trouble."

Karla stared at him. "Clare told me on the phone you had been there. I didn't think – oh, well. It's done now. Matthias will have told him; that's what he does. He is not as - what would you say? He is scarred; more than I am. I guess he still has problems with it all. It looked like that to me the last time."

"When was that? You have been back?"

"I went back to see Peter last year – he was having girl troubles, and I wanted to see him. Matthias pretended I was not there the whole week; did not speak to me, the whole thing. It was strange, but my brother is a little strange, I'm afraid. It was also probably the best thing – I cannot reach him, whatever I try. "

During this last exchange, Andrew had heard the door open behind him. He realised that both their voices had been raised above normal conversation level, and wasn't surprised to hear Clare's voice from behind him.

"I have long wondered about that. He doesn't talk to me when I am there. Of course, I'm always with Erika, and I suppose there are problems there." Clare moved around to sit beside him, and Andrew shifted a little to accommodate her.

"Problems? Only in Matthias' mind. He thinks – this is what I know, but it could be out of date now; he thinks that they are all angry at him still because of the shooting, and that he broke up the family. In his mind, they blame him for his mother's sickness, and he probably does blame himself still. If he hadn't done what he did, she wouldn't have had to protect him, and..."

Andrew was startled, but tried not to show it. "Shooting? He told me many things, but not about a shooting."

Karla stood up and lifted her sweater up. For a terrifying moment, Andrew thought she was going to pull it off – she seemed not to be wearing anything under it, but she stopped when her midsection was uncovered. She traced the line of an old, jagged scar with her index finger. "He could have killed us both," she said matter-of-factly. "It was the worst pain I have ever experienced; much worse than childbirth."

Andrew was the first to react. "Matthias did that to you? He – what? He shot you?"

"Who knows what he wanted to do, but he would have shot Peter if I hadn't seen what was happening." She lowered the sweater and sat down again. "I don't think he really meant it, but it still happened. Then he just let his mother be blamed for it."

Andrew, who had heard Matthias' version of the story, worked it out first. "So, when he went to 'rescue' you; it was him who assaulted you; it was him who was arrested? He told me..."

"It was her. Yes, he still believes that, I think. She accepted the blame, but he was there. I haven't thought about it for a long time now, but that's what happened. It was not really his fault, of course, but still – he shot me. And then, when I left Peter, he tried to stop me ever seeing him again. Maybe I don't blame him for that one, but we don't talk now."

Andrew looked into Karla's eyes, but he couldn't read her at all. "Peter is my son too. Did that never occur to you? Maybe I would like some say in his life? Maybe I had a right to know? Maybe" – and here he faltered, because he wasn't at all sure where this thought was going – "Maybe I could have done something?"

Karla stared at him, her expression unchanging. When she spoke, her voice was calmer, more of a professional's tone:

"I did not think of you, English boy, that is the truth. I was not always in control of my life, but you were not in my thoughts. I needed Peter to get me out of there; after that, nothing mattered."

Clare bristled, and made to say something, but Karla cut her off, her voice back to the strident near-shout.

"You stay out of this, Clare. None of this would have happened without you. You stole the baby which was mine; you made me leave; you took Dieter away from me; you even made my brother come to look for me. You are the cause of all this. Him" – she looked back at Andrew – "I can speak to, but you I cannot."

Clare stood, and Andrew made to stand with her, but she put a hand on his shoulder and whispered "stay; you might learn something more". She walked back out through the door and slammed it shut behind her. Andrew heard her footsteps on the stairs, then the big outside door thud shut.

The room fell silent, then Karla asked if he would like some lunch. Andrew, unsure what was going on now, hesitantly accepted.

The two of them walked back out through the courtyard, and Karla led Andrew down some streets he hadn't seen before. They ended up at a traditional German restaurant in a disappointingly modern-looking building, but Karla assured him that the food was worth putting up with the lack of ambience.

She ordered spätzle for him, telling him that he couldn't come here and not have it. Andrew had a vague memory of eating it once before, and feeling very full afterward, but he agreed to Karla's suggestion with a brief nod.

Karla made small talk about Bretten while they waited for the food to arrive, but Andrew paid little attention to her; he was lost in his own thoughts about Peter and Matthias. Matthias had seemed normal enough to him, but as Anne had pointed out, there was something about his story which didn't quite add up – the more Andrew thought about it, the more obvious it seemed that he knew about Peter; and if that was the case, why the charade? And the whole prison thing had sounded odd to Andrew. If what Karla said was true – and that was a whole other area of speculation – then it made more sense.

He ate under Karla's watchful gaze, and he had a memory of her watching him eat breakfast one day; her gaze then had been predatory, he supposed; now it was mainly curiosity. He gave up the uneven struggle with the food after only getting through half of it, and Karla laughed.

"You used to eat more, I remember."

"I remember you watching me," he replied before he had thought about it. She continued to look at him. He felt it was now or never. "What was it about me? Why did you – well, why me, I suppose?"

She sat back and looked down at the table as she spoke.

"It was clear at the time, but now.... No, I should tell you. I hid from my problems for too long. I needed to get pregnant. It was the only way I could see of getting out. School was finally over, and he was getting worse. I couldn't leave on my own – he told me what would happen if I did. But I knew if I had another life to protect, this would break his spell. Dieter would not do it, which is why...." She looked at Andrew, who did not react, then looked down again. "Anyway, it might have been someone else, but I needed someone who would never know; I think even then I needed this to be just about me – something I could do without anyone's help. And I thought it would be easy – boys are very easily tempted, I thought. In fact, I know it – I see it every day. But not you."

"Not me. So you raped me."

Karla's head snapped up to look at him. She stared into his eyes, but he would not look away. Eventually, she breathed out. "Yes, I did. All my life since then, I have told myself that it was OK, that you were a boy – boys dream about those things happening." She paused, then went on. "But I always knew what I had really done. I don't know what to say."

You could try apologising, he thought, but he said nothing. He didn't want to force it out of her, even when she showed no sign of doing it by herself. Instead, he found himself asking her a question.

"What would the counsellor Karla tell the teenage Karla, do you think?"

"I cannot answer that, because I am the same person. If you ask me what I say to someone who has done this today, I would tell them to look inward, and understand the damage they might have done, but I cannot tell myself this – it is too hard.

"I have my own counsellor; it is the law in Germany. I talked with him about everything, but not that – not how Peter came to be. I did not lie; I just avoided it." She looked away again, and Andrew wondered if she might be crying, unlikely though that might seem. They finished their meal in silence, and Andrew offered to pay, which Karla accepted with a dry laugh.

Outside, it had grown colder. Andrew stood awkwardly, looking back to where Karla was chatting to the restaurant owner. He felt he should try to find Clare, but he felt equally strongly that he still hadn't finished with Karla. A snatch of Shakespeare floated into his mind; something about standing in pause where he should first begin, but it drifted out of mind before he could pin it down. Karla's cough brought him back to the present.

"You wait for me? Even after all this time? It's true what they say about the English, isn't it?"

"What's that?"

"You would rather be killed than be rude. It's silly to make generalisations, but sometimes – it's a little bit true, isn't it? Your body is telling me you want to run away, but here you are – doing the polite thing; the English thing. I wonder – maybe all I should have done was just ask you nicely – perhaps..."

Andrew interrupted her. "Of course I bloody would! All you had to do was be nice to me – show an interest. For God's sake; I was 15. I hadn't a clue what was going on, but I was in awe of you. I think I still don't understand most of it, but all it would have taken was a few kind comments, for you to show an interest in me, and I'd have given you what you wanted. That's..." Andrew stopped, aware that he was shouting; aware that the restaurant owner was staring at him from behind the glass door, and that Karla was looking calmly into the middle distance, as if she wasn't even hearing him. She spoke, much more softly.

"I know. If it makes you feel better, it took about ten years of therapy to understand why I did the things I did then; why I was that kind of person. I always knew the reason, of course, but I never really thought about why I was that way. It was..."

"It was about power. I know that – I knew it then, I think, although I didn't really know about your father then. I just knew that you were determined to be in control."

"Yes, that's part of it. Also, I needed to be cruel. You know that you weren't the only one – just the one who actually got me pregnant."

Andrew hadn't thought about it, but it didn't particularly surprise him. He remembered something Matthias had said – something about being one of a long list. He said nothing, and Karla began to walk. Clare was nowhere to be seen, but he couldn't allow himself to worry about that for the moment. Karla's voice remained at the calm, soothing volume it had been – presumably her counsellor's voice, he thought.

"It was about power, and control, and cruelty. All the things he taught me." As it had earlier, the "he" was almost spat out – *not as cured as you might think*, Andrew thought.

"Almost all, I suppose. I speak good English because of him. And – no; that's it, really. I have this horrible personality, and good English. Doesn't really cancel out, though." For the first time, Karla looked sad, and Andrew felt a twinge of something which wasn't quite pity, but wasn't far off it. He felt he should say something, but all he could think of was that she had done this terrible thing to him, and wouldn't acknowledge it. What did he want? He supposed it was an apology, but he was wary of that thought, because he suspected that an insincere apology would only make things worse. Finally, he spoke.

"Look. I have not had a bad life so far. Most of the things which happened to me were my choice. I married Anne, I had children, I divorced – all because of my choices. I have a reasonably decent job – again, thanks only to me. Something happened to me that summer which wasn't in my control, and I thought I was over it a long time ago, but I never was – and, deep down, I think I've always known that. I wasn't sure about coming here; meeting you again, but I think I'm glad I did. It doesn't solve anything; doesn't make it better, but at least I know. I'm sorry you had such a crap life, and I'm sorry about Peter, because if I'd known about him, I would have done a lot of things differently."

"Don't be sorry – I do not regret anything in my life; it's just what happened, and I absorb it and go on. You understand this?" Andrew wasn't sure, but nodded anyway – the polite thing to do. She continued, "So, I'm interested – you said that at least you know. What do you know?"

"I know that the mother of my oldest child is not actually a monster, which is what I had been led to believe."

"By my brother?"

"Not entirely. You made a strong impression. But yes; if I'm honest, I thought of you as this strange, frightening dream which may or may not have been real until I found out what had come of it. Then I got angry; now, I'm mostly sad. So that's what I know."

Karla stopped – they had reached the entrance to the courtyard – and laid her hand gently on his arm.

"I won't apologise, because that's not what I do. And whatever the situation was, it also was where Peter came from, and I can't apologise for him." A thought struck Andrew.

"Do you love him?"

She stared at him. "Of course I do. But I do not love like most people love, and it seems very strange to most people, I think. I do not need to be in his life to love him."

"Does he know?"

She was silent for a long time; long enough for Andrew to get a little uncomfortable. Eventually, she spoke; her voice a little more fragile than before.

"Yes, I think he does. I left him when he was eight or nine – I don't even know for sure – and in that time, I have seen him perhaps once per year. We don't talk about love – I don't trust my emotions with my family. But I think he does, you know?" Andrew looked past her at the courtyard and the green door at the end of it. She looked round, and commented that she would probably have someone already waiting for her. Andrew stepped back, giving her permission to leave, but she seemed reluctant. He thought of something else:

"What did you tell him? About his father?" Karla looked away for an instant, but quickly returned her gaze to his.

"When he was young, I told him that his father had gone away; I always thought he understood that his father was dead, you know? Later, I wrote to him and told him that you were a one-night stand, and that I was embarrassed about that."

"You never told him about me?"

Karla almost laughed, then caught herself. "No. What good would it do? He had Dieter; he was growing up not so bad. I only remembered that you were Andy, not more. I hate to tell you, but you were only one small part of my life then."

Andrew thought about this, and felt some of his sympathy and understanding slip away. She spoke again.

"Will you see him? Clare told me on the phone that you are going there."

"I don't know yet. I will have to think about it. At the moment, I assume I will."

"Well, if you do, please give him this." She pulled on his arm, and he bent closer to her, expecting perhaps a whispered message. She kissed him lightly on the cheek.

"Best I can do, English boy. Best I can do." She turned and hurried down the passageway. He stared after her until the green door slammed shut, then he took a deep breath, and put his hand up to his cheek. It was dry, and he wondered if he had imagined it. But the kiss had left some kind of imprint on his senses. It had happened.

He was startled out of his musing by Clare's voice.

"Well, come on then. It's a long old drive, and we'll have to get round Frankfurt. Best get going."

He spun around, expecting to see her smiling at him, but she looked tired and older than she had that morning. He wanted her to explain to him what had just happened, but he wasn't sure she had even heard — where had she been all that time?

She read his mind. "I was just over there" — pointing at a café across the road — "I didn't hear, but I saw. Come on, we can talk about it later."

An hour passed in the car before either of them said anything. He had switched the music players, which passed without comment from Clare, and he had put Mahler's 9th Symphony on, which meant that he saw little of the journey, lost in the music. However, only a minute or so into the final movement, he reached over and turned it off. There would be time for that later, he thought, but he was in far too fragile an emotional state to listen to that.

Clare protested, and he tried to explain.

"It's one of my favourite pieces of music, the fourth movement, but I have to be in the right mental place to listen to it. Otherwise, you'll have me sitting here in a puddle of tears."

"You know, a good cry might do both of us some good," she said, but made no effort to turn it back on. Some more time slipped by, the road gradually getting busier as they neared Frankfurt. The silence was no longer companionable – Andrew grew increasingly uncomfortable with it, until it dawned on him that he had the power to break it.

"What happened in there, Clare? Not to me, but to you? You came in; she yelled at you, you left again. That doesn't seem like you"

"I haven't been entirely honest with you, Andrew. She and I had a bit of a shouting match on the phone when I called to arrange this. As you heard, she blames me for everything, and she really didn't want anything to do with me, until I pointed out that, as Peter's father, you do actually have some rights. I'm glad you went first, though – I don't think she and I would have got very far, do you?"

The silence reasserted itself, and Andrew had to force himself to ask another question – all his life he had proceeded in conversations like this on the assumption that if someone wanted him to know something, they would tell him. This approach probably led to his lack of understanding of many things, and plainly wasn't going to work in this situation

"Why does she blame you? It doesn't make sense to me."

"Apparently, she had come to the conclusion during her therapy that nothing which had happened to her was actually her fault. Or her responsibility. Which means that it has to be someone else's fault. Mine, it turns out. Apparently, if I hadn't seduced Dieter, she would have moved in with him, got away from her parents and been happy. I fucked that up, and then everything which came after was down to me. I had the baby which was rightfully hers, and she was left with – sorry, Andrew, but you should know – some stranger's. Her words. Then I was responsible for her running away; I don't remember it quite like that, but in any case, I'd have thought she would have been grateful. Oh, and I was responsible, somehow, for Matthias coming to find her."

"But that's..." Andrew tailed off before using the word 'crazy'. "It makes no sense. She said to me that the baby had to be hers alone; I assumed she meant that Dieter wasn't an option."

"I know. I don't think anyone knows what was going on in her mind, but she's still playing games with everyone; she has to be in control, even when it would make more sense just to tell the truth"

Andrew thought about this, then remembered what had chilled him.

She said something to me which bothers me; how she just absorbs whatever happens and moves on. Seemed kind of sociopathic to me."

"I don't know what it is, Andrew, I wanted to warn you, but I also wanted to see what you thought. I guess she didn't apologise for what she did to you?"

"No. And she even has me wondering if what she did was so bad. Which I know is also crazy, but..."

"She stole your son from you; raped you – you might remember that – and then did her best to fuck up your son's life, too. Who knows? She's probably still messing with his life. I'd suggest that she's not worth it, but that depends on what you want to do about Peter, I suppose. You might even have to have some kind of relationship with her."

Andrew tried to imagine that – sending her Christmas cards, or the occasional email; being involved in the life of this person who was little more than a bad dream to him. He couldn't get his mind to accept it, and after a moment or two, stopped trying.

Clare looked over at him as she pulled out to overtake yet another large German truck. Andrew idly wondered if she shouldn't give at least a little more attention to the road, but he said nothing. She continued to look at him for longer than he was comfortable with, but she said nothing. Finally, just as he was about to protest, she looked back at the road, minutely adjusted the wheel to bring them more precisely into the centre of the lane, and sighed.

Andrew was beginning to get the hang of this conversation thing. "What? What do you want me to say? It was a disaster, but I did learn some things."

"What things? That she's just as manipulative and controlling as she was, but a little more subtle about it?"

"Well, yes – although I could have guessed that. Or at least gone through life without needing to find it out. No, I found out that Matthias probably hasn't told me anything which is actually anywhere near the whole truth; that I mostly feel sad where I expected to feel anger, and I found out that I do want to see Peter, and talk to him at least. If he wants to, I think I'd be happy to be part of his life in some way."

"And if he doesn't?"

"Don't know. I'll cross that one when we get there, I suppose."

"You should prepare yourself for it – he might easily just tell you to go forth and multiply. Think about that, too."

"You're right. It's funny, but I've been thinking about what would have happened if I hadn't come out here back in August. If I hadn't known any of these things; would I have been happier?"

"And?"

"On balance, no. I think. I may not be enjoying every moment of this process, but I'm glad I'm in it. And" – he paused and cleared his throat –

"I'm glad I'm here with you. It's still kind of weird, but I'm glad."

Clare said nothing; she stared fixedly ahead, planning the trajectory of her next overtaking manoeuvre. She checked the mirror, then checked it again, then smoothly pulled out, swept past the slower-moving Volkswagen in the inside lane, and was safely back before a white Porsche barrelled past them. Andrew whistled, but Clare didn't react. He began to wonder if he had said something stupid. After another overtake performed in silence, he decided to say something else, and see where that got him.

"So, Clare, what happened last night? It feels like there's a gorilla in the car with us − were you trying to seduce me, or am I still misreading everything?"

Clare's head snapped round to look at him; he met her stare, even though he was more than a little discomfited by it. She looked forward again.

"I'm sorry, Andrew; I really am. I like you and I was worried about you. You didn't know what you were walking into, but I did, and.... Well, I got it wrong. Can you see how bad I am at this sort of thing?"

"I see it, but I find it hard to assimilate, I'm afraid. Your life may not be lived in the surface, but your surface is very impressive. It's kind of convincing. For what it's worth, I'm just enjoying having a long-lost friend. Mostly."

Clare smiled briefly. He wanted to change the subject, but she had more to say.

"I'm enjoying it too. That took guts today, to go through with that. I'm sorry you didn't get what you needed from her, but I'm still angry with myself for getting you into it, and angry with her."

"Clare, you didn't get me into anything; I went there of my own accord. Why are you so angry with her, though?"

"The last time I saw Karla, she showed me who she really was − a scared, confused girl who had been abused by her parents all of her life, and who was desperately looking for a way out. As soon as I started to talk to her, I could see that that Karla − the one just below the surface back then - was gone. In its place was a nasty, cynical manipulative bitch. And I had so hoped that it wouldn't be the case. She didn't even acknowledge that she had done anything wrong; she blamed me, and now she has fobbed you off. And, damn her, I do feel responsible for it. For all of it. Including dragging you out here to talk to her for no reason. And I know I'm over-analysing it, but − damn."

Andrew wondered aloud at Clare moderating her language, and she laughed drily, then started a sentence several times before taking a deep breath. Andrew had time to be even more alarmed than usual, but she cut him off before he could tell her it didn't matter:

"OK, this is uncomfortable and I'm going to be in denial as soon as I say it, but here's the truth. You ready for this?"

"I think I'm beyond being surprised by the truth now. Go for it."

Clare did seem to Andrew to genuinely be uncomfortable, and he wondered if he could divert her on to something less controversial. The weather, perhaps? But it was too late.

"Andrew, I have done many stupid and unforgivable things in my life. I have a talent for it; it's probably why I'm still single – not that I mind that particularly – and it's why we're sitting here now. I took you under my wing, or whatever you want to call it, mainly because I felt a little responsible for what had happened to you. Sitting there today, looking at her, all fat and pleased with herself, I clearly understood two things. Firstly, that I actually was responsible for you and Peter." Andrew tried to interrupt, but she waved him down.

"Don't stop me now; I'm on to something. I created the situation with Dieter, and I left you open to attack. I keep thinking about this: on that first night, she asked me about you – naturally enough; you were living in her house, after all – and I told her you were a nice kid, probably a bit naïve, and a bit of a pushover."

"Meaning? Not that I'm necessarily disagreeing with you, but..."

"Meaning that she had been wondering aloud which of the boys would be up for losing their virginity. It was a bit of a laugh, I thought; she had Dieter in tow, so I supposed she was talking about this stuff in general, not looking for a victim. And I kind of maligned you. Put the idea in her head, I always thought. The other thing is that as soon as you went in to talk to her, I really wanted you not to be hurt by her again – it was almost a physical reaction. I wanted to leap in and protect you, and I really don't know what that means, or if I'm even comfortable talking to you about it. Sorry, but there it is. The stuff about it being all my fault; that I could deal with – part of me had always kind of thought that, anyway.

"But when I was in there with you, she was clearly not going to give you anything. I liked the way you stood up to her, but the Karla I saw is not there any more, and I'm angry about that."

Andrew said nothing. Part of his mind was turning over the idea that Clare had felt something for him – something other than a desire to tease him, or wind him up – and part of it was wishing he could go back and properly confront Karla. He was about to expound on that idea when Clare interrupted his train of thought.

She announced that she was going to stop – "I badly need to pee, I'm afraid" – and that perhaps they should change the subject after that; give themselves some breathing space. Andrew said nothing, but was glad of the suggestion; he no longer knew what he thought about anything.

Clare stopped at a rest area just south of Frankfurt, and disappeared inside with her enormous canvas travel bag. Andrew freshened up and stretched his legs by wandering around the car park for a while; by the time he got back, Clare was loading the bag back into the back of the Mercedes. He stopped to watch her; she had changed into her obviously more comfortable clothes, including a battered old leather jacket which Andrew wondered about. As they set off again, he asked her about it. She laughed.

"No, it's not the same one. My God, can you imagine? Wearing the same old thing for 25 years? No, this is one I bought at a second-hand market in Wimbledon a couple of years ago. I just like them – comfortable and practical, I always used to say, although a fat lot of good they did me when I was in Canada in the winter!"

They talked for a time about Clare's life and travels, and about how she felt about being more settled in London. Andrew explained how he had been offered chances over the years to move around – his employer was a truly global corporation – but that he felt too tied to one place, and too comfortable with his lifestyle to change – "not at my age," he offered, which caused Clare to laugh.

He thought about this; he certainly didn't feel 40, and remembered his own father at 40 – an old man, grey-haired and balding - he was different, he acknowledged, but he felt positively elderly compared to Clare, who appeared to be still comfortable in youth culture; fond of modern popular music and films, and still dressed much as she had when Andrew had last known her – leather jacket and jeans never really goes out of style, he thought.

As they passed Bad Hersfeld, he felt himself begin to tense. Clare noticed, and asked him what he was thinking.

"I don't know. I'm thinking about this morning, and about how this all came to pass. How it is that you are hurtling me through the German countryside in an expensive silver Mercedes. I'm wondering what it all means. And I'm wondering where I'm going to be sleeping tonight."

Clare looked over at him, as if to divine any hidden meaning to this last statement, but Andrew simply smiled wearily at her. "I mean, you haven't told me what the arrangements are, and I don't suppose – given what I know now – that Matthias has been alerted. Have you booked us into another hotel?"

"No, not exactly, although this place does have a sauna. You remember Liezl's place, of course. Her folks still live there, and they've given us the run of it for the rest of the week. They've gone to their summer place – up north somewhere, I believe – and Liezl's got us all billeted in there. She's brought her youngest – he's only six, and doesn't like to be separated from her. Erika's coming down from Berlin, and you and I will have rooms to ourselves – there are plenty to spare. I don't know if you remember it?"

Andrew did, but not in great detail. He wasn't sure he had ever been upstairs, and he knew he hadn't been to the sauna. He had a vague idea that there were an absurd number of bedrooms, and he supposed it would all make sense once they were there. He felt the tension ease a little, but he needed to talk about what they were expecting. Clare tried to be reassuring, but he wasn't in the mood to be comforted, and worried – more about what he was going to say to Matthias, he realised, than about what, if anything, he would say to Peter.

Clare asked him to put the music back on – "I'm calm now, and I'd like to know about the music which makes you cry, if you don't mind." Andrew had to think about it for a minute, then remembered that it was the Mahler, which he felt spoke for itself. He explained a little about it anyway, and wondered idly how long it would take him to drive to Meiernigg - a place he had always wanted to see – from here. If things get really bad, he thought, I can just escape there.

The music soothed and calmed him, without making him too emotional. He tried to explain that it had less emotional force for him if it was divorced from the rest of the symphony, but Clare shushed him – she was listening intently, and he smiled to see it.

They arrived in Hohenügel shortly before the end of the movement, and Clare pulled the car over to the side of the road as they left the autobahn so that they could hear the end of it. She took several deep breaths once it was done, then turned and smiled at him. "I may have to revise my opinion of a few things," she said. "I never quite saw the point of all that classical stuff, but I may be getting the general idea. Jesus, that was sad, wasn't it?"

Andrew rarely needed an invitation to gush about music, and he gently disagreed with her. "On the surface, it is, yes. He's dying, and he knows it. It is a lingering farewell, but it's also a statement of defiance and intent. I always hear it as the musical equivalent of 'rage against the dying of the light'. I do find it can reduce me to tears if I'm not careful, but I can also find it enormously uplifting if I'm in the right mood."

"Which is it today?"

"I'm not sure; I never quite engaged with it – too much else on my mind, I suppose – but it has calmed me and I think I may be ready for whatever might be coming."

"Well, you'd better be, big guy, because it's coming, like it or not."

A thought occurred to him. "Clare? You promised me some surprises. I think I'd quite like them not to be nasty surprises, if that's OK with you." Clare smiled.

"No promises; they might not even happen, and I can't promise how you'll react. Don't worry, though. Honestly; don't worry. I have a feeling things are going to work themselves out." She fished out her mobile phone and called someone on her speed dial list – holding down one button for a second. Andrew heard a long string of numbers punch itself in, then an unfamiliar, foreign-sounding ring. A woman answered, and Clare launched into some high-speed German. Andrew guessed that this was their arrival being announced – presumably to Liezl. Clare laughed that raucous laugh again, and Andrew sighed. She looked at him as she hung up, and he smiled.

"Whatever happens, Clare – and don't take this the wrong way – I'm glad to have you here with me. I couldn't - wouldn't - do this on my own.

"Me too, big guy. Me too."

Clare parked in what seemed to Andrew to be an expanded and enlarged driveway – he seemed to remember rose bushes or something out front, where there now was gravel. He remarked on it, but Clare remembered it differently, and he let it pass. He had, after all, only been in the house two or three times a quarter of a century ago.

The front door opened, and a middle-aged woman came running towards them. She was greying, and dressed in a way which Andrew thought of as Anne-like; but she was Liezl. Although he hadn't seen her in all those years, he recognised her. She hugged Clare, and then turned to look at Andrew.

"Well, I think I might have recognised you." She stared into his eyes, until Andrew began to feel uncomfortable. "Yes, I can see you in him, too. I think this will be a good thing." She stepped forward, and Andrew almost did the handshake thing again, but caught himself, and bent to offer a cheek, which Liezl ignored, hugging him as tightly as she had Clare.

"So many years," she said quietly, "and so many things to happen to us." She stood back and smiled at him. "Come inside, Andrew. You remember the house?"

Andrew did, and he wondered aloud if the whole family still lived in the same houses.

"No, not all – Erika is in Berlin, you know this. Her father – my grandfather - died some years ago, and her mother moved to be closer to her babies." She searched for the word, then it came to her "her grandchildren – is this correct?" Andrew nodded. "Sorry for my English – I do not speak it so much now. My girls are better than me, I think." She called inside the house for someone called Rudi, then grinned at the young boy who appeared, looking a little shy, at the door. This, presumably, was her 'youngest'. She talked rapidly to him and he smiled, then ran off to where Clare was fishing in the boot of the Mercedes. He returned with an expensive-looking metal aeroplane, which earned Clare a telling off in German, but a good-natured one. The two women were clearly friends – had been since 1978, Andrew supposed. Why were women so good at that, and men so bad? He thought guiltily of Matthias. Some friend I turned out to be, he thought, then thought again. He obviously didn't know the whole truth, so perhaps he shouldn't be so hard on himself.

He went back to the car for his bag, and carried it into the house. Liezl was standing in the enormous hallway – *I remember this*, he thought – and directed Clare and Andrew upstairs. He thought he understood the German instructions, but found that he was heading for the same room as Clare. She laughed at his confusion. "Over there, Andrew – next door to me." He wondered for a moment which had been Anne's room, but guessed it would have been the one Clare was using. He went in to his room, and sank down on to the bed. He could hear Clare moving around in the next room, opening a sliding door, and pulling the curtain over. He got up and looked out his own window. All he could see were pale brown fields. He had a memory of walking through fields with Anne, but wasn't sure if these were the same ones. He pulled his jacket off, and rummaged through his bag for something a little less formal to wear.

As he changed, he thought about Liezl. He had not had many dealings with her – or Erika, come to that – but he remembered her as kind-hearted and cheerful. His clearest memory of her, of course, was the schnapps-drinking morning just downstairs. He thought about that, and understood that he was probably going to have to go back down to that same room now and make polite conversation. He looked at himself in the mirror – well, he should be able to do it; he wasn't actually the 15-year old innocent kid who had last walked out of this house.

Downstairs, Clare and Liezl were in the kitchen, making coffee. He stood and looked at them for a moment – his long-lost friend moving around the kitchen as if she lived there, and Liezl looking awkward and lost in her parents' house. He recognised that feeling; however often he went back to his own parents' home – the house he had grown up in – nothing was ever where he remembered it to have been, and he usually had to ask for help in finding the most obvious of things.

The two women were conversing in German, and he simply listened for a while, attuning his ear to what they were saying, then when a suitable pause developed – they had been talking, naturally, about their respective children – he interjected with an anecdote of his own, which he felt sure he had mangled a little. Liezl carried on the conversation, including him in it as if he spoke good German, and Clare gave him an encouraging smile.

They did, however, switch to English as they sat at the kitchen table with their drinks. Andrew remembered sitting around this table before, and said so.

"Ah, not this table, Andrew. This is not so old. But, yes, the family always gathered around here. You are thinking of the first day, I suppose?"

Andrew wasn't sure, but Clare reminded him. "This is where it all started. That Sunday night – you and Matthias came up here; Erika and I were already here, then Karla brought Dieter. One or two others, I think, as well."

Liezl smiled. "Many more, Clare – always the same. If something is happening, all of the family comes to see. I used to hate it, but now I think it is a nice thing. I like it, but there are not so many of us now."

Clare wondered if they were expecting the entire family tonight, but Liezl laughed. "No. Mostly, they do not know. I think this would be better, no? We have some things to talk about."

Rudi came in to announce – Andrew was able to follow this bit – that Grandma's house was boring, and Liezl went off with him to find something interesting to do. Clare looked at him.

"So, what do you think?"

"So far, so good. I like it here – this house is slowly coming back to me. It has a good feeling to it, doesn't it?"

"I always thought so. And I always liked to visit – Liezl's parents are lovely. You remember that her mother is Erika's half-sister, don't you?" Andrew more or less did. "So if we came down, we always stayed here. Funny – this was the house where I came to terms with my situation, but I never had any negative thoughts about it."

Liezl came back, having figured out how to work the television in the main room. Rudi appeared to be happily watching something loud and violent-sounding. She walked over to a telephone on the side and dialled a long number. The conversation was beyond Andrew; it seemed to be conducted in high-speed dialect, and he asked Clare what was going on.

"Erika, I should think. She's driving down this afternoon. She'll be here soon enough, knowing her – you think I'm a fast driver..."

Andrew smiled. He thought about Erika's drive from Berlin, realising that it would be entirely on roads which would have been inside East Germany when they had first been here. She would no doubt pass by the old border crossing, he thought. In some ways, that's where my troubles began. He tried to put the thought out of his mind, but it was difficult for him to avoid thinking about it, having seen Karla that morning. Liezl hung the phone up, and he asked her when they could expect Erika.

"She has just left Berlin, she said. So maybe three hours, maybe less. She is quick, *meine tante*."

Liezl asked if they had actually been to Bretten that morning, and Clare began to tell the story. As he listened to it, Andrew found it hard to avoid the feeling that this was something which had happened to someone else; it seemed unreal. Clare reached the point where she had walked out, although she seemed less angry about it than she had been earlier. Andrew suddenly realised that both sets of eyes were on him – only he knew what had happened next. He thought for a minute.

"You know, I'm not sure what happened next. She talked about her father and why she is – what she is, I suppose. We talked about Peter a little, and she gave me a - message, I guess- to pass on to him, but I'm not sure if the message was for me, and not him. Also, I – oh, I don't know. I got angry with her, but it did not seem to bother her. She just moved on – that's what she said; 'move on'. I don't know what to make of that. I may never know."

Liezl had listened to all of this impassively. "I think my cousin will never be right. She does her best now, I think, but she – it was all so bad. I want so much for her to come back; for Matthias, too. Erika says I am stupid; nothing will change them, but I still hope."

Andrew asked about Matthias.

"He is here, and he may come to see you. If everything happens, then he probably will come, I think. He needs – oh, I think there is good hope for him. But he finds it all so hard, and he would rather not be here."

Clare broke her silence. "Why do you think he is still here – he could work anywhere, don't you think?"

Liezl smiled sadly. "His father still has very long arms. And his mother is still near to here. He feels responsible for that." She paused, then said in a much quieter voice, "and so he should."

Andrew looked at her, but she shook her head quickly. "For another time, Andrew. Come, let us cook something. We should have dinner ready for Erika – she will be ready to eat!"

The three of them worked in the kitchen for a time, and when Rudi came in again, Andrew volunteered to take him out into the garden with a ball. Rudi seemed unsure about this, but Liezl thought it would be a good idea, and the two of them went out after some reassurance that *mutti* would be able to see from the window.

For the first few minutes, Rudi watched the window much more than the ball, but he quickly thereafter got into the game, explaining endless complex rules to Andrew. The fact that Andrew was able to follow about one tenth of them didn't seem to bother the boy, and the two of them spent the best part of an hour laughing at each other's inability to remember any of the rules.

Andrew wondered when he had last done this, but the fact that he had to think hard made him feel guilty, and he abandoned himself to the simple pleasure of messing around with a kid.

He called time on the game when he realised that he was sweating unpleasantly, and let Rudi lead the way back inside. Clare laughed at him from the kitchen – he supposed he was not a pretty sight. Liezl came out of the kitchen, carrying a large glass of red wine, and smiled at him.

"You should shower and – would you like to sauna? I can turn it on for you while you shower."

Andrew thought about this, but decided it was too fraught with danger, after the night before. He settled for the shower, a change of clothes, and some of the wine.

The three of them settled in the main living room – the same room

Andrew remembered from the schnapps morning, although it had been comprehensively redecorated and refurnished – and talked about their lives, Andrew being careful not to get too involved in tales of his divorce and his relationship with Anne. Rudi would fly by from time to time with his new toy, and on every third or fourth pass, would complain of being hungry.

Eventually, Liezl tired of explaining that they were waiting for *Tante* Erika, and took him off to the kitchen to feed him. Clare raised her glass to Andrew in a silent toast.

"I would have left you alone down there, you know." Andrew looked at her. "In the sauna, I mean. Learned my lesson. You could have had peace and quiet. You look like you need it."

"I do, I suppose. Pity, though – I might have enjoyed another sauna with you." He had meant it light-heartedly, but feared it might have come out wrong, because Clare stared at him, took a long drink, and nodded. "Sorry. I didn't mean – "

"No problem, Andrew. Maybe another time, you think?"

He didn't know what to think, so said nothing.

Erika did finally arrive, with a passenger. Andrew, standing at the window, wondered if it was one of her children. The fading October light meant that he wasn't able to get a good look at the younger woman, and so he was unprepared for her arrival. He looked up, smiling and waiting to be introduced, only to apparently be confronted by the younger Clare. His casual smile, he could feel, had been replaced by a kind of slack-jawed stare. This should have been disconcerting to a stranger, but the woman simply laughed – not quite Clare's laugh, but close enough that he had no doubt who she was. He went to introduce himself, but she got there first.

"You must be Andrew. I'm so pleased to finally meet you! I suppose she didn't even tell you I was coming, did she? She is like that – why am I telling you? You must know. Well, pleased to meet you, anyway. You're a lot taller than I imagined – I thought she was exaggerating, but – well, my goodness."

As Polly gave this speech, she was rapidly encroaching on Andrew's personal space, and he suddenly found himself being hugged just as fiercely as he would have been by her mother. He wasn't sure what to make of this, and looked over her shoulder for an excuse to disengage. Instead he saw Clare standing in the doorway, grinning.

He smiled back, deciding just to let things happen to him for now. Polly stood back, saw the look in his eye, and turned to face her mother.

"Clare! I've missed you! How are you, darling?" The hug she favoured her mother with was every bit as fierce and joyful, and Andrew felt a pang of envy at their easy relationship. He didn't have anyone – not even his own children – he could relate to like that, and he wondered how you got to be like that.

Erika interrupted his thought process, bursting into the room, ignoring the hugging mother and daughter, and coming over to Andrew. He looked down at her. Erika, unlike her – cousin? Niece? He still couldn't remember – was still dark-haired, but looking much more her 40 years than Clare did. He remembered a short, stocky girl, and what he saw now was a short, slightly less stocky woman. He had had relatively little contact with Erika; partly, he knew, due to her shaky English, so he was surprised when she greeted him in fluent and idiomatic English.

"Andrew; it's been so long. Oh; I suppose you've all been saying that all day, haven't you? Sorry – I'm only just catching up. I'm so pleased to have you back here; for us all to be back here." She looked quickly round at Clare as she said this, and Andrew noticed something pass between the two women, but he couldn't quite tell what. Erika offered her hand, very formally, but as he reached out to take it, she pulled firmly on his arm, and he found himself bent over far enough for Erika to manage a much less formal double kiss.

He stood up and looked at her, and for the first time since he had landed in Frankfurt, had the sensation that things might turn out OK. Something about Erika's confident manner reassured him. Bad things were not going to happen while she was around. Erika turned and faced Clare and Polly, who were watching all this with their arms around each other's waists.

"So, when's dinner? Poll's starving, and – well, so am I, if truth be told. We didn't stop, did we, girl?"

Polly laughed "No – we drove at Erika speed all the way here. So I need a large drink, a bathroom, and dinner. Not necessarily in that order, either."

She disengaged from Clare, and waved Erika over to her.

"Come on, Erika; show me where to find it all." They walked out of the room, leaving Clare and Andrew once again alone together. Andrew looked at her.

"Sorry, big guy," she said. "Thought it might be fun to spring her on you like that. Your face, though!"

"I thought there had been an accident with a time machine, or something – she's very like you."

"In some ways. She still tends to dress like me, which says something about one or other of us, I suppose. She's not all like me, though. Good with numbers, cautious, careful, that kind of thing."

"How did she get here, then? You said she was in France, or something?"

"Flew into Berlin this afternoon, I think. She doesn't need an excuse to come here and see what she calls her old dad – I still think she's making up for lost time with him, sometimes."

"But you're not her 'old mum' – I noticed that."

"No, she's pretty much always called me Clare. Doesn't bother me – I think it's because she had to grow up so early, when it was just me and her against the world – you know."

"Not really; I was never 'against the world' much. My kids call me 'dad', and it never occurred to me to do it any differently."

They had walked back over to the window as they talked, and Andrew stared out at the darkening sky; trying to orientate himself in the landscape.

"What you thinking, Andrew?"

"Just that the last time I was here, I didn't stop to consider anything other than my story. I was feeling sorry for myself, I suppose, and I thought Matthias might be fun."

"That all?"

"No." He sighed. "No, I thought he would be able to tell me about Karla; let me put that to rest, I guess. I suppose I just wanted to know that there had been a happy ending; that what she did to me was ultimately pretty harmless, and if I had been dwelling on it all this time, it was because of my sedate life, not because it actually was momentous."

"And, yet, here you are."

"Here I am. And I'm glad I am. I wish I had asked him about the girls – Erika and Liezl, I mean. I wish I'd come over here to see what was going on. I wish – a hundred things, which I can't do anything about. But here I am. And here I am with you. Which still seems weird."

"Freaky," Clare said quietly. She grabbed his arm and squeezed it gently. "Come on, there's dinner to be had. My offspring isn't the only hungry one."

The evening passed in a haze of good food, better wine, and much laughter and memory. Andrew learned more about the strange world of diplomacy than he had ever imagined would be interesting; Polly told them several amusing and possibly libellous tales of the film industry, and Andrew barely thought about any of the reasons why he was back in Hohenügel after all this time.

He didn't want to be the first to retire, but the stress of the day caught up with him, and he had to make his excuses just as Liezl was offering to find her father's expensive brandy. The others seemed genuinely sad to see him go, but he couldn't help feeling that he was something of a spare wheel in the group of women, and he was a little relieved to let them get back to a situation they were comfortable with without their interloper.

He lay awake, however, listening to the merriment and the conversation until it faltered and, with much coming and going, the others also found their way to bed. He was beginning to drift off, when he heard a knock on his door. He sat up, and was about to ask who it was, when the door opened, and a slender figure let herself in.

"You awake, big guy?" Clare, then. He had actually briefly panicked that it might have been Karla, somehow, but relaxed to hear a friendly voice. He realised that he hadn't answered, and that coming into the dark from the lighted corridor, she probably couldn't see him.

"Yeah. Just about – I'm tired, but the brain isn't yet. I'll get there, though."

"I know what you mean. Listen, I thought you'd like to know something before it comes up in the morning."

"What?" His panic, never far from the surface, threatened to break free again, but Clare came over to him and laid a hand on his arm.

"Nothing bad, but when I asked Polly which room she was in, or even if she was coming in with me, she said she had to get going. Staying with Peter, apparently."

Andrew thought about this. "Well, that answers that question, I suppose."

"Sure does. At least, I suppose it does. It means he'll know all about you before you see him, apart from anything else. I can't decide if that complicates things, or makes them easier."

"I can't force myself to think of anything much right now, I'm afraid. Sure it'll all work out tomorrow." He fell silent, but Clare didn't move, perched on the edge of his bed. A thought crossed his mind, but he dismissed it, remembering their conversation in the hotel corridor the night before. Clare's hand on his arm gently rubbed up to his shoulder and back to his elbow. She seemed reluctant to let go of him, and he was quite happy to have her company for the moment.

"Andrew?" she finally asked.

"Hmm?"

"Don't take this the wrong way, but are you – I mean, are you actually wearing anything?"

He laughed. "Well, yes, as it happens. I don't usually, but I'm in a house full of women, including – so I thought – your daughter. I thought I'd better preserve some of my modesty." He paused, then thought he may as well ask. "Why do you ask?"

"Oh, nothing. Well, I suppose I am psychoanalysing you a bit. Back here, no lock on the door – I wondered if you had…."

"Funny; I actually had a flash of alarm as you opened the door – as if it could be her. I'm glad it's you, though." He smiled at her, but wasn't sure if she could see him. He could just about make out her shape, sitting there on the bed with him, and he thought back to the previous evening, in the sauna. He felt suddenly uncomfortable, and cleared his throat.

"Uh oh," Clare said. "I'm doing it again, aren't I?"

"No, actually," Andrew replied. "I mean, well, yes, you are in a way, but I'm actually trying to figure out a polite way to get you out of here, because you're right, and the last thing I need is to mess up our friendship right now."

He was sure he could hear her smile at this. She bent over to him and kissed him, not very successfully, since she obviously couldn't see him, then stood up.

"You're right, Andrew, and I promise I won't – actually, that's not what I mean." She sat again. "Look, I'm the impulsive type, right?"

"I had noticed."

"So, I promise this. I'm probably not going to change the way I am around you – it's the way I am. But if I do cross the line – whatever that means – it'll be because I've carefully thought about it. OK? Deal?"

He thought about it. "Deal. No – wait. If you ever do – you know, cross the line. Well, maybe I won't have thought about it as carefully. You might have to wait for me."

"Deal." She stood again. "Fuck, you're sensible. I wish – ah, fuck it. Goodnight, big guy. Sleep well."

He heard her head for the door, when something else occurred to him.

"Clare?"

"Yup?"

"Is that it? For the surprises, I mean? Am I done now?"

She was silent for long enough that he wondered if he had missed her leaving.

"Well, no. Not quite. Just the one more. One more that I know about. But you'll be fine."

"Why the surprises? I mean, it was great to meet Polly, but why?"

"Because until this evening, I wasn't even sure it was going to all come together. Now, I just figure it might make things easier for you. Or me; I'm not sure which. Sleep, Andrew – all will become clear." She slipped out the door and closed it softly behind her.

If only, he thought, and refused to think about what he meant by that.

Polly was back at the house by the time he surfaced for breakfast. Liezl had taken Rudi off somewhere, Erika had gone to visit the people who now lived in her old house, and taken Clare with her – Clare had shouted all of this through the door to him half an hour before - so Andrew was taken aback to find someone in the kitchen.

"Oh, hi, Andrew. Sorry, did I disturb you?" He shook his head. "Just that Peter is up at stupid o'clock, and for a baker, he doesn't actually have much in the way of food in the house, so I came up here for breakfast. Want some?" She was picking her way through an assortment of pastries which had been left out for them; there were some things which looked suspiciously like cakes on the kitchen side, and some black bread had also been left out. He could smell the coffee which Polly was drinking, and decided that would do him for now. He poured himself a cup, and sat down opposite her.

In the morning light, Polly looked a bit less like her mother than she had the night before, which he found something of a relief. She chatted to him about how much she liked Hohenügel, and how she might even consider basing herself here, if it wasn't for the fact that it was so far from a decent sized airport.

Andrew couldn't stop himself. "Basing yourself here? With Peter, you mean?"

She smiled at him. "Well, if that works out, that'd be nice. But my old dad's here, and I kind of like him. It'd be nice to be around him, don't you think?"

"I guess it would. That's..." He stopped himself. This was, he belatedly realised, way too awkward.

"Oh, I'm sorry. I wasn't thinking. You still haven't worked things out yet, have you? With Peter, I mean. He's – look, I'm not the one you should be talking to, and I don't actually know what he's thinking, but I think he's looking forward to seeing you. So is Dieter, come to that. He's really excited about it all, for some reason." Andrew thought about this, then let it pass.

"Do he and your mother – Clare. Do they – "

Polly grinned at him. "Is the coast clear, do you mean?"

Andrew was alarmed. "No! No, I meant..."

"Don't worry, I know what you meant. And I know what you think you meant, as well." She laughed. Clare's laugh this time; full and uproarious. He smiled in spite of himself. She carried on. "Sorry; I'm a bit of a tease. Can't think where I get it from. For what it's worth, you'd be good for her, but she's not the settling down type. You might have noticed." Andrew nodded.

"But the question was about my mum and my dad. As far as I know, they only ever did it the once. He likes her now; more than he did all the time I was growing up, he says. But he's happy here – you do know he's married, don't you?"

Andrew thought about this. He did know; Matthias had told him, but he had become less and less inclined to believe anything which Matthias had told him, so he had perhaps blotted it out. He felt a sense of relief, and understood that for what it was, too.

"Yes; I suppose I did. Sorry, I'm a little – perplexed – by things these days. I'm not normally like this." Polly smiled at him again. "I'm usually sitting somewhere on the sidelines as life passes me by. I'm not used to all this – stuff."

"I think that's one of the saddest things I've ever heard, Andrew. You're 40, right?" He nodded. "Same age as Clare. She's never sat on the sidelines of anything in her life, I don't think. I try not to. It's a lot more fun this way."

"Oh, I believe you; I just don't know how to change it."

"Stick with Clare. She'll show you."

They talked some more, but Andrew wasn't paying close attention to the conversation; he was preoccupied by what Polly had said. After an hour or so, Erika and Clare came back, bearing supplies for making another enormous meal. Polly immediately prevailed upon Erika for the use of her car, and disappeared off to 'do some shopping'. Andrew went out into the garden where he had played with Rudi the night before, and the two women left him to it.

He walked up into the fields, remembering doing this with Anne on the night of the barbecue. He thought about his ex-wife, without bitterness now. He ought never to have pursued her, he thought – she needed someone a lot more involved in her life, not someone who felt constrained by it at every turn, and couldn't wait to be free of it. He wondered just what it had been which had made him so doggedly determined, and realised suddenly that it had probably been the sex.

His one experience of sex with anyone other than Anne had been a lot more traumatic than he understood at the time, he realised now. Anne was the salve for that; Anne was the one person who wouldn't be predatory, who wouldn't judge him, and who would go at an even slower pace than he would. That was what he was looking for, he saw now. All he wanted was a quiet, comfortable place, where he could curl up and not feel threatened.

He shivered involuntarily, and remembered Anne doing the same that night. He smiled feebly at the memory of it. He tried to remember the first time they had actually has Penetrative Intercourse. It should have been a big deal – for both of them, he thought – but he couldn't quite remember it. Anne hadn't been a virgin. He thought about that. Why hadn't it been an issue? He couldn't remember. He knew that he had been utterly shocked to discover that she actually had slept with Matthias; that he hadn't been the only one for her as she had been for him – *although that's not really true, is it?* he thought - but he couldn't for the life of him remember why her previous experience hadn't been obvious to him at the time.

Naïve and innocent, I suppose, he thought, although that couldn't have been it. Perhaps Anne had convinced him of something. He worried at this for a time, and stopped only when he saw that Clare was watching him from the back door. He smiled and waved to her, feeling a little foolish as he did so. He walked back down to the house, and joined the two women at the table.

The quiet conversation around the lunch table was destroyed by the return of Rudi, full of enthusiasm for some new toy or game he was waving around, too close for anyone to properly see. With an excited yelp, he was off again. Liezl came in as soon as he left, and apologised for his boisterousness.

"He is bored. I should have thought of this – I thought it would be good to have him on my own, but I didn't think about what he would do. He wants his grandparents to be here, and he doesn't understand why they are not. So I have to take him out and bribe him with presents. It's not good, but I do it."

Andrew smiled sympathetically – his experience of parenting children of that age was not so far behind him, and he understood the situation – often, he would find himself alone with his children, and the only way he could think to stop them from fighting with each other or with him, was to bribe them with things they would play with once and then discard. Many a dull Saturday afternoon had been survived that way, with normal service only being resumed when Anne came back from whatever she had volunteered to do on that particular Saturday.

Since he had been under Clare's influence, however, he had begun to reach out more to his children. It was early days, but he felt he was beginning to get through to them, and understand more about how to be part of their lives, even from afar.

He looked around him, aware that he had missed some more conversation. His usual behaviour in groups like this was to sit quietly, attentive to everything being said, but he was spending large amounts of time lost in his own thoughts, and he was aware of missing things which he possibly needed to know. He looked pointedly at Clare, but she simply smiled, then hushed everyone.

"Look at us," she said. "Andrew and his women. It should be a movie, don't you think?" This raised a laugh, and Andrew wondered if they had talked about him after he had gone to bed the night before. He tried not to worry about that, but it added itself to the long list of his concerns, and he sighed. He felt himself begin to panic a little; he felt out of control of almost everything now, and there were a number of questions crowding in on him which he needed time to answer. He also realised that the concern would be showing on his face, and he began to worry about that.

Liezl had said something clever in response to Clare's remark, and Erika wondered if Polly would be able to get finance for this film. Andrew smiled weakly, and stood. Clare looked round at him, alarmed.

"Hey, we're only teasing. Don't worry; we're on your side."

He smiled a little more convincingly at her. "I know. I'm just a little confused – as usual, I think. I'm going to go for a walk; try to clear my head."

Clare stood, even as she was telling him that it was a good idea, and walked out to the hallway with him.

"Where will you go? Do you want me to come with you?"

He shook his head. "No, Clare. I really need thinking space. I am more affected by yesterday than I realise, and I still have a lot to face. I need some space." He paused, then laughed softly. "Listen to me. I don't normally talk like this, Clare. Something is going on."

"I think it's all good, but we'll see. So, listen." She suddenly became much more serious. "Peter knows you're here, right?" He nodded. "I'd suggest that going to see him at work might not be a good idea. Whatever his state of mind, I'm certain that finding you on the other side of his counter isn't going to improve it."

"I hadn't thought about it, but I guess you're right. I don't know when I'll see him – unless you've got that all worked out already – but I suppose the part of me which wondered about going to see him now hadn't really thought it through." He stopped and looked down into her eyes. "As always, good advice. How did I make it to 40 without you keeping me on the right path?"

Clare smiled back at him. "Oh, you had the odd guardian angel, you know." He looked at her, but decided not to try to analyse that statement too much. He turned, found his jacket in the pile on the hooks by the door, and went outside. Clare followed him as far as the step. "Don't do anything silly, Andrew. We'll still be here when you get back. It will work out, I know it." He turned to look at her, but his vision was suddenly and unexpectedly blurred, and he turned away again. Don't think about it, he said to himself. Just walk.

He turned left as he came out of the driveway and just walked for a time. This took him up the hill out of the village, and he quickly understood that he was going to have to turn round and come back fairly quickly. The pavement ran out after a while, and he thought about turning then, but he felt vaguely foolish about it, and pressed on, walking on the wrong side of the road until he came to the overpass. There was pavement here, and he stopped, leant on the rail and looked down at the traffic thundering by below him.

He supposed that it should seem strange to him, since this had been the place where all traffic had come off the road when he had last stood here, but it didn't – a motorway bridge is just a motorway bridge, he thought.

The last time he stood here, though – that brought him up short. That Sunday morning. He stood up and turned to face back the way he had come; the way he had faced when watching Karla vanish into the distance on that motorbike. He had felt humiliated, he supposed, but there had been something else – he had felt oddly powerful. He remembered vividly now, standing here again, that he had felt grown-up. He had dealt with a difficult situation, and he was involved in the lives of adults. He smiled at the memory of it. How little he had properly understood.

What would have happened, he wondered, if he had just given in to Karla that morning? There was no-one else in the house, and it could have been over with quickly. Perhaps she would have talked to him; perhaps he would have been able to reassure her, or to encourage her to do something. He was momentarily arrested by the vision of Karla breaking down in his arms and confessing her problems; of the two of them making plans for her over breakfast, then of Karla packing quickly, firing up the motorbike and making a break for freedom after declaring her love for him, and promising to come and find him as soon as she was settled somewhere.

He laughed out loud at this idea – exactly the way Andy would have thought. Except, of course, Andy wasn't just the hopeless romantic, but also the terrified little boy. Karla had offered him a glimpse of what passes for paradise in the minds of 15-year old boys, and he had panicked. He remembered thinking at the time that if she had showed that much skin to almost any of his friends or any of the boys on the bus, there would have been a quite different outcome.

Now, he wondered about that as he began his walk back. Maybe they were all just scared little boys back then. Maybe the others were just better at hiding it. Clare had said something about it all being more difficult than it seemed at the time, and if it had been difficult for her, then what hope had there been for any of the others?

As he walked, he tried to think about Peter, this giant son who he simply couldn't fit into his world. But this proved much more difficult than he had thought; he kept remembering the last time he had walked this way. He remembered trying to work out just what had gone on up there on the hill. Karla had wanted something from him, he understood, and he supposed he knew what it had been, given what had happened in her bedroom.

He remembered his confusion then, and he understood it now – Karla simply wanted the power over him. She tempted him with what she assumed he wanted, which was her body. When that didn't work; when she figured out that she had a skittish colt on her hands, she had tried, in her own way, to relax and excite him at the same time – she had become almost friendly; encouraging him to try to ride the bike, and offering to take him on an adventure. He realised now that she had been offering him the opportunity to take the lead – alone with her, far enough from the possibility of someone passing by, she had offered him the opportunity to take things at his own pace; to kiss her or something. From there, she could have made it all seem like his idea.

And then she would have had what she wanted, without any of the force. In fact, she'd have had a week to make sure of it; to creep into his bed in the middle of the night – since he wouldn't have locked the door in this alternative reality – and make things a little less uncertain for her. Maybe they would have talked about things; maybe they would have figured out a way to be together –

Andrew stopped himself. This had never been about Karla wanting him; she had simply wanted what he could provide. His romantic self kept doing this; kept embroidering the past until it became unrecognisable, and he shook his head to try and clear it of these odd thoughts.

He had walked back into the village by now, and saw that he had unconsciously headed for the school. There was a buzz about the place; the not-entirely subdued hum of lessons and, somewhere, a game of some kind, signalled by the squeak of rubber sole on wooden gym floor. He stopped and stared at the building, wondering what impulse had brought him here. He sat on the low wall at the front of the schoolyard for a time, clearing his mind of all thoughts. An image came to his mind – Anne, soaked to the skin and standing on those steps, almost flaunting herself to him. What had got into her that day? In all the years since, he had never seen her behave like that again – she remained modest and self-deprecating throughout the years of their marriage – and he wondered again: what if he had been able to unlock that Anne? What if…?

He sighed, and stood. This was pointless. School would be out shortly, he assumed, and there was the risk of running into Matthias before he was ready. He thought for a minute, then figured out where he would like to go.

It took him some time, once in the cemetery, to find the correct headstone. He had thought he remembered where the family plot was, and it did seem familiar to him, but the names were not what he had expected. He looked around him, but there were simply rows of low headstones, mostly in black marble, stretching in all directions – none of them stood out as the one he was looking for.

He walked aimlessly for a bit, then decided to try a more pragmatic approach, going back to the entrance and following each of the paths in turn until he found what he was looking for. The headstone was no different from the family ones on either side of it, but it was strange, he thought, that it was a single stone on its own; Rolf had not been added to any of the other family headstones here. Then he understood why; Rolf was the outsider in the family; he was not part of the local tradition here. Matthias' mother must have been the scion of the family; Rolf was an incomer. He looked at the inscription, as simple as it could possibly be; just a name, and dates, in the German style – it took him a moment to decipher the date of birth as March 1922. Ten years or so older than his own parents, which made sense to him now, otherwise how could he have been in that photograph – the grey uniform and the steel helmet, so familiar to him from war stories and films, suddenly and alarmingly made real by a picture in a family album.

Rolf's picture on the headstone was much closer to the man he remembered – older still than when Andrew had last seen him, with half-rimmed spectacles. He looked what he was; a successful professional man, steely, determined. Andrew wondered how much of what he subsequently knew he was reading into the photograph. He had become aware of another person nearby, and thought that he should probably move on, allow someone else to come and pay actual respects to people who actually mattered to them, but before he could do so, he was surprised by the voice which came from almost directly behind him.

"I knew that it was you, but I could not understand why you are here." Andrew turned, unsure of his ability to recognise the voice – although who else could it be? Matthias stood there, his hands thrust deep into the pockets of what looked like an old and well-worn long black coat. Matthias attempted a smile, but it wouldn't come.

"Why am I back in Hohenügel, or why am I here in the cemetery?"

"I think I know why you are back in Germany. I should not have done what I did before, I think. I do not know why you are here."

Andrew pointed to a low stone bench and Matthias nodded, then led the way. Before they had even begun to sit down, Andrew tried to explain what had not been particularly clear even to himself.

"I think I am looking for clues. I don't think I can ever understand all that happened to me – to us. But I want to find some ideas, and I thought he might have some."

"But there is nothing here."

"Nothing. I thought that something might explain who he was; why he casts such a shadow into my life, but nothing – just his dates, his name, and his picture."

"This, also, is my fault. I was the only one to do anything about him. I thought he should be here. The family did not all agree, but he was my father. So – I made this for him. I could not think of anything I wanted to say to him, so I said nothing."

"What happened to him, Matthias? What made him who he was? Do you even know?"

Matthias thought about this. Looking into the distance, away from his father's grave, he seemed lost in thought. When he spoke, he seemed close to tears. Andrew looked away in an instinctive attempt not to embarrass his friend.

"He was 18. You understand? Just 18. I know this, and I know a little." Andrew said nothing, and Matthias continued. "He was a farmer's son. From just over there" Matthias pointed off to the east, and Andrew turned to look.

"Niederhügel?"

"Not so far away – in the country. You could see the farm from the hill – you remember the hill?" Andrew did. "He was not a soldier, but they made him into one. You understand this? He was in the army in Russia. He told me once – near the end of his life – he told me that he had seen such terrible things. He told me things I could not ever tell anyone, but I know they were true. He was just a boy."

Andrew sat silently, willing to wait as long as it took. Matthias eventually took a deep breath, and carried on in a more normal voice.

"It does not make an excuse for him, I think, but I cannot imagine what he went through. In the end, he was a prisoner for some time – months, I think, not years, and then he was sent back. He told me once about being in Berlin after the end of the war, then he tried to come home, but it was not possible."

"What happened? How did he end up here, on this side?"

"I do not know for sure. He had a friend – Erika's father, you know?" Andrew nodded again. "This to me was strange – in all of Germany, he met someone from so close. They came back here after – in 1948, I think. You could go to the East then, if you had family there, but his family was gone. He did not recover from that, I think. He stayed here – as close as he could be to his home, but someone else lived there, and no-one knew where his family was. He learned to be a teacher – they needed many teachers then – and he married one of his students. And the rest, I suppose…"

Andrew looked at him. "Do you think the war made him what he was?"

"I do not know. He was a terrible, terrible man, but Markus – Erika's father – survived the same things; he was not a bad man. Perhaps it was because his family was gone; perhaps it was many things. I do not know, but I cannot hate him."

"Really? Even after – "

"No. The very bad things which happened to me, I did them to myself." He paused then looked away. "Andrew, I did not tell you all of the truth before."

"I know. I have been trying to work it all out ever since. I guess you will tell me if you want to, but I have only one question. Why take me to see Peter? If I had never seen him, everything…"

"Would be all right?" Matthias was animated now; he faced Andrew and seemed about to stand up. "You think it did not happen if you don't know about it. I needed to be sure. I thought you didn't know, and when you saw him, and nothing happened – from you or him – I thought that perhaps…"

"Perhaps I would go away, and things would go back to normal? Why invite me at all, then?"

"I wanted to tell you. I wanted to tell you everything. My life has been – I do not like myself, and I thought I could make something better. And then you say you are divorced – I did not know this. It changed things for me. I thought perhaps… I am sorry. This is not making sense."

Andrew was puzzled by this. "My divorce? What has that to do with anything?"

"That is one of the things I did not tell you about. I still do not know if I can do this, but I would like to tell you some things. I promise to make it true this time."

Andrew sat in silence. Matthias was looking almost pleadingly at him, but this was a situation he had thought about, and he wanted to be sure he got it right.

"Matthias, I have been through a lot in the last few months. Everything I knew, or thought I knew, about myself has turned out not to be true in some way. I'm in a bit of a fragile situation here, and I need time to come to terms with things." Realising that this probably sounded a bit harsh, he softened his tone. "Look, I know it does not compare to what you went through, but maybe you can understand what I need? Every time I speak to someone in your family, I find out something else which does not quite add up. I know Peter is my son – and so did you when I saw you in the summer – and I know that I am going to meet him at some point today or tomorrow. That's going to be hard enough for me. Please tell me some truth, Matthias. What happened?"

"My family? You spoke to – Karla?' Matthias was disbelieving.

"Yesterday. Clare and I went to see her. It was – interesting." Matthias' face fell.

"So, she told you her story, and now you won't believe anything I tell you."

Andrew thought about this. "No, Matthias. She told me very little, but enough for me to know that you didn't tell me the truth. I'd just like to know about Peter, really. But he is part of your story, too. I just want to find out the truth, really."

"All of it?"

Andrew started to reply, then caught himself. He almost smiled at the memory of the famous 'unknown unknowns' of the year before; he had been involved in more than one heated argument about the whole concept, but here was a perfect example. How could he know if he wanted to hear the whole truth? It was impossible to know what he didn't already know. *How bad could it be?* he wondered. He looked Matthias in the eye. "All of it."

MAY 1979

Matthias was cold. He thought he had dressed for the cold, but the pre-dawn air was wintry, even in May. He could see his breath every time he breathed out, and it hung about him in the damp air, so that he felt as if he had his own private cloud. The idea amused him – to be able to create your own hiding place. He smiled a little, but he did not relax. Until the train arrived, he would have to be in a state of constant alert for his father.

His old man was a light sleeper – learned it in the war, he always said – and Matthias had been sure he would have heard something. Most of his preparation had been done the day before, in that precious hour between the end of school and his father's ritual return. More often than not, Matthias spent that hour somewhere other than in his own home, so as to avoid the worst of the temper which was sure to accompany whatever had happened that day. He knew that the smart comment he had made in class earlier would earn him a few bruises, but the packing – particularly of the one thing he needed to get from his father's desk – had to be done when the house was empty.

Now, waiting for the train in the grey light of early morning, he was in a state of high alert. If the old man had heard him, had looked in the locked drawer, had seen him leave – any of a hundred scenarios he had already obsessively replayed in his mind – then he was as good as dead. If the familiar sound of his father's boots rang out on the steps before the train arrived, then he would be done for, and there was nothing he or his mother would be able to do about it. Any explanation he could give – even the truth, that he just wanted to get Karla back – would not excuse what he had done. He was a dead man.

The train was a little early, and Matthias almost clawed the door open in his hurry to get on. He found an empty carriage, carefully placed his duffel bag in one corner of it, then returned to the door to look nervously back along the platform. No sign of anyone. He had been the only person in the station, as far as he could tell, although another door slammed some way back along the train. He heard a shout, and froze, but it was a guard calling for the doors to close. Matthias pulled the door closed, lowered the window and continued to look out nervously. Even after the train moved, he continued to stare back the way he had come, and it was not until they were safely out in the countryside that he closed the window and could begin to reflect on what he was doing.

He was going to Bremen, to rescue his sister, and he didn't really know why, or how he expected to make this happen, or even what he would do if he accomplished it. He had really only done it because his mother kept asking him if there was something he could do. Some part of him felt that if he could only please her, that he would then break out of the pitiful situation he was in. He knew he had to finish school; had to submit to a few more months of his father, and then he would try to get away.

On his good days, the getting away seemed a simple affair - he would quickly gather up everything he valued, which wasn't much, pull all of his savings out of the *Sparkasse* and leave. He didn't know where he would go, and – on his good days - it didn't matter much. On his bad days, he knew he would never be able to do it; would never even be able to get out of his bed.

This, however, was looking likely to be one of his good days – he had felt that he was in an upswing for most of the week, and when he had survived yesterday with nothing worse than a bruise high up on his right thigh, he had intuited that Saturday would work. If it had been a bad day, he wouldn't have been able to get out of bed to do something as momentous as this, so the fact that he was on a train, heading north, before six in the morning, meant that everything was going to be OK.

And, until he reached Bremen, everything was OK. He knew where he was going, and the trains were on time. It was only a little after lunchtime when he arrived, and he headed out of the station purposefully. He knew exactly where he was going – first to the café, then to the apartment building. He shivered at the memory of the café; the violence of their argument – the first time he had actually seen his father hit Karla; the first time he had properly understood that he was not alone; the first time he had ever seen his father back down, when that thug – there really was no other word for him – with the gun had stepped in between them. He also remembered the beatings he had suffered when they had got home. He supposed it was shame. Shame and frustration. Whatever it was, the memory of it would never leave him. He had decided the next morning just what he needed to do, but his mother's disappearance had thrown all of that into confusion. It wasn't until she was – somehow – persuaded back into the family home, that he could actually put the plan into action. He was going to Bremen, to be with Karla, who surely understood him now. If she wanted to come back, then they would face him together; be the team they had never been, and with the grandson – Matthias had heard his name was Peter – as a buffer, surely they could find a way out of this.

The one thing he knew for sure was that Karla could not stay where she was – it was too dangerous. And that was the reason for what he had in his bag.

He found the café, went in, and ordered a coffee. He sat there for the best part of an hour, hoping that Karla would happen by and save him from having to face the apartment building, but there was no sign of her. He paid for his coffee and left, a little less certain of what he was doing than he had been an hour before.

He knew where the apartment building was, had traced it on a map in the village library, and he found it with little trouble. He walked past it six or seven times before he got up enough courage to go in, then immediately found himself faced with the problem of how to identify the correct apartment. He had a number written down, but it made little sense to him here on the ground – there were, it seemed, no numbers actually on any of the doors, and barely any light in any of the corridors. He walked up and down the stairs for a while, then sat heavily on the bottom step to try to work out his next move.

As he sat there, he became aware of a baby crying, and then – miracle of miracles – his sister's harsh voice, threatening the baby with all sorts of punishment unless it shut up. He followed the sound up to the third floor, then faltered as the crying stopped. He stood there, certain that the noise had come from one of the apartments at the back of the building, but unable to distinguish between four doors, all of which looked the same to him. One of them might have had a faded '5' painted on the wall beside it, but he couldn't be sure , in this light, and he simply stood there, wondering what to do next.

The crying started again, although it was quieted relatively quickly. He had been able to pinpoint the correct door, however, and he summoned the last of his positive feeling about the day, and knocked confidently on it. He had to knock three more times before he heard something, then it was opened a crack. He saw an eye – a familiar eye – look out at him, then the door was opened enough for him to come in. Karla slammed it behind him, and launched into a tirade before he could even think of something to say.

"First, tell me you are alone. I'll fucking kill you if you've brought any of them with you. What the fuck do you think you're doing, coming here? Don't you think I've got enough to deal with, with all this – shit. I don't need another fucking mouth to feed, you idiot. Tell me what you want, then piss off home like a good little boy."

Matthias stared at her through all this, astounded at the condition of his sister and his nephew. Neither looked like they had been clean in months – which in Peter's case, probably meant that he had never had a bath in his entire life – and Karla was not only dishevelled, but only wearing a large and unflattering pair of grey underpants. Peter was sucking listlessly at one breast; the other was sitting there in plain view, the nipple looking red and painful. Matthias realised that he was staring – at his own sister! – and looked away.

"What's the matter, little boy? Never seen real life before? This is what it's like, you know – just an endless fucking grind to keep going one day to the next. Not very glamorous, is it?"

He looked around, hoping that Karla would take the opportunity to at least put some clothes on, but what he saw merely depressed him further. The flat was essentially unfurnished, with only a couple of mattresses pushed into one corner, and an old gas stove leaning against the opposite corner. There was another room off to his left – a bathroom, he hoped – and there were various bags and cases strewn abut the place. Karla was apparently still just staring at him – he hadn't dared look – presumably waiting for some answers. He could sense her fury from where he was, and thought it best to at least tell her something.

"Karla, this is – just a mess, isn't it? I came to see if you wanted to come back – to come home or go somewhere where someone will look after you. It's tearing her apart, you know – not to be able to see you."

Karla laughed at him. "You think so? What makes you think I would go back? Expose Peter to that bastard? No, I think he's done enough damage. I'm gone from there, I'm never going back, and I suggest you don't go back, either. You got any money?"

"A little."

"Good; you can feed us, then you can just go wherever you want. I'm fine here; things will work out as soon as I don't have this fucking leech clamped to my tit all day." As she said that, she detached Peter, and took him over to the mattresses. He was, at least, wrapped in a warm-looking blanket, and he settled down to sleep with little protest. "At least he sleeps most of the time. Wish I could." She walked over and faced Matthias, seemingly uncaring that she was not only essentially naked, but also leaking milk from one nipple. Matthias looked away again, but she reached over to him, and turned his head back. "Go on, take a good look. This is what *he* does to people. This is how low you can get. Don't like the look of it? Then do the only sensible thing you might ever do in your life – get out and stay out."

"I thought we could – "

"Don't include me in whatever you've got planned. I'm out of it, and staying out of it. I'm touched that you care, really I am, but you're on your own, little brother. If it bothers you that much, tell her I'm doing fine, and she can stop snooping."

"Snooping?" Matthias was astounded. "What? Mother?"

"Yes, 'Mother'. I don't know how she gets up here, but at least once a week, she's there – she thinks I haven't seen her, which is touching. I just ignore her – if she wants to get her fun from seeing me like this, then fine. She doesn't dare come near me."

"She drives up to Bremen? How often?"

"I don't know how she gets here – I suppose she keeps it secret - but once a week – Wednesdays or Thursdays – she's there, in the café. She tried to give me money the first time, but she won't make that mistake again."

Matthias shuddered to imagine the scene Karla would have caused, and wondered if the thug with the gun had intervened again. His sister, meanwhile, did at least go off into the corner of the room where the cases were, and do her best to dress in something approximating a respectable fashion.

Once she was dressed, they went down to the café. Peter continued to sleep, and Matthias was entrusted with carrying him. The baby felt enormously heavy and at the same time fragile to Matthias – he did not have any frame of reference for it, but he seemed big for such a young baby. He said as much to Karla, who merely agreed with him. He thought about asking who the father was, but he couldn't make himself say the words.

They ate, and Karla, checking that Peter still slept, offered to carry him back to the apartment. Matthias, however, was actually enjoying the responsibility of looking after his little nephew, and continued to hold him awkwardly, but securely. This time, however, Peter woke and began to cry. Matthias tried to comfort him, but really didn't know how. Karla came to check on him, popped a not-entirely clean finger into his mouth, then declared him not hungry.

"He will need to be changed. You can learn, if you like – it is not so hard, when you know." They picked up the pace after that, and arrived back in the flat with Matthias sweating slightly from the exertion of carrying a wriggling baby. Peter was restless but not particularly unhappy, and now that they were back in the flat, Matthias could smell the problem. Karla took him from her brother, and expertly – or so it seemed to Matthias – untied him from all his clothes, unpinned the cloth nappy, which seemed to Matthias to be full of something alarmingly green in colour, then cleaned him up with it, rubbed some cream or other on him and rewrapped him in a dazzlingly clean replacement. The used one was taken through to the sink in the bathroom, washed out and draped over a door to dry.

Matthias was impressed, and said so.

"Your sister is not so useless after all, eh?" Karla actually smiled at him, and for a moment he allowed himself to think that this might yet all turn out OK. However, the smile faded as quickly as it had arrived.

"Come on," Karla barked at him, "we need to pack. We can't stay here."

"What? Why not? I mean, why leave now?"

"Because she knows where I am; she knows you have disappeared; even she will be able to work it out - she'll be here soon enough. Come on; I hate this place anyway. Let's go."

Karla packed the two cases up with a minimum of fuss – most of what she took appeared to be clean nappies and a few blankets; very few of her own things. Matthias stood and watched this process, but hesitated to join in – he knew her well enough to leave it all alone for now. Once she was done, she retrieved a long winter coat from the bathroom, plucked the still-wet nappy from the top of the door, put the coat on and stuffed the nappy into the coat pocket.

"Come on, then – you carry those; I'll take the leech."

She picked up Peter, who had been gurgling happily to himself, and headed for the door. The two cases were heavy, but not unbearably so, and Matthias slung his own duffel bag diagonally across his back so that it would not interfere with the other cases. They left the flat, Karla taking care to close the door behind then, and headed out to the street. Matthias saw nothing unusual in the street, but Karla seemed unduly nervous, and they hurried towards the station at a pace which Matthias knew he would not be able to keep up. They did not, however, stop at the station, as Matthias had expected.

"Too obvious; she'll expect us to go that way. We'll hitchhike." Matthias tried to protest, but Karla would have none of it. "No, come on; it's easy – I'll show you."

But it turned out not to be easy – partly because Karla would not accept a ride from any vehicle she deemed "too bourgeois", and partly because Peter cried for most of the journey, and even the most well-meaning of drivers tired of it after half an hour or so. They did eventually reach Buxtehude, which was most of the way to Hamburg, Karla's stated destination, and Matthias volunteered to buy them all a train ticket. It was, by now, somewhere around eight in the evening, and they were all exhausted. Karla agreed, although train travel somehow was against her principles. Once they were on the deserted train, and Karla was more easily able to feed Peter – affording Matthias another unwanted glimpse of a cracked and sore-looking nipple – they talked properly for the first time. Matthias was struck by something.

"Karla, what happened to the motorbike?"

"Oh, that. I had to sell it, of course – you think a baby pays for himself?

I got a good price, too, but it is almost gone now. When we are in Hamburg, I will organise something. The group" – that was the word she used, *Gruppe* – "will help me."

Matthias was alarmed. "What group – the ones we saw in Bremen that time? The guy with the gun? Isn't this all dangerous?"

"Not dangerous if you believe, brother. We are a collectivist group; what is ours belongs to all of us."

"Even Peter?"

She flashed an angry look at him. "No, not Peter, stupid. People are not property. Although try explaining that to *him*." Matthias didn't need to ask who 'him' was.

Matthias wanted to know how the group worked, and why they were now going to Hamburg, but she claimed it would all take too long to explain. There was something about 'cells' which he didn't quite follow, and all the explanation did was reinforce his belief that he needed to rescue both of them from this nightmare.

The address she had in Hamburg was not too far from the station, to Matthias' relief, but when they got there, he was less than reassured by what he saw. The flat in Bremen had been dirty and uncomfortable; this place was squalid. Blankets acted as windows, and the walls, such as they were, appeared to be made mainly of cardboard. There were several tall men walking around with poorly-concealed handguns, and the women seemed surly and frightening. He stood there with the two cases at his feet, holding the quietly protesting Peter, while Karla sought out someone she knew and negotiated some kind of living space. He spelt pot smoke, and suddenly felt exactly what he was – an out of his depth schoolboy.

Karla returned, smiling broadly, and introduced him to 'Mario'. The unkempt man with the Italian name took them upstairs to another part of the building – it looked like an abandoned factory or office building to Matthias – and pointed them to a corner where they could be away from the noise of the rest of the building. Matthias was close to collapse from exhaustion by now, and Karla didn't look much better. Peter was, mercifully, quiet for now, and Matthias suggested they all try to get some sleep. Karla agreed with him, and ferreted about in the cases for blankets and something to use as a pillow. They made a kind of nest on the floor, as far away as possible from the window, which was even less secure and draughtproof than the ones on the floor below, and together the three of them – the frightened schoolboy, his tough older sister, and her five week old baby – curled up and tried to sleep.

Peter woke once in the night, and was quickly quieted with, Matthias supposed, another feed. He looked over to where Karla must be, but could only make out dark shapes. He tried to sleep again, but the snuffling noises Peter was making disturbed him, and he sighed loudly and propped himself up on one elbow. Karla didn't appear to have noticed, so he tried talking to her.

"Karla? You remember when I came before? With him?" His sister grunted softly. "I didn't know, before then. Not for sure. I suppose I guessed, but I didn't know."

Karla's voice was soft, almost gentle, as if what she was saying was aimed at soothing her baby. "You thought you were alone? You never saw the bruises? No, I suppose not – he was always careful. Why did you think I cut my hair that time?"

"I don't know – it was the kind of thing you would do – I didn't think it was anything else."

"He used to pick me up by it. When I was small, it was almost fun, but later…. I cut it to spite him. I did many things to spite him, but he didn't know about most of them. I wasn't as brave as I thought I was."

"Why didn't you leave before? You could have gone when you left school."

"Or before. But it's hard – you know that. He wears you down until you cannot think, and then…." She stopped. Matthias could sense that she wanted to confess something, and he waited. "He told me – very clearly, one night when she was asleep. One night before he stopped coming to me in the night." Matthias gasped at this, but Karla ignored him." He told me that if I ever left, he would hunt me down and kill me."

"And you believed him."

"Oh, you bet I did. He is the only person I have ever been afraid of. When you showed up that day, I was ready to die. I thought he would do it right there in the café, so I had the boys follow me there – you remember?"

"I thought they were going to kill us."

"If I had told them to, they would have killed him, I think. But something stopped me; I don't want Peter to be a part of it, so I left it. I thought he would come back, but he never did."

"No, he won't now, I think. He told me many things on the drive home. About himself, about his life. He told me he only had one child now, and that he would not fight it any longer. Then he beat me so hard, I thought I would die."

"Poor Matthias. You must have known he would."

"I thought he would make you come back. When did he ever not get what he wanted?"

"Sometimes, Matthias. She has more power than you think. But she does not use it for us, only to save her own hide. So, no – before you ask again; I will not go back."

"What about Dieter?"

"What about him? He isn't the father."

"But you – he…"

"He thinks he loves me, but you found me and he didn't even try."

"And you? You love him?" Karla was silent. Finally, she almost whispered.

"In another life, I do." Matthias was alarmed by this, but let it go. He didn't really want to be part of his sister's emotional life. All he wanted was to get her away from this, and – and what else, he still didn't know. Peter gurgled softly for a time, then fell back to a contented-sounding sleep. Karla evidently dropped off as well, but Matthias lay awake, watching for the grey dawn at the edges of the windows.

At some point, before it was properly light, Karla got up, pulled on some clothes, then crouched over Peter for what seemed like hours. Matthias watched through half-closed eyes, but said nothing. After she was done communing with her son, Karla came over to him. She stared down at him, then turned away. After a moment's thought, she turned back, bent over and kissed him lightly on the temple. He didn't flinch, afraid to let her know that he was awake.

Karla stood quickly, and walked out without looking back at either of them. Matthias slept a little after that, and was surprised on waking – Peter was crying again – to find that she hadn't returned. He picked his baby nephew up, and tried to rock him back to sleep. He tried the finger test he had seen Karla do the evening before, but he couldn't tell whether Peter was hungry, or just interested in exploring this alien object with his mouth. He thought that he should check the nappy, and wrestled with Peter for some time, much to the baby's obvious discomfort and distress. The nappy was wet but not soiled, and Matthias found himself unsure whether that meant it needed to be changed or not. Since he had already got Peter more or less undressed, he decided to persevere.

He looked around for the case full of baby supplies, but was afraid to lay Peter down anywhere in this grimy room, so carried him in the crook of his arm. Peter cried more lustily at this, and appeared to be shivering. Matthias put him in the case where he would at least have something soft to lie on, but Peter responded to this by urinating over everything. Matthias had an instant flash of fury, which he recognised but clamped down on, and continued to search for a clean nappy.

As he located something clean enough and dry enough to be of use, he was aware of a figure in the doorway to his left. He looked up to see an enormous bearded man – not anyone he had seen before – scowling at him.

"Are you going to shut that fucking thing up?" the stranger asked, but did not stay for an answer.

Matthias worked faster after that, but the nappy he put on was poorly fastened, and he was sure it would fall off at any moment. He found some of the less-damp clothes, and spent a good ten minutes trying to persuade Peter in to them. Once he was done, Peter was still crying, and Matthias felt close to tears himself. He tried rocking again, but this had no effect. He slipped his little finger back into Peter's mouth, and this time felt an unmistakeable sucking sensation. Panicked, he looked around for something; anything, which he could feed the baby. He knew that they only really drank milk, but would he drink water? And did it have to be boiled first? The point was moot, because the only fluid he had was a foil sachet of sugary orange squash, and he knew that wasn't the right thing.

He was also aware of a growing restlessness among the other residents of the building – the knocks of frustration on the walls and floor were becoming more frequent, and the muttered curses had become more distinct and more threatening. He momentarily felt overwhelmed, unable to figure out what to do next, but knew that, as long as he was responsible for Peter, he couldn't allow himself to be consumed by his black mood. He picked Peter up again, stood up, and headed for the door. He wasn't sure exactly who it was he was going to seek help from, but as he walked tentatively down the cast-iron stairs, he fixed not on the pharmacist or health clinic which had been his first thought, but on his mother. She would know what to do. An hour in a train back to Bremen, and all would be well. Karla said she would be there; that's where he would go.

He got no more than five paces beyond the outside door, however, before he was confronted by a furious Karla, who had evidently heard Peter from wherever she had been, and had come running. She grabbed the screaming Peter from him, belted him powerfully across the face with the flat of her palm, then hauled her shirt up, and affixed Peter once more to herself.

Matthias staggered back, rubbing his ear, which was ringing. He had no words to protest, but needed none.

"You fucking idiot! Ten more minutes, and I would be there, but no – you cannot take it. I won't come back to you, so you steal him! Go on, fuck off out of my life! Fuck off back to Mummy and Daddy! See if they'll do whatever it is you want, because I have more important things to do." She made to hit him again, but cradling Peter took a higher priority, and Matthias cringed away from a blow which never landed.

Karla pushed past him into the building, and he stood there, weeping silently for everything and nothing.

Two hours later, he was back in Bremen. He had no clear recollection of the journey, but he had an unexpired train ticket in his pocket, and he held on to that as if it were some kind of talisman. He realised that his bag, with most of what was left of his money, was still in Hamburg. He might not see it again, which wouldn't have bothered him too much, but for the one item in there which he could not allow anyone to know was there.

He walked morosely back to the café where he and his father had confronted Karla, and peered in through the window. There she was!

Sitting on her own in a far corner, with a clear view over everything which happened or was likely to happen in the place was his mother. She looked old; grey haired and grey-skinned. Her posture, of which she had been so proud, seemed to have leaked away from her, and she was half-slumped in the chair, nursing a clear brown mug of milky-looking coffee. Matthias had a sudden flashback to a café in Chester with those same mugs – he had been happy that afternoon, he thought irrationally, and an overpowering emotion surged through him for a moment; he thought of Anne, then he took a deep breath and pushed the door open.

His mother looked up, and recognised him at once, but she did not stir from her seat. He walked over and sat down opposite her, but still she said nothing.

"Mum?" He sounded pathetic and lost, but still she simply stared at him. He began to cry, but this, too, elicited no reaction. Eventually, his mother lifted her mug to her lips and drained it.

"Come on, boy. We need to find her. Show me."

She gave him nothing; barely a flicker of recognition, and nothing else. He could have been a stranger passing on an impersonal message, but he was her only son, wrung out and emotionally drained, sitting across a grubby Formica table from her, in obvious distress and in need of something – reassurance; affection; love – but getting only what he had had from her all his life. He hadn't expected it, but the reality crushed what little positivity he had left out of him. He watched her gather her things up, then mutely followed her as she walked back out on to the street.

He was startled to see his father's car parked around the corner. Startled and then terrified – was the old man here too? His mother looked over at him. "He is in bed. Won't come out. He doesn't even know I am here – he thinks I am in Fulda, as usual. You have destroyed him. You and your sister."

Matthias' mind spun. *We destroyed him? If only*, he thought. *He* - but this train of thought was too difficult; too painful. He got into the passenger seat of the car, tilted it back to something close to a recline, and closed his eyes.

His mother was not a particularly good driver; she got little practice, he supposed, and she tended not to move her foot fully off the accelerator pedal as she changed gear, which caused the engine to protest at every change. He kept his eyes firmly closed as she negotiated her way around the centre of Bremen. He wondered where they were going, since he had said nothing, but his mother suddenly pulled the car over to the kerb, and he looked up. They were at the foot of a tall block of apartments. He squinted over to the driver's side, where his mother was peering hopefully out.

"Not here," he heard himself say. "They are in Hamburg. But she will not see us – any of us."

"We will see about that. You have the gun?" *Shit. She knew, which meant he knew, which meant –which meant his life was over.*

"No." He wondered if he had the mental strength to bluff it out, but quickly found that he didn't. "I left everything there this morning. She threw me out; thought I was kidnapping Peter."

"So, we shall go and get all of it, then. I suppose she is not alone – she has these friends; I have seen some of them." Matthias wanted to ask her about that, but couldn't muster the strength. Let her think whatever she wanted to think. He turned away from her, and pretended to sleep.

As his mother drove, he allowed his thoughts to wander. He thought of summer afternoons, playing in the back garden with Karla. She had been a fun companion for him as a young child; he was terrified of his father, but Karla seemed to be his shelter. He tried to work out when that had stopped; when their relationship had wandered off course, but he couldn't pin anything down. He could hear his mother humming tunelessly next to him, and he thought about her. He had assumed that she was normal, just like all other mothers until he was six or seven, when his understanding of the wider world began to take shape. His aunts were slightly too overbearing for his taste, but it wasn't until he began to relate to the mothers of some of his other friends that he understood that what he thought of as overbearing was, in fact, normal maternal affection.

He often tormented himself with thoughts of what he might have done as a child to lose the love in the one person who was supposed to love him unconditionally, but something about the way he had seen Karla so brutally exposed, and so raw in the last 24 hours had solidified an idea in him. It wasn't his fault – Karla was like that, too. She even projected some of her mother on to herself; calling Peter 'leech', and so on. He felt guilty, somehow, for the fact that he had always been so wrapped up in his own misery that he had not appreciated what Karla had also been going through. Perhaps if they had stuck together, all of this might have been better.

He could feel his state of mind slipping away again – he began to silently berate himself for his behaviour that morning, blaming himself for not being good enough to keep Peter quiet, or to look after him, or whatever it was he had done to provoke Karla so. All he wanted to do now was to crawl into a hole somewhere and wait for his life to be over. Which, if his father got to know about the stolen gun, might be soon enough.

In some part of his consciousness, Matthias understood that he was not normal – that he, perhaps, had some kind of illness which made him behave this way. In his better moments, he could even rationalise this to the point where he could squarely blame his parents for the way he was, and dedicate himself to getting away from them and finding some kind of normality. Today, however, all he could see was that Karla had tried this, had not been able to escape them, and appeared just as miserable, if not more so, than she had been when she had been at home. He let out a deep breath, hoping it might help to clear his mind, but he still couldn't think straight. He recognised some of the signs of what was happening to him – his thoughts becoming fractured and dissonant, and his inability to focus on anything.

Matthias had one solid, proven method of holding it all together in moments like these, and he used it now. He forced himself to think about the previous summer and of a Friday afternoon in Liezl's house, when his guardian angel had saved him. He had been so bad that afternoon, and it had come on so suddenly, that he had been genuinely frightened by it. Everything had been going well; they all seemed to be having fun, then Andy went back to pack, and by the time they were halfway back to Liezl's, he realised that Karla was probably there. He knew he should do something, but was unable to organise his thoughts properly; unable to break away from the group and go to Andy's aid. He just kept walking, a few paces behind the others, willing them to ask him what was bothering him, but they carried on as if nothing was wrong.

Once they were inside, Anne had excused herself to go up and pack, and the three girls had laughed about it, saying that she would be asleep in minutes. He joined in the laughter, but felt almost hysterical about it. His cousins had suggested a sauna, and he had perked up at this, but Erika vetoed his involvement, saying that it was unfair on Clare. Clare had protested, but she had looked uncomfortable, and the other two had closed ranks. They got up to go downstairs, and Erika had patted him on the shoulder, and said something about next time, but he scarcely heard her.

Sitting on his own in the living room, he had begun to unravel. He raged at the unfairness of life in general, and his cousins in particular; he stood up and marched around the room in an undirected fury; he swore as creatively as he could at everything and nothing, but nothing changed. He could hear the girls' laughter faintly from below, and he paced around the ground floor, actually tearing at his hair at one point.

He suddenly remembered about Anne. She was probably the calmest and kindest person he had ever met. Maybe she would know what to do; how to help him. He went upstairs with no more plan than to find her and talk to her. Liezl had said something about Anne liking him at some point, although he thought he understood that she liked Andy more. That did not concern him for now; he simply needed someone to talk to him and calm him.

He knew which room she was in, and tried the handle. The door opened, and he peered in. She seemed to be sleeping on the bed, as predicted, and he let himself in. Just being in the room with her was soothing. He listened to her breathing for a time, and could feel his mind calming. He walked over to the side of the bed and stared at her. She wasn't quite what he would call pretty, but she was kind and solid and reliable, and she was all that he needed right now. From the door, he had thought she was naked, but closer up he could see that she had taken her shirt off - her flesh-coloured bra had given him the illusion of nudity. Standing by the bed, he could see she still had her new jeans on as well. He walked around the foot of the bed to the side Anne wasn't occupying, and then, with no thought for what he was doing; no rationale or even understanding of what drove him, he started to undress.

Anne stirred as he was unfastening his own jeans, and he quickly snapped them shut again, then explained who he was, and why he was there. He didn't mention his mental turmoil, just that he had been alone, and thought he would keep her company. He took her silence as acceptance of this, so he lay down beside her. She moved away from him a little, but it felt like accommodation rather than avoidance, and he closed his eyes.

Anne's breathing returned to its calm, measured pace, and he felt emboldened enough to reach out and touch her. He put his hand on her shoulder, and when she did not recoil, he began to gently stroke her back, trying to avoid the straps and clasp of her bra. After a few minutes of this, Anne sat up and looked at him. He panicked, and tried to stand; tried to explain, and Anne began to scream.

Then the miracle. She stopped herself, looked straight at him, and almost smiled. Her features softened as she stared, and she seemed somehow to understand him. He began to cry; not his usual tears of rage or frustration, but a genuine, heartfelt weeping. His thought processes couldn't quite keep up with his emotions, but he supposed it was because someone had shown him some kindness. She made him sit, and although he was now embarrassed about being shirtless, and what she could surely see, she seemed to simply accept it. She touched him briefly on his back, but the shock of it – so close to the bruises and scabs around his spine which never seemed to heal properly - caused him to jump, and she withdrew. She asked him questions which he really couldn't properly answer, and then she got up, went to lock the door, and after a pause she got back into bed with him. She told him that they were only going to hug, and he began to cry again.

They lay together - like two innocents, he later thought - until he felt peaceful again, and Anne seemed to be asleep. He resumed the stroking of her back, and even tentatively tried to undo the clasp his hand kept brushing against, but he understood that would cross a line, and he withdrew. His left arm was under the sleeping Anne, and he rolled her gently over to extricate it. As he did so, she murmured something in English to him, but didn't fully wake. He looked down at her and froze.

Her bra had moved as she turned, and much of her right breast was visible to him. He leaned his head over, and Anne moved slightly, enough that the nipple, soft and dark against her pale skin, came into view. He stopped breathing, astounded by what he was seeing – although he shied away from nudity because of his bruises, it was not so uncommon to see one's friends or relatives topless from time to time, in the sauna or at the pool. This, however; this was nakedness, and it had caused his mouth to go dry and his heart to pound.

He had intended to kiss Anne gently on the cheek as he got up, but instead he lowered his face to where she was exposed, and – barely touching the skin so as not to alarm her – he kissed her breast, right by the partly exposed nipple instead. As he did so, he felt a calm descend upon him.

His mind was clear; he was able to think clearly again, and he understood that he might have done something terrible, but that Anne wasn't making him feel that way. He stood quietly, so as not to wake her, his guardian angel, his saviour, and looked down on her. She was still just Anne, with the unfashionable hairstyle, and the body shape he couldn't help thinking of as matronly, but she was also the most beautiful thing he had ever seen. He stared and stared, willing the moment to last for eternity, then eventually tore himself away and dressed.

As he left the room, he looked back, and took a deep breath. *Everything will be alright*, he thought, *for someone cares for me.*

Sitting slumped in the car as they drew into Hamburg, however, he wasn't so sure about that. Anne had been the best thing ever to happen to him, although he cursed his wasted time in Chester when, under the eyes of his father, he had been unable to do anything about getting to know her until it was almost too late, and then he had managed to go too far in an attempt to recreate that magical afternoon, and almost ruined everything.

Almost, because once he was home, Anne had begun to write to him; chatty letters at first, asking about him and his family, and what was happening at school, but after a few weeks, more personal, almost intimate, and Matthias had clung to them as if they were the life rafts which would float him out of his miserable existence. She confessed in the letters that once she had thought carefully about what had happened between them that she thought of it as a comforting thing; that she had been able to help him in his hour of need, as she put it, and that she had, on reflection, actually enjoyed what they had done. He didn't know what might come of all of this, especially as she also wrote about Andy in some detail, but he had concrete evidence that she was still out there; his guardian angel who would look over him and keep him safe. All he had to do was to keep thinking of Anne, and let those thoughts blot out the world.

But some days that was easier to say than do. His mother interrupted his reverie by pulling into a petrol station and insisting that he go and use the bathroom – "clean yourself up," she shouted after him, "you look disgraceful." He almost laughed at this, since he knew where they were going, and the better he looked, the more they would stand out, but he – as he had done all his life – meekly complied.

Once back in the car, his mother started to grill him – about his journey, about whether he had planned it with Karla in advance, about how he had managed to get the gun out of the house without his father knowing. He mumbled and grunted his replies in what he hoped was a convincingly teenage-like way, and the questions dried up. The only communication they had from that point was to do with directions. Matthias thought briefly about claiming not to be able to remember, but more than anything, he wanted this car journey to be over. What followed, followed, he thought to himself.

He directed her to the location without having to talk about anything else, and his mother managed to find a parking spot which allowed some kind of view of the front door – Matthias assured her that sooner or later, Karla would have to come out that way, but given that she had obviously been shopping that morning, it might be some time. His mother got out of the car and walked over, but didn't get particularly close before turning on her heel and returning to the car. All she said to him was "sleep now, we will fix this in the morning." Matthias tried to explain that this wasn't a good place to park overnight, but his mother simply stared at him until he stopped talking, then he turned over and closed his eyes again.

This time, thinking about Anne worked and he slept for some time – he couldn't have said how long. When he woke, it was dark, and his mother was silent in the seat next to him. He looked over at her, but she didn't move, just kept staring fixedly at the doorway. After what seemed to him to be an hour of this, he decided that he should at least get out and walk around. His mother didn't react to him getting out of the car, although he heard her open the window once he was walking.

He walked back to the door he had come out of that morning – possibly the morning before, he thought – and looked at it. It appeared to be locked, or possibly even boarded up. He tried to remember how Karla had managed to get in the day before, but all he knew was that she had some kind of knock. He turned away, just as the door opened. A young girl slipped out, and he grabbed the edge of the door. She stared at him, but merely shrugged and turned away. He cautiously looked in, but could see very little.

He closed the door behind him, and was about to walk along the corridor when a deep voice yelled at him.

"Lock the door, idiot!" He turned and stared at the door. As his eyes adjusted, he could make out a long iron bar which obviously slotted into a gap in the stonework at the side of the doorway. It was something like an ancient castle, he told himself, and wondered how it had been arranged. He gently slid the bar into place, then tiptoed inside. The voice thanked him, more or less politely, and he breathed normally for the first time in several minutes.

Karla was still sleeping in the same corner. Peter was curled up beside her, and he contented himself with simply sitting and watching for a while. Then he remembered the bag, and crept over to the corner where he had left it. Karla mustn't have looked inside it, because everything – the money, his book, and especially the cold, heavy object wrapped in an old t-shirt – was still there. He took the gun out and looked at it in the faint light from outside.

He supposed it had been something to do with the war, but since he wasn't even supposed to know about it, he had never been able to ask his father about it. As he looked at it, he wondered about that. Was there anything which could have brought him closer to his father? If he had shown an interest in things his father prized – not the gun, perhaps, but other things – would there have been some kind of bond between them? His thoughts began to race and jumble again; just thinking about the old man could do that to him, and he tried to shut them down, to bring a vision of Anne to mind – his guardian angel would help him deal with this.

He tried to focus on the gun, tried to understand why he had even brought it. All he knew for certain at this point was that it had been terribly important to him to have it, as if it would be able to give him some kind of safety or security. Looking at it now, he understood how absurd that was. It was so heavy, so ungainly, that he didn't even know if he could lift it and point it at anyone with any kind of accuracy. And as for firing it, he wasn't even sure that it was loaded. He wanted to look, but was scared of making any noise which would wake Peter or even Karla. He simply held it and stared, trying to judge by feel if it had any bullets in it. He tried to work out how to fire it – he knew that pulling the trigger alone probably wouldn't actually fire the thing, it would have to be cocked first, and he knew something about pulling the hammer back to load, but his knowledge came from books and toy guns, so he was more than a little unsure.

He began to blur the idea of the gun and Anne in his mind; the idea that if she was here, everything would be fine confused with the sense of security the gun was supposed to bring him. He struggled to think clearly, but knew that the gun wasn't calming him the way Anne did, and holding on to that, eventually, slowed his heart rate and got his breathing back under control.

The more he looked at the gun, the more ridiculous it all seemed. Anyone who saw him point a 40-year old pistol at them would probably just laugh. He wrapped it again, catching a whiff of the oily smell he had first noticed when removing it from the desk drawer the morning of his departure.

He curled up on the floor, thought of Anne, and tried to make a plan. He had intended to come in, get Karla, and warn her about Mother. He thought he would have enough money for them to get away again before she woke up, but he had no idea where to go or what to do once there, and the sight of his sister and his nephew sleeping peacefully there had frozen him. He lay down and closed his eyes. This felt bad – his indecisiveness was almost crippling, and he felt his heart begin to race again. He knew that this panicked state was a reaction to having effectively betrayed Karla, and that the simplest way to resolve it would be to wake her, deal with the consequences of that, and move on. But there was a striking difference between what he knew to be sensible, and what he was actually able to get his mind to instruct his body to do. He had experienced this before, usually in social situations at school, or when debating how to break bad news to his parents, but this was on an entirely different scale, and he was truly afraid of it.

He fought sleep for what felt like hours, stirring himself more than once, and managing to conceal the gun a little during one of those restless bouts, but eventually, and against his will, he slept.

He woke to shouting and crying. He struggled to understand what was happening and where he was – adrenaline coursed through him, but it served to confuse rather than awaken him, and he took several minutes to come to enough to piece things together. The crying had to be Peter, although no-one seemed to be attending to him. The shouting was Karla, and she was shouting forcefully at someone, but not – as far as he could tell – him.

He tried to look up without alerting his sister to the fact that he was awake, but the light coming around the window coverings was falling across his face, and he had to squint and move his head to see anything. He saw Karla in her usual belligerent pose, fists balled at her hips, but he couldn't see Peter, and he couldn't see who she was yelling at. He needed the crying to stop, and he needed to understand what was happening. He tried to make sense of the words, but they were being delivered at such a volume and such a pace that he couldn't decipher them at first. If only someone would shut Peter up!

His fear and confusion was not helped by the sudden understanding that the other person in the room had to be his mother. He panicked properly then, realising that he had failed Karla not once, but twice, and he rolled over, fumbling for his bag. Perhaps he could just make a run for it while they argued. The shouting and the crying wouldn't let up. His mother kept saying over and over "he is mine; you cannot look after him." And Karla, clearly frantic, was screaming swear words and insults. Matthias felt tears on his face; all he needed was time to understand what was happening, but the noise was too much – all he knew for certain was that this was all his fault. Peter somehow found the lungpower to increase the volume of his screams, and Matthias felt something in him give way. He had to stop it. He reached for where he thought his bag was, but instead came up with the gun. He shook the wrapping off it, and tried to stand up. He started to add his own voice to the cacophony, but he couldn't make himself heard.

He looked at his mother, her gaze fixed on Peter, who she was holding, and then looked over at Karla. Neither of them seemed to have shown any interest in Matthias, and he wondered if he could just walk out and disappear. He looked at the door, in time to see Mario and at least one other large bearded man fill it. They added their voices to the noise, and Matthias was sure he saw some kind of weapon at Mario's waist. He lifted the gun again, not sure what he was intending to actually do with it, and this got Mario's attention. He bellowed something about "a gun!" which penetrated Karla's fury. Her head snapped round to look at him just as he reached for the hammer. He wasn't pointing it at anyone in particular, just hoping that he could stop the noise by appearing to be in control of things. His clammy hands found the hammer mechanism slippery, and he fumbled with it for a moment.

Suddenly, he felt, rather than saw, Mario rushing him from the door. *Please just stop Peter crying!* The gun swung round in the general direction of his mother, and at that moment, his fingers let go of the hammer mechanism, and something unspeakably violent happened to his right hand. Mario thundered into him, crashing him to the concrete floor. His head bounced off the floor, but the pain of that was nothing compared to the pain in his hand. He couldn't see, but could hear that the noise in the room had changed appreciably. Peter was no longer crying, his mother was whimpering, but Karla – Karla was screaming in a way he had never heard before. He tried to sit up and see what had happened, but Mario kept him pinned to the ground. He tried to protest, but Mario swung an arm at him, and either the punch or the second contact with the floor knocked him cold.

OCTOBER 2003

"Everyone thinks I don't remember what happened. Everyone thinks I blamed my mother for the whole thing, but this is not true. I have never told anyone this, Andrew, but it is time."

"Told anyone what?" Andrew was only a little surprised by what he had heard – from Karla's description the day before, Matthias' story had to be the truth, or close to it. He didn't allow himself, for the moment, to think about the fact that Matthias might well have killed Peter, even accidentally.

"I never spoke up. My mother took the blame, and I let her. They said that she took the gun, and rubbed her hands all over it – this was when I was still unconscious. They said that she just handed Peter over when the police came, and said "I did this, you must take me away.""

"What about Mario?"

"Are you joking? Whatever he and his group were, they were not legal. As soon as it seemed I was not a danger, they all ran. Karla told me once that she talked to him after, but I don't know the details."

"What happened to you? Were you really in prison?"

"Not prison, no. It was a kind of hospital. It felt like a prison, but it was for my safety, they told me. I – I understand it now; they said I tried to kill myself, but that was never true – I wanted to punish myself, and I hurt myself. Also, I was not able to speak for a time, and then I decided – nobody knows this, Andrew – I decided that it was easier for everyone if I did not speak. I said nothing about any of it for three years, and in that time, I only would talk to Karla."

"And she forgave you?"

"At the time, I thought so. She came to visit, she brought Peter. She told me that she had gone back to Witkreuz, and lived with Dieter. But she hated me too. I don't know why she came to visit."

Andrew thought about all of this.

"So, you know now that you were – bipolar, I think they call it now?"

"Yes. I think I knew then. It seems obvious to me now, but I don't know about then. I thought I was normal. This is not so unusual, I am told."

"But why do you live like this now? Are you well?"

"This is a long question. I do not see my family, because I have told so many – I do not like to call them 'lies', but I have told many stories. I know that they hate me, too. But I live here, because mother is here, and because he is, too." Matthias looked over to his father's grave, and Andrew said nothing.

"I know – it is crazy, but it is the truth. I am here because he is here. I cannot explain it. Karla told me once why she left. She said that her plan was to be pregnant, and to let him see it – she knew that Peter would be a big baby, and – I don't know, Andrew – she knew it was you, even then. I was so stupid."

"But why did she leave?"

"Because of your friend – Clare. I don't know what they said to one another, but it made Karla understand that she must go. She blamed Clare for it all, you know."

"I know – we found out yesterday. Clare says that Karla had already decided to leave, but seeing Clare also pregnant just pushed her to go. The other things – I don't think Clare is responsible, but maybe I don't know everything"

Matthias sighed. "And the thing which is a problem for me – has been my problem all along. She never blamed me. I shot at Peter; I hit her, but she blamed everyone apart from me. I do not know why."

Andrew wondered about this, but said "she doesn't talk to you, though?"

"Not so. I didn't tell you the whole truth. It is me. I do not talk to her. I do not talk to anyone in the family. Not since he died. That was my fault, too."

Andrew stared. "What, your father's death?"

"No, not so much. I never told you what happened to him. This is my fault. All the time I was in hospital, they kept asking me why I was doing these things – why did I take the gun, why did I not stop my mother, why was I not talking to anyone, why I was hurting myself. Finally, I understood something. Even when I was feeling better, I could not face the possibility of being sent home to him. My mother was in prison, Karla was with Dieter. I had nothing – I would have to go back to him. And he would surely kill me. So I knew what I had to do. I told the truth."

"About him?"

"Yes. And perhaps a little more than the truth. They did not believe me at first, but Karla had already said some things, and so did some others who had been his pupils – I think there were some girls who – never mind, it was believed in the end, and they took him away. My cousins have never forgiven me for this – they think I lied. Of course, some of it, I did. I was worried that it was not enough; he would not be punished enough. So I told some other stories. They do not believe me, so I keep away."

"Matthias, you were not responsible for who your father was."

"They tell me this, but I know what happened. I believe that my parents were happy until I was born. I was – ah, what does it matter now? I think that things were normal until then, and after me, he was – not normal. I did this, even if I did not mean to."

Andrew looked closely at Matthias, but the other man seemed to be calm and composed. He started to say something, but Matthias cut him off.

"One other thing, Andrew. Perhaps hardest of all." Andrew nodded for him to go on, and he took a deep breath, then looked away.

"You know about me and Anne?"

Andrew nodded, realised the Matthias couldn't see him, and managed a gruff "yeah."

"All of it? Did she tell you about after?"

"After what? I know you and she - slept together. In Chester. I'm not sure what I think about it, but I cannot be angry. It happened; it probably doesn't change anything."

"This is what I thought." Matthias was silent for some time, and Andrew started to worry. He knew that the right thing to do – especially after what he had heard – was to offer forgiveness, and to move on. He and Anne had not been together at the time, and weren't now, so what did it really matter? However, as he prepared himself to say something along those lines, Matthias spoke again.

"It wasn't the only time. I'm sorry, Andrew, to tell you like this, but I promised to tell you the whole truth." Andrew had a curious sensation, as if he was watching this conversation from afar, but he said nothing, made no protest. "She wrote to me – I said that."

Andrew remembered, and again nodded pointlessly – Matthias was still looking off towards his father's gravestone.

"So, she wrote, and I wrote, and then I was in hospital, and she wrote, but I did not reply; she must never know, I thought. I did not reply until I came out, when my father was gone. I went back home, and I lived in my room for months. It was 1982, I remember. Anne was in Exeter then, I think."

"She was – I was in St Andrews; it wasn't exactly convenient."

Matthias breathed out heavily, then continued. "So, I knew about you and her, and I thought I was happy – it seemed to be good for her. Then she offered to come and see me."

Andrew instantly realised what must have happened. 1982 – Anne had gone Inter-Railing with three university friends; Andrew hadn't been able to afford it, and had spent a miserable month doing menial summer jobs for the council. She must have gone to see Matthias then.

"She came here, I think she hoped to see Liezl, but Liezl was in Italy that summer. Erika was also not here, I remember, but I don't know why. She knocked on my door, and – well, it happened, Andrew. I cannot excuse it; it just seemed as if fate had done something. I needed my – ah, I should not say this."

Andrew hesitated, then encouraged Matthias to finish.

"Well, I thought about her as my guardian – you know. And she was here. We talked, and she stayed overnight – I am ashamed of this, to tell you now. But when she was gone, I came back into the world. Before she came, I had many medicines, and I had therapy; I wasn't truly in the world. She did that for me, Andrew. I should be sorry for it, but I cannot."

Andrew thought about that summer. He had been, he thought, gradually working on lowering Anne's defences. He remembered that they had come close to having sex on more than one occasion, but that one or other of them – he remembered it was Anne, but began to doubt himself – had always backed out. Their relationship had been strained by this, and they had almost parted more than once over the next couple of years. He thought he had been clear about what was going on then, but he was doubting himself and his memories now.

He realised that he had said nothing, and tried to remember what Matthias' last words had been.

"Don't apologise, Matthias. I think you did what was best for you. You didn't owe me anything then. If I have a problem with this, it is with Anne, not you. And I wonder if I do have a problem. I need to think about this."

"Then you must know that there was one other time, and I am very ashamed of this. After that time, we agreed not to be in contact any more. She said that I was able to be myself again, and I didn't need her to help with this. I was not so sure, but she was right. I met Gerda soon after, and I thought my life was normal. And then something happened. Something happened soon after he died."

Andrew looked over at the headstone. *August 1993.* 10 years ago. His children were small then, and Matthias' would have been, too. He tried to remember what he had been doing at that time, but it was a little vague.

"I went to see you. Not her, I don't think, although my mind is not so clear about this. There was a school trip – I should laugh about this, I think – and we were in a place called Havant. I arranged to take some time, and I took a train…"

Andrew interrupted him. "How did you know where we were?"

"Anne wrote to me. Always, when she changed house, she would write.

No letter, nothing else, just a new address. I had kept it, and I saw it was easy on the train, so I went. If you had been there, it would have all been different, I think. She did not recognise me to start with, and then she was surprised, and invited me in. She said you were in America somewhere, and we just talked. Your children were small – like mine, I remember - so we did not have a chance to speak until late. Then, I told her about my father. We did not talk much about anything else; but – oh, Andrew, it was late, and it was a bad, bad thing I did. I did not want to do it, but I could not stop it."

Andrew was silent. He stood and walked slowly over to Rolf's headstone. The old man glowered back at him, and he shivered. Which trip had that been, he wondered? 1993. Probably New York. A pointless conference about technology which was obsolete within a year. He had been bored most of the time, and missed his children. He thought he remembered missing Anne, but wondered if that was actually true. If it was New York, then that would have been one of the times he had come close to being unfaithful. He couldn't remember her name now, but she had been genuinely interested in him all week, and on the final night had given him enough hints. He had got as far as her hotel room door, but had taken a deep breath and gone back down to the bar.

Some unreconstructed part of him now thought that he might as well have done it. He looked over his shoulder, half expecting Matthias to have got up and left, but he was still there, staring sadly back. Andrew shrugged. What did it matter now, he tried to tell himself. He considered Matthias. What a fucked-up life, and if Anne was some kind of comfort to him at times, then perhaps I should just be...

But that was stupid. He *was* angry. He felt betrayed and lost. He hadn't lifted a finger to try to save his marriage, but he hadn't actually gone out and slept with anyone else, either. He tried to work out what he felt about Matthias, but the answer seemed mostly to be pity. He wanted to feel angry with him, but simply couldn't. He needed to talk to Clare. In fact, he plain and simple needed Clare. A thought struck him. He would go and talk to Clare, and something else besides. He walked back over to Matthias, and spoke to him in a soft voice.

"Come on, Matthias. We're going."

"Where?"

"I need to talk to someone, and I think it's time to bring this all to an end, don't you? 25 years is long enough. Let's put all our cards on the table. It's time to reintroduce you to your cousins, I think."

Matthias started to protest, but then shrugged.

"If this is how you punish me, then I accept it. I deserve to have worse, I think, but perhaps you are right. I should face up for what I have done."

Andrew looked at him. "I suspect you'll find that you did nothing, my old friend. You and I are not so different, after all. We have spent our lives sitting back and waiting for things to happen. Well, I wonder if perhaps we need to make some things happen now."

Matthias looked positively terrified at the prospect, but he said nothing. He stood, and meekly followed the much taller Andrew back down the hill into the village.

As they walked, Andrew thought. He had no idea what he thought about Matthias and Anne, and everything else was pushed aside as he tried to understand all he had just heard. He tried several times to find something to say to Matthias, but nothing sensible came to mind. All he knew for certain was that he needed to talk, and he needed, more than at any time in his entire life, it seemed, to take some positive action about something; anything. He felt as if some shackles had been removed – it was time to throw off the old Andrew.

As they came up the drive, he could see Erika's car back in front of the big window – Polly must have returned from whatever her errand had been. He suddenly found himself wondering about her and Peter, and about when he would actually meet his son – until he saw the car, he had managed to quite forget the primary purpose of this trip. This realisation added yet another layer of confusion to his overburdened mind, so it was with some relief that he saw Clare come hurrying out of the door towards them.

Clare was smiling, but her words were not exactly what he had expected to hear. She raised her voice as she came towards them, and he had no difficulty hearing her.

"Oh, Andrew, no. *This* wasn't the plan. This wasn't it at all. Damn. Just when it seemed to be coming together. Hello, Matthias, by the way. You're looking well." Clare returned her attention to Andrew. "Shit, big guy, you actually went and took some initiative. Well, you never can tell, can you? Look, don't take this the wrong way, but this complicates things a little. You'd better come in. Both of you. Bugger."

Andrew smiled in spite of himself, and followed. As he crossed the threshold, however, his smile died. Coming from the kitchen was a very familiar voice, and he almost stumbled. He grabbed Clare's arm before she could go and announce their arrival.

"Erm, Clare? Actually; this complicates things a lot. I *told* you I didn't want any more surprises."

"Yes, well, I'm sorry about that, but I didn't know for sure until this morning that she could even make it. We're all here now, though; we'll have to make the best of it. Drink?"

Andrew stared at her. "Yes, please. Large one. Lots of alcohol in it. And I think you'd better take Matthias somewhere until I have had a chance to talk to my ex-wife"

Clare grabbed the bemused Matthias' arm, and dragged him off to the main living room. Andrew decided that he'd better get the drink himself, and while he was about it, warn everyone else that he'd somehow managed to mess everything up. *This*, he thought, *is what happens when you try to take the initiative.*

Andrew walked into the kitchen with the intention of carrying this off nonchalantly, but as soon as he saw Anne, he was stopped in his tracks. She was – different. She was chatting animatedly with Liezl, laughing and running her fingers through hair which had been cut short, waved in some way, coloured and styled. She was wearing a sweater he didn't recognise, one which suited her very well, and a pair of jeans. He simply stood and stared. Anne looked over at him and smiled. No – grinned.

"Andrew! You like it? I'm terrified, to tell you the truth, but I'm stuck with it now." *She's been drinking*, he realised. She was holding a large glass of red wine, and she looked very pleased about something. He tried to find his voice, but what came out was slightly strangulated, and he had to start again.

"Hi, Anne. You look great, actually. Where are our children?"

She smiled, took another sip, and then explained how her mother had come down for the weekend, and the children were probably either running rings round her by now, or terminally bored already.

"Neither of them has called me yet, so it's probably not too bad. Mother wasn't sure she could get away until yesterday, which is why no-one told you until now. And I thought it might be a nice surprise"

It's as if none of it ever happened, he thought. *She's pretending that we're just long-lost friends back together for a fun weekend. Or something else is going on.* He stared at her, then managed to find the open wine bottle, poured himself a generous glass, and drank half of it. She came over to him, and he turned to face her. She was smiling, but her eyes were telling a slightly different story. He had to tell her something, he realised.

"Anne, we need to talk. Not here; somewhere quiet." Anne looked quizzically at him, then turned back to whisper something to Liezl. The German woman smiled cheerfully, and pointed. Anne told her that she remembered, put her glass down, then motioned for Andrew to follow her.

Out in the hallway, he expected her to head outside, or up to a bedroom, but Anne turned left, and headed downstairs.

"Come on, Andrew; this'll be fun. I've been thinking about it all week, and I don't want to miss any opportunity."

The famous sauna. He hesitated, then looked back to where he could hear Clare's voice. She was talking animatedly to someone in rapid German, which he struggled to follow, but it appeared to be a potted life story, so he supposed she was talking to Matthias. He heard Anne walk on, and turned to follow.

The sauna surprised him. For some reason, he had expected a small box in one corner of a dark cellar, but this was as bright and clean as any hotel he had ever been in. Anne closed the door behind them, and walked past him. He stood and watched as she undressed without any of the self-conscious folding of arms about herself which he remembered. He looked at her, perhaps slightly slimmer than when he had last seen her naked – *and how long ago was that*, he wondered – and he tried to analyse his feelings. He wasn't aroused by the sight of her – she was, perhaps, too familiar to him for that, or perhaps he was too upset by everything else which had been going on – but he liked to see her; she seemed comfortingly familiar to him.

He also undressed, found a towel, and followed her into the sauna. It was, to his surprise, already hot. Anne had placed her towel on the bench and was arranging herself on it. Andrew stepped past her, being very careful not to touch any part of her, and sat, slightly sheepishly, on the end bench. He kept the towel over his lap, but quickly realised that this was silly – he would be much too uncomfortable, and he wasn't about to embarrass her. He moved the towel beneath himself, let out a long breath, and waited.

Nothing happened, and he understood that this was part of what was going on – he needed to take the first steps. He needed to talk about Matthias, but he couldn't work out how to raise that particular subject, so he asked her about her journey.

"I flew to Frankfurt this morning. Polly met me, and we drove up. She thought you were a bit subdued after yesterday, but I told her you were often like that."

He winced; Anne was normally much less direct than this, although the divorce process had uncovered a lot of these feelings; perhaps she felt able to simply say them now.

"I was subdued, Anne. I still am. We met Karla – did Polly tell you?" Anne nodded. "It was not far short of a disaster – I still don't know what I learned. She's not what I expected, and she told us some stuff about Matthias which I was shocked by…"

"The gun?"

"You knew?"

Anne seemed about to elaborate then closed up. She folded her arms about herself, and suddenly seemed a lot more like the Anne he had been married to.

"Anne, I know a lot of things now. I don't pretend to know the whole story, but I know some things. Whatever you were about to tell me probably won't surprise me. Not now."

Anne looked at him, and slowly lowered her arms. "I was afraid of that. I had to have a certain amount of Dutch courage just to get here, I'm afraid."

"I noticed. And the haircut? The jeans?"

"No, that's something different. That's mainly down to my therapist and the need to break out from who I was." Andrew looked at her.

"Didn't you try that once before?"

"I was a child, Andrew. A scared, lonely and confused child. I had to go through so much to get to where I am now, and I am going to grab hold of it. That's really why I'm here. If that Friday hadn't happened; if I'd gone home with my new self-image and no bad memories; no consequences, then I think I'd have been a much different person."

"And me?" Andrew felt almost ashamed to ask, but he needed to know.

"I don't know, Andrew, really I don't. Perhaps we'd have been lovers for a while, then moved on to what we really wanted. I just don't know. But that supposes that you hadn't been fucked up by that Friday, too." Andrew let out an involuntary gasp, and Anne smiled at him.

"Oh, I know all the bad words, Andrew. And what other word would do for that situation? You were – a mess. I never knew why; I always thought it was just your personality. That's why, when you told me about Peter, I got so upset. If I'd known…. Well, things would have been different."

"And you really think we would have been 'normal' – whatever that means – if we hadn't both had those experiences?"

"I have no idea, Andrew, but as I got older, I came to see it that way more and more. I never particularly enjoyed penet – sex; and you never seemed that bothered, so I didn't really worry too much about it. Now, I think we both missed out on a lot, but it's too late to go back."

Andrew stared. This was the first time that he could recall having any kind of meaningful conversation with Anne about sex, and he was all at sea. He was aware that she hadn't seemed to enjoy sex all that much, and he had never had any idea why. For himself, he recognised almost from the beginning that the experience with Karla had made him frightened of it in some vague way – he enjoyed it, but it always felt somehow slightly wrong or something to be afraid of. He was only now coming to see just how much damage that must have done to them both. He began to feel sad about that, but then remembered what he had needed to talk to Anne about.

"Anne, I need to talk to you about Matthias." She paled a little, he thought, and looked away. "I've been talking to him. Just now. In fact he's upstairs." It was Anne's turn to gasp.

"He knows I'm here?"

"Well, so far, I'm the only person he's talked to, and I didn't know, so…". He paused. "But Clare's talking to him right now, so I suppose it's possible."

"Probable."

He thought about this, then agreed. "Probable. She doesn't know what I know, unless…" This was it. He had to bite the bullet now. He looked up and stared at Anne until she met his gaze. He normally felt uncomfortable holding eye contact with anyone, but it was important that he see her reaction. She stared at him, and he could almost have sworn she was afraid.

"He told me the whole story, Anne. All of it. The gun, the prison hospital, the part where you slept with him in our bed. Everything." He watched her carefully, but she didn't react. He supposed she must have been expecting this, even to the point of not being affected by his uncharacteristic bluntness. She held his gaze, but her voice was soft and a little shaky.

"If it makes any difference, it wasn't in our bed. I couldn't – oh, Andrew, I can't explain it to you. You'll never be able to understand it – *I* don't understand it. It was never meant to happen; we had both promised, and even while it was happening, I felt that neither of us wanted it. And I never told anyone. I was - I am – so deeply ashamed."

Andrew had been calm up to this point; he kept telling himself that he could be rational about it; it didn't really matter any more. He had not had long to absorb this news or to figure out his reaction to it, but he genuinely believed that it didn't matter. In spite of this, he could feel an almost primal urge to get a full confession from her; did she enjoy it? Did they do things which she hadn't wanted to with him? Were they just overcome by animal lust and tore each other's clothes off in the hallway? Did he bend her over the kitchen table? Did – but this was futile. He took several deep breaths and calmed himself. He needed to focus on what was important – before Anne and Matthias met, she needed to know that her secret was out. A thought struck him.

"Anne, you said you told no-one. Does that include Clare? Because if she doesn't know, then she probably doesn't really understand the depth of the shit we could be in here."

Anne continued to stare at him. "That's it? No anger? No righteous indignation? You find out something which should have torn you apart, and you're worried about whether Clare knows? No, Andrew, she does not know. We are friends, but not that close – I'm sure there are things she hasn't told me over the years, too."

"I'll be angry in time, Anne; I'm sure of it. Part of me is raging at you right now, but where's the benefit in that for any of us? Anne, there's a problem, and I didn't understand it until I spoke to Matthias this afternoon. He has some issues, which I thought I was cleverly addressing by getting him to come here and face his cousins after all this time, but I didn't know that you were here, and I really didn't factor Clare in, either. I need to go back up there and talk to him; we need to do this differently."

Anne laughed softly. "Andrew, I think you're over-reacting. Matthias has some issues, sure, but talking to all of us here will probably be the best thing for him. I'm truly and deeply sorry that you found out about us from him – I should have had the courage to tell you at the time; life would probably not have been so different now if I had, except that I wouldn't have had to live a lie for so long. I definitely should have had the courage to tell you before now; before you came out to meet him back in the summer – I didn't sleep that entire weekend, expecting you to call and tell me that you knew. But now – now, I think we should all sit down and try to heal things."

"How do you think he will react to seeing you here?"

"Just fine, Andrew. We're all older and wiser now – he didn't want anyone to know, either; it'll be just fine." Anne stood and stretched; Andrew wondered if that was his signal to get up as well, but she was coming over to him. She stood in front of him and stared at him. He finally understood, and got up, a little shakily. Anne embraced him, and he, after a moment's hesitation, reciprocated. The feel of her skin, so familiar and yet so strange, produced mixed feelings in him, and he tried to pull away before anything else happened which he might regret.

Anne held on to him, though. She murmured an apology into his chest, and he sagged slightly against her. He didn't dare move his hands, which were lightly resting on her upper back; he had a clear understanding that Anne was trying to get him to forgive her, and not doing it particularly subtly. He remembered his humiliation at Karla's hands, and how he had resisted giving any sign that he was complicit in what had happened, and he felt the same impulse now; *just stand here, and it will pass – you'll still have the right to be angry.*

He thought he heard some movement outside the door, and tried to pull away. Anne relaxed her grip a little and looked round in time to see Clare step into the sauna. Clare stared at them, then smiled.

"Oh, I'm sorry – do you want me to go away?" Anne laughed at this, startling Andrew, and stepped back from him. Clare was wearing the swimsuit she had worn at the hotel, for which Andrew was grateful, but he still felt uncomfortable and vulnerable, and clumsily wrapped his towel around himself.

By the time he got himself covered up and seated, the two women were sitting comfortably side by side. Andrew's equilibrium had been badly disturbed by all that had happened, and having Clare in the room was not helping. He started to say so, but stopped himself – what he really needed was to understand what Clare might have told Matthias.

Clare was telling Anne about Matthias, so Andrew felt able to interrupt.

"Clare, did you tell him Anne is here?"

"Of course; he seems delighted, although I think he's a little shaky – a bit much, after all this time, I suppose. Liezl is not sure how to talk to him, but Erika's doing a great job – I actually think this has been a terrific idea.

Just imagine: the six of us back together in the same room..." she trailed off, perhaps understanding that the six of them in that room might not be quite such a fun memory for the other two. Andrew stared at her.

"Clare, there's a little more to it than you know." He looked pointedly at Anne, who then had to explain to her friend about the whole of her involvement with Matthias. By the time she was done, Andrew knew more of the details than he had been prepared for, Anne was crying, and Clare was plainly dumbfounded. She had not known about the InterRail visit, either, to Andrew's surprise, and he wondered if she understood what she had just heard.

"Clare, the problem is that he's not just shaky; he has some issues which will not be helped by having Anne here. He sees her as – his words – his 'guardian angel'; I spent a couple of hours with him this afternoon, and I'm worried. As long as we're down here, I suppose it's not too bad, but..." Andrew didn't get to finish the thought. The door to the sauna was thrown open, and Polly stood there - fully dressed, to Andrew's relief, but pale and agitated. She had eyes only for her mother.

"Clare, you need to come back. He's got a knife, and – and I don't know. I think he wants to hurt himself mostly, but Erika's there with him, and – shit, mum. Come and sort this out!"

Andrew stood up and Polly, registering his presence for the first time, looked round at him. Belatedly, he understood that his towel had dropped, but he was in no state to worry about that. He asked Polly where Matthias was, and ushered them all out. Polly told them to meet in the hallway, and ran off through the door. Clare was already half dressed, and followed her daughter out without even properly drying herself. Anne and Andrew took a little more time, but did so in strained silence; Andrew all the while fighting the impulse to say something along the lines of 'I told you so'.

By the time they got upstairs, everyone bar Matthias and Erika was in the hallway. Liezl had Rudi in her arms, and was staring at the door to the living room; everyone else was staring at Andrew, or so he felt. Clare spoke first.

"Andrew, just how bad is he? Is he threatening suicide, or worse, or is he just freaked out by all this, and needs to be calmed down?"

"How should I know, Clare? I don't know him at all – I think he's capable of anything, but someone needs to talk to him."

"Will you do it?" Clare looked at him almost pleadingly, and he tried to formulate some kind of excuse before Anne's hand on his arm stopped him.

"No, Andrew; I'll do it. This is my fault, and I need to mend it." Andrew stared at her, then understood what he needed to do.

"We'll both do it, Anne." He took her hand and walked towards the door. Clare began to say something, but cut herself off. Andrew reached the door and pushed it open. Matthias was sitting on one of the sofas, holding an ordinary-looking kitchen knife. The knife was resting on his thigh, pointing straight up into the air. Erika was facing him, and thus had her back to the door. Andrew panicked momentarily, but then heard Erika's voice, asking Matthias in German who was there. He replied in English.

"Don't move, Erika. It is Andrew, and, I suppose, Anne. It is good to see you again, Anne. I think now you are here, it will be fine for Erika to go." Erika stood and looked at Anne and Andrew. She smiled warily and gave a vague, non-committal hand signal. Andrew didn't know what that meant, but felt strangely reassured by it.

Erika spoke. "I will stay, if that's OK, Matthias. There is nothing so bad that we cannot fix it, I think. Just talk."

Matthias had not taken his eyes off Anne. "No. You go out with him, and I will talk to Anne for a minute. Then you can come back." Erika shook her head, for Andrew's benefit, but Anne spoke up.

"OK, Matthias; that's fine. Just put the knife down, and we'll talk." Andrew focused on the knife, which did not move for what seemed like hours. Then, slowly, Matthias laid it on the table between the two sofas. Anne breathed out, let go of Andrew's hand, and moved over to where Erika had been sitting. She looked back at the other two, and motioned for them to leave. Reluctantly, Andrew did so, Erika following him slowly.

Back in the hallway, everyone bar Clare crowded around Erika, looking for details. Clare took Andrew aside and hugged him.

"Sorry, Andrew – I should have listened to you. Will she be OK in there, do you think, or do we need to call someone?"

"The police? No, I think the danger's past. He's put the knife down, and we can go back in in a couple of minutes. Just Erika and I, I think, but we'll see." Clare held on to him for a few moments longer, then turned to look for Erika. Erika had already told the story once, but repeated it in English for the benefit of Clare and Andrew.

"He came in to the kitchen to look for an apple or something to eat. Liezl gave him what he needed, including the knife, and he walked back out – did not speak to Liezl or to me, except to ask. Remember, we have not seen or spoken to him for years; so I went after him, only to talk to him. He closed the door, then said he would cut himself unless I listened, and he would cut me if I tried to stop him. He blames everyone for what he says is the mess, but mostly he blames himself – if he had not gone to get Karla, this would all have not happened."

Andrew looked round to where he had closed the door behind them. "And now, he has Anne there and he is blaming her? I'm going back in." Clare grabbed at his arm, but he evaded her. He walked over to the door and pushed it open. Anne had moved to sit beside Matthias, and he had his head on her shoulder and was weeping softly. Anne spotted Andrew, and waved him away. He retreated, but left the door ajar, and stayed close.

For a long time, nothing happened. The crowd in the hallway were silent, looking at Andrew and the door; the two people inside were murmuring to each other, but Andrew could not hear what was being said. Rudi, getting bored with this, began to squirm in his mother's arms, and she let him down to go and play in the garden. He ran off happily, but the commotion had obviously disturbed Matthias, who said something.

Andrew heard Anne reassure him, then begin to talk to him about how it might be best for everyone to talk. There was a long silence, and Andrew felt he could stand it no longer. He pushed the door open and walked slowly into the room.

Matthias had picked the knife up again at some point, a detail which Andrew had missed on his previous visit. He was holding on to Anne, with the knife perilously close to her left ear. Anne seemed oblivious to this, and was talking softly to him.

"It's going to be fine, Matthias. No-one is blaming you for anything, and if we can all talk to each other, there will be no more secrets. We can all go on with our lives."

Matthias said something, and Anne pulled back a little.

"Well, you've lived without me for all these years, and you have a family who love you, don't you?" Matthias nodded. "So, don't worry. They will help you. We will help you. We can all be here to help, if you let us."

Andrew walked slowly into the room. He was very uncomfortable about being there, but he knew that he had to do something; to overcome every impulse and act. Anne looked up at him and shook her head. For the first time, she became aware of the knife and winced sharply. Andrew wondered if she was hurt, but Matthias sensed his presence and sat up, removing Anne's ear from any immediate danger. She reached up and felt the side of her face; Andrew saw a drop of blood, and this overcame his noble impulses. He now had to fight the urge simply to run away. He spoke, his voice less shaky than he had expected.

"Matthias, come on. Put the knife away. Anne is here; we're all here. We want to help you, and you can help us."

"Me? What can I do? I am useless. Everything I do turns to shit. Look at me."

Andrew reached the sofa, and sat down facing Matthias. "I need you to help me. I am here because I need to meet my son. Only you can help me do that. Come on, old friend. This feels bad now, but we can heal things; make them better. All you have to do is let us in." Andrew was not convinced by his own speech, but he saw Matthias waver, and he tried to signal to Anne with his eyes that she should try to get the knife off him. She stared back at him uncomprehendingly, and he shook his head quickly.

Matthias tensed, pulling Anne closer to him.

Andrew came close to panic, visualising Matthias harming Anne in response to whatever he tried to do. He tried to find calming words, but nothing came to mind. His default response to every situation, wait and see, reasserted itself, and he folded his hands in his lap and waited.

Anne pushed against Matthias, and complained that she was uncomfortable. Matthias relaxed his grip on her, and she sat up, careful to look only at Matthias. "Now, put the knife down, and we can talk. How does that sound?" Matthias looked at the table, then at Anne. At that moment, the door behind Andrew opened, and the room filled with voices, Clare's most prominent among them. Clare walked up behind Andrew and put her hand on his shoulder. Matthias looked alarmed, but still in control.

Clare spoke. "OK, this is enough, I think. No-one wants this to get out of control. Let's put everything aside, and just talk. Open the wine, and let's all just relax. I apologise for not telling you everything that was going on" – was this to Andrew, or Matthias? Andrew looked up at Clare to try to understand, but he couldn't tell from her expression what she was thinking. "Can we come in, Matthias? Can we sit down?"

Matthias looked at her, then let go of Anne altogether. He stood slowly, with the knife in his hand. He looked for a moment as if he was ready to lay it down, then he looked over at Clare.

"It was you. It was always you. Everything which happened; you were the one. Karla said it, and I did not see it before, but it was all your fault." Clare moved around the sofa to face Matthias, but he didn't falter. "You seduced Dieter, and made Karla do – the thing she did." He waved at Andrew." You told me that Anne liked me, and said to me that I should look after her. You told me that I must walk away from Anne. You told Karla to leave home. You did – you did all these things. It is your fault."

Andrew understood what was about to happen before he even saw it; as Matthias straightened, he was already rising from his seat; had he not been so tall, everything which followed might have turned out differently.

Matthias took a half step towards Clare, avoiding the end of the table, and suddenly swung his arm back. Andrew shot to his feet and launched himself at Matthias. The arm holding the knife was halfway through the swing by the time Andrew reached it, and he couldn't be sure if Matthias had thrown it or not. All he knew was that he had to stop this. He grabbed as much of Matthias as he could reach, and the two of them crashed to the floor. Andrew could hear the table going over behind him, and some colourful swearing from Clare and, he thought, Polly.

Then he had to deal with the fact that Matthias was underneath him, and struggling. Matthias made no sound, but thrashed furiously. Andrew's greater bulk and the fact that he was mostly on top prevented any serious attempt at escape, and as Andrew held on, Matthias gradually subsided.

The bear hug seemed to Andrew to calm into a kind of embrace, and after several minutes, Matthias began to breathe normally. The initial shock was wearing off, and Andrew became aware that he had banged his right knee mightily, and that there was a sharp pain in his left arm, up near the shoulder.

Matthias said something to him, but he didn't hear properly and had to ask him to repeat it.

"You are hurting me now. It's OK; it is over. I can be normal now." Andrew tried to push himself up on one arm, but it hurt to do that, and he sank back down.

"No more knives, Matthias. Just friends. All you need is someone to love you, and we can do that. But you have to let us." It was Clare's voice, calm and measured. Andrew took a huge breath and forced himself to sit up, using Matthias' back as leverage, which had the effect of keeping his adversary pinned to the ground. He looked up at the alarmed faces looking down at him, and tried to smile. His legs were shaking, and he really needed a drink now. Clare reached down to help him up, and then he reached down to Matthias.

Matthias stood carefully, and looked around him, as if he was looking for an escape route. On an impulse which took him by surprise, Andrew grabbed on to Matthias again, and hugged him.

"It's OK, Matthias. Stay with us; we can work it out. No-one wants you to get hurt here. But Clare's right – no more knives, and no more blame. What happened is over now. We need to move forward." Andrew had no idea where that had come from, but it sounded right as he said it. Matthias nodded, and Andrew let go of him. It was Erika who stepped forward, and took charge of Matthias, getting him to sit down. Clare picked up the knife from the floor, and gave it to Liezl, who motioned Andrew to follow her, then walked out of the room.

Liezl led him to the kitchen, and then surprised him by telling him to take off his shirt. "You're hurt, Andrew. We need to look at it." He looked at his left arm, which was stained with shockingly bright blood – his own, he supposed. Pulling the shirt off was difficult until he remembered Karla's trick. He pulled his right arm inside the sleeve, then, wincing at the pain, pulled the whole thing quickly over his head with the left hand.

Liezl fussed over him, cleaning what turned out to be a fairly superficial wound and then dressing it. Andrew sat there, on a kitchen stool, and thought about nothing in particular. Once the bandage was on, Liezl nodded to the kitchen door, and Anne came in. The two women hugged briefly, and then Anne came over to her ex-husband.

"I'm sorry, Andrew. I'm truly, truly sorry. I did this, and I thought I could just pretend that it didn't affect anyone else, but it did. Thank you for what you did – I was so stupid."

Andrew heard himself reply, although he had no idea what he was about to say: "No you weren't, Anne. You were human. You have been the one good and true thing in his life. It's not your fault that he is so in love with you; it's not his either. Perhaps things might have been different if we'd been different people, but then we wouldn't have been in this whole mess. I don't know what I think about you and him, but you didn't do it out of malice; you did it out of love."

"Not love, Andrew — compassion, perhaps. I never loved him; not like he loved me. Not like I loved you — or used to. I'm so sorry." She leaned into him and kissed him, then turned away.

Polly was next to visit the dressing station which the kitchen had become. She ran over to Andrew, threw her arms around him, kissed him wetly on the neck and thanked him profusely.

"For what?" he heard himself ask.

"You saved Clare's life, I think." He was stunned by this. He hadn't seriously thought that anyone's life had been in danger, but perhaps he hadn't allowed himself to think of it that way. He tried to laugh it off, but Polly's slightly desperate hug was disconcerting, and he tried to stand, knowing that would shake her off. Polly stood up and smiled at him. "I never asked — are you OK with me and Peter? I mean — oh, that sounds silly."

"No. No, it doesn't. But I hardly know either of you, so my opinion is not so important." As he said this, he realised that he actually still had not met his son, and wondered how that would happen, or even if it would now.

While Andrew and Polly were talking, he was aware of Liezl on the phone in the corner, arguing with someone. His German was not up to the subtleties of the one side of the conversation he could hear, but she seemed to be urging whoever it was to come over as soon as possible. Gerda, perhaps — it might be for the best if Matthias was removed from the situation. He decided to worry about that later. Instead, he looked at Polly.

"Are you bringing him here? Do I get to meet him?" Polly kept smiling.

"I think that could be arranged — as long as you're up to it." Now he was standing, Andrew could feel that his knee was more painful than he had realised, and he sat down on the stool again.

"I think I'll be fine, but I might need some ice for this knee." Polly looked down at it in alarm, then interrupted Liezl to ask after ice. While that process was going on, Andrew was hugged briefly by Erika and then Clare, who murmured in his ear, "Thanks big guy. Later, though. OK?" She pulled back to look at him and smiled. He nodded, and then sat back to allow Polly to tend to his knee. He briefly worried that he might be required to undress again, but the ice was applied externally to his jeans, and he was able to relax to a degree.

Once he had been proclaimed fit to walk, he went back through to the living room. Matthias was still there, sitting sadly on the sofa, with Anne and Erika opposite him. The women were chatting to him softly, but Matthias was not particularly engaged by the conversation, or so it appeared, and Andrew hovered on the edge of the room, before Anne noticed him and motioned for him to sit down. Andrew asked Matthias if that would be OK, but the answer he got was noncommittal.

He contemplated leaving the room again, but at some level he understood that tackling Matthias like he had done had changed something; he had rights here, and although he didn't fully understand Matthias' situation, he was sure that sitting back and waiting for things to happen was not the right choice. He sat next to Anne and looked at Matthias.

He recognised that he was feeling uncomfortable in the face of having several difficult questions to ask – in the heat of his divorce from Anne, he would get to a point like this; ready to ask painful questions, but unable to say anything. He swallowed hard, then asked the question which was most pressing.

"So, were you trying to kill her?"

Matthias paled. He looked away, and Andrew thought he had blown it. Anne had stiffened beside him as he asked the question, and he knew exactly what she was thinking; that the hard work she and Erika had done had just been undone. Matthias looked slowly back at all three of them, then shook his head.

"No." A long pause ensued, during which Andrew had to resist the impulse to proclaim that he was happy to hear it, and could they all go out and have a beer now?

"No; I did not intend anything. It is hard for me to explain, I think. I can feel my father inside me, and I have to fight him. It is why – look." He pulled his left sleeve up, and Andrew gasped to see the various scars on his forearm. "There are more. This I can do to stop myself. Gerda keeps me alive." Andrew heard a sound from beside him, and surmised without looking that Anne was crying. He felt oddly bereaved by that, but ignored it.

"So, what were you doing? With the knife? A cry for help?"

"I cannot explain it."

Andrew stared at him. "I'm afraid you're going to have to try, Matthias. We should be calling the police right now – tell us why we aren't." Andrew felt somewhat panicky at being in this position, but he knew that for Anne's sake, he had to carry on; see it through. Then he stopped himself. *No; not for Anne. For Clare.*

Matthias looked down at his feet. He was hard to hear properly, but the room was utterly silent otherwise, and Andrew was sure he understood enough.

"I can control myself now. I have medicines, and I am good. I had to pass tests so I can work with children, and it is not so hard. I told you I teach, but that is not quite right – I help, and this is OK. This – thing – only happens when too many things happen all together. I get scared, and I know I can hurt people, so I hurt myself."

"But you were about to throw the knife at Clare. You managed to hurt me" – Andrew pulled up the sleeve of his shirt enough for Matthias to see Liezl's bandage – "I don't know if I can believe you."

Matthias looked up. "No. I would not throw it. I think perhaps I would have hurt myself badly; my mind was telling me to make it stop. She – Clare – was the excuse. I think perhaps you saved me, not Clare."

"So we should call a doctor?"

"Perhaps it is a good idea, but it is not necessary. It has passed; I feel normal now. I am deeply ashamed, but I am normal. When this happens to me, it is like a storm – it goes past quickly."

Andrew wondered what he was supposed to do next. He looked out the window, surprised to see that it was dark. Anne turned to look at him, but he knew he wasn't finished with Matthias.

"You do know that it is no-one's fault, don't you? A few months ago, all I knew of the whole thing was that I had been raped by Karla" – he felt oddly liberated, saying that in company – "and I wondered if it had been my fault. Now, I know all of the other things which happened that summer, and it's just a normal human tragedy; we all made mistakes; we all had experiences which were out of our control, and we all learned to live with them. I think if we'd all known the whole picture, we'd have done things differently, but it was what it was."

As he said all this, and wondered if he really believed it, he heard footsteps behind him. A full wineglass was passed to him, and he reached over to take it, brushing Clare's fingers as he did so. This time he did feel something; some essence passed between their fingers, and he wondered if Clare had felt it too.

Matthias was looking up at Clare, who was standing more or less where she had been earlier. He seemed ready to break down and cry, but Clare walked over to him, and extended a hand. He took it, as if to shake it, which struck Andrew as absurd, but was then pulled to his feet. Clare embraced him in the normal Clare way – *fiercely*, Andrew remembered thinking of it – and Matthias held on to her. Clare spoke softly, but loud enough for everyone to hear.

"I've been thinking about it, and I am to blame for some things, so I'm sorry for those. But we're all to blame for some things, and mostly we're to blame for not talking. So Liezl and I have agreed; we hold no grudges, but we're going to talk. All of us." She released Matthias and went to sit beside him. Liezl came around the other end of the sofa, and sat on Matthias' other side. Suddenly, there they were – the six of them, together in this room. Andrew almost said something about a bottle of schnapps, but stopped himself in time.

They were silent for some minutes, then slowly they began to talk. Matthias told his story, mainly for the benefit of his cousins, who had never heard all of it before, and there was much weeping and hand-holding. Clare talked about her travels, and about Polly; Anne confessed again to what had happened between her and Matthias, and Andrew finally, and with a great deal of hesitation, told the story of how Peter was conceived. After this, the room fell silent.

It was Erika who broke the silence.

"We should have a toast, I think. We did not think of it at the time, but we should have agreed to meet here after 25 years, and see what had become of us. We are still here; we have many things to be proud of, and we should salute that. And we should salute the brave people who have talked today. I did not understand all of what happened, especially with my own family. I knew he was a hard man, but I did not want to believe that he was a monster. I did not know what Karla could do, and I am sorry about that, because I know she is a good person underneath.

"And I am most sorry because we could have been better friends, and we failed. But here we are, and we can start again. Cousin, I have missed you, and I am so happy to see you here and to talk to you." Matthias was staring at her and smiling. Andrew felt that something had passed over – he still had unresolved issues, but perhaps they were not as important as knowing that the six people in this room could eventually put the past behind them and move on.

There was a gentle knock at the door, and Polly quietly announced that Rudi was bored and hungry, and that she really ought to go and get Peter now. Liezl jumped to her feet, and began to organise things. Andrew stood and walked slowly to the window. In the dark, he could imagine that the view was what it had been a quarter of a century before. The fence would have been just over there, to the left, and he craned to look for it, expecting to see the floodlights, but there was only darkness. He half expected someone to come and say something meaningful to him, and deep down he wished it could be Clare, but perhaps everyone felt he needed some solitude.

He turned to face the room and looked at the activity. Matthias was talking quietly to Erika, who had an arm about his waist; Clare and Polly were making a fuss of Rudi, who was delighted to be the centre of attention again, and Anne...

Anne was still sitting in the same place, staring at him with a wry smile on her lips. He looked at her; the woman he had spent most of his life with, and he wondered how he could have missed so much. She looked younger than the woman he had been married to, and he thought about the person she might have been. *No sense in that,* he told himself, *there's no going back.*

He fought a sudden urge to ask Liezl to stop all the preparations; to just allow the six of them to spend the rest of the evening together, but the spell had been broken, and he knew that he could not avoid what he had, after all, come here to do. He went over to Polly and asked if he could come with her to get Peter; now that he had broken through his protective screen of inertia, he felt he should do something with it.

Polly looked uncertain, but after some thought, agreed to it, and led him out to Erika's car. He stood by the car and breathed the cool air, wondering where this calm assertiveness had come from. He looked back at the house, but no-one was paying any attention to what was going on outside, and he felt that he had stepped outside the world for a moment. He decided to enjoy the experience, and see where it took him.

Polly drove almost as quickly and efficiently as her mother, and they were outside Peter's apartment building before Andrew had properly gathered his thoughts. He looked over at Polly, who smiled encouragingly. "Come on, Andrew, let's get it done. Then we can all relax, don't you think?"

Andrew wasn't quite so sure about that, but he agreed anyway, and they got out of the car.

Peter was waiting for them inside the main doorway; he smiled warmly at Polly, went to hug her, and Andrew relaxed a little. Then Peter noticed Andrew, and aborted his embrace. He straightened, flicked a nervous sidelong glance at Polly, then walked over to Andrew and extended his hand.

Andrew looked into the eyes of his son, and tried to identify what he felt. Nothing concrete came to mind, and he reflexively took Peter's hand. As soon as he made contact, however, he knew that it was wrong. *My own flesh and blood,* he thought, then disengaged and opened his arms. The two men, of similar height and build embraced awkwardly. Andrew was aware that he was pushing his own interpretation of events onto Peter, but the younger man seemed to be reciprocating, and Andrew at last felt that, perhaps, this would work out.

He understood that he would have to be the one who broke the embrace, and as he was wondering how long it should last, understood that that thought alone probably meant it was time to stop. He stepped back, worrying that it might have felt like he was jumping away from an uncomfortable position, but Peter was smiling. Andrew wondered how good Peter's English was, and tried to remember what it was that he wanted to say. Peter beat him to it, though:

"So, Polly says 'this is weird'; is this correct?"

Andrew smiled; Clare would have said 'freaky'. "You are right; I think I had a long speech worked out, but I don't think it's the right time or place."

Polly grabbed them both by the arm and ushered them towards the car. Peter automatically went for the back seat, but Andrew diverted him to sit beside the driver, then instantly regretted it as he tried to fold his legs into a rear seat which was presumably designed for children. Polly laughed to see him struggle, and for the first time that day, Andrew also felt like laughing. He wondered if it was nerves, but he felt calm enough.

Once they were all seated, Polly turned to look at Andrew.

"I thought we'd go to the bar first – just enough time for you two to talk. So that you're not surrounded by chaos." Andrew felt this was thoughtful and said so; Polly pointed at Peter. "His idea, not mine. He's the sensible one."

Andrew smiled, but couldn't find any well-organised words, so said nothing.

The bar was as quiet as it had been when Matthias and Andrew had met here another Friday night three months and a lifetime ago. Andrew paid for drinks, and then Polly wandered off to find the jukebox – or so she claimed. Father and son regarded each other, then Peter asked about Andrew's other children, and the two of them began to talk. The conversation was disjointed and stilted – Peter's English was passable, but there were several areas which they both struggled with, and it wasn't until Polly came back that they had someone to help them make sense of it.

As they talked, Andrew dimly registered a song – had Polly put it on the jukebox? It was something he hadn't heard consciously since that summer of 1978; it was even possible that the last time he had heard it was in this very pub. He registered it, and returned to the conversation.

After close to an hour of polite and interested conversation, Polly looked pointedly at her watch – it was getting on for eight o'clock, and she had apparently promised to return them before then. Andrew looked at Peter, who nodded.

"I am ready. It feels OK, I think. How is it for you?"

Andrew thought about this. He really didn't know – how did one react to meeting one's child for the first time as an adult? He kept trying to see himself in Peter; in his gestures or his approach to things, but he wasn't sure any of him was really in there. Despite that, he liked this young man on a level deeper than just politeness. He realised that Peter was waiting for an answer, and that Polly was clearly intrigued.

"I don't really know, Peter. I am so pleased to meet you, and I am happy that it feels normal. But it will take me a long time to understand it properly. I do not think I am ready to think of you as my child; does that make sense?"

Peter nodded. "My father is Dieter – that will not change. When I look at you, I see myself. This is strange, but I think that I like it. Since I knew about you, I have to change what I think. My mother told me when I was small- she said to me you ran away and did not want me. I believed this for a long time. But Polly has told me about you, and I have to think another way. I saw you in the summer, and I did not know what to do – I wanted somebody to do this for me, I think. My uncle said it was you before you came, and then he changed his mind, I think. He did not introduce us, and I was not so sure. So it is good for me to see you here. And I am happy – I want to know about you."

Andrew looked at him in surprise. Peter was his son, after all. "This feeling – you want to let other people do things for you – this is what I have given you, I am afraid. But today I have learned that I can do things for myself. Maybe I can help teach you how to do this."

Andrew felt sure that Peter hadn't properly understood this, but it felt very important. As they walked back to the car, he tried again, but got no further, and Polly told him not to worry – there was all the time he wanted now. Andrew considered this, then squeezed himself into the back seat – over Peter's protests – to begin the final part of his journey.

As Polly drove, Andrew silently figured out the song he had heard – 'Follow You, Follow Me'; Genesis. As he contemplated it, he found that the entire bus trip came sharply into focus in his mind – remembering the song seemed to indicate to him that he had remembered everything he ever would remember about those two weeks, even if it was a song he had barely registered at the time, and which he had scarcely, if ever, thought about since.

They arrived back at the house to the promised chaos. There were two more cars in the driveway than when they had left, and Polly had to park close to the street. The three of them walked up the drive, and Andrew wondered how they must look, the two enormous men flanking Polly, who was by no means short, but who must have looked child-sized in comparison. He smiled at the thought of it, and was still smiling when they crossed the threshold.

Liezl was waiting for them, looking slightly more ruffled than Andrew had ever seen her before. She started to explain to Polly that dinner had now got somewhat out of hand, and that in the interests of keeping the peace, she needed to explain what she had done. Andrew, who had been close to feeling relaxed up to this point, began to worry again.

"It is no longer the six of us," Liezl said to Andrew. "I invited Gerda to come and be with Matthias, and this seems to be a good thing. Also Dieter is here – I suppose Clare told him, but in this town, it could be anyone. But I also called someone else. I did not think she would come so far, but she is coming, I think. Andrew, I need to know if it a good thing. When

Matthias was so bad, I called Karla. She argued, but she said she would come."

Andrew stared. He was still preoccupied with how he felt about Peter, but dimly recognised that this might just be a very good thing. He shrugged. "Liezl, I am beyond being surprised by anything now. If she comes, she comes. It has been an extraordinary day already."

Andrew wasn't sure he had ever been in the enormous dining room before, but he was somehow not surprised to discover that there was more than enough room for the ten adults now gathered, although he was astonished to discover just how much food had been prepared in the short time he had been away. He stared at the table, wondering if there was a seating plan, then wondering about any number of seemingly unconnected things which hurtled through his mind one after the other.

Clare came up behind him and her touch – she grabbed his arm – calmed him a little. He turned to face her, and caught his breath. Here, tonight, after all that they had been through, he saw her for who she really was. He felt he was seeing her for the first time, not as a dimly remembered crush, or as a fantasy construct which he could project his imagination on to, but as a friend and companion; someone who had, however expertly or otherwise, conducted him through some of the most difficult things he had ever done, and who had come out the other side still happy to know him, and still full of whatever it was which made her so much fun to know.

He stared into her eyes and held her gaze. Clare grinned at him, and clutched his arm a little more tightly. She was about to say something, and Andrew, drawing again on his new-found reserves of assertiveness, put his free hand up to stop her.

"Don't say anything. I need to tell you this." Clare looked momentarily worried, and it was Andrew's turn to grin. "Not whatever you're thinking. I need to say thank you. This has been the most – extraordinary, I think is the word – extraordinary few days of my entire life, and you made it happen. One day, I'd like to talk to you about other stuff, but right now, I need to say thank you." He smiled, then bent to kiss her. She stopped him.

"Just a minute. No kissing until I sort this out. *You're* thanking *me?* The person who is responsible for this whole mess in the first place?" Andrew looked at her, but she seemed serious enough. "And the person who provoked a knife fight earlier. I think I should be thanking you, don't you?"

Andrew paused, then bent to her again. He kissed her briefly, shook his head and said, firmly, "no. No, that's not it at all. No blame, remember?" As he straightened up. Liezl came in, carrying more plates and dishes, and he sprung back from Clare reflexively, which caused her to laugh.

Oh, the laugh, he thought, trying to suppress his mixture of embarrassment and something which felt like desire. He caught himself, thinking that he still had no idea what she thought of him, but supposing that it was not as much as he might hope.

Clare was still holding his arm, and she utilised this fact to cajole him into helping out with the carrying. By the time he was done with that, most people were seated, and he couldn't clearly see where there was room for him. He looked around, but only Erika was paying him any attention, and she waved him over to sit between her and Gerda.

He nodded and complied, but then spent the first part of the meal in the middle of a rapid German conversation which he only partly followed, and in no way felt able to contribute to. He looked over at Clare from time to time, but she was happily chatting to Dieter and to Peter, and he could think of no way of asking her the things he needed to know.

Once the main course had arrived – Andrew was startled to discover that it was a fair approximation of a large shepherd's pie – Erika made an effort to include him in the conversation, and he did his best to make small talk, but he was frequently distracted by the sound of Anne laughing, clearly enjoying Peter's company. He would not be able to relax until he understood a little more.

In the absence of understanding, he helped himself to more wine, until his bladder forced him to excuse himself. As he emerged from the bathroom, he was surprised to find Clare, sitting on the floor in the corridor outside. He briefly registered that this was exactly what the teenage Clare would have done, and he smiled to think of it. He made to sit beside her, but she stood up.

"Don't make your knee any worse- I'm already feeling guilty about it as it is." He tried to protest, but she waved him away.

"Don't, Andrew. It's fine; I'm mostly teasing you – I seem to be quite good at that. But I had to come and see if you are okay – you seem distracted."

"Small bloody wonder, Clare." He was astounded to realise that he had said this out loud. *Ah, well, all part of the new me,* he thought, "I'm in fear for my life in there. I have no idea who knows what; if I say anything about Anne to Gerda, will she kill me, or what?" He thought he sounded a little like a petulant child saying this, but that was, in some way, how he felt. Clare smiled.

"Ah, yes. Hadn't thought of that. Let's see. Dieter knows all about pretty much everything, thanks to his daughter, who has always felt that honesty is the best policy. He has, of course, kept up with Matthias all this time, too, and I'm sure he knows at least some of the truth about Anne. Gerda; well, it turns out that Matthias told her – years ago, after he came back from" – she paused, and looked away – "that time. They came close to divorce, apparently, but it's all more or less forgiven now, I think. She didn't know about you and Peter until a couple of hours ago, though, so if you're getting funny looks, that'll be why. Anything I've missed?"

"One or two things, but they can wait." Clare looked at him oddly, and he realised that he had also said that out loud. "Sorry, Clare, I'm a little - something – right now; I don't even know what it is."

"Emotional?"

"Probably, but it doesn't feel like that. I don't know. Can I ask you something?"

"Sure thing, big guy."

He smiled at that – that was something he could get used to. "Can I have a serious talk with you about things? And soon; I'm worried I'm about to screw everything up again."

"Things? Any time. And you're not. Really, you're not."

She pushed off from the wall and the bathroom door was shut behind her before he could ask her what that meant. He shrugged, then walked back into the dining room.

Andrew had no sense of time after that, and it may have been close to midnight when the doorbell rang. He looked puzzled at first, then remembered. Liezl went to get it, but Andrew jumped to his feet.

"May I? he asked. "It'll be for me, I think." Liezl looked at him, then nodded. Andrew walked out into the hallway just as the bell rang again. He had it in his mind to try humour; to answer it with some caustic comment about wearing the bell out, but remembered in time that he had been drinking in convivial company, and the person on the other side of the door had not. He opened it slowly, and smiled. He spoke softly.

"Hello, Karla. You might not believe this, but I'm really glad to see you."

Karla was dressed much as she had been earlier in the week; she looked tired, which was not surprising, Andrew thought, and she did not return his smile. Instead, she pushed past him, and he closed the door behind her. He turned to look at her, and she was staring at him.

"I suppose everything has been resolved now, and it is all one happy family. No point in my journey. I suppose; you can tell me."

"There's been one person missing, Karla. Until now." She ignored this.

"I heard he tried to kill you – is this so?"

"Not really, Karla." For some reason, he found it important to keep using her name. "He tried to hurt himself, we think. He is much better now, but he will be glad to have his sister here. I think" – here Andrew's nerve failed him. He had been about to tell Karla that Matthias still relied on her for protection, but he wasn't at all sure it was true; for some reason he was desperate for Karla to be a full part of this gathering, and he understood that he might be overdoing it. Karla stared at him.

"So, why am I here?"

Andrew only hesitated for a heartbeat. "Because many things have been said today, and the most important is that we cannot change the past, but we can, perhaps, come to accept it. This means that we are all trying to leave blame behind, to accept what has happened, and to go on. You told me that was how you like to do things, but you did not seem to be at peace with me. You are here because Liezl thought you would be good for Matthias, but I need you here as well; I need to look you in the eye and know that it is okay.

"You need to make peace with us all, I think. To forgive Clare, and to apologise to her – she is not to blame for anything. You need to tell Peter the truth; he already knows it, but he needs to hear it from you. And; well, I hope you can figure out what I need from you."

Karla was still staring at him, and Andrew felt more than a little shaky. He had not intended to pour all that out in one burst, but once he had started, he had the clear impression that he would not get another opportunity. He kept his eyes fixed on Karla's; she had been looking straight at him, but now she was looking down and past him. She said something, but he didn't catch it. He kept looking at her.

"I said, I'm sorry." If he'd expected fanfares and the lifting of a heavy weight, he was disappointed. He mainly wanted to break down and cry, but he held that in check.

"Accepted, Karla. I don't know if we understand the same thing in that 'sorry', but I accept it anyway." He stepped forward and made to embrace her, but thought better of it. Instead, he bent down to her ear and whispered, "you can let the mask slip now. We all know the truth. You're not to blame any more than anyone else."

She stepped back, and glared up at him. "Far enough, English boy. Once there was a mask; now, it is all me. He is to blame for that, and you cannot change it. But I will try. For my brother's sake."

"And your son?"

"Him too. And, maybe a little, for you. But don't push me." Andrew nodded, then took her coat. He had no idea what to do with it, and by the time he had found somewhere to park it, Karla had opened the dining room door, and he was treated to the full range of emotions on the faces of the others. Anne was clearly stunned; she must have been remembering Karla as she had been, not as she had been described. Matthias was overjoyed, as Peter appeared to be to a lesser degree, while Dieter appeared to be in shock. Karla turned to Andrew.

"You did not tell me that Dieter was here."

Andrew shrugged. "Didn't get the chance. Not a problem is it?"

She thought about this, while everyone looked on. Dieter slowly got up from his seat, but before anything could develop, Karla turned to look at him and spoke.

"No. Not any more. Perhaps I understand, a little." She took a deep breath, and looked back at Andrew. He waited for her to speak, but she merely shrugged one shoulder. In that gesture, he saw the girl she had been, and he also felt that he perhaps understood something. Dieter was still standing, and now, seeing that the danger was past, he walked slowly over to her.

Andrew was the only one close enough to hear what passed between them, and he wasn't sure that he had understood it, but it seemed to him that Dieter had apologised, and that Karla had reciprocated. There was more to it than that – there had to have been – but something important had passed between them, and then Karla walked over to her brother.

Not to her son, Andrew noted.

Matthias stood, and brother and sister hugged for several minutes. Andrew heard some sniffling, and looked around for the culprit, absurdly worried that it might have been him. When he could see no sign, he understood that it must be the only person whose face he could not see. He looked at Anne, who smiled at him, then at Clare, who gave him a little clenched fist gesture which caused his heart to do somersaults.

Karla broke the embrace with a demand for a drink and, first, some tissues. Andrew only recognised the tension in the room once it had been broken by this remark, and he suddenly felt faint and drained. Maybe, just maybe, he had got something right.

Later that night, after Polly had taken Dieter and Peter home, and Gerda had shepherded Matthias and his sister away, Andrew sat on one of the sofas in the living room while the four women talked loudly in the kitchen. He imagined briefly that he was being mocked for avoiding the clearing up, but he found that, for once, he didn't much care what others thought of him. Something had happened to him, and he wasn't sure whether he would be able to deal with it, but on the whole, he liked it.

The others filed back into the living room shortly afterwards, and made to settle in, but Andrew was tired; his arm was throbbing gently and his knee was stiffening. He stood, a little shakily, and excused himself. Anne stood as well; she echoed his sentiments and everyone agreed that it was probably time to go to bed.

Andrew used the bathroom before anyone else had made it upstairs, and he was undressed and sitting on the edge of his bed when there was a knock on his door. He looked up, expecting Clare to put her head around it, but nothing happened. He walked over to the door, glad of the pyjama trousers he had decided to bring.

He opened the door to find Anne standing there. She told him she had forgotten to bring toothpaste, which he recognised for the fairy story it was – the idea of Anne forgetting anything was laughable. He invited her in, and climbed into bed. She sat on the edge of it, and looked at him. He smiled, and she seemed to relax.

"Well, I'm glad to see you smile. I am worried about you, you know." She fell silent again, and Andrew wondered why she was here. After a time, he thought she might have been ready to leave, but she suddenly spoke, as if deciding to get the thought out there before her nerve failed her.

"It was right here, you know." He didn't, then after a moment, he did.

"In this bed?"

"I don't know; chances are it's a different bed, but perhaps not. It still seems like a dream. I had no idea what I was doing, but it seemed important to look after him. How stupid I was."

"Not stupid, Anne. You were just being you. He needed help, and you were able to give it."

"But I've never been able to understand it – I could have talked to him; he wasn't a threat to anyone – I knew that at the time. That first time; here in this room – it led to what happened back home. I helped him in the most stupid way I could have dreamt up." A long pause. "Do you think you'll ever be able to forgive me?"

Andrew answered before he was properly able to think about his answer. "I suppose I will, Anne. I'm not angry, but maybe I will be in time. I was earlier, but that was shock, I think. Funny thing is, I do understand. I know why you did it; even that last time, and I don't really blame you."

Anne looked at herself in the mirror. "Can you explain it to me, then? I've spent months in therapy, and all I've got to show for it is this haircut, which I don't really like – it's not me."

"You are whoever you want to be, Anne." This sounded trite to Andrew even as he said it, but to his surprise, he realised that he meant it. "You had a moment of abandon which wouldn't have happened except for what you did in this room, and you've spent your whole life trying to turn it back. All you need to do is admit to yourself that nothing will ever change that moment, and you'll be able to move on."

"I don't know about that, but I'll think about it. Want to hear something funny?"

"Go on."

"I kind of wish we weren't divorced. I've finally found the Andy I loved all those years ago, and he's been right under my nose all this time."

Andrew had to fight sudden tears at hearing this. "Don't, Anne. We've moved on. There's no…"

"Going back; I know. Just a thought, that's all. Wish we could have talked like this all that time, though."

He sat up and reached out to touch her arm. "Me too, Anne, but I'm not sure it would have made a difference. We weren't who we thought we were. It was doomed from the start, I'm afraid."

Anne made to get up, then evidently thought of something else.

"What did you say to Peter? He's a lovely boy – man, I suppose. I really enjoyed his company tonight. He seems very relaxed about all of this."

"I don't really know, Anne. This whole trip was set up to get us together, and we spent an hour in the pub talking about the children, and I don't really know what else. I wanted to fix all my attention on him, but I kept thinking about Matthias, and all of you here with him. I'd really like to see him again."

"You've got time enough, I think." Another long pause. "Well, I'm going to bed now, before I do something else I'll regret in this bed." She stood and smiled at him. Andrew half expected a kiss goodnight, but perhaps Anne felt that would be too dangerous, and she left with only the briefest of backward glances.

Andrew lay back on the bed and stared at the ceiling. He knew it had to be the middle of the night, but he couldn't sleep. He was glad to have spoken with Anne, but he was also mildly dismayed – he had had a plan, and it was probably too late to carry it out now.

Five more minutes of staring, however, convinced him that the old Andrew would simply have given up, but the new one should try a few things out. He got up and walked to the door.

Clare's door was not locked; he hadn't expected it to be. He peered around it, but the room was in darkness, and he stepped inside and closed the door behind him without knowing whether there was any point to what he was doing, or whether he was actually being something of a stalker. This thought seemed to sober him up, and he reached for the handle again, only to be stopped by Clare's voice.

"Was about to give up on you, big guy. Come talk to me."

He felt his way across the room, slowly becoming aware of his surroundings. Clare's room was smaller than the one he was in, although the bed seemed to be of a similar size. Her voice was fuzzy, but warm and inviting.

"Want to know something funny? This is the bed that used to be next door – in your room. Liezl told me earlier. So this is…" she stopped. "Shit, listen to me."

"No, it's fine. Until just now, I thought I was sleeping in that one."

"Well, now you can." This startled him.

"What? Did you just…?"

"Sorry. Kind of slipped out. Don't feel you have to." He reached the side of the bed, and felt for a space to sit down. Clare moved herself and the covers, and his hand briefly brushed her bare legs. He supposed he was meant to just get in with her, but he hesitated and sat on the edge.

"Sorry, Andrew, I'm not good at this; I may have mentioned that."

It was Andrew's turn to inject a long pause into a conversation, and he used the time to muster his thoughts.

"Clare, what do you think of me? I only ask because - well, I ask because I don't know what the fuck I'm doing here. I hear your voice, and I appreciate what you're doing, but I still see Karla. Maybe not as clearly as I once did, but she's still there."

Clare sat up. Andrew's eyes had sufficiently adjusted for him to see that she was not wearing any kind of shirt. She held out a hand to him, and he took it in his own.

"I know, Andrew. I kind of meant this to happen. Don't know how sensible it is, but I'm not Karla, and maybe you need to break that spell. I'd love to know what you said to her tonight, by the way." As she spoke, Clare moved Andrew's hand towards her, and brushed it gently against her side. "Not pushing you to do anything you don't want to, but if you do, I'm up for crossing the line."

Andrew thought about that. "Clare, I don't understand. What's changed since Frankfurt? Since last night? Since lunchtime, come to that? Why now? Not that I'm not – well, I can't help thinking this is wrong, too. It doesn't cancel out, you know."

"Maybe. And maybe it does. I'm working hard, here; you'll have to give me a bit of room. Just an idea I had, really. Shit; I'm not making a lot of sense, am I?" She paused, but Andrew couldn't think of anything to say to that, and she picked up again. "So, here's the thing. Something did change today – I'm as surprised as you, I think, but when you saved my life down there, it shook me up."

Andrew looked at her. He could see her face now; she was serious and calm. He still wasn't sure what to think, but he smiled at her. He stood up, breaking the contact, and walked around the end of the bed. He pulled back the covers on the other side, but did not undress any more than he already was. He slid into bed, and lay down beside her, putting an arm around her waist. Clare turned herself to face him, but otherwise did not move.

"I didn't save anyone's life, Clare, and you know it. Well, maybe Matthias', but even then, I don't know how serious he was."

"Well, I'm not so sure, but even if you're right, you put yourself in harm's way on my behalf, and I suddenly had a vision...." She stopped, and Andrew wondered if she was crying. "Sorry; I just thought about being alone all this time, and it suddenly seemed to me that having someone to look out for you might not be such a bad thing. And; well, you've changed. You're changing – I liked the old Andrew, but he was a bit passive for my taste. The last couple of days I've seen a new Andrew, and I think I could get to like him a whole lot more."

Andrew's head was spinning. Some part of him registered that he was lying in bed with a naked Clare, and that it would be easy just to lean over and start something which he had longed for for weeks. No, scratch that; he'd longed for it since he had been fourteen, as far as he could tell. And yet...

"This is not such a clever idea, though, is it, Clare? I mean – Anne's just across the hallway; we're both in a strange emotional place, and – well, you told me yourself about fuck 'em and forget 'em. I'm not ready for that."

Clare hugged him closer. He could feel her breasts pressed against his chest, and he could feel his resolve waver.

"Just hold me, then, big guy. It's fine. We'll deal with it all another time."

He thought about this, and he thought about himself. He thought about Karla in her bed that Sunday morning, and how he had been changed by it. He thought about Anne in this bed with Matthias, and he thought about what that meant. He thought about Clare and the ferry; he remembered the feel of her when he awoke that morning, and he thought about the fact that they seemed to have come full circle.

As he lay there, 'Follow You, Follow Me' came back into his mind. He allowed the memories of 25 years before wash over him as he thought about the song, and when his mind somehow dredged up some words about fears drifting away in the night, he had to fight back tears.

He felt Clare's breathing even out, and he realised that she was drifting off to sleep. He smiled and lay with her for a time. As he did so, he remembered some more. He saw Anne's face smiling at him, as it so often had done. How often he'd resented her smile! All she had ever wanted was to make people happy, and he had worked so hard at being miserable. He thought of Matthias, and of how they were not so different. Matthias had a kind of manic release for his frustrations; Andrew had only self-pity.

But here he was. In spite of everything; in spite of who he was, or thought he was, this beautiful person had invited him into her bed, openly and with genuine pleasure. He looked at her. "I think you were wrong," he murmured to her. "You were the one I needed. Just took me half my life to work it out. Don't take this the wrong way, though." He had no idea if she had enough consciousness left to hear him, but he felt he ought to excuse what he was about to do.

He disengaged from her as gently as he could, and stood up. A faint light from somewhere made Clare's body appear to glow, and he wavered for a second or two. Then he folded the covers back over her, and tiptoed to the door. As he opened it, he heard some sound come from the bed, but he couldn't identify it. He waited, but nothing else happened, and he took that as his cue. As he walked back to his own room, he saw that there was still a light coming from under Anne's door. He paused before that door, but took a deep breath and turned to his own.

Andrew slept for much of the following morning. From time to time, he was aware of movement and noise elsewhere in the house, but none of it directly concerned him, and he kept drifting back into sleep. Eventually, he was woken by Clare, who brought him coffee and a pastry, and made to leave again. He thanked her, and she turned back.

Clare came over and stood by his bedside. She looked serious, and Andrew began to worry that he had missed something else important by being asleep for so long. He was about to ask her what was wrong when she took a deep breath and looked him in the eye.

"Meant what I said last night. I'm up for crossing that line. I've thought about it, and I'm still sure I'm right." She leant over and kissed him on the cheek. "And that was a smart and lovely thing you did last night. Don't doubt yourself so much, Andrew. Your instincts are good."

She smiled at him, a different smile from her usual easy grin and one he hoped he'd have the chance to get used to, then she too left him to it.

It took him an hour to make himself presentable enough for his firstborn to see, so when he did make it downstairs, Peter and Polly were holding court in the kitchen. Peter was telling a long tale about his uncle, and it took Andrew some time to understand that he meant Matthias. He listened respectfully, not wanting to interrupt anything, and let his ear become attuned to his son's speech. He tried to hear himself in the unfamiliar language, but he wasn't sure. As Peter talked, Erika looked over to Andrew, then back and forth between the two tall men. Once the story was told, Erika broke in.

"So; I don't know. They are both tall, and there is something about them, but are you sure?" He thought she was serious, but then he noticed her smile. She was teasing, and he knew better than to fall into that trap. He shrugged, but Polly took the bait.

"Oh, there's no doubt. There are certain physical similarities.." she began, then flushed deep red and buried her face in her hands. Clare caught on to it first, followed by most of the others; their laughter was uproarious. Peter looked a little perplexed, and Andrew also took a moment to realise that Polly had seen him in the sauna the day before. He then also turned a fetching shade of scarlet, which provoked more laughter. Clare came over to him, and took his arm. He wondered what he should do, then settled for canting his head over so it rested on top of hers. Anne looked at them thoughtfully, but Andrew felt more at peace than he had done in a long time, and he simply stared back at her.

After finding himself some lunch, he walked out into the garden. He stared out over the countryside, trying not to think of anything in particular. He heard the back door, and looked over, expecting Anne to come and talk to him, but it was Peter who emerged. Father and son regarded each other, then Andrew smiled and indicated that they should walk.

They walked, and at last properly talked. Peter talked of his childhood and of how Dieter had raised him. He talked of Karla, and of Matthias, and he tried to explain how he felt to have another father. He started to tell the story of why Karla had left them, but then suggested that Andrew ask her about it. Andrew mostly listened, but there came a time when it was his turn to explain. They were standing at the crest of the hill, and Andrew was trying to pick out where the fence had been, when Peter asked him why he had come back to Hohenügel in the summer.

"I didn't know, Peter. I think I perhaps understand it now, but I had no idea what I was about to uncover. I needed to face something which had shaped my whole adult life." Andrew wasn't sure if Peter would be able to follow his thought process; he wasn't sure he understood it himself.

"I thought I was a relatively happy person. You know; good job, good marriage, nice family. But I was shocked by the bitterness in Anne when we divorced, and I had thought about that. I wondered if I could understand it if I came back here; back to where it had all started. I wasn't sure what I wanted, but I knew I might run into Karla, and I think I wanted to know something from her.

"She took something from me that day, and I never understood how important it was until I was back here. Of course, I also didn't know that she had given me something as well." Andrew turned his head and looked at his son. "I mean, you're not 'mine' any more than you are 'hers', but parents see their children in strange ways. Sorry, that's not very well expressed."

Peter shook his head. "Fine. I understand."

"So, I came hoping that Matthias would be still the cheerful friend I thought I remembered, and that maybe I would find Karla, happy with her life, and ready to tell me that she was sorry for what she did, but I didn't expect the things I found. It was as if I had pulled on a thread – I kept pulling, and things kept unravelling. You understand what I mean?"

"I think. I know; go on."

"I wanted to understand why I was the person I was; understand why it had all gone so wrong with Anne, and then be ready to move on. Instead..."

"Instead, here is me."

"Here is you. And almost everything since that weekend has been worth the journey, I think. I just wish it hadn't been so painful for everyone."

"Not for me. I am happy. If not for you and your friends, no Polly, and I never know who is my father. Sorry for my English. All is good, yes?"

"You know, Peter, I actually think so." They walked back, Andrew feeling something change within him as they did so.

The women – 'Andrew's women' they kept referring to themselves as – assumed that the rest of the day would be spent sitting around, drinking coffee and chatting, but Andrew knew he had unfinished business. Erika and Liezl were keen to see their long-lost cousins, but also respectful of their privacy; Andrew understood this, but also knew he did not have the luxury of time – he needed to see them now.

Anne volunteered to come along, but Andrew knew this was the last part of a long journey. "I started this, I have to end it. Thank you, though. I appreciate it."

Anne smiled and then walked with him as far as the road. On an impulse, he turned and kissed her. She pulled back, but held the smile.

"I already told you, Andrew – I set you free. Do something with that freedom, but don't cling to me; I'm not who you thought I was."

"I know that now, Anne, and it makes me sad. But I'll get used to it."

He turned and walked away, fighting the impulse to look back. The Anne he married would have waited for him until he was out of sight, but he was sure he heard her footsteps on the gravel as soon as his back was turned.

Matthias' house was further away than he remembered; more than once he was sure he had missed a turning, but eventually he found it, navigating by the church spire which he remembered so vividly. He thought about how he would normally walk past several times before getting up the courage to approach, and wondered when that had started, but he walked confidently up to the door and knocked firmly.

Gerda answered, and smiled to see him. She motioned to the back of the house, and he walked through, wondering what he might find.

Mathias and Karla were sitting in plastic chairs in the back garden. They may have been talking, but they were silent and looking away from each other when he stepped out onto the patio. Karla looked round first, but said nothing. After a few seconds, Matthias followed suit, and smiled.

"My friend! I am pleased, because I thought you might be at home before I saw you again." Karla looked at her brother and almost automatically corrected his English. Matthias looked startled, then laughed.

"She always did that. I cannot tell you how good it feels to hear her do it again." Karla looked less convinced, but it was she who bade Andrew sit, and he did so gratefully – he was still tired from the emotions of the previous day, and the amount of walking he had already done had not helped the situation, or his still painful knee. Gerda came out and looked at them all, then ducked back inside. The three of them sat there for some time as the silence grew more uncomfortable, then Andrew broke it.

"I suppose there are two things I want to know," he said, not looking at either of them. "I am not sure if you want to talk about this, but it feels important to me."

Matthias looked tired, but nodded.

"Why didn't you tell me before? About Peter, I mean."

Matthias smiled thinly.

"That was the idea. Why I came to see you, but you were not there. Karla had gone, and I thought it was the right time, but instead..." He did not finish the thought.

Andrew had more or less come to that conclusion himself, but he felt better hearing it directly.

"But I was in New York, and so..."

"And so I made things worse, not better. I am sorry, Andrew."

Karla asked what the other thing was, and Andrew had to think for a moment.

"Well, it is not so important, but I do not understand what happened with you and Peter – why did you leave?"

"I think it is important. I think it explains a lot of things, and it shows that your son is a good man." Karla seemed emotional, and Andrew wondered if he even had the right to ask about it.

Brother and sister looked at each other, and then the two of them told the story together: Karla had been wild and out of control – in her own words – for years even after she was supposedly settled down with Dieter. She would fight with everyone, and one day had provoked Matthias into attacking her.

"When I saw this, I knew I had to go. I was scared of him" – pointing at Matthias – "as much as I was ever scared by my father. My father lived in him, and I had to get Peter and myself away. But Dieter would not allow it, and Matthias took his side. So I went. In a few months, I sent for Peter, but he would not come. Until last night, I could not forgive Dieter or Matthias for this."

"But it was not us," Matthias explained, "Peter was only 10 or 11 years, but he knew. He wanted what was right for him, and he knew. We did not influence him. He made the choice. And every year after that, we would make sure he saw Karla, even after she was recovered, but he felt he was at home here."

Karla, her eyes red, agreed with her brother. "He was a good boy, and he is a good man. I think maybe this is because of you. It cannot be because of us. He made the right choice."

They sat for a while as Andrew tried to absorb all of this. Everything seemed to boil down to this: Rolf Schneider had been some kind of vicious brute who had damaged his children – and presumably his wife – beyond repair, and no-one had talked about anything. Ever.

Karla took a deep breath, and looked at Andrew.

"Come with me, Andrew" – had she ever used his name before? "I want you to see something."

She stood and walked inside with a confident familiarity which surprised Andrew until he remembered that this had been her home, too; once upon a time. She led him upstairs, which alarmed him for as long as it took him to realise that he was much bigger and stronger than she was, and considerably more worldly wise than he had been the last time they had been in this house together.

Karla led him, as he had suspected she might, to what had been her room.

"Look at this. It is still the same. Matthias says that after I left, she wouldn't allow him to touch it, and once Matthias was here, he just kept the door closed. Stupid, no?"

Andrew looked at her. "No. Not really. Whatever the rights and wrongs of what you did, you didn't ever finish your life here, and I think that your brother needed you to do that properly. Don't you agree?"

"I do not know what to think. I mostly feel old and tired, being here. I want to move on, but this is – not good, I suppose."

"No, Karla, this is good. This is what you should have done years ago. For everything that happened, all Matthias needed was for you to forgive him. I guess you never did."

"I am not good at these things – no-one ever taught me how." Andrew looked away, suddenly afraid he might feel sorry for the woman who had cast such a long shadow over his life.

"You managed to say the right thing to me last night," he told her.

"I know; I think you forced me into it, but I suppose that is a fair exchange." She walked into the room and sat on the bed. Andrew stared for a moment, then remembered that she had sat exactly there the first time she had ever spoken directly to him. Everything flowed from that moment.

"So, what now? What do you want from us now? You know the truth. It is not pretty."

Andrew drew a deep breath. *Let's see what comes out,* he thought.

"Karla, what was in your mind that first day? Do you even remember it? You lay on that bed, and tried to seduce me. What was going on? Apart from the obvious, I mean."

Karla barked out a dry laugh, then seemed to understand that he was serious.

"I don't remember so clearly now, but I thought I wanted revenge."

"For Clare, you mean?"

"Of course – I could take it out on you. She did what no-one else would have the guts to do – she fucked my boyfriend. I was not used to that."

"And Dieter?"

"I thought I loved him. I even forgave him, in a way. But she – I don't know. Maybe in the end, she got what she wanted."

Andrew thought about that, then thought some more.

"You know, Karla, I believe she just might. Took longer than you think, though." She looked at him, puzzled, but he felt no urge to explain. "Go on," he said.

"I told you – I saw something I wanted, and I took it."

"And me? What I wanted?"

"Oh, come on! You were a horny teenager, weren't you?"

Andrew looked at the floor. "Only in my dreams, Karla. I wasn't what you thought I was."

Karla's voice moderated; she sounded almost contrite. "So, I got it wrong. I knew that as soon as – as soon as it happened, but it was too late. I should not have done what I did, but I was…. I was desperate, do you understand that? Do you remember the bruises?"

Andrew's memory of Karla was that she had been luminous and unblemished, but he forced himself to think harder. Something nagged at him.

"Your ribcage – on the left, I think. It was purple."

"And my legs, where he used the belt."

"I never saw that, Karla. You kept it from me, I think"

She was silent. He felt no need to say anything, occupied as he was with his thoughts. Eventually, she spoke again.

"You want to know something?" She didn't wait for an answer. "I provoked him to hit me. I wanted a scar or something on my back. That would have worked, I think. But he wouldn't do it, and I was so frustrated. I remember why. Now I think about it, I remember why. I bought a swimsuit – for the pool. It had no back, because I thought it would stop him. I did it to myself. So he hit me on the backside, where no-one would see."

"But why? Why did you want a scar?"

"Because it would be easy to seduce you. Once you saw it, you would be easy."

"Or terrified. Which I actually was."

"I remember. I got you wrong. I got many things wrong." She looked up at him, and took a deep breath.

"I mean it this time. I am sorry. Sorry for what I did to you, and sorry that you had to find out like this. I have many reasons, and perhaps some excuses, but it was wrong. On Thursday, you said to me that all I had to do was ask. Well, I understand that, but you need to know – I was never able to ask for anything. Not from anyone. Can you understand that?"

Andrew thought about it, then slowly nodded his head.

"So; here we are. Is this – does this help you? This is what I am supposed to do; to help people."

Andrew looked away. He would have to think about it. He looked down at Karla and tried some kind of smile.

"It might, Karla. There might be some ghosts still, but perhaps they will not frighten me so much."

Karla stood and made to leave, but Andrew took her place on the end of the bed.

"Go on", he said, "I'll be down in a minute. Karla looked at him, then reached a hand out and squeezed his arm, right where the knife wound was. He winced, but said nothing, and she looked at him quizzically. He stared back at her. "Thank you, Karla. I don't know what it means, but thank you." She half-smiled then left him alone.

Andrew sat on the bed for several minutes. He tried to burn the memory of it into his mind; this was where it had started, and he wanted to be able to have it clear in his memory, because he had no intention of ever coming back to it. He tried to picture what might have happened if Karla's back had been striped with welts from her father's belt. *Probably would have run a mile*, he thought.

"Still, we'll never know now," he said out loud, then shook his head. *A bit old to start talking to yourself*, he chided himself, then stood and left the room without looking back.

Once downstairs, he couldn't wait to be free of the house, and he worried that he had seemed rude, coming here and disrupting what had been going on. But Matthias seemed unperturbed. They stood on the front step together, and shook hands this time. Matthias made a remark about not being so awkward as before, and Andrew smiled at the memory of their previous parting.

"Look after yourself, Matthias," he said, then worried that it sounded banal. "I don't know what else to say. Please keep in touch with me, and please make the best of your life – you deserve it." Matthias thanked him, and turned quickly away. Andrew understood that, and made to leave.

Karla called out to him, and he turned to find himself roughly embraced by her. He stood there and endured it at first, then slowly folded his arms about her soft, broad back. She mumbled something which he didn't hear, but he responded with what he thought was the right thing.

"He is a wonderful person, your son. You did that, and you must be proud of it. You are closer than I am, so watch over him for me – I'll know if you don't." Now he was ready to break down, so he pulled himself clear and walked away.

He thought he could do it without looking back, but he couldn't help himself. The door was open, and he could see them, brother and sister, side by side but not touching. He looked away and walked on.

MAY 2008

Anne is sitting in her garden, enjoying the late afternoon summer sunshine. She knows she should be making dinner, but her children will probably not be home to eat it, having spent the day with their father, and she considers going out to eat. She flicks once more through the glossy celebrity magazine she picked up for the train journey home this afternoon, and smiles again to see Polly and Peter, in the background of some expensive-looking film premiere.

Anne is more or less content with her life, six years after her divorce. She thought she would never love again, but there have been men in her life, and she wonders if the most recent of them, someone she met through work, might be worth pursuing more seriously.

This causes her to think again of Andrew and Clare. She had not expected anything to come of their relationship, but somehow they have stayed together. She remembers how hurt she had been, that weekend in Germany, when they had obviously slept together in spite of their protests to the contrary, and she thinks, as she often does, of how she saw Clare take his hand as they queued up to get through passport control that Sunday evening. She has never told either of them, but she heard what Clare said as she did so, and the pain of that moment still lives with her.

But this is almost the only pain in her life now, and she has remained friends with both of them, although more distant than she might otherwise have been. Her children have grown up strong and independent - although not independent enough to actually leave home yet, she thinks with a wry smile - and she feels as if Peter and Polly are also in some way her children.

Liezl is a closer friend now than Clare, and they talk almost every week. Liezl it is who keeps her abreast of what Matthias is doing, and she is always glad to hear that he is happy and well. Out of the blue, he and Gerda had a baby about a year after they had all visited, and Anne feels in some way responsible for that, although she cannot explain it to herself.

And, perhaps most surprising of all, she has become friends with Karla. Karla the hellion, who turned out to be Karla the earth mother, and then finally revealed herself to be Karla the scared and confused teenager who had never quite been able to shake off her fearful upbringing. Anne had had no contact with her in 1978, and only spoke a few words to her 25 years later, but a connection was made in their shared concern for Matthias, and out of that has come a strange and unexpected friendship. Anne does not know what to make of it, but she has, at last, learned to stop worrying about things, and just to let them happen.

She thinks of Matthias more often than she probably should, and she expects that she never will come to terms with what he meant, and means, to her. Sometimes, late at night when she cannot sleep, she remembers what it was like to be held by him; what it was like to be so desperately needed by someone, and she allows herself to shed a few tears for all that she lost. She still blames herself for the way she was; she can see how events and upbringing have shaped others, but she has always accepted full responsibility for who she is, and cannot bring herself to consider that she has also been affected by external forces.

She sighs, cross with herself for letting her thoughts wander again, as they seem to have been doing more frequently of late. She thinks that perhaps it is something to do with the time of year, so close to the time – now thirty years before - when they all piled on that rusty old bus and set out for what they expected to be the adventure of their lives. She stretches and tries to shake off the memory of Hohenügel and all that transpired there, but some memories aren't really memories at all, and cannot be shaken off.

She shivers, and looks at the sky – an early summer storm may be building, she thinks, as she notices the birch trees at the end of the garden begin to shimmer and shake. She picks up the cushions from the plastic chair she has been sitting on, and remembers to take the magazine, which she intends to send to Karla. Anne looks around her garden again, smiles, and goes back inside.

ABOUT THE AUTHOR

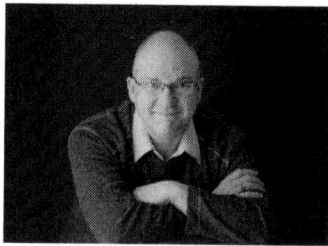

Richard Watt was born in Aberdeen, Scotland in 1962. He emigrated to British Columbia in 2007 and was regularly published in the *Prince George Citizen* newspaper. *Going Back* is his first novel.

Made in the USA
Charleston, SC
24 May 2013